Kiti on Ice

An Historical Tale of the Traditional Inupiat

by

Phyl Manning

PublishAmerica

Baltimore

First printing

ISBN: 1-4137-0685-1
PUBLISHED BY PUBLISHAMERICA, LLLP
www.publishamerica.com
Baltimore

Printed in the United States of America

DEDICATION

To the memory of Ivan L. Manning,
who supported his wife in more ways than she knew.

VIEWPOINTS

"Stunning prose. In *Kiti on Ice,* Manning transports us with high drama to the High Arctic. This breathtaking and chilling chronicle of life in another time and place is a special story that no reader will forget."
Claire Braz-Valentine, Playwright and Poet

"Amazing stuff! *Kiti on Ice* is a unique addition to the small-but-growing pantheon of real woman heroes—forced by necessity and empowered by innate talents. . . . Manning has carved an astonishing new character out of what hardly seems promising source material: the perpetual ice and cold of the far frozen north. Kiti is cool."
Kent Lee Brisby, Director of Asian Story Theater (San Diego)

"Rare and delicious! Here's a quest adventure with a strong female protagonist, a tale that grabs readers and holds them in icy thrall."
Walter Mayes, Librarian and Co-author of *Valerie & Walter's Best Books . . . a Lively, Opinionated Guide*

"My laughter was out loud, and my tears were in awe of the universal qualities we humans share. Anxiety and pain and determination anneal a woman powerful and inspiring. Although this Inupiat dwells in a culture, time and place alien to most, Kiti is *all* of us—a new literary heroine."
Jenny Kay, Editor and Teacher

"Using characters that walk off the page, *Kiti on Ice* lets us feel the warm breath of a seal, whiff the aroma of whale blubber, shiver in frigid temperatures. . . . Manning weaves her reader into the icy fabric of the Arctic."
Chicki Mallan, Travel Writer and Author of *Moon Handbooks: Yucatan Peninsula, Belize, Colonial Cities*, et. al.

CHARACTERS

(IN ORDER OF APPEARANCE OR MENTION)

ORIGINAL FAMILY AND VILLAGE (Inland)
SUKITILAN: Only daughter of Pichikut and Narluk
PICHIKUT: Mother of seven; spirit of one
MAQ: Village Midwife and Pichikut's Friend
NARLUK: Much respected *angakok* of inland people
NUNA: A dog to die for
AJAK: Nuna's pup
PALUNGA: Youngest of the five brothers older than Sukitilan; disappeared
        on tundra
OOJULIT: Eldest son of Pichikut and Narluk
PAJUK: Next-eldest son of Pichikut and Narluk
(KARIKIT): One of two middle sons, lost on floating ice
(MAMAK): Other of two middle sons, lost on floating ice
IYARPOK: Lead dog ("The Laughing One") in contention with Nuna

ON THE TRAIL
KITI: Young woman on a dangerous mission
ARAJIKA: Baby of unusual circumstance
TUK: Young man who has recently lost his family (Coastal)
TONRATU: One of two who visit Kiti (Inlander)
ODLERK: Other one of two who visit Kiti (Inlander)

TUK'S VILLAGE (Coastal)
PUSIK: Woman who nurses and befriends Kiti
ITOK: Village hunter and husband of Pusik
ANJUK: Old man who is self-appointed leader
KANERK: Storyteller who reveals the tale of *Chikut*
(CHIKUT): Heroine of Kanerk's tale at the Walrus Feast
(MUNKUT): *Chikut's* father in the tale
(KOLOKI): Water serpent in tale of *Chikut*

THE ICE VILLAGE (Coastal)
ERTOK: Spry old woman who remembers Pichikut and is now Kiti's closest
        friend
POMAKUT: Husband to Ertok
ISUMAK: Popular child among villagers
ADLA: The stranger who wanders in from barren grounds
SAGAK: The wise but not so old man whose counsel is sought

Part I:
Pirtok!

Expectations

The mother died when the baby was born. Actually, the woman Pichikut died before the birth. Near the end, her only daughter Sukitilan stood over her above the special birthing ledge of ice within the arching walls of the snow house. *Can a healthy infant arrive after labor of two sleeptimes and now a third day starting?* the young woman wondered silently. *And if it happens that a child comes after all this toil, and if the mother dies as she herself predicts, can it be that the infant will then be laid out naked in the wind to freeze?*

No, their father Narluk—all-wise *angakok*, a shaman honored widely among *Inupiat* of the caribou—would never commit this terrible act his wife foretold. Not when he knew that a snow-death was against her wish. Especially not when he learned that arrangements for feeding a motherless child had been made carefully and long before this time of birth. . . .

The left hand of Sukitilan lay buried in folds of the robe that warmed her mother, her *Ananak,* this laboring Pichikut. The daughter took comfort from the white bear fur made soft and malleable with human saliva, urine and great effort. Her right hand reached up and lightly tugged scar tissue at the gnarled slick lobe of her own ear as she watched her mother snatch shallow breaths raggedly . . . over . . . once again . . . no more?

"Someone must push!" Sukitilan scolded softly through tight lips. "A woman needs to help the babe be born."

So hot. Condensation rolled down the circling wall to make runnels underfoot. Sukitilan used both hands to lift the neckline of her *illupak,* the light pelt undergarment worn uncovered inside shelter. Air reached her skin, and she exhaled slowly in relief. Her lungs wheezed from hours of breathing the stale breath of village women who suffered with the revered wife of their shaman—this present pain along with their own still-remembered childbirth. *Very, very warm,* she thought now. She pushed straggling strands of long black hair behind both ears, once more allowing the middle fingers of her

11

right hand to rest against her lobe.

Two sleeps ago, when Pichikut's compressions had signaled that a baby would soon try to be born, Sukitilan the only daughter went out to summon Maq, the midwife, wizened and tattooed, with red-rimmed eyes and skillful hands. All five other women of the village accompanied her—were loyally assembled still, and each providing heat.

Sound, too, Sukitilan realized when most of it suddenly ceased. She looked around. Somehow, the women seemed to know that the critical time had finally arrived. Chatter faded, laughter diminished and then stopped entirely. That early sound was now replaced by earnest chant and the snapping *click-er-click* of amulets. Rhythmically, one flat voice and then another called out the names of good *Inuit* men and women now gone to the spirit world. Identified aloud were free shades no doubt eager to live again by entering an infant newly born.

The child would emerge when it heard the proper name, and that last name called was likely to be the spirit that controlled. It would protect and guide the early breaths, the first precarious days until it proved itself, prevailed over other minor specters as guardian of the new being throughout its life. *The Way of the People*, Sukitilan reflected: *peeusinga*, the way of *Inupiat* who lived here inland, far from the Sunrise Sea.

Pichikut had told her daughter what to expect. She said also that her own people on ice islands far north at the top of the world secured a guardian spirit at the time of birth in the same manner.

"And does it happen that those upon the frozen islands also leave a motherless child alone to die?" Sukitilan wanted to know. She could still ask such direct questions of her mother, her *Ananak,* but only when they were alone. Others? Them Sukitilan was far too old to query—not her brothers, certainly not her father Narluk. Nor could she question villagers and violate their privacy—or she would receive for her answer a softly exhaled *Hoo-oo* of censure or at least a disapproving look—head tilted sideways with a long stare from eyes black as wet berries. She must not intrude on the delicate inner spirit of another.

"Perhaps yes," Pichikut answered directly, as was her way. "A newborn can be set out to die—if the small one is doomed otherwise to suffer a lingering death from lack of food and care."

"That would be a kindness," the daughter admitted. "But if provision has been arranged?"

"Then perhaps *no,* for all *Inuits* love their babies."

Sukitilan, now beginning her twentieth winter, was long-legged, lean by nature—and would therefore not ever be considered beautiful. Also, her right ear lobe was notched and glossy with a scar. She took comfort in the disfigurement, though, and her bare right hand touched it for reassurance. Here was a legacy from an animal attack when she was a toddler scampering out of her mother's hood. *This was **proof** that good luck rode her shoulder.* Also, this was a permanent bond with the great white sled dog Nuna—the very one whose great-great sire as a pup had leapt upon the child to savage her ear.

No, the only daughter of Pichikut would not even consider a double death of mother and infant, she reminded herself now, in spite of *Ananak's* prophecy and in spite of *peeusinga,* the *Way of the People.* And no *need* to. She looked down at the still form of the woman before her and swallowed. Of course a vigorous child would soon arrive; and naturally Pichikut would live; and all would be in harmony as before except that Sukitilan would no longer be youngest in her family and her village. A strange, choking sound came from the young woman's throat.

Maq, the midwife clasped Sukitilan's shoulder, and squeezed in sympathy, but the young woman shrugged her hand away; then bent to test for her mother's breath upon the tender skin of her own eyelid. Nothing.

"*Ananak*! Mother!" she hissed without regard for the great discourtesy committed by addressing another person so directly. "**Pichikut!!**" Perhaps she could shock the woman into seizing back her departing life spirit. Surely no fate more harsh than present circumstance could come from this offense.

But the beloved form before her on the high birthing ledge lay motionless, and Sukitilan despaired.

Suddenly, Maq reached deeply into the birth channel and brought forth a red, squirming mass that clenched as air struck flesh. A weak bubbling sound from the infant became a lusty protest even as the old woman nipped the cord and tied the ends. She pushed the squalling child into the hands of Sukitilan without a word; then turned away and scuttled out through the hide baffle before others in the snow hut knew what had happened—before they realized that all their utterances and amulets were not enough to anchor the spirit of this mother. Before they themselves dived into the tunnel and disappeared.

"Someone needs help—" Sukitilan protested, as she watched the village

13

women go so hastily. She fell silent as she saw the flap stop swinging, glanced around the empty *igloo* that was home. She understood their haste, of course, for Pichikut had predicted this very panic. She would die in an unsealed place, she explained to her daughter. Villagers would believe that the woman's spirit, angry at having to depart, would now be loosened upon the community. And although people honored and respected the wife of *angakok* in life, they were likely to fear her deeply in death because all knew her spirit to be uncommonly strong.

Pichikut had also reassured her daughter that neither she nor anyone had anything to fear. "No logic lies in thinking that a spirit who protects someone throughout life becomes suddenly sinister when death occurs."

Alone in the *igloo* with the spiritless body of her mother and the fretting baby brother, Sukitilan tried to stop shaking. *Pichikut, a daughter trembles with misgiving about everything **except** her mother's spirit—which is most awfully welcome in this place!*

As she had been drilled, the young woman automatically bathed the child in snowmelt, long ready as it warmed above the seal oil lamp. The first and likely the last bath he would ever have. Yet another boy, she saw, and sighed. *Six* brothers for Sukitilan? The baby quieted as she wrapped a soft hare skin around him, then sucked mucus from his nostrils. Feeling helpless, she studied the hiccupping newborn in her arms. The next step was to take him to their father, as her mother had directed. She would present the infant to Narluk, and the result of that meeting would control Sukitilan's own future and the baby's.

Ananak had commanded so much. . . . Here was Pichikut's Plan, now in effect. *A healthy newborn—male or female—is to be kept **alive**,* she told her daughter often; for she herself never did expect to withstand the birth of this seventh child. The daughter looked down at the husk of her mother, the tortured body now in respite following so many hours of anguish. Pichikut had been exhausted, flesh and soul. She welcomed death, Sukitilan knew, as a quiet finish to this existence, perhaps to be followed by a little rest before her spirit commenced the next life. And the daughter would not wish to take this well-earned interlude from Pichikut—even though the young woman quaked at the thought of continuing without the strong woman who had guided her for so many years in a variety of ways no other mother could. At least, none that Sukitilan had ever known or heard about.

The sister laid her baby brother on robes atop the *iglerk,* the family sleep ledge that shelved out to cover nearly half the snow house interior. She hurried

14

to put outdoor clothing over her *illupak.* She placed each furry pants leg into a waterproof *kamik,* the moisture proof, warm boot that fit her feet like skin. Then she plucked up the newborn and placed him deep inside her parka front where he would rest warm, supported by the taut drawstring.

Cradling the little one, Sukitilan crawled past the baffle and through the tunnel until she came up into the darkness of a winter morning. She listened, heard nothing—the dogs were gone out with hunters on the trail. She nodded with satisfaction. No one would see her go—good! Except for her father the *angakok,* village men were somewhere on the trail to find food—her two remaining brothers also, despite their mother's circumstance.

And right now, village women were inside their *igloos* packing up, busily preparing for a move by sled to flee as soon as possible from the detached spirit of Pichikut. Narluk and his two grown sons still at home would seal this snow house when they returned today, would even build a small new shelter for the single night of sleep—but everyone including the family of Sukitilan would be gone before this time tomorrow. No one would grumble, for moving was a part of life for every *Inuit*—if not to escape unbound spirits, as in this instance; then to find a better region for the hunt or to elude a troublesome predator or a maddened trail spirit. *Pirtok,* no one can undo that which has already happened.

Sukitilan hurried away on foot from the seven scattered half-moon shapes of glowing snow houses, a fair size for a winter village inland. She thought that Narluk would be at the place he usually sought for solitude. She needed to show him his sturdy new son when she gave the sad news about Pichikut— *or would a villager already have searched him out?*

Breaking trail to walk north in the near-blackness of this early winter day, Sukitilan reviewed her mother's scheme. The woman's predictions were unfolding as truth—*Ananak's* death, desertion by fearful villagers, great vigor in the newborn baby. Before this dark day was finished—eh, soon! —the daughter would surely know whether she must actually carry out her mother's desperate design: Pichikut's Plan... *Rescue the newborn from a tradition-bound Narluk. Take the trail north and east alone with the baby and Nuna. Keep the infant safe and healthy while eluding any who might follow. Finally seek asylum at the ice island village of Pichikut's own origin.* The design seemed almost simple as she reviewed it now. But it wasn't, and it would not be, she knew.

Secretly, *Ananak* had been instructing and training her daughter over

15

numerous moons, developing and practicing the necessary skills despite the young woman's protests. The pregnant woman had drilled her over and again on what were likely to become *essential,* life-protecting capabilities. Above all, she insisted, was patience.

To teach this quality, *Ananak* had Sukitilan fidgeting as she hovered above a spear-drilled hole in lake ice which her mother insisted was the breathing hole for a seal.

"It happens that the hunter must make no sound and cast no shadow moving on the ice," Pichikut whispered.

After long hours of surveillance, Sukitilan thought that she would explode like a carcass on the tundra heated in summer sun. "No seal will ever rise in mere lake ice!" Sukitilan muttered. "This time of great discomfort is for nothing."

"Nipjarnok! Hush!" her mother commanded. And not until two days around one full sleep had passed, *Ananak* leaving and returning silently as she managed family matters at the *igloo,* was the girl free to go and rest upon the warm *iglerk* at home.

"And if *nathek*—that small, oily, delicious but most wary seal—rises in such small time as this," her mother said as she dismissed her, "then the hunter is indeed fortunate."

"It happens," Sukitilan retorted, "that this woman will not *ever* be so hungry as to hunt for seal."

Pichikut tilted her head and considered her daughter for some moments. Then she snorted. "It is at least hoped that the person will not expect seal on freshwater ice." Then she laughed aloud, a joyful, unrestrained sound that echoed off icy mounds and boulders nearby.

Skills considered crucial included ice fishing, even though Sukitilan like most Inupiat did not much like the taste of fish. Also necessary was use of the sturdy little killing spear designed by *Ananak* to be light and manageable. And more complex but still essential were ways to rapidly assemble and use the compact harpoon crafted with much skill long ago by a maternal grandfather called Munkut to fit the hand of then-young Pichikut.

A unique aspect of the requisite training of a daughter included practice in ways to dilute the rich lactation of a sled dog—for the anticipated trip was meaningless unless the baby remained hearty. Also, the young woman must know the killing spot on every food creature that might present itself along the trail or at the Sunrise Sea. Sukitilan used the spear and the harpoon to slay many a snowdrift bear and caribou. She loved being out with her mother, for they both enjoyed most of the play-games..

But surely all of this instruction and practice were pointless when pertaining to the care of a baby and assuring that the infant with its sister and a sled team could survive alone on the trail. *Her mother would not perish in the coming childbirth. And if she **did**—which of course she would not!— then certainly the family must continue as a unit.* So Sukitilan told herself. Often.

"How is it," the daughter demanded of her mother, "that *Ananak* knows so much about the trail?"

"It happens that Pichikut beginning as a child was sole huntress for parents overripe—"

"—*Hoo-oo* . . . no brothers!" Such a household was unimaginable to someone who had a surfeit of these siblings.

"Not even one, for the child fruited from the old womb of an aging mother, who with her husband had long ago despaired of having children."

"And Pichikut's father found no food?"

"An artisan, as the harpoon can prove. But then, most men can make weapons with some skill when the need arises." *Ananak* laughed; then continued. "It was said among the villagers that old Munkut always met with disaster when he took the trail. Even as a youth, so the story went, his step was heavy, his arm unsteady, the mercy of his heart usually overriding the rumble of his gut."

Sukitilan was silent. Such men normally became *angakok*—her own father being an exception; for Narluk was honored as having prowess on the hunt as well as celebrated shaman skills.

Her mother went on. "The loving husband and father, this Munkut, of an always-hungry family." Pichikut smiled. "So the daughter blest with fortune on the hunt found food for her family and team until her parents died."

"—And after that—?"

"—Provided for herself and some few needy widows and their children until she married and left the village."

"*Ananak* used the words 'fortune on the hunt—'"

"—Yes. She knew herself to possess great good luck on the trail—as does her daughter."

Sukitilan said nothing. All know that skill and courage have little meaning without good fortune as well. Did *Ananak* truly believe that her female child

17

possessed this *luck*? This unsure creature, who quaked daily beneath the burden of her mother's demands?

But Pichikut only concluded her tale. She was a young woman alone when she met and married the mighty shaman Narluk. They went west and mostly south to live among his inland folk on landlocked tundra. She never again had to make the long journey to the frozen sea.

Her mother's differing origin would account, Sukitilan reflected, for the disparities in thought and practice between Pichikut and villagers here. Her mother reasoned a situation instead of always blindly following *peeusinga, The Way of the People*. She expected the same of her children. More like Narluk, though, all but Palunga among her sons kept to local custom. She wondered now, would the daughter also disappoint? Never mind, she was too young—or at least entirely too untried to know.

With the infant quiet in her parka, Sukitilan picked her way carefully around hard-frozen drifts. Blowing snow made tracks disappear. She stumbled, slipped back down a steep rise, nearly fell, gentled the startled babe, steadied herself and regained balance; then chose another route to bypass the hummock.

It would be good to have sent a brother to find their father, not subject a newborn to the fierce north wind. *What use were brothers*, she thought crossly, *if none were ever present at a time of need*? She had moments to consider those five older brothers as she pressed into the frigid gale. Oojulit and Pajuk were the two who remained, the only ones at home with the family. Fine hunters both, they were considered brave by villagers. They would be good providers for their families if ever they married. But both seemed content for now to satisfy their urges with impermanent choices among girls and women from other villages or from travelers off the trail. Sukitilan sighed. But then, she too enjoyed the *iglerk* pleasure of some man—and she too had no desire to marry. No one she had met so far caused her to forgo the relative freedom of her present life in exchange for children and unshared domestic responsibility. *Ai-ee!* A man held small mystery for her, not with five older brothers. And besides, Pichikut needed her—well, always had. Even with only Oojulit and Pajuk on the hunt with their father—eh, the endless hides to process for clothing and *kamik* and boat covers. . . . The meat to be distributed fairly among those villagers was not as successful. Pichikut had been clever, though: she would give two hides of equal quality to a village woman for curing and preparation. Only one needed to come back to Narluk's family. The women were delighted. But even so . . . her brothers needed to find wives!

18

Why did they not marry? Perhaps they were too accustomed to their own family unit and unready at this moment to exchange the very comfortable present for the unknown. Both brave and proven on the trail, they were accustomed to a pleasant niche in the family.

Sukitilan snorted. They should marry *soon*. Their sister could not provide—would not even permit them the domestic ease they took for granted. For a time at least, and probably forever, Sukitilan would lack her mother's speed and grace and expertise within their home. They might now—very shortly now!—wish to find themselves women of their own to take over the hard work of preparing skins, of making and later mending their apparel.

And the brothers had recently demonstrated their desire to distance themselves from household crises. Both had gone out especially early and with grim resolution on these three mornings of travail for their mother. Like *angakok,* the intrepid warriors fled the snow house to escape the pain and waiting. The sister smiled inside the tightly drawn parka opening. Bravery manifests itself in settings other than the hunt.

She loved them, but wished that they were here and useful right now. Oojulit so serious and Pajuk the joker—not serious at all. Yes, she was quite sure. . . . Her growing up with six men in the family probably explained why she had no wish to marry. The male of her human species held for Sukitilan no wonder and small potential for romance. Several men, some still young, had come to the village to seek her father's counsel; then stayed on to meet and talk with *angakok's* daughter. But although she agreed to bed them when they asked, and although she thoroughly enjoyed those nights in the furs, her parents observing and making suggestions, her brothers joking and teasing, she certainly found no one she would want to marry. Nor was she so beautiful and charming that they stayed to pursue their cause. Tall and narrow were not qualities sought for in a woman.

Five brothers until this day. The middle two, Karikit and Mamak had been away, now commencing the second winter, almost too long to expect their return. They had been with villagers on an ocean hunting trip about this time twelve moons ago—perhaps too early in the season and before sea ice was stable. A crashing blow came up during the sleep, according to those who witnessed the catastrophe, and the grounded ice on which they camped broke off to become *situ,* a loose floe, traveling northeast before the wind. Still, they had with them robes and hunting bags and trail packs with food and extra clothing; also, their sled and team. On the same *situ* were three more experienced men and several dogs separated from their sleds. Hope remained, therefore. Karikit and Mamak might yet manage to return to the family.

And then young Palunga, only a couple of winters older than his sister, had walked out to search for his brothers when they were not back by winter's end. In the thaw of late spring, he had left dogs and sled behind as useless on bare ground. Her favorite brother. Palunga, youngest of the five . . . funny and helpful, always troubling himself for others. Twenty-one winters old when he strode away, hunting spear in hand and trail gear rolled up into a sleep robe across his shoulders and steadied by a strap across his forehead. He did not return to the village, and hope dwindled as summer bloomed briefly and faded. No one could survive winter here alone without sled and team. Next to Pichikut, her *ananak,* the girl had loved Palunga best.

Sukitilan came over a rise and saw her father in stark, unmoving silhouette against the roil of pastel colors, pinks and yellows, blooming in the northern sky. She had seen him here before in this same place and with a similar stance when solitude for serious thought became his goal. He stood at the crest of a rock-strewn cliff above the frozen lake. So alone! So powerful! So helpless. The young woman shuddered, tried to reassure herself by putting both arms down to support the infant resting above her belt. She had a mission set by her mother, and she was trusted to carry it out.

But was this the right time to take the step she planned? The right place? Furtively, she positioned herself beside a high hummock of drifted rock to watch the furs of mighty *angakok* sweep away from the moaning north wind and reveal a figure tall and thick and motionless. Here was the mighty shaman, healer and magician renowned for his great skill who with his vast store of knowledge now stood in retreat. His magic from the sea and sky and land could neither relieve the suffering of his wife nor compose her fluttering spirits.

Sukitilan was not yet close enough to read her father's face, but she knew from experience that his features at such time as this would be fixed as stone. She could see from here that his body was a stiff continuation of the rocks on which he stood. His mind and spirit—who knew where! She waited for some signal that he was once more unified, for all know it is dangerous to disturb *angakok* in his separated state.

Sukitilan drew the face of her hood even tighter to discourage the still rising wind and ward off the ground flow of stinging ice pellets. She squinted to protect her eyes and still observe her father in the unreality of northern glow. Perhaps someone had found him earlier, told him of Pichikut's death.

Whoever that might have been would presume the child dead or dying. No one but *Ananak* and her daughter knew *The Plan*. None but these two realized that provision was already arranged for feeding a motherless infant in a village without lactating women. It would be like Narluk to decide, even after he was informed of his wife's death, not to move from this place until Oojulit and Pajuk came for him. If this were so, he would not welcome the interruption of his daughter for any reason. *Was all of this about Narluk true,* Sukitilan asked herself, *or was she imagining such thoughts as an excuse to avoid confronting him?*

She watched. *Angakok* was not astute about details of home and family. He was a kind and reasonable father, yes, not given to sullen moods or violent outbursts. Certainly, he was a good provider—especially so with grown sons to help, even though now merely two took the trail where five had been before. But Pichikut had often prompted him to wear furs before going out in winter cold. Indeed, and surely unique among *Inupiat* men, he had to be reminded to *eat.* Sukitilan sighed. These vital cues were now *her* obligation.

Sukitilan waited for the rigid form atop the cliff to move and show himself to be fully joined. She lingered while the spirit lights beyond slowed and finally turned to brief, rare flickers. She stayed while a watery sun peeked above the south horizon at mid-day, gave its bit of glow while it rested a few moments, before sliding down to leave the land in darkness once again. She watched until her feet were numb with cold and her body trembled—with fatigue and with such swelling fear as she had never known. For the first time—seeing *angakok* so aloof and removed—she believed that *Ananak's* dire predictions could possibly come true. That this shuddering young woman might have to go away and not return. . . . That secretly and undetected by family or villagers, Sukitilan might have to carry out Pichikut's Plan. She and the white bitch Nuna. Instinctively, her mittened hand covered the place on her parka located at her right ear.

The baby became restless. He moved and wriggled; then cried. The wail filtered out from the neck of her tunic and rode south on the wind. Narluk would not hear the cries, true, but the infant must be attended. She turned away. She would find some way to see her father privately when he came home. The longer he delayed, Sukitilan decided as she trudged back to the village, wind finally at her back, the more time she would be able to spend at sorting in the snow house before the family missed her presence. So many tasks, her mother had set for her!

Grief welled higher with each step back to the village—*spirits, help this*

21

terrified young woman. Apprehension threatened to drown her thought and will. She fought against the weakness of self-pity, tried to push away anxiety that threatened to close in and stop her breath. She stilled sharp resentment over her mother's willingness to die. And she stifled the ugly inner voice that accused the baby. *Whatever in the land or sea or sky made Pichikut believe that her youngest, weakest child could carry out this Plan?*

"Here lies honor," Pichikut assured her often throughout the moons of training, "to be trusted with such great responsibility."

Sukitilan would fight the automatic tears. She preferred by far to circumvent such distinction and remain the pampered little sister in the family.

"Most unmarried girls," her mother would say with laughter in her voice, "spend spare moments giggling and rolling in the furs with this and that young man."

Did *Ananak* jeer? "Our small village has no young men except brothers of this very household," the daughter would remind her *ananak*. To lie with a relative was not permitted.

And then be reminded back that she, Sukitilan, had so far shown no long-term interest in visitors who stopped along the trail, either. In fact, she seemed to shrink away from serious talk with males not members of her family. And although she did not decline *iglerk* opportunities with strangers offered by her father—indeed, often delighted in the very prospect—possibilities beyond the sleeping shelf were quite another matter.

The more successful the man as hunter, the more burdened would be his wife with the never ending pressure of support tasks—butchering and proper distribution among villagers of the various cuts of caribou or fish or hare or other creatures taken; processing of hides including careful chewing to insure supple pelt to make clothing, boots, and sleep robes; preparing animal bladder to receive cubes of blubber and make the golden lamp oil. Yes, and forming warm, waterproof *kamik* for every foot in the family. Never ending? Ah, the maintenance and repair of everything.

Her own family of men would have kept the only daughter also occupied every moment she was awake—if Pichikut would permit them to do so. But she would not. "Sukitilan has the necessary skills. Let her hone them later. A woman's life is long."

Why would any female from a family such as hers ever consider taking on still more *igloo* work? Especially someone like her who hated routine and could find food independently? Who emphatically favored hunting over chewing

22

pelt and tending a lamp? Who picked at every opportunity a strenuous labor out-of-doors like *kayak* building over any of the possibly softer but so-repetitious indoor jobs?

In her subtle way, *Ananak* had encouraged her. Most parents and especially mothers would worry over a daughter who did not like to dream of men and spend their time refining domestic skills. But Pichikut was amused, not alarmed. She did suggest, though, that the daughter's attitude might change someday.

Let her hone domestic skills later, so Pichikut had said. Well, *now* was *later*, Sukitilan reflected. *What would happen on this day?*

Sukitilan slipped into the snow house where the sinew wick burned low. She shrugged back her hood; then retrieved the baby, laid him on the fleecy *iglerk*, opened out the hare skin wrapper. This new *Inuk* was perfect, she decided. All parts husky and well formed, intact, bright eyes trying hard to focus. When chill wind struck the boy, he howled, tiny fists beating air, body pink with resentment and getting pinker as his ire increased. How much easier would her own life likely be, she reflected, if this infant were not so robust. She quickly tucked the wrap around him. The lusty shouts ceased, and the two regarded each other.

"Eh," the sister said softly, "a babe knows what he wails for, stops crying when he gets it." A good quality in any person, she decided. This seventh child of Pichikut was hefty, bound to become a mighty hunter like his father and his brothers. She did not dare to dwell fully on the question, but wondered at the crisp edges of her mind: *Who will someday be the ones to teach this child the secrets of the trail? If not his father or brothers, might it then be his big sister?*

Sukitilan propped the child on a wrinkle of robe so that he could sense motion nearby as she worked. Three caribou haunches that leaned against the ice wall inside were half-thawed from the long vigil with so many people in the snow house. These, she dragged out to the harness porch so that they would re-freeze. This ice-block porch blistered out from the side of the tunnel as protected shelter for storing leather straps and harness not in use. Much as dogs love to run before a sled, they eat their leather lines at any opportunity. Near the baffle-protected exit from inside, she stacked clean waste and oil bladders along with bags containing water, food and permafrost. Most robes from the *iglerk* were folded and ready. All of these effects would be needed for the quick new *igloo* that Narluk and his sons would build tonight and also for that inevitable move by everyone tomorrow. Everyone?

By herself, as well? Please, spirits, let her father abide by the wishes of Pichikut.

To keep everything safe from dogs, she would wait until her father and brothers returned before she took outside all this that she had packed. What remained inside would never be missed and—should she indeed have to journey separately in solitude—would provide far more than she could carry on the small sled she had already selected from the rack behind the village. *Palunga's* sled. She felt good about that.

Sukitilan looked over at her brother, now asleep. Soon, she must take him to Nuna. A sudden thought shook her. *Does this child have a special spirit for protection?* Who could remember what name was last called before Maq brought the babe to air? Now the young woman battled a whole new apprehension—but no. If Pichikut had thought the matter important, she would have anticipated it, planned for it or at least warned Sukitilan against its happening. *Can it be that birth and spirit matters sort themselves naturally?*

"If the babe is vigorous," Pichikut said so very often as the time of birth approached, "then male or not, it is to live." And then the mother herself died leaving with her daughter the burden of nurture and protection for the infant. Yes, resentment was among the whirling storm of passions that blew through her mind.

"Eh, *pirtok*. What is done cannot be altered." Sukitilan's bare fingers rubbed the puckered lobe of her right ear. "With or without a guardian spirit, the child must be saved," she murmured to the sleeping baby and to the weeping walls.

24

Making a Move

Sukitilan clasped the infant to her, both arms around him tightly. Eh, poor babe—would they soon have only each other? He smelled moist and fresh, cuddled down although his head moved to each side, mouth pursed and sucking. Hungry at last? So time to start the next part of Pichikut's Plan. Humming a chant for reassurance, the young woman laid the wrapped child gently onto an old bear fur on the otherwise empty *iglerk* by the lamp. For a moment, she watched the boy watch her.

Before her father and brother had sealed what they now considered to be Pichikut's *igloo* exclusively, Sukitilan had placed outside the tunnel all that she had separated as family belongings; certainly the best and biggest robes from the sleeping ledge, the sturdiest bladders and hide bags with most of the food supply, frozen flesh wrapped well enough to keep the village dogs from scenting and plundering it immediately. She had meekly crawled out of Pichikut's place following the death—as expected by her family and the villagers—but then returned by way of a secret entry hacked through the back of Nuna's *igloo* into the harness porch. *All part of the Plan.*

Now, while people thought she was seeking solace from Nuna for the tragedy of her mother's death, Sukitilan could finish the final, personal packing—could select from the small hidden hoard all that she hoped not ever to need. She could, in the unrelenting darkness of the afternoon, bury old blankets and extra bladders up by the sled and *kayak* rack on a drift-protected snowy mound south of the village—could do everything needful around whatever time the baby required.

Her family had first sealed the corpse of Pichikut in the original house and were now busying themselves with construction block by block of the new shelter. Here was a time-consuming task in which all *Inupiat* men take pride, despite in this instance, the temporary nature of the building. As Narluk and his sons worked, she could finish her tasks here; then surreptitiously return as often as needed in the sleep time by coming through the hidden entrance of the lopsided little snow house for Nuna. One that she herself had built. This

25

late afternoon, she was grateful to the spirits for winter's daytime darkness.

Sukitilan dressed rapidly in outdoor furs, rolled the glowing wick onto the top of an oil bladder, dropped a soapstone travel lamp into an inner pocket on the side of her fur trousers, her *silipak*. She plucked up her restless brother and stuffed him down the front of her parka where once more he lay wriggling against the drawstring at her waist. Later, she would have him in a proper hood for carrying on her back. Her mother's *amaut* at first, she supposed—for in spite of Pichikut's urging, the daughter never had made one for herself. Why should she, when this time—the occurrences of this day—would not, could not ever *be?*

Two sleeps ago, the morning that Pichikut's time began, Sukitilan had taken the first real step toward carrying out the Plan. She had kept that promise exactly—well, almost—when she removed from the lead dog Nuna five of her six fat puppies, still unweaned but two moons and more in age—certainly large enough to feed on flesh, not milk. She collected them carefully into a ragged robe hoisted over her shoulder.

Whining softly, the canine parent padded behind her as Sukitilan walked out into the village with her burden. "These great hulking creatures should have stopped taking their mother's milk long ago," the young woman explained to the anxious dog. "It happens that someone got extra meat for extra time so that she would produce ever more milk for the strapping pups."

Now she coughed delicately to call the people in the first snow house. Then she added softly to Nuna as they waited, "For them and for their mother's coming task."

Nuna cocked her head and quieted, but an occasional whine still escaped.

"It is not a good thing," Sukitilan admonished her, "to care so strongly that some cranky spirit is challenged to take away that which is beloved." The young woman drew breath on a sob and wondered where those words came from. Not from Pichikut, who always loved without restraint. From the immature Sukitilan then. The child who had lost three brothers and her mother—and now might lose her home.

One snow house at a time, Sukitilan distributed five pups among villagers who were delighted with the gifts. "A dog from *angakok's* clever bitch. What great good fortune is this?!"

What she did not do, something counter to the Plan, was remove the sixth and final pup, her favorite Ajak, the "small blizzard," a yellowish gray fur ball brindled black and white. Oh, Sukitilan and her mother had argued formerly

26

on that matter with heat and frequency.

The daughter would say, "It happens that Nuna is likely to lose heart if all her young are suddenly stolen away."

"That dog is to have but one obligation," the woman would retort.

Now, with her mother dead, Sukitilan felt a niggle of conscience about the disobedience. She had taken advantage of *Ananak's* inability to check on her. Still, it was she herself, not Pichikut, who must live with the result. She fingered her ear. Surely, Sukitilan understood Nuna better. *And did not the mother encourage her daughter to think for herself?*

Other problems were more critical at this moment. What if the sled dog would not accept a human child? Or he not accept her? What if the milk did not agree? Sukitilan's legs began to quiver, and she felt the baby at her waist stiffen in response.

"Milk is milk!" Pichikut always insisted when her daughter worried aloud during the final moons of planning. "The child will have no other source of nourishment."

Sukitilan sighed as she knelt down at the hide flap and cradled the newborn with one hand to keep him from bouncing along the ice floor. Now she crept on two knees and the available forearm through tunnel, harness porch and canine *igloo*, outside blindly into black, breath-stopping cold.

Yes, she herself had built Nuna's crude snow hut at her mother's insistence, all in preparation for Nuna's imminent litter and for the dog's upcoming task— as well as for experience in technique likely to be serviceable on the trail. Narluk, with both brothers at home, scorned the effort. Only a dog would live in such a place, they insisted. But only a dog needed to.

Pichikut did not ridicule. "Here is someone who can build a snow house with her first try," she announced with pride. And to her daughter privately: *"Let them laugh! Men need to think that males alone can build igloo from crisping snow."*

Sukitilan spoke with soothing tones as she crawled up from the short tunnel and through the baffle to Nuna. The dog whimpered in distress from overladen mammaries. The woman groped around the ragged robe she had placed here. She rubbed and patted the remaining pup. Ajak was asleep, breathing noisily, belly distended, gorged with milk. Speaking to the big dog softly as she worked, the woman brought out the still-glowing wick and travel lamp, poured in a bit of seal oil from the bladder to produce a mere glimmer of light unlikely to be noted from outside; then plunged her snow knife through the low arch of roof to make a nostril for smoke to escape.

Nuna scented the human baby immediately, pushed repeatedly at the front of the woman's parka with her nose, whined.

"Patience!!" Sukitilan laughed and gently withdrew the infant in his wrap. He shuddered when cold struck his forehead and broad cheeks.

The dog sniffed with interest, stretched her nose gradually closer, pulled back a moment at the unaccustomed scent, finally gave the infant face a tentative lick. Then another.

Sukitilan placed the baby near one of Nuna's swelled and dripping teats. She rubbed milk on the baby's lips while she watched the dog. The bitch was gentle as sled dogs go, but still would be protective of her one remaining child. She could in a flash purge life from the infant if she perceived a threat.

Sukitilan recognized a dog's power all too well. Again, her mitt went to her ear. Only a minor disfigurement. She still remembered walking out from their summer tent when she was—what? Four winters? Three? And although she knew to avoid the tether lengths of staked sled dogs, she had no fear of free-running, frolicking pups. The young of sled dogs were treated like *Inuit* children—encouraged to explore, roam free and active without restraint. Regardless of their mischief and destruction, no one said *No* to the small ones. One day soon, these young dogs and humans alike would be taxed by grave responsibilities that lasted for their lifetimes. But not yet, not yet. . . .

The ancestor of Nuna was the largest pup among the spring litters—fastest, strongest and most daring. He leapt up playfully on Sukitilan and latched his tiny teeth upon the lobe of the child's ear. Immediately came screams and blood from the little girl, and shouts from all adults who saw what was happening.

When the excitement ceased—with the puppy disengaged from Sukitilan and the child comforted, an indignant Palunga brought out his killing spear. The little dog must die for attacking his sister.

His mother Pichikut stopped him. "Stay. A dog child only played."

"—But no dog may harm *Inuit*, and once it has—" Palunga raised the spear again.

"—Stay. See how he was not frenzied by the wound."

This was true, as all could observe—family members gathered round and villagers as well.

"—Still, he licked the bloodied ear—!" Palunga turned frowning to argue; then swung back and lifted the spear once more.

"—Stay. He did so only to minister to the child. The pup is large, true, but

28

still young and filled with fire. He has no understanding of his strength."

Frustrated, Palunga turned to his father for support.

"It happens that a boy must heed his mother for a few more years." Narluk evidently agreed with Pichikut, and their youngest son lowered his weapon. *Angakok* continued: "The pup may yet become a bright star in the sky." And he had, for he had sired outstanding pups—and here was Nuna, finest of them all.

Palunga muttered imprecations on that day, Sukitilan remembered now, but in time learned to love the dog as he continued to attain size and strength, developing gradually into the perceptive, eminently sensible leader of Narluk's strong team—then breeding sons and daughters of similar distinction. And now, long after that damage done to the ear of the family's only daughter, the powerful Nuna and Sukitilan seemed to have a special bond.

In the tiny snow hut, the big dog nosed down once more to sniff curiously; then gave a quick wash to the baby's face. The child did not protest. Sukitilan placed him closer, and his small jaw began to work when his mouth touched the nipple, but he did not surround it with his lips. *How long*, she wondered, *before a new being—an* Inuk—*knows to suckle?* She patted Nuna, and spoke to her softly. The dog gave Sukitilan's face a quick lick also, before returning her muzzle to the baby and gently nudging him closer. But although the tiny mouth still moved, the baby was asleep.

Nuna accepted the child. The woman knew that she could trust the big dog with her baby brother. The infant would readily learn to eat when he had an appetite—and she knew that, too, for *Ananak* had said it would be so. She looked over at slumbering Ajak. She must take the puppy with her every time she left her brother to feed, at least for now. She picked up the human baby and replaced him in her parka front, secure against the drawstring.

"Soon, we'll try again," she promised Nuna as she doused and collected the lamp; then moved forward into the harness porch and sealed tunnel.

The body of Pichikut nearby, Sukitilan finished automatically what she had started earlier and talked through with her mother often before: sort and packet, weigh and analyze all that was before her. She realized suddenly, overwhelmingly, what a comfortable life she had lived up to now. She understood for the first time how much luxury she had accepted as her due. Splendid parents, for one thing. Big Narluk, sought out for *angakok* skills, honored by inland people everywhere. And unlike many a shaman who used his talent to trick or cajole for personal gain, Narluk was honest, truly concerned about those he thought of as "his people"—and was a fine hunter as well as an affectionate, although often, preoccupied father. Probably most satisfying to Sukitilan, though, was joyful Pichikut—often singing, filled with fun, making jokes, telling wondrous tales—a favorite of the villagers, a dependable source of nurture to her family. The two remaining brothers, as well, sober Oojulit and humorous Pajuk, brave and fortunate hunters both . . . although Sukitilan did wish now, as often in the past, that those two would find wives to cure and process, sew and mend the many hides brought home from the hunt. Especially now.

Unlike most others in the village, for she had listened to the stories, Sukitilan had never in this lifetime known great hunger, had never been wet and miserable in a summer tent nor starved and freezing in a winter snow house, had not been truly lonely ever . . . not until this very day.

Pichikut was gone. That sober thought cast its shadow. Her mother had borne six boys beside the one daughter—many children, for *Inupiat*. With the parents, nine should now be in the household. Only five were present on this morning, and five again would sleep tonight—the newborn to replace *Ananak.* . . . *How many in the family* igloo *for tomorrow's sleep?* the woman wondered. *Still five, or merely three adult males?* Her stomach tightened. Her breath stuck in a suddenly stone-dry throat.

Pichikut was dead. Sukitilan laid her hand on the soft little form resting against the drawstring of her tunic. She scowled. This one had changed everything. . . . Because of him, their mother's spirits fled. Because of him, Sukitilan might have to leave her home. Eh, surely not. Pichikut had revealed her vision of the future, though, a prophecy that was accurate thus far.

Not the child's fault—no infant demands birth. Sukitilan dropped her hand from the sleeping babe within her parka. Although she liked the whole idea of being someone's "big" sister for a change, she did not at this moment feel friendly toward the brother. Must her comfortable life now change completely? And if so, could she survive? The little one, as well? Pichikut always said *Yes*, took great pain to insure that her daughter gained skills needed not only for the home but also for the trail. But must everything be put together *now*? Sukitilan shivered, not from cold; and her bare hand went up to rub the scar on her ear.

As she worked to lighten the prospective sled load, making last choices, her wick burned down to sputter and smoke. She reminded herself once again that tending a seal oil lamp would be yet another new duty for her in the family. She must keep it going day and night within the winter snow house, often in the summer tent or lean-to besides. And if she were not with her family: then what about light and warmth for a small party on the trail? *Her little band,* if she must follow Pichikut's Plan? She swallowed hard and tried to keep her lower jaw from trembling. Through tears that stubbornly collected in her eyes, she had to find reserve flint rock and tinder to take on the trail. . . . Where would her mother keep it? For temporary use, she tightly twisted moss gathered last summer, dipped this fresh wick into oil; then held it on the glowing old filament until it smoldered. She thrust all but the lighted tip into the golden fat. The snow house brightened, and so did her outlook.

Eh, perhaps she could find extra supplies in Pichikut's *Big Feed* . . . her mother's exclusive property forgotten and untouched up to now. This cache always built into the side of whatever they called home could not be used by any but the ranking woman of the household—only by the keeper of the lamp. And now the head woman in this family was Sukitilan. A surge of excitement warmed her as she undid the sinew lacing the top of *Ananak's* bag in the alcove, a pouch generous and tough, made from thick splits of walrus skin. She dug down into the first packet. Cured but uncut caribou hide, soft and light as snow goose down was rolled neatly. She removed it, and placed it on the end of the sleeping ledge.

Then she exclaimed, *"Ai-ee!"* with pleasure. Her cry disturbed the baby, and she patted him awkwardly. Here was precious wolverine pelt—yes, the dark coat from ferocious *kapvik,* to edge the face opening of parkas. The one fur which would not collect ice. No matter how sharp the wind, how severe the cold, how heavy the blowing snow, the hollow hairs of *kapvik* fur stay clear and warm. Every parka of each person in her family was lined with it. But such wealth as that which lay before her would allow trade with strangers for food on the trail—if she should ever find herself upon the trail, that would be—no. This foolish woman-child must cease playing . . . *Probably not,* she warned herself. The remainder of *Ananak's* predictions could easily prove true. Sukitilan might have to take the child and run. She must prepare her mind as well as the little sled upon the knoll behind the village. *Ahmi,* who can know the future?

In a bladder she found surplus household items. Prudent Pichikut! Coils of sinew twisted in different thickness for tying, mending, fishing, even fine strands for the repair of open wounds. And a small soapstone lamp she might take along the trail for emergencies. Eh, she'd drag the whole *Big Feed* out to the rack right now, and bury it with other supplies to pack. All the contents were likely to be as useful as that seen so far. She looked around. Not much remained. Beginning tonight and lasting until complete disintegration by winter storms, this snow house with everything in it would belong to the shell and memory of Pichikut alone.

The young woman's eye fell upon the old harpoon that her mother had brought with her from the far north. It was short and possessed a handsome toggle of carved walrus ivory. The father of *Ananak* was an artisan of skill, an accomplished maker of tools and weapons—but in a land and at a time when every *Inuk* made his own. Old Munkut was no hunter, at least not at any time Pichikut admitted to remember. That weapon must also go on the sled. No man in this household used it, so none would miss it, even though each brother had claimed it as a child. Palunga as the youngest boy was the last to wield it before becoming strong and skilled enough to proudly make his own. She, as a female, was not permitted officially to use a harpoon, not even this abandoned one. Among the inland *People of the Caribou*, to do so as an adult was sure to bring misfortune on her village. Or so some noisy people thought. She could not even carry this small one on those times that she, with Narluk and her brothers, had trekked far east in winter to hunt near and on the sea ice. But that did not mean she could not smuggle it from the village and practice secretly!

Pichikut always laughed and said that what brought galloping good luck to her own *Inupiat* of the frozen seas and ice islands far north could not possibly usher in calamity at this place. And then, her mother proceeded to teach her privately. . . . Alone in the *igloo, Ananak* showed her over and again how to disassemble, then reassemble this harpoon until the girl could do so with amazing speed. Out of doors and in secluded places, the older woman coached her daughter in its use. Sukitilan remembered the long hours of drill with the weapon. She had practiced on tundra snow and icy rocks with this harpoon that fit her hand as well as the new killing spear Pichikut had made for her. Except that her mother called those white mounds *caribou* and *bear, walrus* and *whale*, pointing out imaginary heads and legs, fins and flukes—then insisting that her daughter strike only vital spots.

Ah, and may the clever woman possess good fortune in the hunt! she would say over and again, not only when they used the weapons but also when they took the trail or even worked together in the snow house.

"What is meant?" Sukitilan would demand. "It happens that a daughter is already considered lucky on the trail! Everyone knows that even a tireless hunter, besides having great skill and valor, is undone without a whopping portion of good luck."

Pichikut would laugh but not explain. Her daughter would blush with embarrassment over having complimented herself.

She must make amends for boasting. "It does happen that she is not very quick with weapons," Sukitilan would then admit, for she knew herself to be hesitant about attack. Besides, her brothers frequently pointed out this flaw. "Still," they often added, "creatures good to eat present themselves when she comes on the trail."

True—fish, birds, hare, especially caribou—all happened to be nearby when she was with the hunting party. Even Narluk said so. Each brother had told her privately that having her along insured their finding game.

But no matter how much Sukitilan spluttered and complained or even boasted, Pichikut would laugh and then repeat, *"May the girl have fortune in the hunt!"*

Sukitilan moved silently in darkness to get the last trail needs and finally the *Big Feed* up behind the village into the drift. She would later load and lash only essentials onto the sled she had selected—Palunga's sturdy little bone sled too long unused. She knew that she would continue to think of it as his— if she truly did have to take the trail—and would then feel less alone . . . if being alone actually became—*irk! Stop that!* It is necessary to prepare and pack for a long and difficult trip in solitude. For a cold, dark journey filled with danger. *Always be ready for the worst*—she could hear her mother's voice echo in her ears—*and thank the spirits if destiny smiles instead.*

Top priorities included food, oil, her own fully outfitted hunting bag which included sinew and bone needles for repair of clothing and boots, plus medicine herbs and everything needed for fire-making. On the trail, she must, of course, have a snug *upluk,* a nest for the infant with Nuna and Ajak—some robes anchored firmly on top but protected by a close-tied barrier to cut the wind. Certainly, the main weapons would be hung secure and ready on the antler handles of the sled—her spear and a sharp knife. She would make space for the whole *Big Feed* if possible. She now knew that she was not likely on this night to have time for appraising every treasure in its depths. Doing so later, in a family hut or even on the trail, was sure to be a pleasant task guaranteed to reconnect her with Pichikut.

Creeping down the snowy slope from the rack to the village, she spied Narluk and her brothers still working on the temporary snow house. She walked up. "A daughter will be pleased to chink the cracks," she offered. Perhaps she would find opportunity while working near her father to broach the subject of the baby and to test Narluk's response.

The man grunted at her suggestion, motioned her back without looking up from his work. He stood in the center of what would soon be the new structure and skillfully placed from within the blocks her brothers on the outside cut and brought to him.

"It happens," tall Oojulit told her, "that a young sister has done well to assemble the family's belongings."

She warmed in his praise, but discovered with dismay that she was relieved to put off telling her father about the child. More and more, she feared Narluk's reaction, since his response would circumscribe her future. Anyway, so she told herself, she must try the baby with Nuna once more; then return to the sealed hut one final time. She planned to scrape clean the blood-soaked and by now frozen sleeping robes used for her mother, include them for her possible journey to make the day nest cozier and trail nights more secure. Then, on the hill south of the village, just as practiced in Pichikut's Plan, she had to make a final check while she mudded and iced runners; then packed up and lashed everything securely.

"It happens that effort may be wasted," Sukitilan once told her mother, "if the sled is readied for travel even before a father's attitude is known."

Pichikut's retort was sarcastic, quick and impossible to debate. "A father bent on destruction is sure to stand and wait patiently for his daughter to prepare her runners and lash her load in order to thwart his plans."

Of course she had to be ready. *Ee-ee, Yes.* Time would be short if she was forced onto the trail. She decided now that the readier she was, the less likely she would have to employ her preparations. She sighed. So much was up to her, however the next hours turned out. If she was able to stay with her family, she had to keep everything going smoothly in the temporary *igloo* they built today; then all along the trail with the villagers, and finally in the new place after they settled, for however long they stayed there.

. . . Or for however long *she* stayed. She wanted to ask Narluk when the people or at least he and his family planned to go, but she dared not. At four winters, even five, she had been free to ask all questions that came to her. But now a young adult, she was expected to observe, to imitate, to improvise, to experiment—but not ever to rudely query. One must not disturb the calm center of *Inupiat* with questions. Nor may one tempt fierce spirits and invade another's privacy by direct address, especially with a loud voice.

She slipped up the hill behind the village to the rack. Perhaps Narluk would accept his new son. Perhaps all this secrecy and dread and preparation were without cause, and she would not have to go. Perhaps her mother's Plan was the wild enterprise of a fearful spirit . . . except, as all who knew her would agree, Pichikut possessed a bold and independent essence few could match. She was not a fearful woman. It was her daughter who was timid, Sukitilan reflected. It was the young woman who was haunted by anxiety, who was by nature cautious to a fault—and presently close to panic. It was she who at this moment wished she were any place other than here and at any time other than now. She snorted. And it was this very one who spent good energy chewing and re-chewing over and again that which could not yet be identified and swallowed.

Irk! Stop! *Do each task in order, one by one, as you were taught.* Sukitilan piled melted permafrost clay along the sliding surface of each whalebone runner on Palunga's sled. It froze immediately. Using her sharp snow knife of fire-hardened bone, she sculpted the mud to make a reasonably even coating two fingers deep along the length of each runner; then carefully with a trembling hand carved off each bump and nubbin. Next came melted snow, warmed in her mouth, spit along the sliding surface layer by layer, each coat freezing on contact and polished with a scrap of cured caribou hide until the shallow crescents gleamed in starlight. Now she dug once again through the icy drift where she had stowed supplies. Travel lightly as possible, she reminded herself once again, for the sake of the dogs as well as the sled. But given that requirement, equipment must be complete, especially anything not likely to be found upon the trail. And the order of packing was nearly as important as the content. She must, of course, make a flat space on top for the *upluk,* the nest to contain her passengers. She was still glad she had saved back Nuna's pup. Atop the heap also, securely tied but easily accessible, must be her hunting bag. Here were extra weapons, special herbs in case of injury, flint and precious tinder to make fire on the trail, sinew for fishing and mending, amulets—all her means to secure food and overcome disaster. Along with the weapons carried close at hand, the contents of this bag stood between herself and whatever fearsome creatures of the trail might challenge her presence, whether animal or ghost or—more frightening to a woman alone— human. Sukitilan shivered.

Discovery

The child ate greedily with much snuffling and smacking of lips. By the second feeding, Sukitilan had learned to thin Nuna's rich milk in order to let the infant drink without distress. Pichikut had suggested the dilution. She had warned her daughter to look for too-short nursing time, a hardened belly or other signs of stomach pain. It was not difficult, Sukitilan discovered, to warm in her own mouth a little water from the drinking bladder and transfer it to the mouth of her brother from time to time.

She picked up sleeping Ajak and dropped the pup down the front of her tunic. A three-moon sled dog could be jealous. The infant was no match for a resentful pup, and Sukitilan did not want her brother harmed if Ajak awoke. The human child had finished drinking and now lay peacefully in his wrap against the warmth of his foster mother. Sukitilan turned away and let herself through the back wall of the snow hut into the empty harness porch; then up through the sealed tunnel to Pichikut's *igloo*. Above the broad *iglerk,* she had earlier fastened strong sinew collected from the *Big Feed*. No one must know that she was here, especially now that the hut was supposedly sealed, and she dared not light the travel lamp she had found in the *Big Feed* until, feeling her way in darkness, she had used robes to build a tent where she could work. No flicker of light within the death hut betrayed human presence inside, for she had gone out earlier to check critically from every angle. The small lamp was freshly fueled, and she adjusted its wick to a bare glow, sufficient for her purposes when she left this place and worked beside the rack while her family slept.

Later, Sukitilan lay in the new snow house and listened to the rhythmic breathing and snores around her on the *iglerk*. After blocking the big snow house, or so they thought, as final resting place for Pichikut, and after finishing this new and smaller structure to house them tonight before they moved on with the village after sleep, Narluk and the brothers Oojulit and Pajuk had placed inside it everything the young woman had stacked out on the ice. They all took a meal before rolling wearily into their sleep robes. So difficult, this day . . . for everyone.

Still, Sukitilan knew that she should have insisted on telling at least Narluk about the child. She should have somehow made a time, forced *angakok* to listen. Pichikut would have found a way. The daughter sighed, climbed with stealth from the warm furs and put on her trousers and parka, adjusting the sleeping baby before stepping into her *kamik*. Tonight, she would find small opportunity for sleep.

Silently, she went from the *igloo* into cloud-troubled starlight and picked her way to Nuna once again.

As before, she left her small brother with the dog and tucked the overfed puppy inside her parka before she crawled on through. She could spend needed time with the shell of her mother. Awkward, this ranging in and out through Nuna's low snow hut on three appendages instead of four, always having to support the weight of the baby or else the puppy to keep them from dragging along the ice floor. The effort was worthwhile, though. She very nearly had the bloodied robes scraped, now; and all her surreptitious supplies and equipment were up at the rack by Palunga's sled. Not that she would need—no! A woman must stop her dreaming. She would have to go or *not* have to go. Of course she hoped the latter; who would not? And if it happened she could stay—ah! In a mere moon's time, perhaps less, she could confess to her father and older brothers all the useless preparation that took place on this day and night, all the plotting and planning of the many moons past. *Ee-ee,* they would sit by the fire and laugh as she spun her tale.

Sukitilan doused the travel lamp and poured the remaining oil back into its bladder. She brought down the robe walls, dropped the rolled sinew into an inner pocket of her tunic.

"Forgive me, *Ananak,*" she murmured as she lifted the last sleep robe from the still form. She spread it onto the big *iglerk,* scraped vigorously in darkness to remove frozen blood. This fur, with the two cleaned earlier gave three extra robes that no one would miss, for her family thought them left with Pichikut. Extras to make the special nest for Nuna and her two charges . . . all for the trip she would not, after all, ever need to take—no! She tried to smile but found that the corners of her mouth turned down and quivered. Yes, everyone would laugh together about such foolish fears—for she would never dishonor her mother by revealing that the Plan was Pichikut's.

As the sleeptime deepened, Sukitilan crawled and dragged and stacked and balanced and tied until she found herself so tired that she had to force each footstep and plan each motion of her mittened hands. Her spirits were still at war. She felt herself separating into pieces and losing parts—painfully—

like some captured creature butchered while still breathing. Who would be so cruel? She could no longer find the loved and loving daughter adored by family. Gone was that cheerfully dependent young woman whose every need was fulfilled. Instead, the husk of an untried youngster played awkwardly at being an adult.

Within herself, Sukitilan identified also a dull *Inuk* with vacant eyes who believed all she was told and did what she was drilled to do, a slave to her female parent. This one tread tediously as an instinct-driven insect back and forth through the secret door, up and down the glazed hill, behind the village.

And still another part was mere shadow—too undefined to see a shape, to see that which her *ananak* recognized, spoke of and rejoiced in . . . a sturdy *Inupiat* woman that Sukitilan herself had never sensed at all until today. This part of her was unseasoned, yes, but adventurous and clever—so Pichikut always said—a being who observed and even ridiculed its counterparts, that aged child and the mindless drone. This one had imagination, could improvise as necessary. . . . Pichikut had not, for example, told her female child to take the three birthing robes. Nor had she said to explore the *Big Feed*. Yet, the wise woman would approve.

One final fragment throbbed and writhed within Sukitilan, threatening now to surge to the front and destroy everything else. Here was frenzy—horror at what might be coming, insurmountable panic, sobbing helplessness. This part foresaw doom and disaster, worried continually, was unsure of every move, unwilling to do anything that could not be undone. This *kussuyok,* this coward, trembled at each turn, expected nothing but disaster. It was the *kussuyok* who made each motion so exhausting.

It is good to ponder and plan, Pichikut had told her only daughter once when she grew weary of the girl's apprehensions and misgivings, *but the mind must be married to muscle. A good Inupiat woman does not welter in thought without action.*

So moving, *doing,* busy at the sled, Sukitilan monitored these persona that churned within her like the roiling spirit lights now flickering overhead. *Was she doomed forever to be composed of warring parts? Who and what would she finally become?*

A piece of her knew, for instance, that she should have been fearful in the abandoned snow house, should have been terrified of newly homeless spirits thought by everyone in her village to be wandering and angry. Yet, she had felt only comfort there. . . . At this time and under the present circumstance, she would rather be in that snow house with the husk of Pichikut than anyplace else with anyone else she could imagine. She wished that she could hide there now, until all the important decisions were made.

Once more nestling between robes on the *iglerk* with her family, but still fully clothed except for *kamik,* Sukitilan came out of a light doze into heavy dismay. The baby was awake and crying. She patted him, but he only wailed louder.

Narluk stirred.

She removed the baby from her parka and thrust him deeply into the sleep robes. He continued to squall.

The long sleep breaths of Oojulit and Pajuk shortened. Both shifted restlessly. She heard no sound at all from where her father lay on the far end near the lamp.

Sukitilan dug into the robes and turned sideways to muffle sound with her body. She wanted to disappear with the child into one of the furry wrinkles, and pull the cover after her. She addressed the infant with a whisper in his ear: "It happens, silence is needed here," she told him severely.

But his cries escalated. Could he be hungry or in pain? Yet, he did not seem distressed. His stomach was soft, his muscles relaxed. What he was doing, she decided as the weeping continued, was exercising his lungs.

"Hush!" she whispered. *"Nipjarnak!* Be silent!"

At that moment, the sleep robes that covered her were pulled up and away. From the corner of her eye, she saw in flickering lampglow that her father towered above. Quickly, she stuffed the howling child once more into her parka. *How long had she thought to keep his existence a secret? What a fool she was, what a* **soospuk***!* She dragged a fur across her.

"Trim the lamp wick," Narluk told her.

Sukitilan came off the ledge reluctantly, the baby still in full cry. **Pirtok.** What's already happened cannot be undone.

Although she kept her head down, her eyes on the lamp, ministering to the wick as the snow hut brightened, she knew that her father stood by her once again. She sensed his turning away to get his furs from the bladder, heard him put them on over his *illupak.* Sukitilan felt like some outlandish creature—herself directly from the sleep ledge and now betrayed by still wearing outdoor furs—standing gap-mouthed before her awakened family with a sustained howl arising from her bosom. Adding to the bizarre effect, she saw her every motion as the lamp cast shaggy shadows onto the arching walls and roof.

On impulse, she withdrew the infant in his furry bunting, held him out.

Now the father could behold his new son—could see how sturdy the child was. Narluk knew certainly that the baby had healthy lungs. The cries ceased immediately as the eldest and youngest members of the family studied each other.

The big man cleared his throat, started to speak, and cleared again. "This babe was born of Pichikut?"

"Ee-ee," Sukitilan said softly.

Silence. Then, "Emerging before or after the spirits left her?"

"After."

Narluk stood motionless for so long that the icy terror of foreboding once again crept up to chill the woman. She felt such agitation flow through her that it was difficult to stand on her shuddering legs. Pichikut had described what Caribou *Inupiats* consider to be kindness for a motherless child. Sukitilan might blame this little one for their mother's death. She might blame him also for unwanted changes in her comfortable life. But the babe did not mean to make trouble. And unlike other little ones who could not go suckle at their mother's breast, this infant would not waste away and die. He would be saved by Pichikut's Plan. He had his sister watching over him. He had Nuna feeding him. To kill this healthy child—even quickly and without pain—would be no kindness.

"Give me the baby." Narluk reached out. He already wore his mittens, Sukitilan saw. He had finished drawing on his furs while she stood in that frosty fog of fear. He was ready to go outside. Sukitilan raised her head slowly and saw the terrible resolve flickering in his eyes. Narluk also had a Plan. Once again, Pichikut's prediction would prove accurate.

"Pinnak, don't!" She turned away, thrust the infant back into her parka. Angry bellows resulted. She had seen before she turned her back to them that both Oojulit and Pajuk sat cross-legged on the sleep ledge, furs clutched around them for warmth. Neither said a word.

"Give the baby to me!!" Narluk's voice was hard, without inflection.

Sukitilan trembled—not with fear of what her father would do to her but of what she knew he planned for this tiny brother. She would not turn around. She would stay forever with her face to the wall—stay until she awoke to find that the whole family was still living in the large snow house no longer sealed. Pichikut alive. The baby born normally. All would be as it should be . . . and this dreadful, endless day and night would be only her bad dream to be picked over and analyzed and finally told aloud and laughed about.

Narluk's hand touched her shoulder gently. "The daughter must deliver

40

the babe to its father."

"Why?!" she demanded. She knew the reason. Could he say the terrible words?

"So that the father can do with it—"

"—*Not* it. A boy!" she blurted, once more producing the child, but cradling him with both arms so that he could not be snatched away. "Narluk's *son!*" She turned to the man slowly, arms locked around the baby. Here he was, for full view. "A hearty, healthy child." If she had a name for him, he would seem more permanent. It would help also if she could name the spirit most likely to be protecting him. Again she tried to remember—*what was that last name called before Maq took the baby from his dead parent?*

Narluk glanced at the infant, and then looked away, his decision clearly unchanged.

"He is well-fed," she said, "and will continue to be so."

"That is impossible." The man stretched out his arms once more.

"*Owka!* No!" She pivoted once more, placed the baby in her parka with wildly shaking hands. For a wonder, the little boy ceased his cries.

"A daughter must obey her father," the man urged quietly; then added, "and her mother would wish it."

"–*NO!*" She looked at Narluk. Dark shadows around his eyes were emphasized by flickering light that came from the lamp below. She knew he was saddened by the loss of his wife; by what he planned for the infant, by his daughter's resistance, too. Sympathy for her father glimmered, but she snuffed it out.

"Pichikut planned ways to keep her last child alive."

Narluk answered nothing, but his arms lowered slowly.

"Nuna is gentled for her task."

"Nuna . . . ?!" His voice trailed off.

"Already, she accepts him, and he her."

More silence, and then, "No . . . not possible—*Hoo-oo* . . . a human suckled by *kringmerk*? By a dog? *Ai-ee!!*" He was speechless with dismay and disbelief.

"He'll be healthy—he's already healthy! Cared for by his sister. The father will see!" Sukitilan glared at her two brothers still motionless in their robes, eyes huge with shock. "The brothers will see, as well as the whole village!" Her voice broke into sobs. Then she resumed her plea, repeating former words and adding gradually, amid hiccups of strain, the special provisions Pichikut had made. Leaving Nuna's litter with her to suckle for nearly three moons so that the dog's milk would be sufficient. The woman's love for her yet unborn child, the sustained effort to train her daughter in caring for an infant, the daughter's reluctant effort to learn.

What she did not tell Narluk was the Plan. Her silence on that subject was not by design but instinct. Had she reasoned, the whole scheme would have been exposed, as pleas and promises bubbled like a spring freshet from her mouth into Narluk's deaf ears. She did not tell him that she was packed and ready to go. That if necessary to save the baby she had promised to leave the family forever. That she would run fast and far with the child if her father insisted on heeding tradition without regard for special circumstance.

Later, she thanked the spirits for channeling her loose tongue.

Finally, the words ran dry in her parched mouth, and she stood sobbing across the lamp from Narluk. He moved toward her, his voice soothing and deep. "If a woman in the village could suckle the child . . . " he began; then stopped. A hopeless possibility. No woman here had born a child in twenty-five winters.

"—Nuna can suckle—" she gasped for the fiftieth time.

"—*Owka!* No, she cannot. Certainly, the babe will die—if not soon, then late—!" His voice broke off, and Sukitilan realized that he had put one hand inside her tunic from below while the other fumbled with the outer drawstring. She had allowed herself to be cornered at the end of the sleep ledge behind the lamp, and she felt violated.

She flung both hands under the child and tried once more to turn away, but too late. Narluk's nimble shaman fingers released the string as he forced her arms up.

"Far better," he continued in the chanting tone his voice had assumed, *"that the infant find death before it learns to savor life."*

"*Aa-gii-ii!* NO!" she implored, trying but failing to sound like Pichikut. She felt her little brother taken from her. Narluk eased him away from under her parka with one of his huge hands while with the other he caught and held both of hers.

She stood shaking and sobbing afterwards, as her father stooped down to the old hide baffle that guarded the doorway of this new *igloo*. She heard her voice continue to repeat the previous protests and rationales. But he and the baby were gone. Her big brothers, she saw, had dug beneath the furs to feign sleep.

"Someone sees the two brave hunters hiding from someone less than half their size!" she spat, her bare hand grasping at her ear. Palunga would not hide, she reflected. He should be here with her now. But these two would never deny their father, regardless of any personal feelings. They supported him out of fear. She sighed, still rubbing the lobe. No, out of respect. And did she then not respect Narluk? Never before had she defied him. Nor did she want to now. But in this matter, his blind following of tradition made no sense. Pichikut had explained often the reason for leaving a motherless babe to freeze. Ice death was rapid, painless . . . final. . . .

Not for this one, though . . . . *Ananak* had said her child was to live. But then—ah, kind spirits please have mercy!—she left it for her daughter alone to resist Narluk. Oh, Palunga! How often today had Sukitilan thought of that youngest among her elder brothers? Sensitive, kind even when ruled by mischief, his abiding sense of fun controlled by strong principles about what is fair and just . . . . He surely would have joined this confrontation—and stood gamely beside his sister.

But like Pichikut, Palunga was gone. He had walked out alone on bare ground in the springtime following the winter before this one, looking for the two brothers who had floated away. He had left his sled and dogs, for ice was melting fast and would not support runners. He took only his hunting gear. And he did not return. Narluk with Oojulit and Pajuk searched for him along the coast of the sunrise sea, braving savage tides. They found no trace. And now a new winter had begun. How could he or anyone survive without dogs and sled? Yet in his sister's mind, Palunga remained very much alive.

And here was cowardly Sukitilan once again imagining when she should be doing. She leaped across the ice floor to where she could pull *kamik* over her light slippers. That she wore her outdoor furs—her *silipak*—when she came from the sleeping ledge must have startled her father, certainly the brothers.

Now she dived into the tunnel, crawled from the *igloo*. She did not go for a weapon. Instead, she made her way around to Nuna's snow house. *Why was everyone in this village so old?* she raged. *Why was no woman young enough to put this baby brother to her breast?* She would be glad to leave this place!

Nuna greeted her with a short whine of friendly greeting when the woman stuck her head past the baffle into the tiny ice room.

"Come!" With Ajak asleep on the ancient fur floor covering, the parent joined her readily. The dark night snapped with cold but was at this moment without wind and lighted once more by greens and pinks and blues swirling high in the north.

"It happens," Sukitilan told the bitch as they followed Narluk's tracks across the tundra, "that we must find where he put the child; then hide ourselves until we're certain he is gone." If they arrived too soon, her father would see them coming. And this—absolutely!—must not occur. A second opportunity to save the child would not present itself. He would dash the baby on a rock, if pressed, just as she had seen him and other hunters out of kindness end a baby seal or bear whose mother was taken in error.

Nor must they be too late, she warned Nuna, *or the child would be stiff and spiritless*. She focused ahead on her father's big *kamik* prints. She did not worry overmuch about meeting Narluk coming back, for she knew that he was more than likely to walk over to the rocks above the lake and there quiet his distressed spirit. For this drama tonight would trouble him greatly. Once more, she pushed back her nagging sympathy.

The man should have listened. He should have respected the memory of his wife enough to at least consider her wish. He was closely tied to local ways, Pichikut had warned. His own son must be set out to die because the babe was motherless and no village woman could suckle him. So it was done always. *Peeusinga*. That another arrangement was made did not matter, even if it was viable. Narluk could not project himself beyond the custom of his people, and his wife had known this to be true.

Pichikut had always been a reasoning and reasonable woman who thought—logically—for herself. How Sukitilan missed *Ananak's* quick understanding, her impish smile, the flashing dark eyes which accompanied smooth and decisive motions. And the strength—she especially missed her mother's strength. Up to the right ear went the young woman's mitt. Tears fell and froze on her face. Stifled sobs and hiccups broke the silence until Nuna returned across the tundra to walk beside her and stare up curiously from time to time.

The girl patted the dog's head, and the two kept going. Nuna kept her nose pointed upward in the air, probably scenting her foster child. But Sukitilan picked out tracks, occasionally glancing up to keep a lookout for Narluk, just in case.

It was, of course, Nuna who found the boy. As they started up a long rise, the dog suddenly raced ahead.

"*Nipjarnok!* Silence!" Sukitilan called softly; then stumbled along behind, unable to keep up. *Where was her father? He must not see or hear them.* She at last spied the dog on the crest, hunkered full length on the ground, pale coat on pale snow but shaggy fur in silhouette against the roiling lights in the north. *To give warmth?* Sukitilan scrabbled beneath the big creature to find her brother. He had lain naked upon his white hare bunting. Cold, yes, but not yet frozen. His arms moved slowly but his head twisted from side to side, lips puckered and sucking. She had disturbed his feeding. Sukitilan plucked him up, unwrapped him, tucked him into her parka, and secured the drawstring. She shook the bunting, rolled it up and put it inside also, beneath her arm to warm.

"Now we go for team and sled," she told Nuna, as they started the long walk back. Pichikut's Plan.

Halfway to the village, the baby began to cry once again. No weak whimpering, either, but lusty shouts of outrage. He wanted his meal. When Sukitilan had taken him out from under Nuna to place him inside her parka, he had in silence accepted the change for welcome warmth. Now, though, he made great noise. She sighed. No sound must awaken the people when she returned to the *igloos* deep in the sleep time. Especially, no alien sound of a babe. Nor must her family stir, as Sukitilan entered and left the village silent as the shadow of a red-throat loon.

She clicked her tongue to bring Nuna back; then laid herself down on the tundra, spreading the folds of her parka and trousers as wide as possible after she withdrew the child. Onto spare fur, she placed her brother newly rewrapped in bunting. Nuna understood her own function immediately and lay beside them.

What an eater, this little boy . . . *Kargolarpok!* What a great smacking of lips, what noisy satisfaction . . . Sukitilan smiled as she skimmed clean snow to warm in her mouth for thinning the too-rich canine milk. She listened with pleasure to the sound of feeding, and she delighted in the sight of Nuna nosing down to lick the child affectionately. Here was a time to think, without other action required, and she savored the moments, and turned her thoughts forward to make final selection on which among the dogs of her father and brothers she should take for her team. Nuna would always be her choice for lead—but Nuna had other responsibilities, now.

What of **Iyarpok,** the *Laughing One*? The one that had been Palunga's lead dog, was now claimed by Oojulit. The creature would feel comfortable with his former master's sled. He was large enough to command respect from other dogs, reasonably intelligent . . . but with fierce views. Never mind, a lead dog needs strong will. Iyarpok was aggressive but not vicious. He might do well. She grinned in the dark, glancing up at the one star still visible, beyond the crest of—*what was that?*

45

A shadow bobbed at the top of the rise they had just descended. An animal? Some predator—no, she made out fur trim on a smoothly rounded sphere. A person? Not Narluk, for he would come striding down on them directly. Perhaps some spirit wandering in the sleep time—not malicious, or Pichikut's Plan could not be working so well. Here might be a helpful guardian—oh, she would consider the matter at some other time. Identity other than *angakok* did not concern her, and she turned her eyes away. Sukitilan's bowl for now was full to overflowing. Only three lumpy morsels remained to chew. . . . She must get home, get harnessed, and get away.

The woman's eyes burned as moisture collected on inner corners. Poor, pathetic child, she mocked herself—no tears. . . . She had no time to be a *kussuyok,* a coward—not now. Later, perhaps. Her chin still shuddered as she tightened her jaw. She knew exactly what remained to be done. She had rehearsed each act of preparation with Pichikut as many times as she had toes and fingers. More deliberation—let alone tears of useless self-pity—would only delay her; and speed or its lack could mean success or failure. She must move automatically as the moon and stars, regardless of obscuring clouds that were her feelings.

On impulse, Sukitilan lugged from the leash porch of the abandoned *igloo* two more bladders of permafrost—permanently frozen earth. In the summer season with warmer temperatures and occasional sunshine, upper layers of permanently frozen earth softened slightly. She remembered digging the mucky stuff from beneath shallow-rooted grasses on the tundra. She would take what she could carry to thaw above the travel lamp and pack sled runners as needed. She had to mud and ice the runners several times each run while they made a bumpy winter trail inland, all depending on snow cover, so Pichikut had warned. But then her mother promised that when Sukitilan got onto smooth saltwater ice, one packing each day would be enough. On the trail when she ran out of permafrost, as was inevitable, she would with great difficulty hack out and heat some more. She dragged the bladders up the rise. These would insure her having no delay along the trail for half a moon at least.

Her mind at ease temporarily, knowing that she was accomplishing what must be done, she relaxed. A certain possibility floated into her head softly as wind-borne gossamer—a possibility that soon became a comforting ***probability***. Here was an idea that brought energy and a brightening spirit. . . .

She tested every lashing on the sled, rechecked the runners prepared hours ago. She jerked up and sideways on the loaded frame, tried to topple it.

The cargo was balanced. Good. She laid out on the snow nine separate harnesses she had attached to the sled earlier. They made a rainbow arc with the longest lines at center for Iyarpok. She went down to the village for the *kringmerk,* the sled dogs of her family that she had decided on. The advantage of having no team of her own was that she knew the temperament as well as each dog's working style from having driven every team at various times. All the dogs knew and accepted her. Oojulit would not be pleased to lose his lead dog. Yet, her muddling all three teams by selecting the best from each meant more confusion if anyone in her family tried to pursue her. The best dogs would be gone, and creatures mostly unaccustomed to each other would suddenly be forced to work together. She must take only the one lead, though, or she would create within her own team a chaos unlikely to resolve itself for many moons. Nuna would hate having Iyarpok in her place; but she should be preoccupied with her family. . . . Still, Sukitilan would tie her to the sled nest for the first few runs.

The young woman selected two more good dogs from the team of her eldest brother, dug them from their warm drifts, bought their silence and cooperation in following her to the sled in the same manner that she had wooed the others—by offering frozen prime parts from a haunch of caribou. Delectable pickings for anyone, a banquet for a mere dog.

The creatures were unlikely to eat well on the trail, not at first. In the next days, Sukitilan planned to feed them and herself at every rest break only frozen char—no one's favorite—fish caught last summer, dried and cached secretly for this purpose under Pichikut's supervision. Freshwater fish were small, lean fare normally consumed in summer when neither *Inuit* nor dogs were working hard or fighting frigid temperatures; or else it was bagged for emergency rations in time of winter famine at home or on the trail. She would have no chance to hunt during the early runs while she used speed and cunning to lay a false trail for followers.

The dogs were nervous, unaccustomed to the new sled and to each other. One by one, she hitched and reassured them, talking soft nonsense in a soothing voice. She fought back her own shudders of anxiety that rose up once again to shake her at departure time. *Think carefully. Review what is loaded to go and what is left behind,* she told herself. *It will not be possible to return if a mistake has been made.* She balanced the inner churn by allowing herself to consider the possibility—no, the *pro*bability!—of identifying the guardian spirit for her small brother. She worked to control a rising excitement.

At last, she took her snow knife from the loaded hunting bag and went back to the village and the only snow hut she had ever built. "Nuna, come!" she commanded softly. The big white dog rose obediently but whined back at her sleeping pup when she got outside. *How did she sense that Sukitilan now proposed more than a short walk on the tundra?*

The woman crawled into the snow hut, swooped up Ajak, and then used the snow knife to hack down the secret door in back. Outside, she slashed the small *igloo* into an untidy drift. She caught Nuna's eye and raised her chin abruptly. Nuna was at her heel as she went up the hill with the baby in her tunic and Ajak wriggling beneath her arm.

Sukitilan finally felt calm. Very likely, *Ananak's* dispossessed spirits had found their new home immediately after her death. *In the baby.* Why not? Clearly, she remembered calling out her mother's name as the woman died. What she could not remember was whether the village women were still chanting other names. Probably—but even so, Sukitilan stood closer to Pichikut than the others—and was therefore louder.

Having the woman's life spirits within the child would account for much . . . Sukitilan's ease in the snow house with the lifeless shell of *Ananak.* the child's energy . . . his willingness to accept Nuna. His lusty shouts, too, would be Pichikut's contribution, Sukitilan decided with a grin. His survival of intense cold while he lay naked on the hilltop. Yes, she was convinced; *the vigorous, lusty spirits of none other than Ananak protected this boy!*

Sukitilan arranged her passengers, Nuna first with a double lap of strapping to restrain her along with stern instruction to be quiet and stay put. The dog already disliked not being harnessed, her agitation obvious; but she obeyed. Then the woman placed Ajak beside her mother. Finally, she removed from her parka the babe in his bunting, laid him deep into the warm shelter and studied the unlikely trio. She covered all of them first with an old bear fur but permitted Nuna's head a peeking place. Then she loosely arranged the ragged fur salvaged from Nuna's snow hut floor. She checked the food bags once again and counted six sleep robes beside those which made up the *upluk.* Yes, the travel lamp. Pichikut's *Big*—no!—now *Sukitilan's Big Feed.* They were ready.

She ordered the dogs to their feet in the rainbow hitch. Huge Iyarpok was proud in front, wild to start, straining on his lines against the forked antler set deeply in ice to anchor the sled. The woman picked up the long whip of braided walrus hide.

"It is well that a mother accompanies us," she told them all softly. She felt new strength in the belief that she was not nearly so alone as she had thought. And that so far, she had followed the Plan reasonably well. She expected to hold the sled handles and lope behind the runners for a time, just to be certain that the load did not shift or slide and that her three passengers—no, *four* counting Pichikut—rode comfortably. Then she would take her spear and run forward with the dogs to leave behind her on the trail all the terrible events since her last sleep. *"Pirtok,"* she muttered, "none can change what has happened in the past."

"And so it begins," she said aloud as she raised the anchor and lifted the long whip to let it lightly lash the surface of the snow beside the team.

MEETING

From the crest of a hill, Tuk watched in the deep twilight of late morning as two young men not much older than himself moved around their camp. It seemed to him that he was always an observer, these days, never a participant. Perhaps that condition could soon change.

"Hoo-oo!" he complained softly. Had he missed the great Narluk again? Only one remained of two sleds he had seen before the sleep. He left his own team staked at the sheltered ditch between two ridges, invisible to the other camp; then moved on foot up the shallow hill, an icy gale scouring his face so that he pulled at his parka string to narrow the opening. The unbroken snow cover was tight, wind-blasted, uneven but still slick and treacherous.

He slipped, fell, got up laughing at himself, and moved on. "It happens that the man of nearly twenty-five winters who dreams himself a fully formed *inuk* is as clumsy as a new-born seal."

Last night, he had located, by the glow of their lamp the very strangers he sought. He stopped to make camp, then, keeping the wind in his face to assure that the others were safe and to mask his presence from their teams. No need for a power battle among dogs after his had been so long on the trail. They no longer reacted to strangers. They were hungry. They were tired. So was he. The team seemed to share his anxiety, as well. Alien scents had been their fare since spring, when he and his family journeyed deep into the mainland tundra from their coastal home. Nearly three moons ago. Sadness flooded him like sucking tide. But he must separate himself from such feelings. *Pirtok,* none can change that which has occurred.

When he got to the top of the north ridge, he looked back fondly at the furry creatures on which his life depended. The corners of his mouth turned up. The dogs would likely leap and sing to celebrate return to familiar scents and sounds and sights, so long had they been gone from coastal shores. Ah, the sea. He too would rejoice when—and *if*—he could go home.

Even without his family. They were gone. *"Inueruttyok,* the people are gone." Tuk heard his spoken syllables bounce and echo like a lonely cliff bird

50

calling as it flew above deserted, wave-washed boulders. Fifteen sleeps since he had buried his parents and small sister under rocks above the frozen ground . . . and then awaited his own end.

Except that he did not die—did not even become ill, at least not yet. After the tragedy, he had first moved northeast toward sunrise sea ice and his own island village. He yearned to be there; among the laughing, happy *Inupiat* he had known all his life. But then he stopped. *Would he jeopardize the very ones he loved? Would he cause their sickness and death?* He pondered the matter for three sleeps before making a hard decision. He would turn back and travel further on this barren, unfamiliar tundra to seek out *angakok,* to find some shaman who could tell him whether a malignant spirit rode upon his shoulder.

Pushing memory behind, Tuk now found himself still studying each dog below him with affection. Too many to feed, he knew. His father's eight together with his own six. He should have picked out the best, butchered the rest—he had little to carry, and all of them could use the food!—ah, but *which* six or seven to keep? At the time, Tuk excused his lack of prudence by telling himself that he would observe them on the trail, see which among them worked well with the others. So he harnessed all fourteen, and they pulled together in harmony and as fast as *Nigituk,* the tireless south wind, each trying to outdo the other. They worked up spectacular appetites, as well. . . . But he knew soon after starting that all of them including himself would eat or starve together. These *kringmerk* were his friends, his only companions. Perhaps he would feel differently when the hunger beast gnawed deeply at his belly.

So he staked the big team last night, built a tiny trail house, forced himself to be patient about contacting the strangers. Time enough tomorrow, when all were rested, for him to approach the shaman called Narluk whose trail he had followed now for eight sleeps. Timing was important. The child inside him wanted to leap over the crest of the hill immediately. That youngster wished to shout his need at the top of his lungs, to stir up the strangers as well as their dogs at the very moment he found them. But the thoughtful person who remembered that the quick way to do a thing is rarely best—the Tuk-He-Was-Becoming—knew to wait. It happened that an ignorant and troubled young man needed information that only a shaman could give. It was fitting, then, that he present himself with dignity on a fresh day.

So here was morning, very late and finally glimmering light on the far south horizon, but no shaman to be seen. He snorted. So much for mature decisions. *Or might so many difficulties be sent him by phantoms of the trail to serve some strong purpose?*

Narluk. Great *angakok* of the inland barrens. The shaman whose name was recommended first by so many. He remembered his difficulty over inquiring of people without putting them in peril. He learned right away that it was impossible to keep physical distance between villagers and himself. In that sense, these *Inupiat* were like those he knew at home. He tried entering a village only once—but then panicked as first children, and then men and women, came boiling from their summer soddies to welcome the visitor. Remembering the horror of his own family, all of whom had sickened and died within a single sleep—all harboring base spirits so hot they consumed themselves and their hosts—the young man turned his team and raced at its head as far and fast as possible.

He must avoid villages until he knew himself to present no danger. He reasoned that he could better control the rare meeting with a hunting group along the trail. So as winter began and he came across sled tracks, he would note the paw prints and follow until he encountered someone on the trail. Every hunter he found—Tuk ever careful to stay safely downwind at least a sled's length back—recommended Narluk. What a powerful shaman he must be! By now, the young man pictured him tall as a *kayak* upended, wide as a musk ox in full fur, age-wrinkled as a walrus and wise as the most venerable she-bear. Tuk must find him—*only* Narluk!—to learn what risk for others attended him on the trail.

And now, at last, the man was surely nearby. Tuk turned away from his dogs, walked toward the strangers' encampment. He hurried forward when he saw that the men had spotted him and were coming to meet him.

"A stranger is welcome!" greeted the smaller of the two as he came close. He was short, heavily muscled, but seemed to spring tall with energy at every step. He might be Tuk's own age, perhaps older.

Tuk stopped, raised his arm and hand, palm out, fingers pointing up, to ward off the approach. "It happens that someone may carry sickness," he explained. He was downwind, but still—who knew how far a malignant spirit might leap?

The rangy man looked older than his brother and came to stand towering over the first.

"This magnificent little fellow is called Pajuk, and the gangling collection of bones beside him is his brother Oojulit." His voice carried on the wind but was soft. It is never good to draw the attention of trail spirits by speaking a name loudly.

The smaller brother smiled.

Tuk introduced himself, thinking as he spoke that angular Oojulit was too fleshless to withstand a famine. *Ai-ee,* too slim to miss a single meal. . . . Yet, he seemed hearty. "Someone searches for Narluk," Tuk said.

"As do two others!" Pajuk laughed, his broad face folding inward to a grin. "It happens that a father went to hunt and left two lazy sons asleep rolled in their robes."

Oojulit cleared his throat, his features sobering. "These days, *Angakok* walks often while others snore and dream."

"Yes, and this worries an elder brother," Pajuk told Tuk, still smiling, "but the younger knows this to be his father's *way,* now that—"

"—A matter which holds no interest for the traveler," Oojulit interrupted smoothly.

Pajuk closed his mouth.

Tuk wanted to protest. He wanted to say that he was extremely interested in their father, having heard so much about him and having tried so hard to find him. But something private was here. He could sense pain tucked in behind the voices, even Pajuk's, so he only smiled.

"It happens," Oojulit said then, "that Narluk's family has too much food for the lazy dogs to carry. It is necessary that a guest come help to eat a meal, poor fare though it will be." His eyes moved past Tuk to scan the dim plains and hillocks beyond.

Pajuk chimed in again. "Eh, terrible stuff. . . . The family hunts but never *finds,* as someone is about to learn." He laughed easily, good spirits restored.

Tuk chuckled. It was pleasant to hear someone speak in the traditional manner, belittle himself and his hospitality—and then most likely produce a feast.

Pajuk wheeled as if to return to his own camp. But Tuk was intent on staying downwind of both brothers. He first, and finally Pajuk, waited impatiently while the tall man continued to study the land to the south, the direction from which Tuk had come.

"If a visitor has dogs," the tall man said at last—and who could be on a trail in winter without a team?—"it may be that we can find a few old harness straps for them to chew."

Tuk got into the droll mood, even though he had fed his dogs their usual meager fare before leaving camp. "Someone's scrawny, mite-munched creatures would be pleased for a change to have a meal so substantial." Actually, the response was barely understated. Tuk had fed them what he fed himself—fish exclusively, which they and he ate without gusto. It would keep them alive, but it offered too little fat to protect them from the frigid temperatures. He could offer his team nothing but summer staples, for he was taking small time to hunt during his search for Narluk. Nor was he skilled at capturing prey on inland tundra. He had enjoyed no success at all in his search for local, unfamiliar game. When he followed the tracks of large-foot white hares, the animals popped up and spotted him; then disappeared before he gauged their proximity. Twice, he had seen small groups of caribou, stragglers at least a moon behind large herds. But never had he managed to decrease the distance between them and himself, even though neither herd appeared to be alarmed. Eh, why should they be? Only an ignorant alien followed them with his play-spear.

He had seen the occasional muskox also, *oomingmak,* but was fearful of their speed and the ferocity described in legends. These mysterious creatures with shaggy pelts that flowed outward in the wind could be found on his familiar coastal plains, as well. His people did not eat them, although he with others plucked up and saved the long strands of their discarded fur from prairie grass and rocks. He remembered his father telling of a villager who, as his father phrased it, *searched for muskox until the creatures caught him.* The hunter did not survive the encounter.

Oojulit returned to his camp while Pajuk trotted back with Tuk for sled and dogs. By the time sled runners were iced, sled loaded and team harnessed, the wind had shifted, now rising from southeast. The younger brother moved ahead to remain downwind on Tuk's request, but the two still managed to visit. Pajuk turned everything into a joke, and Tuk moved along enjoying the jerky conversation, delighting in the rhythm of human speech.

"Can it be," Pajuk asked, "that a traveler plans to catch a whale for his many dogs to carry?"

"No, someone goes to find a boulder that contains a cave," Tuk replied, "for the herd of dogs and one man to shelter from the icy inland wind." As if his coastal plains were likely to be warmer.

And so went the senseless prattle building amity between the two. Soon, now, Tuk would get a shaman's answer to his question about infecting people. And meantime, here was welcome camaraderie.

Tuk's father always said that someone's spirits behaved strangely after many sleeps alone upon the trail. Someone solitary for too long fancied enemies that did not exist, he said. Such a person twisted natural events. *When an*

54

unsuccessful search for food becomes calamity directed at the lonely hunter, he must seek out someone to talk to. In those days, his family would recognize unreasoned fear, even hostility, in a stranger long isolated on the trail. That same person might later relate frightful interaction with trail spirits and even real or imagined monsters seen along the way, and would most likely laugh as he told the tales. At such time and regardless of the storyteller's skill, Tuk could barely imagine the adventures described, for he was never lonely in those days. He was hardly ever alone. He had parents. He had a younger sister who never stopped chattering.

Recently, though, he did understand. Only a few sleeps back, he had convinced himself that the stars vanished behind clouds and the snow skittered wildly along the ground in order to obscure the winter day deliberately, so that Tuk would once again leave the trail and be lost upon featureless barren ground. He needed this Pajuk and his brother, he realized now, as much if not more than he needed their father.

Now close to the new camp, Tuk tried to push back anticipation of good food to come. He carried on his sled the remaining fish and berries saved by his family during summer, all before the terrible sickness. But here was early winter, and a person needed good animal suet—not fish and berries—to meet the increasing cold from each day. So did the dogs. Perhaps Narluk and his sons would serve caribou plump from a summer's graze on tundra grass. Or they might have bear or even—eh, his mouth streamed water at the thought— seal or walrus, even whale that had given itself on a trip to the coast last spring. Perhaps the man and his sons were returning from sea ice now? But no, he wondered about their travel south and east and all alone. He had the impression, as he spoke to hunters along the way, that Narluk had a large family, all or mostly sons. Where were the others? But of course he could not ask. One does not rudely pry out thoughts from the private center of another.

He had been told that *three* sleds of the family had left the village—one was missing? What did Pajuk mean when he reported that his father *now* walked while others slept? Tuk thought back upon his search. After making the decision to find *angakok,* and after hearing time and again that Narluk was the person he should talk to, he had gone south and west to get to the man's village, taking direction from hunters along the way. All knew him. All recommended him as they stood downwind to talk. Then when he finally neared the place very late in a sleep time, he had to stop when he saw a young mother suckling her baby outdoors and accompanied by a huge white dog. He followed her on foot to the cluster of snow houses glimmering in starlight.

In fact, he saw her silently leave the village soon after. Quick and confident of movement, capable with the team—*an unusual sight among inland Inupiat, a woman alone with a sled*, he thought at the time. Not so uncommon, especially with widows, among his coastal people. What was peculiar, though, was that she left with no one attending her. And she moved slowly, silently, until she got well away from the *igloos*. Then she vanished southeast at top speed. A curious matter but not his concern then or now. He had gone back for his own team, later found a rolling knoll where he could see the collection of glowing *igloos* and wait out the sleep time before approaching Narluk.

But Tuk had been weary, and had slept late. The village was on the move when he awoke. Whole families streamed north and west along a common trail. He questioned a hunter driving a heavily-laden sled with one old woman perched in robes on top. Narluk's village, yes. But their *angakok* was gone, the *Inuk* told him. Their shaman with his family had left very early, perhaps even during the night. Odd, the villager conceded, but the shaman may have been called away by someone who reported urgent illness. The important man having recently lost his wife, he may well have decided to take his family with him. He would certainly seek out this village on return, the man said with pride, "for *Angakok* has lived among these *Inupiat* for many years." Three large sleds and a small one not used recently—all gone, the man reported. Then he walked back with Tuk to point out tracks leading southeast from the village. One set had left earlier, they both noticed as they studied the imprints.

Narluk's trail had not been hard to follow until two sleeps ago when a shrieking north wind brought tight new snow cover. Tuk lost time then, while he cast about to pick up tracks, finally grateful to Imana, his father's lead dog, a creature that seemed entirely certain of the way.

Now at Narluk's camp, both teams were fed, and then staked well away from each other, most dogs rapidly digging into drifts to spend the night. Tuk's team was drugged silent but blissful after its vast and unaccustomed feast on caribou. Tuk, himself ,was relaxed for the first time in many days, his belly truly satisfied by good red meat and his mind mostly at peace. Narluk would surely arrive soon, for the sleep time approached.

The three young men put their two sleds in a wedge against the wind, draping both with heavy hides and robes to protect the lamp from a gale moaning up from the south. They sat on heavy robes, some belonging to their guest. Tuk thought it strange that the inlanders he observed seemed to prefer a drafty tent or lean-to like this along the trail instead of troubling to make a cozy snow house. But of course he made no comment. He detected quiet Oojulit glancing anxiously to the northeast, the direction of the sled tracks that Tuk had noticed this morning. Once, Pajuk mentioned that his father would face a stiff wind on return. That was all. They spoke of other matters as they got to know each other without ever asking questions.

Then out of the blackness which was a late winter afternoon appeared two dogs, one pale gray, the other rufous and brightly reflecting lamplight as he bounded to the brothers. Oojulit called each by name, and they devoured the food he offered.

"A father has loosened these to find us," he told Pajuk. Tuk sensed alarm beneath the mild words.

And Pajuk was already on his feet, pulling the sled out from hides and robes, rolling up furs, icing runners rapidly.

Tuk got up also and was piling his own robes when Oojulit came to him.

"It is best to move the camp, since a father took only his sled and dogs with spear and hunting bag—"

"—No robes!?" Tuk exclaimed, for intense cold rode the wind, and a storm was likely.

Pajuk shrugged. "Narluk is not one to plan deeply for the future," he grinned, but Tuk could see by lamplight that his eyes had gone narrow with concern.

No one would take a winter trail without robes, Tuk thought—ah! except some powerful *angakok* who could burrow for warmth into the center of the earth. . . .

Oojulit walked over. "Does it happen that our visitor might plan to let the wind blow him as it will?!" He pointed northeast, the direction of Narluk's trail.

Tuk raised his eyebrows, *Yes.* He picked up his water bladder, iced his runners.

"And can his team carry more than it brought?"

"Ee-ee-ee! Certainly," Tuk said, excited. Not only would he soon see Narluk; but by coming in the company of his sons, *angakok* would be all the more likely to take time to speak with him. "These dogs have eaten such good food—they could now pull sun and moon with all the stars behind." Even Oojulit laughed, for Sun and Moon, though brother and sister, are mortal enemies and can never be together in harmony. Tuk unstaked and harnessed his dogs immediately, spread his own robes and few remaining supplies on the bottom; then stacked and tied additional packs brought to him by Pajuk.

"A father will put these on his empty sled," he assured his visitor, "when the dogs have shown us his whereabouts."

They cleared the camp completely. Not long after Narluk's pair of dogs arrived, these same two on long lines raced back to lead the way. They moved with speed, for *Nigituk* the strong south wind thrust them forward.

In full dark of late afternoon, the two path-finding dogs stopped at last, flopped onto the ground and eyed Oojulit expectantly for food. Pajuk gently probed suspicious white mounds until he uncovered part of Narluk's team. Five dogs staked apart came out on lines reluctantly at first from shallow nests in snow. Each barked welcome to its mates and challenged Tuk and his team of newcomers. The shaman would have had to help dig the holes, Tuk realized, for drifts here had a thick ice crust. So Narluk was healthy enough, probably uninjured when he arrived.

"He took ten dogs this morning," Pajuk worried aloud. No rounded drifts remained.

Oojulit nodded. "It happens that three are missing."

"Someone wonders how many were sent to find his sons."

The three young men probed in the darkness. Blasts of snow now came horizontally on an escalating gale amid moans and howls. A smoking ice fog spread along the ground and confused what small vision was possible. Soon, it would be impossible to see anything. If they had not built a trail house of ice blocks, when the storm gathered full force, they would need to attach themselves to each other with sinew to avoid losing the others.

Tuk unharnessed and staked his team, used his snow knife to break the crust so each could make a shelter. But he held back Imana. He prized this yellow lead dog for special qualities—a keen nose and great good sense. It was he, with snout raised to taste the air; that led him to Narluk's party after a snowstorm obliterated the trail. Now once again Imana tested wind, moving off toward a jumble of boulders. Near a cloud-like drift piled on the lee side of the stack, he stood and whined. Tuk followed but saw nothing. Then the dog sat down and sang, teeth bared, muzzle high and maw open, his eerie melody blending with the gale.

Such was Tuk's faith in the dog that he called for Pajuk. He even forgot to stay downwind as the two excavated carefully with their flat snow knives. Each would first probe gently with his blade before vigorously scooping snow. Now came a faint wiggle from the other side. Pajuk drew back, transferred his snow knife to the other hand and grasped his spear from the ground at his feet. If they disturbed a white bear with cubs, she would come whirling at

58

them. Tuk, though, took comfort in knowing that what they had heard was not Imana's bear song. Nor were the dog's hackles high.

The head of a sled dog emerged at last; then another and one more. And now a man Tuk realized must be the long-sought Narluk erupted from beneath the snow and stood up groaning. The young man stepped back in awe as the huge man stretched stiffly. He was nearly as big as Tuk had pictured him—taller even than his elder son, very nearly as tall as a *kayak* on end, and certainly thick as a young walrus. When he rubbed frost from his face, though, the visitor could see that he was not nearly so old as his reputation suggested.

"Eh . . . the sons finally arrive!!" He squinted to look beyond Pajuk, only glancing at Tuk, until his eyes focused on his eldest. "It is good for a family to be together," he grunted.

"It is good also for a family to *stay* together—not wander off without a word," Oojulit responded.

Tuk had the feeling that the words referred to more than his father's straying from camp.

Then Narluk walked up to Tuk himself and smiled. "A visitor!"

Stricken, for he had forgotten his problem in the excitement, and now may have endangered these people, Tuk moved downwind quickly. "It happens that someone needs wisdom from a great shaman," he said.

Narluk chuckled. But before Tuk could say more, Oojulit broke in. "A father is well?"

Again Narluk laughed. "The graceful hunter could not return to camp," he explained, "because it happens that he fell through lake ice warmed by a runnel. It became necessary to get dry."

That explained it, Tuk thought. Some dogs staked, some sent for help; then three holed up in a snow cave to share their warmth to dry the man.

Oojulit nodded. "One has heard that warm springs can thin lake ice invisibly in unexpected spots."

"*Ee-ee,*" Narluk agreed, "and this eager old man ran before his team—his sled and dogs stayed comfortably dry."

"A father will someday remember to take at least robes at all times," Pajuk preached in a singsong voice, as if the sermon were an old one, oft-repeated.

"*Kringmerk* is far warmer than a robe!" Narluk insisted.

"But perhaps less comfortable to lie upon?" Pajuk asked.

Later, before anyone took advantage of the snug warmth in the lean-to they built in front of Narluk's ice cave, the man listened to Tuk's worries.

"How many sleeps since stones were placed above the empty vessels of a family?" he asked.

"Fifteen," Tuk said slowly, fighting sorrow brought by the memory.

Narluk looked over at his two sons. "It happens that a small *igloo* is needed now, nearby and downwind to the north. Our coastal cousin is bound to be more comfortable in a snow house."

Tuk shuddered. Then *angakok* believed he still carried sickness? "Is it possible that a careless *inuk* has already contaminated his new friends? He forgot to keep distance during those moments when he with Pajuk dug at the drift."

The man shrugged. "We shall soon know." He reassured Tuk by placing a mittened hand onto his arm. "In such instance, we shall also discover whether *angakok's* herbs and amulets have potency." Narluk's voice broke off, and a faraway look came into his eyes.

But of course the medicines were powerful. . . . Here was a strong shaman, and Tuk could sense his force. Unlike some he knew among his own people, noisy braggarts full of empty wind—whose magic beyond trickery was limited to sensing a time when a village he served had been especially lucky in the hunt and was planning to have a feast. Narluk was soft-spoken with steady eyes. He had a family. He took part in the hunt . . . earned his own way *and* ministered to those who needed him.

Tuk relaxed and went to chink the seams on the small *igloo* just now finished by Pajuk and Oojulit. Later, behind a protective wall of ice that enabled the big oil lamp to burn outside the main shelter, Tuk stood up to tell his story.

"Late in summer, the two strangers came. They arrived after the first heavy snowfall, as this man with his parents and small sister prepared to join their winter village on the sea." His movements were first of drifting snow; then of wrapping and patting and tying packets on a sled, finally of people who approached.

"Must have been coastal *Inupia*t," Oojulit said, "not our caribou people."

"Ee-ee," Tuk responded. The taller son of Narluk could not have known where the visitors came from—but see how gracefully he got the information he sought without asking rude questions? Tuk placed the method in his memory for later use.

"When they returned at summer's end to build their *igloos* near the sea, the men said, dog-people came to visit. The heavy-eyebrow *kalunait.*" Tuk drew himself up and stomped about, working his own brows.

"Ee-ma! Oh yes!" said the three rapt listeners. All knew about these

exiled dog-boys of their sea-queen Sedna, even though none but Narluk had ever seen one.

"It is likely that they came on land from their giant floating *kamik* which chases whales," the shaman added.

Tuk shrugged. He did not know. "Besides food and skins—" supplies *kalunait* were said always to want—"the men requested walrus ivory on which to make pictures with fine black marks—that's what the strangers told us."

Oojulit looked up with a thoughtful frown. "Called by them 'scrimshaw'?" he asked his father, and the man lifted his brows to show agreement.

Tuk noticed that Narluk had taken from his parka pocket an amulet of miniature knives, none sharpened but all shaped smoothly from various colors of soapstone and attached to each other with braided sinew through holes drilled smoothly in the handles. The man fingered them absently as he listened.

Tuk resumed, carefully tailoring his tale to the trail on which he had set himself, not veering off into his feelings of sadness for lost family or into resentment of lethal visitors. "The *Inupiat* visitors told us that all in their village had sickened and died—all but our two guests. '*Tokoyok,*' they told us, 'a village is dead.' They said whole families died together in their snow houses built on sea ice."

"One has heard before of savage spirits brought by *kalunait,* Sedna's heavy-eyebrowed pups. They come up from the south and sometimes bring sickness which strikes suddenly," Narluk agreed.

Tuk continued his story. The two survivors had sealed the village snow houses and come inland to flee malignant spirits. "'Burning specters snarled within our people,' they told us. 'Then came much coughing as the body attempted to expel them. After that, nothing—all dead on their sleeping ledges, none left to nurture them, none left to be nurtured!'"

The strangers had been invited to go hunting with Tuk and his family before moving on, and they spent the span of several sleep periods upon the trail together. "Then after they were gone, it happened that the sickness of their village occurred as well within someone's parents and sister." The young man kept his voice steady and fastened his mind on the sound of the words, not on their meaning.

Narluk was silent, waiting for Tuk to say more. When no further words came and the young man sat down, the shaman spoke with great sympathy, still fingering his amulets. "Somone needs to know how long the two survivors were on the trail before finding Tuk's family. Also how long they stayed to visit and to hunt."

"Twelve sleeps before they came upon us, so they said." Tuk watched Narluk's face in the lamplight. "Then at camp, and finally hunting on the tundra—" the young man thought back carefully—"four more sleeps or so, as it is recalled."

Narluk deliberated; then cleared his throat. "To be fully safe, the visitor called Tuk should continue to stay downwind and separate, whenever he is with people—for yet one more half moon." The man smiled.

Relief flooded through Tuk. He could start home. . . . He would need more than half a moon to reach his village from here. And to meet anyone along the trail would be unusual—unless he deliberately followed tracks he crossed, as earlier, when he searched for information about *angakok*.

"A wandering man has not caused sickness for others, then?" Tuk had to ask, even knowing such a direct query to be discourteous.

The big man sighed. "These hot spirits are hard to understand. Still, if someone has taken all along his way the same precautions practiced here—"

Tuk raised his eyebrows and sucked in breath simultaneously, to communicate an emphatic *Yes*.

"—Then the cruel spirits which sat upon the two visitors, and which may be riding Tuk's shoulder now, could not easily go to another."

Tuk waited to see if Narluk would say more.

The man looked at him; and then over at his silent boys and back. He cleared his throat. "Wiser men than this *angakok* have observed that these evil spirits are not great jumpers on an icy trail." He stood up, plucked a couple of robes from a walrus hide packet and moved back from the fire more fully into the lean-to.

That was it, then. Tuk would go due east in the darkness of a new day. *He should proceed straight as possible to the coast*, he thought. His experience with procuring food—his fair ability in the hunt—was based mainly on knowledge of sea creatures. He did not do well with inland game. *Ai-ee!* Only fish and berries until then.

He looked over at Pajuk and chuckled. "Inland *Inupiat* would laugh to have seen someone's family from the coast chase caribou off the tundra, last summer." They had run a long time, his father and he, and had caught nothing but a weak calf already panicked by young wolves.

"Ee-ee, and all would laugh to see our inland family clear every coastal rock of seals," Pajuk said.

Both burst out laughing as they took turns imitating themselves on the chase of unfamiliar prey. Each had honed special skills for capturing creatures well known to his people. And neither knew much about the other's.

Oojulit grinned. "For this hunter to capture a seal, the creature would need to be tethered to a stake."

"—Or perhaps weak and dying," Pajuk agreed.

All three roared.

"It happens," Narluk rumbled from within his robes, "that an early start is needed after sleep."

The three got up. Tuk wondered about the purpose of this trip for *angakok* and his sons. Their destination was something he was not likely to learn, since none had so far volunteered information and of course he could not ask. *Who would carry so much food on a mere hunting trip? How would animal spirits recognize a need and make themselves available? Would he ever meet these men again? Ahmi, who knows the future?*

He walked over to his tiny snow house and, before crawling inside with his robes, took pleasure in its glow from the small lamp lit within.

Part II
Wild Prairie Run

DECISION

Sukitilan raced south and mostly east on hissing runners. She planned to mislead pursuers until new snow hid her tracks completely. Then she would veer north along the coast. If fortune rode the trail beside her, she would be near the sunrise seacoast by the time her tracks disappeared. Pichikut had filled her with instructions about travel on *tuwak,* the coastal ice. About its many advantages, and how important it was to her goal. Saltwater ice was smooth, she told her daughter, dependable—necessary if the young woman was to cover the vast distance to Pichikut's village in the moons of protective black winter, which assured ground cover for a sled. Sukitilan must not mind the booming of the ice, her mother said. Nor must she tremble at the great cracks and mighty splashes, for these were adjusting pressure ridges and the natural stress of labor as icebergs were born of parent glaciers. To ward off encroaching panic, she now reviewed the lore as she raced before her sled along with the dogs.

In spite of Pichikut's instruction and her obvious familiarity with, and therefore preference for, sea surface travel, Sukitilan dreaded it. That smooth ice her mother spoke of could also be treacherous. It could—and did!— break away from the mainland in large pieces to float away forever with two of her brothers. Or it could snap into smaller bits and spill its occupants into the black water—sled and contents, dogs, people—all pulled down by Sedna the *Sea Queen* to disappear without trace beneath the silent surface. And it could conceal with its whiteness and unending pressure ridges the great white bear that hurtled from a cave, a boulder or a drift of snow, even up from an open lead within the sea itself in search of meat.

Eh, these were not good thoughts. . . . She had promised to reach frozen saltwater as directly as possible when her tracks were gone, and this she must do. Sukitilan tried hard to concentrate on the present, attempted to fix her focus on detail in Pichikut's Plan. But each hour of travel away from home had so far increased her foreboding and the sinking sense of loss. The trip so far was like stretching the loose end of a supple sinew firmly fastened

67

to her family'and village: the tension increased with distance. For a while, she feared that the band might pluck her up—*twa-a-ang!*—and plummet her back home to face disaster. But as time passed, she feared the band would *not*—that it would snap apart and leave her forever separated, solitary on a hopeless trail. Palunga's sled, as it turned out, gave no great confidence. How fortunate had *he* been? As time passed on the lonely trail, she even began to doubt that her mother's strong spirits lay within the helpless child.

She had convinced herself by now that she fought not only her *angakok* father . . . but also *peeusinga*—the custom established by *Inupiat*—at least the caribou folk, her own people. All very well for Pichikut, she supposed. Her mother had been an experienced adult when she came from ice islands far north. Her differences were several, but long ago accepted in the village of her husband. The woman could afford to be confident; also now dead. But here lay folly for a daughter who shared none of these advantages. . . . What a *soospuk* she was, what a nitwit. . . . All alone, barely a woman, only the nineteen full winters, who dares not only to tangle with tradition but also to invent a trail into unknown territory!? Eh, a senseless fool!

She backtrailed. She would return to the place where her village had been; then follow tracks from there to find the new location and join the group. She struck a trail back parallel to but distanced from her former path. Perhaps even now—and certainly by the time she found her people—Narluk would have put his grief behind him and thought the matter through. He would have considered and agreed with his wife's wishes, and would realize that his youngest child need not die. He would in fact be relieved to have another chance. Would be grateful that his daughter had protected the infant. Would welcome the baby *and* Sukitilan into the family once again.

Throughout the return, though, especially during mealtimes and sleeps, the spirit of Pichikut peered out at her daughter accusingly through the great black eyes of her son . . . so it was, or so Sukitilan fancied it to be. She avoided looking into the face of the baby as she cared for him. Then after the third sleep on the way home, something caused her to turn away once more, this time fury overriding fear—now for the first time fully resolute.

She slept part of one night among sheltering rocks on a high embankment. A shrieking northeast wind awoke her, and low clouds hurtled in. She became anxious to get underway before gale and ground blizzard delayed her. She attended her runners, packed up ready to continue her way home, north and mostly west.

But from her sleep ridge, during a lull in the wind, she heard the voices of Narluk and her brothers. She silenced her team; then spotted her family as it carefully followed her own early trail.

"Aa-gii-ii!" she raged, "No . . . It cannot be." So determined, Narluk? So resolved to kill? How dare he be so strong against the wishes of his wife? All the trouble taken, first by Pichikut and now by Sukitilan herself. The target of her fury split itself in flight—as if two geese at the point of a single arrow destroy the aim as they separate and wing to different destinations. Those three below her, yes. But also, how *weak,* this female. . . . So filled with fear and such sorrow for herself that she gave up and turned back despite her promise? Despite knowing what was in store for the little one? Despite her small brother's right to live? And despite all the planning and the effort to make sure that he survived?

The cold wind snapped at her cheeks as she watched the travelers disappear, bare specks south and east. Then she lifted clenched fists to the sky. "Spirits, make time stop and roll backward!" the young woman shouted.

"Come, snow. . . . May the wind rise, bring swirling fog and blinding flake!" she chanted.

> Let *Ooangniktuk,* the great north wind
> Meet in this place
> With *Nigituk* of the south!
> May they circle in a drumming duel,
> Well-matched, thumping through the tundra—
> Howling in their anger—
> Neither able to subdue the other. . . .
> *Let them come!*
>
> May they wear their snowflake mantles,
> Thick to coat the rocks and prairies,
> Muffling a sled trail well.
> May their labored breath while dueling
> Fill the land with ice fog circling—
> And their groans from struggle
> Pierce the air to frighten all who hear!
> *Let them come!*

69

May the two *Big Winds* collide
With clashing power
To make a storm as violent
As the tempest
When land first began. . . .
Let them come!

Never before had Sukitilan called up weather. Perhaps a mighty storm was fated to arrive on that day. Or possibly, the spirit of Pichikut lent its great influence to her plea. But halfway through her day's run, this time turned and heading due east and back again toward coastal ice, she had to feed and stake the dogs, help them dig their drifts for shelter. Within Nuna's large snow cave, she made room for herself and the babe, as well. The blizzard raged for three sleeps and rearranged the landscape.

Narluk's following her was not *such* a surprise, she realized in the comfort of the ice cave, when her rage had stilled. But she felt violated. She fumed not only for herself but also for Pichikut and all *Inupiat* women who lived their lives in shadows cast by men. When she first saw her family below, her fury was without limit. She hated the thought of Narluk's chasing her like prey, the brothers blindly aiding—all moving slowly, carefully and with confidence. Well, in this hunt they would not find success!

Afterwards, as time on the trail passed and her outrage transformed into cold determination, she saw with greater clarity. What had she expected? *Angakok* is more closely tied to custom than most. In fact, *angakok* often himself directs *peeusinga,* the *Way of the People.* Pichikut had predicted Narluk's action, foreseen it clearly despite the love she bore her husband. Narluk's tiny son was motherless. It is the father's responsibility, among the caribou people, to end the infant's life to keep it from suffering. The man's honor was at stake.

Eh, let him search. . . . The power of this recent storm now past would have covered her tracks completely. She had turned back, yes. She was ashamed of her cowardice. But now she was committed absolutely to a course of action. She would find her mother's people, those who lived upon ice islands in the north. Her father and brothers would have no inkling of where she had gone. Not soon, at least, and perhaps not ever. . . .

East she went, and rapidly, half a moon and more until she reached the sea. She took only a little time to hunt and fish. Sometimes, she was successful—other times, no. But her small brother and her dogs did not starve, and of this fact she was proud. She moved cautiously, at first, making sure each night to camp in a draw surrounded by rocks or high hills so that her presence was hidden from any who might search. Very gradually, the childlike rage directed at her father, the fury directed at her brothers, turned to jaw-clenched strength that hardened her muscles and braced her resolution. She still feared Narluk's power—as she should, for his influence spread far—but she no longer cried on the trail. Nor did she wake in her sleep time shaking uncontrollably. Sobs still came sometimes before she slept, and still she trembled at the unknown land and alien conditions that came with each new day. But she now looked back with disbelief at the frightened child who had begun this trip.

Most sleeps passed in the shadow of boulders or some shallow cave, checked first to see that it was not home to some other creature. She trusted Nuna for this inspection. She found a fine, sheltered cave at one sleep time, clean and clear, large enough to shelter the whole team and herself, yet small enough at entry to block for shelter from the wind and cold. When she called Nuna over to examine her find, though, the big white dog crouched low, hackles high and ears back. Furtively, she looked behind her to the left, and then to the right, a deep growl building.

"It happens that the white bitch is keen," Sukitilan murmured as she patted Nuna's head. Both turned away and left that place, putting distance between the cave and their sleep stop. As they jounced along on rocky terrain, Sukitilan wondered what Nuna had sensed. Only two creatures, she decided, would elicit such response. White bear, perhaps with young, or wolverine. She decided that they must have found a bear cave, because the pungency of wolverine would be detected even by her feeble human nose. For the hundredth time on this trip she wished that Nuna could talk. Her nose and ears were exceptional, even for a dog. She was perceptive and wise, sensing and responding to the moods of those around her, human as well as creature. Sukitilan had no doubt that the dog reasoned—she demonstrated this ability almost daily. *So why not speak, Nuna? Why not share a wise dog's great knowledge with an unseasoned woman on the trail?*

Perhaps some day following the sleep, the big animal would come up to her and say, "It happens that an extra ration of food is necessary." Sukitilan smiled. Should that day come, she would not be overly surprised.

Inland tundra smoothed its deeper wrinkles to become rolling coastal plains.

They slept outside with a lean-to of uncut skins on a floor of robes. Pichikut had explained that an *igloo* was the best shelter when Sukitilan reached the sea. Increasingly, for sleeps where the ice was right, especially if storm threatened, she built a tiny snow house just for practice, found it to be a snug mound impervious to gale where she could curl up with her brother and his foster family. Ajak was plump and frolicking, too rough to leave alone with the baby. But as days passed, the pup learned to tussle in moderation—even as the human child developed strength and resiliency. It helped also that Ajak possessed her mother's tender heart.

After thirty-eight sleeps with cold deepening and now only the briefest and most pale mid-day light, Sukitilan knew that she must stop to secure food. The nine-dog team specially picked from those owned by her family worked together peaceably enough. Iyarpok, the *Laughing One*, ranged ahead and center in the arc-shaped hitch. He seemed to sense Nuna's rivalry and was unfriendly in cunning ways. He did not dare confront the huge female. He knew that she would shatter his bones if sufficiently provoked. So instead, he nipped at Ajak if the pup came close when her mother was somewhere else. Sukitilan worried that he might also consider the human child a target. The sled dog might someday misjudge Nuna's location or her mood. He had so far been a steady leader, never brilliant or intuitive, but strong and biddable. He would be hard to replace before Nuna could wean the babies and be ready.

She warned Iyarpok off sternly whenever she saw him near either of the young ones. "Nuna is larger than Iyarpok, far wiser—half again as clever as this *Inupiat* who speaks," she informed him.

The grey-and-black dog cocked his head as if to understand.

"More important, she is a mother—fierce as a she-bear to any who might bother her pup." Sukitilan thought about that. "Who might bother **either** of her young," she amended. Besides which, she thought silently, any dog that threatens the human child will die by Sukitilan's own spear.

Eh, how savage she sounded!

The woman knew the personality of each animal in the team. She used the strengths of some to compensate for weaknesses in others. Although they may not previously have run together, all knew her and understood her wishes. She rarely needed to use her voice and never the whip of split and braided walrus-skin that she had brought along to slice the air if some command required emphasis.

Sukitilan understood the wishes of the dogs, too. Chief among these involved an absolutely insatiable appetite. Provision available, they would devour all until they vomited, re-ingest that and look about for still more food. Nor did they fatten, for the team was hard-working and Sukitilan worked them hard.

So it was that as they sliced across the last ice of wind-scoured prairie to finally reach the coast, the woman knew that she must stop and stay awhile to replenish food supplies. Their first glimpse of the sea was illuminated by spirit lights churning in the northern sky. She looked at the flatness that stretched before her, now a swirl of pastel reflections. She saw also the black strip far out from shore, something Pichikut called a "lead"—a sparkle of black water which formed a boundary between grounded coastal ice and the traveling ice beyond—the huge, floating and forever rearranging islands of *siku*. Food was here, on and under ice as well as in that somber lead, very likely all along the boulder-strewn shoreline. Sea birds and their nests were here, though no eggs would be found in the vertical sea cliffs of this dark season. Perhaps the shy seal was nearby, a half-grown pup . . . all unfamiliar prey, even though *Ananak* had described and drilled her in the source and capture; then the use of each creature part. She must find a way to seek out whatever was here.

Shelter first, she told herself, and then—she could not keep her eyes from straying inland—the inevitable search for food. Far back upon familiar inland tundra—lost to her now and perhaps forever—was customary prey eager to give itself to any *Inupiat* who was fortunate in the hunt. No. She must utilize the sea and coastal prairie creatures; for soon, these would be all that were available.

Sukitilan sang as she used the snow knife to break through ice to seawater and make a rough circle. She told herself to be silent, but then forgot as she set herself to widening the hole. She was happy. She had made discoveries. Like all inland people, she was timid of the sea. Even though her village might travel often within a day or two's sled run of salt water, and even though she had actually come with her brothers to explore the coast, she never before had found an opportunity to drive dogs on ocean ice. Once past the tidal crack near shore, it was smoother even than freshwater ice in lakes and rivers, just as her mother had said—and being without rocks, much smoother than land. Goose-down smooth. If they could drive north on *tuwak*—the solidly grounded sea ice—and sweep over or around whatever pressure ridges they could not avoid, she need not mud or even ice her sled runners more than once during a full run between sleeps. Once more, circumstance—this time condition of the ice—would be as *Ananak* had described.

She prepared a string of caribou sinew, threaded bait and line through the ice hole, caught herself singing again. Pichikut had reminded her, *Fish are transient visitors. Not like the cautious seal, intelligent, an animal which will avoid its breathing hole for one or two full sleeps—perhaps forever— when it detects sound or moving shadow on the ice above.* Fish, therefore, were easier to capture. Still, she must be quiet. She glanced over at the sled where the infant slept cozily in the nest with Nuna and Ajak. The team dogs were scattered out, unharnessed, relieved to relax, of course, hungry and hopeful. So was she.

A tug on the line she held in her mitts told her that a fish was tasting and testing. A glance at the fur float combined with a new, steady pull informed her moments later that the bait was to his liking. She pulled hard without jerking. The creature below fought the now-imbedded sharp bone hook. Continuing to hold the sinew curled around her mittened fingers, she brought the fish up smoothly, hand over hand, until it slipped onto the ice and flopped a few times before going rigid with cold. Two of the dogs hurried forward, and her hand motioned them away. They stepped back reluctantly, sprawled onto ice, gazed steadily at the catch, a slim but substantial silvery fish nearly as long as the leg of the one who had caught it.

"Someone must have many more of these before it becomes possible to eat," Sukitilan explained to her waiting team, and furry ears pricked forward. She restored her freshly baited line to the sea, and then looked down to address the single fish sprawled on the ice.

Our thanks to *Sea Queen* Sedna for her offering,
And all of us accept, for we have need!
Grateful also are we for *tuktu,* the graceful caribou
Who gave its sinew for the line,
Its bit of bone for carving of a hook.
Even *kapvik* do we thank, the fearsome wolverine
Which answers for its dark and violent deeds
To none but *Paija*—
This *kapvik* gave his piece of pelt with air-filled hairs
That float . . . to tell the tale upon the surface
Of what is happening below.

Again, a slight pull made her check the fur bob and ready herself to set the hook. She was singing once more. . . . Perhaps fish enjoy poetry, the breath of *Inuit*? Are attracted by a melody? Or perhaps—breathing a song or not—Sukitilan was someone who would always be successful in the hunt. So said her family, and so said she!

When seventeen fish lay like driftwood by the hole, she motioned to the dogs, gave one entire fish to each, and they retreated happily with their frozen prizes. They would gnaw and warm their dinner bite by bite, eyeing her reproachfully because it was fish instead of hare or caribou, but down every morsel before she was ready to harness them. She cleared the front end of the sled and dropped all but one of the remaining fish onto the base of caribou ribs. Each icy corpse made a hollow *thunk* that reverberated off the nearby shoreline cliff. As she put her hunting bag on top and adjusted Nuna's nest, she gave the white dog an extra fish, herself first cutting up and chewing some small portions for the pup Ajak. She wondered, *Why do dog parents not feed their young with solid food like wolves?*

"If, near the sea, a person wants to make her igloo *on the land,"* Pichikut had said, *"then it happens she must go far enough and high enough to escape rogue ice and tide."*

The girl could not then imagine a time when she would wish to build her sleep time shelter on sea ice. . . . With her team well fed although not satisfied—not *ever* satisfied by fish—and with each dog separated and staked, Sukitilan returned to the sod-backed lean-to she had built on ground high above the tidal crack at shoreline. Would she ever trust sea ice to support them through a night? Certainly not ever on a night like this, with *Ooangniktuk,* the merciless north wind, wrathful once again.

Often, she awoke during sleep time with anxiety mounting as a storm wind shrieked. Tonight was no exception, and once awake, so she remained, fingers at her ear, rubbing the lobe, cradling and soothing it. Her mind rambled, picking a berry from this bush, and then that one, never stripping a whole plant to collect a meal of anything. She wondered idly whether her success in hunting while she lived at home might have been some kind of shaman trickery by Narluk. Or perhaps her brothers' elaborate bluff to give her confidence. But then, so she reasoned as she lay sleepless in the screeching night, would Pichikut not know? And if *Ananak* knew, she would not abide such nonsense. And if the daughter were *not* fortunate on the trail, then certainly her mother would not have expected so much of Sukit—no, *not* Sukitilan. . . .

She must take another name, and soon. She was so different now—and striving to be more so—from the terrified child-woman who fled family and village. Changed outside as well as in. She had chopped her long hair off to shoulder length because it got wind-tangled when her hood lay back, and then became a dangerous source of perspiration on the trail when her hood was up. She possessed even less flesh than when she started, and what remained was firmly toned, muscular as a man. Never mind her ugliness, being tall and sinewy instead of round and comforting, for she had never aspired to possess great beauty. She had eaten sparsely on the trail because there wasn't much to eat. Also, eating by herself was not much fun—she would be glad when the baby could share a meal with her, could talk or at least listen with some understanding.

Many nights, after a day's run and after the dogs were staked and fed, she would roll into her robes and forget to eat at all—or be too tired to cut and chew. Her face was wind-burned, leathery to the touch in contrast with smooth numb patches where frost had bitten the tips of her nose and both cheekbones. She knew that these would appear colorless to an observer.

And inside this new person, this *not*-Sukitilan, was a stillness born of solitude. A new tranquility that came from being—along with her small brother and her dogs and sled—the only marks upon the snow so far as her eye could see in any direction. A hush that stemmed from knowledge of her growing strength and capability. The old panic visited her imaginings less often as time passed. She now knew that those late night fears were mostly without base. She could solve problems as they arose—if not successfully, then at least acceptably—until a better solution came to her as she gained experience on the trail. For food, she could catch sea birds and fish, at least those. She could successfully hunt caribou by going inland if summer came before she reached the top of the world. Staying by salt water, she would manage somehow to find seal when seal were here, perhaps even walrus. When she found other people—and she would find them!—she could help take whale in spring, as she was anxious for the opportunity to prove herself *to* herself.

She and the baby would survive to find Pichikut's people. Oh yes, the Sukitilan who began this journey no longer existed, and tomorrow she must find a name for the woman newly born amid ice music on the trail.

She had no doubt, anymore, but that the coastal *Inupiat* in the high islands her mother had described would help protect the baby—would safeguard Pichikut's last child. In fact, they would take over as his family. So her mother had promised. *A woman is free of responsibility for the child after she finds her mother's village,* the woman said, *for people there treasure little ones even as wolves cherish their young.*

76

"Do they, then, not set a motherless infant out to perish?" she had persisted.

"They do," Pichikut said slowly, *"but only if continued life for the small one is without hope."*

"Then, how are these islanders so different?"

Eyes narrow in thought, her mother had picked her words carefully. *"Like our people here, they would not see someone suffer—especially not a baby—with no prospect for good life."*

"Suckling a dog . . . ?"

"—They have strong prohibitions, as we do here—most of which were ignored long ago by a bedraggled and rebellious young girl—a nuliajak—*bent on survival. Using a dog to feed an infant when no other provision is possible? Perhaps untried before, for this woman never heard of it—except the reverse, when Queen Sedna used* Inuit *milk to suckle her dog litters . . . so probably acceptable. . . . In any case, the child can be weaned before his sister reaches the islands of Pichikut."*

Sukitilan was assiduous. "Under such circumstance—Nuna's milk might be allowed here in our own village as well!?"

"No." The woman frowned; then shrugged. *"Differing from inland, her coastal Inupiat might be less hard-pushed for food in winter. They are perhaps more willing to gamble on feeding an extra mouth. If a child is cared for and prospering—"* she lifted both shoulders and ducked her head as her voice trailed off. *"Ahmi. None can say the future."*

Sukitilan was convinced by her mother that Pichikut's village would at least take the child. Right now, though, with confidence inflated by the remarkable fact of their survival to date, the young woman thought she might not need their help. Perhaps she could take care of—what name? The child too must have a name. She could not call him *Pichikut,* for no one carries a parent's name, even in such special circumstance. She liked the sound and thought of *Ajak,* a storm-whipped sprinkling of snow. Liked it so much that she had already used it—never dreaming that she might need it for a brother—to designate her favorite among Nuna's pups. Once given, she could not now take it back. . . .

Late the next day, bearing a dozen extra fish and a smiling face, Sukitilan with dogs and sled approached her lean-to under the roiling greens and blues and pinks of spirits tumbling at play in the northern sky. *Someone was in her camp.* One person stood in light that had to be generated by his own lamp. He was not tall enough to be her father or Oojulit. Not thick enough to be

Pajuk. Her dogs barked. Excitement and challenge rang in their outcry, not alarm. Sukitilan silenced and slowed them. Nuna stood up on the sled, braced against its movement. She was growling, hackles raised. When the sled stopped, though, her collar fur settled; and although she remained standing, she made no further objection.

The woman walked up to rest an arm on the dog's back. She had long ago ceased to tie the big husky. "A good mother will protect her small ones," she murmured with approval before she faded back to the weapons in her hunting bag. A stranger and his silent team stood looking at her and her team. The inspection went both ways.

Normally, a traveler among *Inuit* is a welcome sight, no cause for fear. *Inupiats* can and do arrive unannounced from any quarter in any season at any time, day or night, secure about receiving a hearty welcome. They might come alone or in family or hunting groups, might temporarily join a village or merge with hunters on the trail. Although they *always* arrive unexpectedly, since no means exists to communicate ahead, no one ever expresses surprise, for that would be discourteous.

Still, Sukitilan had been long on the trail without seeing so much as a sled track—nothing and no one since that morning long ago when she spotted her family following the marks of her earlier passage. Nor did she yearn for company, not consciously, focused as she was on surviving long enough to reach the high islands before spring thaw. Still more angry about her family than apprehensive, she did not want to consider whether someone would be sent by Narluk, especially so soon. Shrewd and artful himself, her father was likely to dispatch someone similarly cunning—a well-seasoned man—who would look like and pretend convincingly to be someone other than an emissary. Would Narluk possibly select someone this young? The stranger had grave features but an unlined face. His eyes were steady and seemed to be without guile. He too had the stillness of the trail about him. Yet . . .

She had no time to build anxiety. She viewed first with pleasure and then with trepidation the fur-clad human figure that stood beside her lean-to. On either side of him lay a shadowy lump. Seal, she identified by squinting. Saliva flooded her mouth. She smiled. Might oil for her lamp be forthcoming? Light and warmth—how she missed such luxuries!

"Someone would build an igloo for the woman, except that this shelter seems sturdy and the weather mild."

Eh, he had recognized her as a woman. . . . Back in her village filled with aging people, she as an unmarried female was still considered a child.

78

She liked it that the stranger's voice was deep and rich, his sounds carefully produced. His inflection was like Pichikut's had been—eh, *coastal Inupiaq. Wonderful sound,* the young woman thought—then reminded herself that she had heard no human voice at all except her own in a very long time.

"Kinaowit?" she asked. What is the name to which someone answers? Ah, she knew her error even as the syllables were uttered. Not only was she rude to ask rather than wait for him to reveal the information; but also if this stranger gave his name, then she must in courtesy give him hers. What name should she give? *Not* Sukitilan.

"Only genuine *Inuit* concern themselves with names," the young man laughed. "It is necessary to thank someone for proving that she is no spirit of the trail. The hunter standing here is called *Tuk.*" And in a few moments, when she did not return the courtesy, "The woman's name, then? And that of her child?"

"The *child?!"* burst from her lips. Her brother was asleep in the robe nest on the sled. He had made no sound or movement. How did the stranger know about a baby? She looked to his sled and saw the tracks behind it leading from northwest. No instinct within her signaled fear. Or did her ease come only from anticipation of the coming seal flesh and oil? She sighed. *Ai-ee*—at least, he thought the infant *hers,* so he did not know much.

She must not seem to hesitate, so she drew herself up and lifted her chin while she made two quick decisions. A name for her brother? Something close to but not the same as *Ajak.* Her own new name was easy—she supposed she had already decided what it would be.

Proudly, "This one speaking is called *Kiti,"* she told him with great dignity and thought, *But not often, and not by many.* "And a mother's child"— what was similar in sound to the name of his milk sister? "—is *Arajik!"*

There, done. Her little one had a name at last, and so did this new female in her desiccated skin. The sound of each title spoken aloud gave pleasure. *Her* little one? She shrugged and smiled. She had now confirmed Tuk's misinformation on origin of the baby.

"Kiti," the young man repeated, rolling each of the two syllables with equal stress, softly in the back of his mouth. He knew it would not do to speak a human name too loudly out-of-doors for fear of tempting spirits bent on mischief.

Then, "It happens that someone foolishly brought with him some small and possibly rotten seals that lay abandoned on the trail."

The old Sukitilan and now this new Kiti were impatient with the long-winded approach to presentation of a gift. No seal ever just lay deserted—not for long, anyway—not with ravenous predators including *Inupiat* craving the rich flavor. And the only way such a carcass would rot in winter would be for *Inuit* to cache and deliberately rot it to get that special, succulent flavor and texture. Her mouth weltered in contemplation of fat red meat to come.

"Someone would be most grateful," he continued, "if the woman would take some of the meat—perhaps to feed her least valuable dogs?"

She smiled. *"Nakorami,* Thank you." She watched as he expertly butchered the larger of the two. Fresh, certainly not rotten, and of fine size—*nathek,* the petite, sweet-fleshed creature with tallowy blubber to produce much oil for lamps. Regardless of the stranger's origin, heedless of his intent, she must accompany him on a seal hunt. She had gone with her brothers, but they were never successful, knew little more than she about capturing ocean prey. On the trail returning from the sea, in fact, her family always had to trade in order to get seal and walrus meat. Local hunters more knowledgeable about sea mammals were happy to get variety found with caribou or sea bear; were delighted with one of Pichikut's fine parkas trimmed around the face with *kapvik* fur, the hollow filaments from the pelt of wolverine. Kiti must also try to learn what else this Tuk knew about her—and do so without asking any more questions.

The visitor shared the liver, and she ate the delicacy hungrily with deep appreciation. Never before had she been so honored. The two *Inuit* had their fill of seal while both dog teams gorged on the rich flesh. *How could Kiti get Tuk to demonstrate his methods for hunting seal?*

After light conversation without revelation, the stranger spoke seriously. "Skin and blubber in these creatures is too heavy for a lazy hunter to haul," he complained. Kiti knew his comment was not only an offer of more food and oil but also her cue to invite him to travel with her. Here was a pleasing man. But was he an agent to *angakok?* One so cunning as to assuage her anxiety by deliberately indicating misinformation on the child? Still . . . why speak of the baby at all, in that circumstance? Certainly *Arajik* would have revealed himself in short order. So if not through Narluk, how did Tuk know of her small brother's existence?

Or again, might this stranger be some youthful rogue male cast out by his own people for some unspeakable misdeed—and now preparing to prey on her? Pichikut always told her that someone could avoid deception by listening carefully to hear a certain echo in a voice. *The imposter also tends to show great zeal in all matters,* she had said. But mostly, the daughter was to listen

80

to her inner response. So said *Ananak, Pay attention to the silent secret voice*. And in this instance, Kiti felt nothing amiss. She decided that Tuk was most likely to be exactly what he seemed—a young coastal *Inupiat* hunting alone for some unknown reason. She quite suddenly knew herself to be so lonely that she wondered whether she was even in touch with her inner warning system. Kiti had more faith at this moment in *Nuna's* secret voice, and the white dog seemed complacent. See how Nuna was making friendly overtures—unusual for her with anyone other than family!—by pressing her nose under Tuk's arm as he walked by.

Kiti's brain, though, told her to be cautious. She had her knives and spear, knew how to use them, even the harpoon. . . . But oh, how she did long for congenial company! Instead of inviting him to share the trail, though, she rummaged at her sled for small bladders and intestinal sacs in which they could store seal meat. She would accept some packets of meat and oil for herself if he insisted strongly, as she hoped he would. She could reciprocate with—what? Fish was no great gift to any but a starving *inuit*. Perhaps some *kapvik* fur, mending and apparel repair if needed. Her mouth watered at the prospect of meat. Now she watched closely as Tuk cut the other seal to make an oil bag—a process that her mother had rarely found opportunity to undertake, and which Kiti had never taken the trouble to watch. Her own family along with many other inlanders traded caribou and processed hides with coastal *Inuit* to get the golden oil already formed in plump bladders.

Beginning at the creature's mouth, the man sliced delicately beneath the skin, sliding it back expertly as he cut so that he finally had a seamless and liquid-proof pouch into which they would together stuff cubed chunks of blubber. From the *Big Feed*, Kiti took especially sturdy sinew to tie off the opening. Within that pouch would develop a supply of the oil that would light Tuk's lamp, brighten his meals and warm him in a trail house. Well yes, if he pressed her strongly, she would also accept oil. . . . *How long would it take*, she wondered, *to become liquid for the lamp?*

And yes, she decided, here would be a good person with whom to share the trail. A coastal man. But could she travel with someone who might later be her undoing? Why not postpone any decision about inviting him—just wait and see? Continue right here at this fish camp for two or three more sleeps, stay alert to danger if it came, and give this stranger time to reveal himself.

That night, the wind was calm for once, fog hovering thick, and Tuk rigged a ragged hide across the front of Kiti's lean-to. All humans plus Nuna and Ajak were cozy around the travel lamp that burned Tuk's oil—for he had by now seen that she herself had none. She had been without for many sleeps—but he did not need to know that much. If he urged strongly that she accept oil: then yes, indeed! She could reciprocate with wolverine pelt, for she noticed that his *nuilak,* that fur which trims the face opening of a parka, was handsome enough but only fox, prone to icing up in storm and serious cold.

Tuk had by now observed that Arajik—how easily *that* name came!—took his milk from a sled dog. He had made no comment. His eyes had not so much as widened in surprise—for Kiti had watched carefully—the first time he saw Nuna nurse the infant. Perhaps Tuk had seen them on the trail previously? That explanation was the only key to his initial knowledge of Arajik's existence, barring Narluk's instruction. Certainly, that prior sight was a solution to this mystery, a clarification that she wanted to accept. Eh, of course! He probably had known already that Nuna suckled the child.

Arajik. Her brother had a name. She thought happily about how, each time the snow was right, she would from this time on adopt coastal ways and cut blocks to coil up a little house before each sleep. *If* she had seal oil for light and warmth—eh, what pleasure might be coming!

She looked across the lamp at her guest. Before entering the small shelter, he had removed his outer furs—his *silipak*—and beat off encrusted snow. Then he scraped and folded the apparel, placed it neatly into a bladder he had earlier carried inside. A tidy man. His eyes were half shut as he sat in his *illupak,* his underfurs, cross-legged on robes. She saw a sturdy, well-built *Inupiat,* possibly twenty-something winters, twenty-five at most—no older than Palunga would be now. How could anyone like this, so generous and sociable and pleasant, be guilty of deceit? He had broad cheeks and a ruddy, clear complexion, soft smile creases around his mouth. Fully open, his sparkling dark eyes were centered in whites like new snow and surrounded by pale arcs of unreddened skin. During even the brief light of this season on the trail, he must always wear his *idgak,* his snow spectacles. These would be carved from bone or walrus ivory or even from precious driftwood scraps. They would have tiny, horizontal slits through which to peer and thus keep ground glare from blinding him. It being winter, she had not thought to pack such goggles for herself. As a result, the rims of her own eyes were sore, and she knew that they must be crimson. She would have to craft something by springtime, when once again the sun showed its face each day for lengthening periods to reflect on snow that still lay on the ground.

They chatted back and forth, and she continued to observe the newcomer. On the upper edges of Tuk's cheeks were white patches that matched two fingers on his bare left hand. The snow-walker had touched and then released him, for here were marks of recent frostbite. Similar pale marks probably showed in the numb places on her cheeks.

As if suddenly aware of her scrutiny, he lifted his eyes to study her as well across the smoking lamp. *What did he see?* she wondered. Her too-short hair glistened, that she knew, turning under at her shoulders. Perhaps a good point. But she would never be plump enough to be beautiful, even though her full, rosy cheeks—so Pichikut assured her often—gave promise of fine facial flesh to come. At home, although not gaunt as now, she still had always been lanky, already tall as her tall mother and towering over other village women. Not ever round and comforting as *Inupiat* women should be.

Kiti brought herself back to the present. A question must not be asked, but she needed an answer, anyway. "It may have happened that someone saw a person fishing on the ice today," she suggested.

He raised his eyebrows, *Yes*. "A hunter stalked seal on high rocks. He saw a woman take her team far onto ungrounded ice." His words held no rebuke. She knew even when she started out this morning that she might be taking a chance by going so close to the open lead. Just how much danger lay there, she was uncertain. Ice must be easier to slice through for fishing where it was not so thick. And most likely—so she reasoned then—fish would be more plentiful in open water. And had not the success of her fishing on this day proved her correct? She had offered the fresh char to accompany seal for their evening meal. But Tuk insisted that she save the fish for emergencies on the trail. He must not like it, either. She would go out by the lead each day she stayed here before continuing north, do so with or without a comrade. Beginning tomorrow, after the sleep . . . ah . . . unless . . .

She took a deep breath. "It may happen that seal is abundant near this camp." She had gone southeast to the coast for seal with her brothers two winters back. They had insisted that she hide herself and be silent. But even so—or possibly *because* she obeyed and stayed far from the seals, so *Ananak* scolded them later—they captured nothing.

Tuk sucked in breath, *Yes*. "On this day, at least. *Ahmi*. One cannot know the future."

"It could happen that two hunters can enjoy double the success of one." He did not need to know that her experience was so limited. Nor did he need to know that she wanted to learn from someone who came from the coast, someone familiar with sea creatures.

His eyes crinkled at the edges, but he did not laugh aloud. "Perhaps." She

83

remembered that *Inupiat* women do not normally refer to themselves as hunters—even if they hunt.

Later that night, although they shared the robes and sleeping place, Kiti made no signal of willingness to share more, no move to extend the courtesy common on the trail. Why not? She was no maiden, certainly, and knew she would enjoy a lusty romp in the furs. Here was a compelling man, balanced in form and mellow in manner.

Well, for one thing, he had made no overture—but even if he had, she would have turned away. She already liked him—and she did not wish to like him more until she knew with certainty that he did not come from her father.

Still, she was curious, and she warmed herself and put herself to sleep by imagining what he might be like. She was aware of and sometimes a participant in activities upon the sleeping ledge at home, especially when one or another brother brought in some visiting woman to share the *iglerk*. But she herself had never sought out males from off the trail. Nor had she begged to expand her acquaintance of men by accompanying her family when they visited another village or joined with other groups in summer camp.

Still, she always agreed when someone asked her father to have her for the night, and he in turn asked her. And each time, increasingly, her body had reveled in the play. But always, she kept her mind and manner separated. She wondered now whether she could keep this kind of distance if her partner were someone like Tuk. Villagers remarked on her cool bearing, sometimes within her hearing. How was she to learn a woman's secrets with such rare opportunity, to receive advice and counsel from others on the sleeping ledge of her own home? How, without great experiment and practice? Still, most of the villagers were much older, tolerant of someone whom they considered still a child. Eh, and the daughter of *angakok*, besides. *Pirtok*. So it was, and no help for it. The girl excelled in other ways. . . .

It was Pichikut that the daughter listened to. And Pichikut sent the same message in a dozen ways: *Life can be long. No hurry.*

Kiti woke up early. On impulse, she crept out to the sled and got into her mother's clothing. She proudly shrugged on the softly flowing *silapak* with *amoutik,* the trousers with adult woman's parka that had the extra hood, the *amaut,* for carrying a child. Everything was much too wide, but hardly too long at all. She pulled the pants high and then flapped the waist over and down before she drew the string as tight as possible. The parka fit like walrus hide would fit a seal. It did not—quite—drag the ground because she was after all nearly as tall as her mother had been although not so round. Arajik was resting and at peace when she plucked him up and cuddled him, pressing her nose into his fat cheek. She carried him with her to the sled, then lowered him gently into the deep hood that opened to her back. He nestled down immediately, perhaps pleased by unaccustomed skin contact. The girl now busied herself with preparation of her sled runners.

Tuk crawled out through the hide baffle of the lean-to just as Kiti finished a final ice coat. She was proud of her work, for the parallel strips glistened in bright starlight. When she walked over to the lean-to, though, Kiti realized that she had made a mistake by putting the baby into the *amaut*. All had been well while she bent to attend the runners, but standing up and having Arajik swinging in the tip of the carrier made him bounce against her buttocks with each step. He did not complain—in fact, his muffled chortles came to her. But the dignity she had planned to display was breached, and Tuk stood open-mouthed.

"It happens that the babe is not yet large enough for this hood," she explained. Any *soospuk* could see that the problem here lay not with the size of the baby but rather with the fit and sheer volume of fur clothing obviously not her own.

Tuk turned suddenly away to undo and fuss with fastenings at the front of the lean-to. His next words were muffled. Kiti listened as she twisted the *amaut* around and scooped Arajik from the hood. Then she plucked up clothing that fit from her sled and went back to the lean-to.

"Can it be that two hunters will soon go for seal?" her visitor asked finally. His voice was grave, but she could see in lamp glow that his eyes danced with mischief.

85

Seal!

Seal can be captured in two ways. A hunter may go out on ocean ice and search for an *aglu,* a breathing hole around which at certain seasons is built for newborn pups a circular ledge below the ice surface but above the water line. The breathing holes—and one animal probably has several—are used and kept open by the seal. They are invisible, or nearly so, to anyone who searches from above. Even the huge white bear, whose great joy in life comes from capture of a seal and whose effective although time-consuming technique for hunting these creatures has been copied and adapted since the earliest *Inuit,* even this astute predator has difficulty finding *aglu* on ice above the sea.

If good fortune rests on the hunter's shoulder—and perhaps luck comes from a hungry sled dog with a sharp nose—an *aglu* can be located. Then the hunter sets up a harpoon on bone crosspieces, takes out the killing spear and knife, puts a few layers of bear pelt between *kamik* and ice, balances a fur float in the hole . . . and waits. Sometimes for only part of a day but more often for two or three sleepless nights and intervening dark days, the hopeful *Inuit* stands silent, motionless, hunched over the *aglu* to make the least shadow possible. He endures.

Or at least, Kiti remembered, *she* endured. Perhaps the seal would finally come. Or not. How many hunters had she heard about found frozen, stiff and spiritless over an *aglu* on sea ice?

The other method to catch seal is faster but even less certain and involves the rocky shore. When the sun is bright, or even in winter when moonlight bathes the coast or lights display in the northern sky, seals in small number may pull up onto craggy boulders above the tide. There, they take an air bath to rid their fur of louse-like saltwater hitchhikers. If a hunter is lucky enough to find the creatures out of water, and if this hunter is sufficiently skilled to get close, then several seals might give themselves in a single encounter. So whether in water or on rocks, seals are never easy. Intelligent, wary, suspicious—but oh, so worthy of great effort!

* * * * *

Late on the second morning after Tuk's arrival, just as a pale strip of light showed shy and delicate, low on the southeast horizon, Kiti followed the man up an icy trail, creeping along, slithering like some legless creature, slowly . . . . So far, the furry mammals well forward on a stone-strewn point seemed not to sense approaching danger.

In a roundabout way, Tuk had asked earlier whether a young mother had ever before hunted seals.

"Yes, on both rocks and ice." True, but that was all she had done: *hunted.* And even so, she had participated mostly as an observer. This morning she must educate herself about searching out seal when she was alone on the trail. She would not admit to Tuk that she had never even *seen* someone capture a seal, and she was relieved when he did not require specifics. Not one seal ever gave itself. Not to her brothers, certainly not to her. Nor even to Narluk, so far as she had ever heard about. Not even close. She had so far mentioned nothing of her family to Tuk, and she did not plan to. *She still did not know how much he knew about her.*

Kiti's neck ached from watching the soles of the *kamik* of this man who crawled along in front of her. Expecting glare on snow and ice in a clear sky after the stars faded—and even those very few minutes of the hazy, early winter sun glow before it faded totally could damage eyes, he assured her— Tuk had given her a pair of his own *idjak,* slitted goggles carved elegantly from driftwood. Her eyes ached anyway. They did not throb from the sun, which even now faded into the southwest only a few degrees from where it had first stained the sky. But rather, they hurt from trying so hard to follow and copy every move made by the hunter in front of her. Eh, would she now, as Pichikut had so often petitioned the trail spirits, truly *be successful in the hunt?*

When Tuk stopped going forward and rolled onto his side, she wondered at the action. And when he became frenzied, with an arm bent at the elbow while keeping a mittened hand close to his side, she became even more curious.

She edged up to be even with him. They were now so close to the herd that wind might carry her voice to the seals, so she whispered her words directly into the hood at his ear. "Someone is well?"

He continued to wag his elbow, but more slowly, gradually turning so that he faced her. His quiet voice came to her. "It happens that a seal is vigilant."

She raised her eyebrows, *Yes. She knew that.*

"But also, it may be that seal eyes cannot distinguish details of shape at a distance."

Again, Kiti's eyebrows arched. New information, credible, but what did it have to do with Tuk's odd behavior?

As the man realized that the conversation was not concluded, he sighed. "Many the fine and fortunate hunter who lost his shot at seals upon the rocks."

He was watching her eyes, and she knew that some response was expected, some sign that she grasped his thought from the few words given. Nothing came to her.

"—Because," he continued finally, "the hunter forgot to *scratch.*"

"—Scratch," she echoed woodenly.

"Scratch!!" Tuk's elbow became more energetic as it changed angle to fan a new spot.

Kiti lay staring blankly at the flailing arm.

"To rid oneself of itching pests."

The woman was mystified. She felt no need to scratch anywhere. The trail contained no troublesome insects during winter.

Even more patiently, Tuk continued, "It may be that a creature suspicious but blurry-eyed is reassured to see approaching figures scratch like any other basking seal."

Ah! Kiti scrunched back to her former position, grasped her trousers firmly, then thrashed her elbow with great energy back and forth. She must become a seal, must try to envision juicy clams on the ocean floor. She must roll a little, sluggishly, as she had seen these ahead of them do, must be a seal awkward on land and away from its element. Must stretch and preen. And especially, now that the space between *Inupiat* and seals was lessening, she must remember to *scratch*? She did her best to imagine an itch where her fluttering elbow might reach—which was no place—and chuckled softly until Tuk doubled back to peer at her.

"It happens that what seal lacks in eyesight is compensated for by acute hearing," he told her softly. "True seals do not *giggle.*"

Kiti forced herself to become quiet, determined to become a good—no, a superb!—hunter of seals. But a broad grin split her face.

At last, the two reached high, rocky headland that contained a jutting table that tilted slightly downward to overlook a narrow lead of open water. Their progress now must be even slower; for stones on which they crawled could easily shift and alert their quarry. Kiti knew this part of seal chase on land from hunting with her brothers. She remembered the intense cold, too, that overtook someone creeping slowly along the ice. Today was no exception, even though she tied the drawstring on her hood especially tight to prevent the entry of a freshening wind. Her view opening was only half the size of her palm. She had stuffed extra moss and qiviut—the wild warm wool of muskox—into her *kamik* before leaving camp this morning, but her toes were without feeling. She heard the sea lash onto rocks below, where the lead sizzled so close to shore. She was too cold to shiver. She must not think about the chill, must not fear proximity to pounding waves. She must think only of seals—their shape, their killing spot, the taste of them as well—and she must continue to *be* a seal . . . eh, did seals ever feel the cold? Perhaps not, with their three *Inuit* fingers' depth of blubber under warm fur.

. . . And she must not listen to the wailing wind. She must not notice boiling clouds as *Nigituk,* the strong south wind behind her, blustered in its aerial sled lashed high with storm. Too bad that the only approach for the hunters was on the wind. The mammals they stalked would surely smell them soon and seek shelter in the sea. She must continue to inch forward, head up, squinting through her hood opening, to guide herself by the soles of Tuk's *kamik.*

Then she saw the young man stand up smoothly. Clutched in his right hand was his killing spear and in his left, a fire-hardened skinning knife. Kiti copied him to rise with one fluid motion. She carried similar weapons, hers made of bone instead of Tuk's less brittle driftwood. Because the two hunters were obscured by loose snow circling on itself and parallel to the ground before the howling wind, the seals did not take alarm—but Kiti knew that in one more moment . . .

Tuk shouted as he leaped among the creatures and drove his spear into the nearest beast, withdrew the weapon and thrust into another. Kiti scrambled across the rocks to drive her own shaft into one more seal as the beasts twisted and blundered clumsily to reach the cliff drop-off. On the glaze of droppings that fouled the ledge, they rammed each other in panic as they flopped toward safety in the sea. Kiti thrust again but missed, realized that for the first time ever, she had not—and did not now—hesitate before attack. . . . She stabbed again, successfully—and saw Tuk do the same.

Five beasts. . . . Two by her own hand. Pichikut was right—Kiti could do what was necessary in the hunt, now that she herself knew the gnaw of hunger. Euphoric in triumph, she wiped her spear on snow, watching Tuk so that she could join his ceremony of thanks. As she bent to clean the knife, she felt a stone slide beneath her foot. The knife flew from her mitt and struck rock dully as she fought for purchase. Then she was skidding on the slippery decline, feet-first after the seals. She scrabbled for a handhold, for leverage of any kind, but felt herself continue to glide helplessly. As her feet went over the edge, she consigned herself to Sedna and the sea, praised the spirits that Arajik was not here in her tunic—would Tuk care for him now? But before she could speculate about the thought-question, her clawing mitt also slid across the slick edge and she dropped toward water and the babble of panicked seals splashing below. Falling free she wondered if seals might eat people as people eat seals. . . .

Kiti felt, rather than heard, a rhythmic rumble that she gradually recognized as surf pounding rocks. Her ears were filled with the shriek and moan of the still-approaching storm above her. She no longer heard seals barking. Her hips and legs bobbled in water, but her waist and upper body were on flat rock. She had not yet been accepted by the sea? She ached, those parts of her not numb; but she felt as if she were still all together—and so, so cold. Of course, her feet and legs had been without much feeling before she ever reached the herd. Going for seal was a cold business on rocks *or* ice. And now, in water as well.

Ai-ee! Five seals, up there. Tuk would have fine provision for Arajik and himself, for Ajak and Nuna and both teams. Worth the chill? Absolutely. Worth dying for? Umm . . . she wondered when and where her spirit would begin anew. Wind-borne ice pellets struck the bit of face exposed by parka and cut into her passive reverie. Cautiously, she raised her head to look around. Rocks and pebbles were strewn upon the ledge on either side of where she lay. Boulders jutted at odd angles from the cliff before her—play-toys of some untidy giant child. The relatively shallow but undercut cliff she looked up to inspect, the one over which she had fallen and now viewed from below, gave way—as she had noted earlier—to less daunting verticals on either side. She raised a mitten to brush ice from her face, but the movement slid her further into water. She then lay perfectly still, flat as she could. Waves poured around her, but the low ledge where she clung seemed to be protected, receiving only a mild surge. *Pirtok.* Who can question what happens by chance? Frivolous fate that she could not change.

Tuk would think her washed away. How could he investigate from the slippery ledge? *Why* would he? She would not know to search, were he here and she above. She would presume that he had disappeared forever beneath the dark surface, as had other *Inuit* before, as would many more in future. She would believe him taken up immediately by the Ocean Queen, would assume his spirits to be busily preparing at this very moment for return to his people in some new form. If she were the hunter left above, Kiti would not risk sliding off the cliff recklessly to investigate what was, after all, a familiar tragedy . . . nor would Tuk.

She called out, realizing as she shouted that her voice could not be heard above the sounds of sea and squall . . . even if someone were listening. She shouted anyway, and louder. Shrieking gale overhead, slapping, sucking surf below . . . *whoosh* . . . *splash* . . . *gurgle.*

This would be the end of her life-day, then; the finish to the brief new *Kiti* who existed by this name for only two sleeps. Also the end of young Sukitilan, for whom this would have been her twentieth winter. Sometime soon, the tall tide which Pichikut had described with such awe would come to collect her, offering her once again to Sea-queen Sedna. Kiti closed her eyes, and pulled in upon herself. She wished that Tuk and she could together have thanked the seals for giving themselves. She wished that Narluk had not been so stubborn about Arajik. That Arajik had possessed a name from the start. She wished her mother had not died. She wished that Pichikut had not left her coastal *Inupiat* so long ago. . . .

Tuk had not spoken of his origins, but he must be of these same people. His speech. His ease on sea ice. The *idjak* he had given her, formed from precious drifting wood still tucked into an inner pocket of her parka, now poking at her ribs. What a waste, to sink with them, when so little sunlight pierced the sea! Carefully, so that balance was not disturbed, she dug out the spectacles, held them. Perhaps if she released them they would float onto some bright beach one day. Then it might happen that someone who had need would find and use—*ahmi!* Who can tell the future? But *idjak* such as these were too valuable to drown. She put them back, resolved to set them afloat as she herself slid beneath the dark water.

Wood. She wondered where it came from. Only coastal people could find much of it. Tuk's spear of wood with blackened tip. No sled runners of bone, as with her inland people, but again wondrous wood, substantial, that drifting or shore bound material almost never seen in any size on tundra waterways. She wondered for the hundredth time what manner of creature left such bones.

Tuk would of course take Arajik to his coastal *Inupiat.* Perhaps by chance even to Pichikut's people? How strong was her mother's spirit in the baby? And although the people of the ice islands could never know that Arajik's mother was one of their own, the child would be safe with them. So *Ananak* had promised.

She remembered with relief that she was wearing the skillfully constructed clothing fashioned by her mother. How tight the stitches of her boots and trousers. . . . She was embarrassed to recall her own slapdash work, required to be undone and done again not once but three times, sometimes four, *Ananak* still dissatisfied even then.

Tiny stitches with sinew stuffing every opening can make the difference between breath and death for Inuit, Pichikut would tell her. Now Kiti understood those words. She vowed that when she lived again she would sew only the tiniest stitches that did not ever pierce pelt fully.

Lived again? But might it be that the time for finishing this life had not yet arrived?

Arajik! Here she lay on stone and water . . . passively awaiting death. But she had an obligation—a baby, her small brother . . . and had she even *tried* to save herself? Arajik needed her. . . .

Eh, to move at all might slide her fully to the sea. But would that not be preferable to having tide drink her slowly? "What a *soospuk!*" she muttered aloud. What a nitwit!

She must not let loose her grip of both mitts pressed on the ledge. But could she gradually draw those chilled legs and feet up to the rock? She still had feeling in her hips—and for all she could tell, that part of her afloat might still be dry inside.

Bit by bit, she brought her knees up, slowly curled her *kamik* around and onto the ledge; then loosened the tunic drawstring and tucked her legs inside, beneath her, to get warmth and feeling. Doing all this smoothly took strength, control, great effort, much time—and then at last was done. She raised her body up to get belly above knees; then crouched low, completely free of the sea, still pressing as much of herself as possible against the ledge. With a cautious mitt, she rubbed along the side of first one calf and then the other, finally massaging feet and ankles hard but not so vigorously that she lost balance. Ice fragments driven by wind flew in the tiny opening of her hood to sting her eyes. She clenched them shut.

At last, she decided that her feet and legs might hold her up. She peeled away the frost that sealed her eyes; then tightened her parka opening even further, and finally stood bent against the wind. She squinted up to inspect the rock wall before her; then looked in both directions where jutting boulders tilted out and downward to the sea. North, to her right, the ledge itself seemed to widen but was pounded in half a *kayak's* distance by the full force of wave action from a building tide. She could attain it, but she would never manage to resist those wild waves, not even by inching along on her stomach. *How fortunate was the graceful seal hunter,* she thought now, *not to have fallen in that place instead of this.*

South, then, into heavy wind. Bracing against the cliff, she felt her way inch by inch, squinting eyes meanwhile searching upward for a place where the hill descended to her ledge. Those seals got up to the rocky point by land, she reasoned. True, a seal can leap up with force to bring himself above water level—say high as a single *Inuit,* at most. But no seal can leap to the height of two or three people, no, not the distance to the top of the cliff before her—eh, presuming that she was now directly beneath the point from which she had fallen. The seal herd could easily have bounded onto this low ledge on which she crawled, though, even juveniles, and then chosen an indirect route to reach the stars and spirit lights—much as she should do right now.

South, then, along this narrowing shelf. She bumped her head on a sharp outcrop, explored its upper surface, and tried to dislodge the formation with a sudden yank. Solid. Why not clamber up, and then trust to luck that she could find another gripping place and yet another . . . and finally, gain the top? Certainly not what seals had done, but she was no longer a seal.

"Ai-ee-ee!" she shouted one more time; then saved her breath. . . . If Tuk were nearby and if he heard her, he would believe her shout to be the wail of some sad wandering spirit. *Pirtok.* She took off her mittens, and thrust each into a soggy parka pocket. For this climb, she needed sensitive bare fingers.

Energy coursed through her as she climbed, strength and balance beyond any she had ever known. She could clamber to the moon if the stars would make a ramp. Power centered in her hands and arms. Her fingers should be numb by now, but they were not. Kiti would survive this accident, return to Arajik, continue with this same life for a while longer.

In a crashing gale that continued to fling stinging particles before it, she slowly climbed, discovered toeholds, handholds as she went—fortuitously— each lucky find perhaps her last . . . moving carefully, taking time, waiting for lulls in wind to allow vision. Up. Over. Up again, zig-zagging. At last, her nose level with a lower grade of the same rocky hillock where the seals had been, she pulled herself face down and gasping onto the icy ground amid swirling snow already beginning new drift around boulders.

Safe from Queen Sedna and the sea. Here she was—feet and legs and now hands also suddenly numb with cold. She replaced her mitts, clapped her palms together, slapped them against her hips; then tucked them under her tunic and finally down inside her trousers to the warmth between her thighs. Her furs were wet where they had floated on the sea—*kamik* and *silipak,* boots and trousers, stiffening as the salt water froze. Still, she did not think that the ocean had actually seeped through the inner fur-skin, the *illupak,* to her skin. Hard to tell, because they were saturated from perspiration born of fear and great exertion in the climb. A shudder jolted her. She must find shelter. The old drifts were hard-grained granules impossible for burrowing, now topped by nomadic crystals rearranging constantly before a wrathful wind.

She must get warm and stay that way until her clothing dried. She had no food, no sheltering house or robes, no dogs and sled . . . no weapons. She stood up, braced herself on a boulder to keep from yielding to the gale. The threatened storm had arrived in earnest, a tempest rushing by on an unbroken howl of air from the southeast. Up here on the exposed point, the stinging particles peeled her face. Once again, she tightened the cord to close her *nuilak,* the face opening of her parka, this time to a peephole the size of a lemming's eye. Eyes were useless, anyway, in the black and writhing air. She felt her way as a blind creature, stooping to assess the ground, grasping to pull herself along on boulders, up the last bit of incline from the south to the killing place. The tilted bedrock where seals had been was now frozen dry, for she could feel the abrasion on the soles of her *kamik.* The surface was studded with ice particles, far less treacherous than before; but she moved gingerly, nonetheless. It would not do to fall through some widened crack back to the sea.

Then she stopped, astonished. In the lee of giant stones, it was possible to see pale mounds lined up together like a family on its *iglerk.* All five seals. Her killing spear and skinning knife were side by side, outlined with snow on a rock nearby. Tuk had not taken any meat—well then, how *could* he, *soospuk* Kiti?—without at least a team? He had only pulled the carcasses high to ease loading after the storm. . . . He would certainly return.

How long, she wondered, had she lain on the sea ledge before her spirits collected themselves and brightened? Perhaps not so much time, she decided; for even with the building storm, some quarter-glow glimmer of mid-day remained. It had seemed the duration of a full sleep, maybe two, that she had lain inert—first surprised to be alive, next discovering herself unhurt but helpless; then feeling sorry for herself and waiting to die—and finally knowing that she must make an effort.

She peered about to find shelter. Besides driving snow, she saw nothing

94

beyond the white lumps of seal, her own weapons and the surrounding boulders. She stumbled over to drop shivering onto the nearest carcass. Big beasts, this one perhaps a third of a *kayak's* length. Warmth would be inside, she thought dully, for creatures of the ice and sea are well insulated—except, she thought, for puny humankind. She looked around once more, but now could recognize nothing, as the frost-hardened snow granules swarmed and swirled to create an opaque low fog. Shelter might exist. Nearby could be a cave among these very boulders; but even the captured seals were no longer distinguishable. She felt around to find them. Drifts were building. Even if the snow were right to make a snow house—which it was not—she would freeze before she finished building. Anyway, she had foolishly left her broad snow knife back on the sled. Then as her body quaked with chill while the storm blasted her, an idea came.

Why not *make* a cave?

She must have shelter, or she might as well have stayed on the rocks below. Her whole body shuddered with great rolling quakes as she crept over to retrieve her weapons; then crawled back across the seals to find one surrounded by other carcasses and therefore protected from the gale. She made a long incision in the belly, carefully removed viscera and guts, rapidly separated out the bladder-like materials that could later be used for containers and floats. Then she flung the still steaming remainder over the cliff edge. Let sea predators feast, she thought, for it was best not to invite land carnivores, however unlikely they were to come in time of storm.

She would crawl inside a seal to warm herself. If any predator sought out the seals during the coming sleep—and if any were so greedy as to select the largest creature in this group—it would be surprised, would it not? She placed her killing spear and sharp knife inside the opening; then slid through the cut to lie beside them in the moist, bloody cave she had created. Relief. Out of the wind at last. Snug and protected, she listened to the moan and shriek outside, the driven pellets *thud-a-thudding* into the pelt around her; and she felt wind gusts tug at the carcass. She was in a warm place. Her body heat would keep it so. After sleep, she would have to scrape her furs carefully to get them soft and pliable again. *Pirtok!*

She must think through what was likely now to happen. What would Tuk do when he thought Kiti lost to the sea? What would *she* do, were she Tuk? Go back for the one sled they had brought this morning—her sled bearing Arajik, Nuna, Ajak. Tuk would drive the team up here, *her* team. Why had he not cut into even one of the seals—ah! Less likelihood of losing all. No ravenous, always-foraging white bear would be drawn by the scent—no sly white fox, no wolf, no insatiable wolverine. She hoped she would have been so clever, were the situation reversed.

Tuk had drawn the seals together, for he was a tidy man. She liked that. It would have been he who found her weapons, too, for she remembered that she had thrown them as she slid. His plan would be to collect everything when he came back.

Was it too much to believe his rapid return to the sled was to care for Arajik? She had felt restive from the very start of the seal hunt about leaving the baby for so long. But Arajik was as safe with Nuna as with her. Eh, that a young male stranger abandoned fresh meat and took trouble for a mere babe was too much to credit. Tuk had gone back to shelter from the storm. He had gone back to see to the closest dogs—hers, since tracking far into the face of the storm would be impossible. He would feed them, be sure that they were safely sheltered from the weather, and no doubt worry about his own *kringmerk* back at camp. Then he would harness the team when the blizzard was spent, and he would bring the sled up here to transport seals. He could do the butchering at his leisure, anywhere. He could pack and fill with blubber those empty bladder bags from camp that they had with such anticipation collected this morning before they set out.

"*Ai-ee-ee!!*" The cry wrung from her lungs automatically, the sound startling her in her primordial shelter. *Would her sled team pull for Tuk?* Each dog had such different temperament, such unique personality. They needed to be run with a certain order in the harnessing—no question, Iyarpok would rip the throat of any dog that tried to take his spot. Lacking Kiti's hand command, Nuna too must be restrained. In fact, the girl had lately wondered whether Nuna could ever peaceably become lead again if Iyarpok remained on the team.

Eh, and why did she worry about something over which she had no control? Tuk could harness the team or not. The dogs would obey his commands—or not. If not, he would have to return on foot to the lean-to for his own sled and dogs. A long walk. . . . Both teams would be hungry, but they would survive. And soon to come—what a fine feast to compensate!

She hoped the sun would shine a little at midday after the storm . . . hoped Arajik was well . . . hoped Tuk was not someone sent by Narluk . . . hoped she would find Pichikut's people . . . and that her new little family would survive. . . .

96

Sound awakened her, and not the howl of wind. She was disoriented. Momentarily panicked, she struck out wildly as she found herself restricted on all sides. Then the opening slit in the seal skin let her bare hand feel the cold of outside air, let her see dim light. Memory returned. The storm was past. What was the sound?

Spear in hand, she emerged with caution, quiet as possible; she let her eyes accustom themselves, and again heard movement nearby. *Not bear or wolverine*, she beseeched the spirits. So wolf? He and she might share a meal. Then she saw Tuk. His back was to her, and he was at the sled by the cradle *upluk* with Arajik. The baby was shouting with his usual morning exuberance. He would by now badly need a change of bird skin on his bottom. Plus, water must be warmed to dilute the rich canine milk. Would Tuk have observed this practice? Would he think to do it himself? He would not know her reason. They had exchanged no words on the subject.

Kiti stood up stiffly, stretched her cramped muscles; then picked her way over the icy rocks. "It happens, someone needs to find clean clothes," she told the man.

Tuk wheeled to stare at her, incredulous.

"Ah! The visitor was skillful to harness Kiti's team and bring it here," she said. "A woman is pleased." She pushed past him and went to Arajik. But she did not want to touch the baby, covered as she was by seal gore. Instead, she spoke softly. He quieted his shouts, eyed her gravely, smiled, and then began once more to exercise his lungs in great glee. A noisy one, this last child of Pichikut.

Ignoring Tuk, for she knew he wrestled with disbelief, Kiti tried to reassure him by walking and talking normally, by attending normal tasks. She dug into the filled bladder packs lining the sled until she found her mother's *amoutik,* the parka which had so embarrassed her that first morning after Tuk arrived. Only three sleeps ago? She was once again a different person, her body having now been declined by Sedna. Should she select yet another name? No, Kiti suited her. Far back in the mouth, strong—a carrying sound. She shrugged from her matted parka and trousers; then looked down at her undergarments to assess their condition. Her own extra set of *silipak*, she realized even as she inspected in dim light the fully dry and reasonably unsoiled hare skin and *ptarmigan* she wore, were still at the lean-to in their base camp. She had brought Pichikut's clothing on the sled yesterday only because she wished to take no chance of losing the garments to a dog that came unstaked or to a hide-hungry wolverine.

Shivering unclothed in the wind, she put these on; then shook out and shrugged into the oversized furs. She glanced surreptitiously at Tuk as she drew up the waist and lapped it over, tightened the strings and knotted them. The young man was lifting empty bladders from their store, now starting up the rocky hill toward five seals that awaited butchering. He had not yet spoken to her.

The girl laid her sullied furs to freeze atop the sled load, stood to catch the eye of every sled dog scattered in the snow. As each gave evidence of recognition—wagged a tail, pricked ears forward to note her attention—she looked pointedly at the clothing; then frowned at that dog. Delectable as the pelts might smell—bloody leather with fur!—each animal now knew that the apparel was not to be chewed. Nuna, she need not bother to tell. Kiti sucked breath into her lungs and raised her chin to show satisfaction. The message was clear.

On the craggy top of the hill, Tuk stood watching. "Does it happen that this person someone sees is real or some cunning spirit?" he demanded finally. That he questioned her directly indicated the depth of his disquiet.

Kiti laughed as she came up, reached out to apply pressure on his sleeve. Human touch, perhaps impossible for a specter. "Mortal Kiti stands before Tuk. She can show her bruises from the fall."

The boy gazed at her steadily, his jaw working. "Then the woman must forgive this ignorant hunter," he said softly. "A foolish boy thought her spirits flown absolutely when she slid from rocks and disappeared. He even heard the splash."

Perhaps, but more likely he heard seals. Kiti raised her eyebrows, held them up. *Yes*, emphatically. "As would anyone think and hear."

"An ignorant young man looked and listened near the edge, closely as he dared—but saw only frothing waves. He heard the bark of seals for the first few moments. Then no sound more but wave wash."

Again she raised her eyebrows, *Yes*. "Nor would Kiti linger longer, were she above and Tuk below," she tried to reassure him, "especially with a storm arriving and a long walk waiting. And a babe neglected through the day." She watched Tuk's eyes to see whether Arajik had been a factor, but she read in them no change of expression.

Her words seemed to relieve him, however, and the two set to work at loading.

The butchering of one seal accomplished at the lean-to, all dogs fed festively. Fire danced on a freshly twisted wick in the travel lamp. Kiti beat and scraped her furs, put them on, folded her mother's garments back into their bag. It was time to share experience across a meal of sweet seal.

"A hunter thanked the creatures for giving themselves?"

Tuk sucked in a ragged breath, *Yes*. "Right after the capture, before returning to the sled." Kiti recognized that the man was not yet fully at ease with her, uncertain still as to whether she were *Inuit* flesh or phantom. *Pirtok*. Time would convince him—seeing her do what all people do naturally—the many unconscious and automatic claims to humanity.

The woman cut raw seal meat and blubber away from her lips with a quick flick of her *ulu,* the sharp semi-circular utility knife. Tuk did the same. Let him talk a bit, and let Kiti respond before she tried once more to get answers from him without asking questions.

But Tuk was pensive and given to few words on this night. After he finished his meal, he got up and walked over to observe Arajik suckling Nuna. Ajak, the pup was now weaned by Nuna's insistence; but she liked to cuddle up to her mother and foster brother. After a time and without comment, Tuk returned to the lamp and sat on robes. He seemed self-absorbed. Kiti knew he still questioned the miracle of her survival. But she had no way to help him other than to be her own human self. She found her thoughts beginning to scatter, now that the marvel of her continued existence was receding. *She* knew herself to be the same mortal, certainly no visiting spirit person. *She* knew she still drew breath and lived—but what else operated in this moment? Yes. She guessed the answer was quite simple: Pichikut's daughter, so far at least, was—indeed!—*most fortunate in the hunt.*

Storm clouds had cleared completely, and the moon was bright. Both teams of dogs were sated with seal meat, now silent in sleep. Arajik nestled in the front of Kiti's parka while the girl worked at sewing her own *amaut* attachment, the small child's hood-pouch that would fit within her own parka.

Here was a good time for discussion. She had already decided during the meal, when Tuk was not forthcoming, that she had little to lose by asking those questions she needed to ask in order to keep from bursting like an over-full bladder.

"What did a hunter plan to do, with Kiti gone?"

"He was not fully certain," Tuk answered slowly.

"About the baby," she prompted him.

"Yes."

Someone was uncertain about the child? What could be uncertain about the dilemma in which Tuk had found himself? He was obligated to care for Arajik. . . . But she forced herself to be silent as she waited for more.

Then, his lips moved and his voice was low. "It happens that a hunter should have helped someone in mortal trouble—but then did not."

That was worrying him? His lack of action on her behalf was centering his focus? Guilt? Kiti tossed her head impatiently. "As a woman said before, Tuk did exactly as any other reasonable person would have done. What Kiti herself would do. All realize that no chance of survival exists, none at all, for those who slide into the sea. No *Inuit* can swim. But even if a person could somehow buoy the head above the ripples so that breath were possible, cold water will paralyze a human system within moments. Soon, the body ceases to do what it has always done for itself—even stops drawing breath. The heart ceases to beat. And shortly after that, the *Inuk* in water lets loose all protective spirits and sinks."

"Yet a woman *did* survive, inexplicably, and should have had Tuk's help."

The man was finally talking, but not about important matters. She laughed. "It happens that someone troubles himself needlessly.... Kiti has always possessed capable helping spirits, and she is always success—eh, *fortunate* in the hunt."

He sucked in breath to agree. "The girl—the woman—displayed great cleverness, to make her *igloo* of a seal." His tone belied his words. He sounded sad, lost.

He wanted her to need him, was that it? An aspect of the male that Pichikut had told her about, always chuckling at the irony. That Kiti survived without Tuk's help was a spear with two sharp sides in his gut? *"Every female knows that it is the woman who processes and chews the hides for boats and robes and clothing—which she then makes to size and keeps in good repair."* Pichikut's words. *"And she it is who bears and rears the children, who keeps the household going and ministers to the body and the soul of every member. It is her responsibility—*as a young daughter has noticed and complained about quite bitterly—*to obtain and store oil for light and warmth, a woman's disgrace should the supply run out when blubber or even tallow is yet available."*

"Yet, it is the woman who eats last or not at all in time of famine," the young Sukitilan would say.

"What the man does in exchange for woman's succor is hunt. If he is

100

skilled and fortunate, creatures give themselves readily, and all men—most women as well—feel that the activities of life are properly balanced. If the man lacks skill or if he is unlucky, he will die and his family will die before him."

"All know this to be true," Sukitilan agreed then.

"But when a woman hunts with skill—through necessity or through predisposition, as in the case of Pichikut and her daughter—and when she is favored by the spirits of the chase, then men believe life's balance is disturbed."

Kiti remembered asking, "But is it not always better within a family to have the greatest number of hunters possible?"

Pichikut laughed. *"Of course, so long as all of them are men. So young Sukitilan must never seem to be too skillful on the trail."*

Kiti frowned.

"Eh—fishing is fine. Berry-collecting in season, also. But never hunting that requires valor and strength, skill with weapons. At least, never among the barren lands Inupiat."

"This ignorant young woman fails to understand."

"A daughter must consider . . . has someone seen a man chew hide to soften it?"

"Never."

"Of course not, no more than birth a baby—-but also, has someone ever seen a man carry on his back an infant child who continually drools and spits and voids?"

The girl laughed aloud at the image of dignified Narluk so burdened, even within the *igloo.* *"Ananak* says that this is so among those of the inner barren ground. Does she mean that coastal people view the matter differently?"

"When this woman was a child whose aging father was helpless on the trail, she had to hunt or starve. She soon learned to go alone and thereby hide her ripening prowess."

"The family used what their daughter brought?"

"Absolutely. The mother knew that her only child had fortune in the chase, as did the other women in the village. But the father believed, as did every other male, that Pichikut took the sled she had made out onto the ice until a trail spirit she had subdued loaded the sled by her command."

Slowly, "It happens that it was necessary for them to believe this thing?"

"Yes," Pichikut said softly, *"and it is therefore also necessary that no*

101

woman of this household appear to have particular prowess in the hunt."

Kiti focused on the tormented young man who sat across the lamp from her. Then she grinned. "Would someone prefer that Kiti perished when she received no aid from the other hunter?" she asked.

Tuk frowned at her impertinence and did not answer at first. Then he smiled briefly. *"Owka,* No."

Perhaps this visitor was not of coastal *Inupiat* at all. With Pichikut, no topic was ever too grim for laughter. She changed the subject. "A woman puzzles over what the man says was meant to be done with Arajik."

He was silent for a long time. Kiti checked the new wick without losing her fire, and twisted several more fine sinews for later use.

"Take the child to his own village," Tuk said finally, "if the village could be found."

A vast shiver shook Kiti, and then she turned to stone. A voice that sounded as if it belonged to someone else asked: "And how would someone know that village?!"

He looked up, startled by the tightness of her tone. Once more, he did not reply immediately, only went back to watching the lamp flicker. At last, "A traveler first saw Kiti and her babe lying on the prairie late in the sleep time," he said, "then followed her small party to a village—to assure safe passage, he might say, but mostly for his own purpose."

Kiti's chin went up. Her breath came short. "Tuk has tracked someone all this way on the trail?"

He shrugged, shook his head. *"Owka,* No. Only come across her later, once again by accident . . . and recognized her then."

Kiti's thoughts spun. "Can it be that it was Tuk whom Kiti saw on the crest of a hill that night of her departure, as she lay on ice with the newborn babe and Nuna?!"

"Newborn?!" He was astonished.

"Ee-ee, that same day."

Tuk raised his eyebrows. *"Hoo-oo."* Most women did not take the trail immediately after giving birth, especially not alone.

"And someone has perhaps stalked Kiti ever since?!" He had already indicated no, but the girl was thinking fast and not attending his words so much as searching for the truth beyond them. If Tuk saw them only on that night while she waited for Arajik to suckle Nuna, then he truly did not know much. Their activities on the tundra would have been in shadow. Nor was he likely to know that the baby had earlier been set out to die.

Yet he knew about her village moving, and that would be more than he could learn by following her to the sleeping town and then returning immediately to the trail. She tried to control a surge of anxiety. And if he knew more about her village, then he might know Narluk and her circumstance. He might have been sent . . . white anger suddenly burned through her. No matter what he saw or did not see, he admitted knowing of the village. . . . And because he followed her that night, he knew that she departed alone—rapidly, in darkness.

And yet—and *yet,* he had such small respect for her that he would return the child, after her death, to the very village he had seen her leave in secrecy? She leapt up, glaring.

"The newcomer must ice the runners, pack the sled, harness the team and leave this place."

"Tonight?!" He was stunned. Here was a joke, surely.

Her fury somehow related to his plan for the child, and she had not thought it through. She only knew that Tuk represented possible danger. He had already seen too much, if Narluk had sent him. He must go away.

Tuk stood up slowly, consternation on his face. "This visitor planned to return Nuna as well, so that the child would not starve."

"Go *now*." Kiti's voice was cold. "Take the seals. This hunter has no need of them."

"But—?"

He was without words. Good. Let him figure out her reasons in the desolation of his lonely days. He would take the child back *even knowing* she must have strong reason for escaping in the dark of night. Was she—was every woman—only some diversion never to take seriously? *Hoo-oo!*

Then, once at the village—no easy task finding it, she reflected, for by now it had certainly moved but he seemed to know that, too. But once again a man among men, would he not agree with Narluk that small, healthy, hearty Arajik must die?

She picked up her killing spear and drew herself up to look as fierce as possible.

He watched her without words, his handsome face expressionless.

She turned to the sled and withdrew the harpoon, held it high, though pointed to the ground. "And should Kiti see Tuk ever again—" she shook both weapons, and the harpoon toggle rattled—"she may not allow him to live!"

He squared his jaw, and firelight flickered in his eye, perhaps anger there as well. "Just this, before departure. A person meant no harm. He saw a beautiful young mother safely to her village; then watched her leave alone with sled and babe."

Suspiciously she said, "Someone still wishes Kiti to believe, the meeting here with Tuk was only accident?!"

"One recognized the woman on the ice, that's all—off and on for several days—"

"—Then why did someone not make himself known sooner?"

Tuk hesitated. "He had good reason. . . . Please do not ask."

"—Go *now!*!" Her voice came out a shriek, and staked dogs around them lifted their shadowy heads to observe. Nuna growled from the sled.

This man, Kiti believed, could destroy her life by destroying Arajik—he was *her* child, now, and so she regarded him. Tuk could let her father know where they were. Then he and her brothers could pursue. She should kill the man here—now!—leave his body on the ice for predators and birds, or drop it into the lead.

One small cool voice inside advised caution. Tuk spoke with the tune of coastal people. It might be that he did *not* come from Narluk, would *not* report back to him. A part of Kiti stood aside to observe the rest of her. How easily her thought had turned to killing. Unreasoned violence . . . certainly not *peeusinga,* not the *Inupiat* way. Was this great violence in her beyond the custom? Or was such ferocity found in every species by a mother whose young was threatened?

She brandished the harpoon and lowered her voice to make it even more savage. "Go!"

He iced his runners with the small bladder of water Kiti kept warm by the lamp. He packed his sled, harnessed his dogs; then turned and spoke once more.

"A traveler hopes Kiti's husband will soon return and protect his fine family."

Did she hear a wistfulness in his tone?

He looked at her evenly for a long moment, but she did not respond other than to lift the harpoon higher. Could she do it? Oh yes. And that she knew herself capable of dispatching an *Inuit* life spirit frightened her.

Tears came later. They washed from her eyes and froze onto her face. Why? After all, Tuk had taken with him only a little of the seal meat.

The Ḫunger Beast

Trail time north became a haze of ice fog and storm. Each day, each sleep, as winter darkened and deepened, became routines of **non**-routine—whiteout so severe that she must halt or take the risk of driving her team into the open sea. Stopped, she would claw out a cave in whatever drift she found by touch. That failing, she would dig a pit in ice and even dent the frozen ground—for endless wind scoured higher levels bare of malleable material. Sometimes the surface under her *kamik* was only rock-hard permafrost beneath perhaps a skid of ice.

She would settle the dogs, often by simply staking them in a draw on barren prairie with tails wrapped around their noses. Then she would snug the baby into her tunic and crowd among sleep robes with Nuna and Ajak, the pup now bigger than Arajik but dependably gentle with the boy. Sometimes, Kiti would drag the loaded sled across a pit she had hacked into some declivity. Days on end brought whirling snow—rarely new flakes falling, more often white crystals already present rearranging themselves before the wind. Snow seemed to plummet *upward* from the ground. Visibility at such times extended to less than the full team fanned in front. In a whiteout, she could not see her mitt at the end of her arm.

Cold, cold, cold. On the trail, she tied a soft ptarmigan skin across her nose and mouth, then pulled the hood opening tiny as the eye of a fish—and still dared breathe only through her nostrils, for fear of freezing her lungs. In camp at night, or in whatever passed for camp, she could press her face into, and breathe through the wolverine *nuilak,* the fine fur trim on her hood. She laughed when she remembered how, on finding this wondrous pelt in her mother's cache, she had thought she could always trade it for food. Where? With **whom**?

She wanted to travel on the smooth grounded ice along the coast. But in fact, she rarely ventured there because its groans and cracks were so alarming. She recalled tales about whole villages that actually lived on sea ice for the three full moons of blackest winter. If the people did not anticipate spring breakup correctly, they could get stranded, lost forever when stable *tuwak* became nomadic *siku*—when the mooring thawed so that formerly grounded ice began to float. Then it traveled south and east to who knew where. And always melting, getting smaller all the way. It was on one of these newly wandering bergs that her middle brothers Karikit and Mamak disappeared. Palunga, it was, who had vanished alone on barren inland tundra as he headed for the sea. Thus, only Palunga was at all likely someday to reappear. And as new winter deepened, the chance for that diminished.

If Tuk were truly of coastal *Inupiat*, he would know about ocean ice. . . . Why had she not asked him? The spirits knew, she had asked him nearly everything else that came into her head during the time they were together. In fact, she had sounded like a child of four winters, she thought now, for too many of her questions were not cloaked in the attire of a statement.

By each sleep time, Kiti was exhausted from unloading the sled to ice the runners; then re-loading—three, four, five times in a day's run, always depending on the number of jagged rocks that jutted up through too sparse snow. It depended also on whether she could stay on frozen cover so that her runners did not strike barren ground. The sled might be gliding smoothly in the now continual dark of night and day, skim up onto a rise—then grate sharply on earth scoured bare by gales. Disaster for pack and ice on runners. And if the runners themselves were to be saved, they required immediate attention.

Kiti placed her seal and fish store in bladders; then bound everything in bags. She had heard of people using their food supply as a sled without runners, hitching it up to be dragged across snow by the team. She always wondered how people harnessed their teams after the travel party consumed the "sled."

One night, the four of them including the two dogs were huddled among robes in a shallow pit she had slashed down into ice. She covered the top of the hollow with a ragged hide made secure by the heavily loaded sled bridging the top. Then she slid into the cavity and rearranged the covering. She awoke late in the sleep time to hear the fear song of her dogs . . . rhythmic, sustained moaning with a trembling edge of panic. Something or someone fearful to them was nearby. She rolled clear of robes, put on mitts, then grasped her spear and knife. No head space in the hole allowed her to sit up, and she lay there alert, every sense tuned, listening, sniffing—*what was that stink?*

When the wind abated for a moment, she could hear movement at the sled above. Reaching up, she pressed with a bare hand the ragged robe on which the runners rested, felt vibration counter the gusts of wind. Not bear, not wolf—for either of these would first attack the staked and helpless dogs. Then *what?*

Nuna was growling deep in her throat. Now the white dog extricated herself from Ajak and the robe, and by standing gradually, she pushed upward with her croup and shoulders against the rough hide ceiling. That failing to move the sled, she rolled onto her back, trying to dig her way through the restraining pelt. But her claws caught in patches of repair, bringing part of the old hide down on all of them. The dog pawed through ragged folds to rise once more, this time to heave directly against the bottom of the sled.

She began a song of treble yelps, high, hysterical, punctuated by snarls. Once again, she was on her back, paws working this time at the crossbars. Only the weight of the laden sled kept her from pushing it away. Even so, the runners began to slip and Kiti feared that the load would shift and bring the sled with its cargo down upon them. Kiti whispered at her to stop; then reached up herself to steady the runners. She wanted protection. Nuna would be trapped, as well as she—good. . . . This dog had to survive.

Gradually, over and beside the sounds of the dogs, the girl heard other noise—low, uneven grunts of effort, muttered growls—eh, glottal hissing . . . *kapvik?* Yes, that odor could be wolverine . . . She had smelled it only twice before, both times from a distance.

Kiti kept one hand firmly on a runner cross rib, grasped her spear with the other, ready to thrust if the creature should try to come at them. "Nuna, drop!" she commanded, and the dog subsided in the shallow hole, still rumbling, clearly displeased with the order but obedient.

Kiti could now hear splitting and ripping overhead, gulping, gnashing, the pops of tearing cord. The creature should not eat their food—***must not*** chew the lashings, devour the bags and bladders, consume the precious oil—

"—*Owka!* No!!" The girl slid up beside the sled as she had entered the pit, came surging from the sleep cavity, spear swinging before her, the knife somehow clutched in her other mitt. *"Ai-ee-ee!"*

The creature that crouched on the sled load was a mass of dark fur that blew out so steadily that its outline was a blur, even in bright moonlight and the slow shimmer of spirit lights. At one end of the triangular blotch of rippling pelt was an acute angle impossibly low for the size of the animal. Small eyes glittered above bared fangs glinting white in a mouth agape, growling far back in the throat and hissing at the same time.

"Khssh-shh! . . . kssh-shh . . . kssh-shh . . . shh-shh . . . "

The shadow with indistinct edges crouched to turn continually and face

107

her, now lurching forward, reeling back; then shooting out low and fast as if to strike before it faded back. Kiti leaped along one side of the sled, around the end, then along the other, herself darting up, withdrawing—circling, circling rapidly, never presenting a target. Her body was taut, alert to looming danger, tuned to each motion of the raging creature. The spear was ever pointed at the beast, braced hard against Kiti's shoulder, pointing forward and a little down to impale *kapvik* if it actually lunged up at her.

"*Kssh-shh-shh!*"

She realized gradually that this hissing servant of the devil spirit *Paija* was *slow*. It kept turning, yes, was menacing indeed. But dark *kapvik* was awkward as it rustled 'round to meet her attack. She knew from hunters' tales that no wolverine was sluggish when those fearsome teeth and claws fastened into flesh. But as she leapt and circled, shouting, the creature had a hard time staying face to face.

Kiti also realized, as her eyes adjusted to nearly nonexistent light, that the animal had already chewed away the lashings that secured the load. It had pulled food bags from their bundles, torn them open—created the sort of mindless, evil havoc for which *kapvik* was known. The only true criminal of her land . . . the only living creature which would destroy purely for pleasure.

"*Ai-ee—ah-ah—Ai!*" she shrilled as she moved ever more rapidly to taunt the struggling animal twisting on its short front legs, trying to stay high on the strewed packets still remaining on the sled. The body was nearly as long as a sled dog but bulkier and with much shorter legs. Why would it not run away? She was taller, her head well above that gaping mouth even when the wolverine stood here on the sled packs. True, she was not as strong as this terrifying beast—but she was armed and she was at least as angry. The thing should scurry off. Kiti had no need for its fur; and no creature she knew or ever heard about would eat the meat if *kapvik* sprayed. The wolverine itself? She doubted it.

Just go in peace, she thought. *Take whatever can be carried, and go. It may happen that this woman will throw more, and she will be generous.* Brandishing the spear, she wished that she had some idea of where to thrust if *kapvik* did attack. Lacking knowledge, the throat was best. But crouched as the creature was, even the pointed muzzle arrowing to the sled, it exposed no throat or chest. A killing stab could probably be made behind and somewhat above the left foreleg. But neither could the creature's legs be distinguished clearly from the body mass. Too much hair. Too much movement. Too much wind. Too much excitement.

"Ksshh-shh!"

How long the grim dance lasted, Kiti did not know—she leaping, bobbing, shouting; and *kapvik* pirouetting in cadence to his hissing growl, the team at last silent as they watched. But then the creature lurched suddenly and a horrid stench met Kiti's nostrils. What had before been unpleasant to her nostrils now became eye-watering fetor. She watched with disbelief as *kapvik* ejected a foul liquid from beneath its raised tail. She saw or imagined the steam spreading across opened food and what few packets remained sound.

"OW-KA-AA! . . . **NO-OO!**" she shrieked. On inspiration, she placed the spear tip inside the creature's mouth as it hissed and pressed hard without stabbing. The wolverine gagged, backed up, slid off the far side of the sled; then turned to scuttle off to south and west onto the prairie. Kiti could have pierced its throat, but she wanted no further reek of wolverine at her camp. She could in fact run to overtake the animal, separate it from its odorous spirits. But she lacked heart for slaughter without need . . . for killing only in retaliation for the giant weasel's doing what the wolverine does naturally.

Instead, Kiti retched beside the sled. Arajik in her tunic shouted in dismay as the musk reached his nostrils. *Arajik?* She had carried him throughout the encounter. Had the wolverine come at her, it was Arajik in the front of her parka who would have taken the impact of those fangs and hooking claws.

Great heat flooded through Kiti, and she felt suddenly as if she could ride the moon. To use the surge of energy, she ran past the gagging dogs toward sea ice, away from the stench, away from the fleeing wolverine—and away from the grave problem that now awaited her. Strangely, her one coherent thought was that she must hurry to complete the *amaut,* the special hood for her brother.

She returned to camp at last, near-frozen, hip-high fog following in a swirl from off the lead. Pale pink spirit lights with a dancing crimson hem above the near north horizon towered over them and swirled gently. They were oblivious to the wild drama recently played out beneath their glow. And of course were unaware of the calamity which had befallen Kiti's camp.

Nuna, with Ajak, sat waiting well away from the fetid sled, a reproachful glint in her pale eye, and a questioning cock to her head.

"Did odor reach the robes?" Kiti asked soberly. If the terrible liquid had dropped upon their sleeping furs, they would have to accustom themselves to the smell, as no more coverings were likely to come soon.

Because her nose rebelled as they approached the sled, Kiti turned her head to breathe with her mouth through the fur—oh yes, *wolverine* fur—that trimmed her hood. The staked dogs were stretched at the farthest limit of the thongs which held them, facing away, complaining in low moans, not even turning at her approach.

She smiled. "First thing, we'll move a team upwind," she promised them. But doing so delayed only briefly the enlightenment she feared and the necessary job she hated. She must take stock of damage.

The sleep robes, for a miracle, were not contaminated. The food was. Two wrapped packets on the lower layer of the sled might be usable, for the creature had only ripped the hide coverings without yet actually having torn the bladders when its ravage was interrupted. Food, Kiti thought, she could replace in time—but gone was the security of having good packs of seal meat remaining from the hunt with Tuk. Gone also was the reserve of bags and bladders for storing extra provision against the inevitable time of need. All of the lashings were ripped and chewed, no longer usable. Repair would get her nothing more than a mass of stinking shreds and knots. Walrus hide. Split and carefully twisted tight and strong—how could she replace walrus hide? The precious containers, all but those two bladders that had been at the base of the sled, were beyond help. The pouches of blubber and seal oil, thankfully, had been in her hunting bag at one end of the sleeping trench. As had two more drinking bladders. She could still ice the runners. They could still have light and warmth within their shelter every night . . . to accompany their growing hunger. Until she replaced the bladders—could actually capture big game on her own—there would be no way to preserve anything she might seize beyond daily use. Without containers, the dogs would take any meat, even fish. Predators would come.

Pirtok, she thought, *there is no helping what has happened.*

For five sleeps, she stayed on that same prairie by the sea. There, she hunted without success. Even Nuna could find on ice no *aglu,* no breathing hole for a seal. And though it snowed without wild winds to sweep away ground cover, she found no creature tracks to follow, not even hare. Not lemming. On the first new day, the dogs refused the meat that had been opened but not actually defiled by the wolverine. On the second day, and with no other food, they ate of it reluctantly. On the third day, they gobbled what remained and looked for more. There was no more. On the fourth and fifth days, they went hungry. As did Kiti. Only Nuna got food. The woman was now desperate.

She knew that all of them needed good tallow or blubber—animal fat—to withstand the cold. But she was not even catching fish, and the sea ice appeared devoid of life. It was as if an angry Sedna had taken all sea creatures to her palace in the bottom of the sea.

Should she butcher a sled dog? She needed the nine she had. Without transport, all would perish. Only Ajak could be considered surplus, and that pup was too small to satisfy more than Kiti's appetite. Not that she would *have* appetite, where Ajak was concerned.

They must leave this place, then continue north while they had energy. *How many hunters died along the trail from lack of food,* she wondered. *And where was Kiti's great good **fortune** on the trail?*

So they moved on sea ice within sight of land . . . or else on land in sight of sea ice. They went slowly to conserve energy and to stay alert for sign of game. Dark days dragged by—sometimes with storm, other times with starlight and a moon, often fog, never a glimmer of sun. A little snow might come during sleep. Or more likely, existing snow would rearrange. Gale winds drove it low above the ice on land and sea.

Up a pressure ridge they went; then down. Always searching for tracks. Would she tackle a white bear? *Yes.* A walrus on the rocks beside the sea? *Yes, yes.* . . . Seals? *Come, seals.* . . . "*Ai-ee-ee!* Food!"

In a desperate gamble with disaster as the stake, she finally ran the sled far out on smooth sea ice. She no longer had energy to repair runner icing after they struck rocks on land. The coast had shown itself barren of game— and all too often for her sled, barren of snow as well. Perhaps, now that the dogs were truly hungry, one might sniff out an *aglu* near the lead. . . .

Her trail party would stop for rest and she would fish through ice . . . but again nothing, nothing except dark and cold and always the hunger beast gnawing at her belly. She felt faint and dizzy when she moved. *Close the eyes and tend the inner spirits lest they bolt,* she ordered herself. Sleep, sleep, slow the body processes. Did Palunga hunger so, she wondered often in the night, as he walked silent and alone upon the tundra? Did her favorite brother feel the torment of a gut so empty that his spirits tried to flee such an inhospitable host?

And then one morning, strangely, when she rolled from her robes, no craving for food remained. A lightness in her head let Kiti see whatever creature she sought. Only it wasn't there. She would lift her killing spear and hurry forward. The bear or ermine or even caribou on sea ice would continue to stand as she had seen it. But no substance met her weak attack. These were only pictures floating on the surface of her troubled eyes.

Danger. . . . The lead, the open water was too close on their right as they dragged north. Black water. Ice could be thin. She must turn away from this empty river of salt. Yes. Search elsewhere. Sleep. Run with the team when possible, lighten their load, help to push the sled. Even Nuna's food was near an end. . . . Palunga? You, whose sled and dog a sister drives . . . you who know the agony of starvation—eh, *what must Kiti do now?*

And then before her on the ice was first one mound and then a whole village of snow houses. Silent. No glow welcomed strangers. Another fantasy, she thought—and like the others, it would not be tangible.

They drew closer. The mounds were still there, although her dogs did not react. But why would they? They would not imagine what she would. Besides, they too were torpid with hunger and fatigue. Kiti closed her eyes and shook her head to clear her mind. But still, when she opened them, a hunting camp lay scattered on the ice. The girl moved up to touch a wall, be certain that the first *igloo* was real. She felt substance, and so coughed weakly outside the tunnel. No response. But who could hear above the shrieking wind and cracking ice?

She coughed louder at another porch. Still no answer. Sleds leaned on their sides against the arching walls. People could not get far in wintertime without them. Perhaps the villagers hunted nearby. She tried to make her fogged brain reason. The sleds were here—where were the dogs? And especially the *Inupiat,* where were they? She became alert.

"*Ai-ee!*" she tried to shout, but the call came out a whisper. Still her team showed no excitement. Kiti crawled into a snow house. But the dark was too intense, and she came back. She staked her dogs, emptied the sled of its light burden, and upended it on impulse to later make her own lean-to sheltered from the wind. She got fire going in the lee of a sunken porch at one snow house; then pushed the travel lamp ahead of her as she crawled down the tunnel once again. Nuna nosed along behind her, and Kiti was grateful for the company.

Inside, she saw three still figures upon the sleeping ledge. She touched the woman and knew no spirit warmed her. Nor the man. Nor the half-grown boy. Turning, Kiti looked around. Two seals on end were near the tunnel opening. A *Big Feed* nested in the wall near a dark, untended lamp. Nuna whined, and Kiti reached back to reassure her.

She left her lamp burning there, but dragged a seal out. Her need was great and immediate. She cut it up for Nuna and the team with a little for

112

herself. The dogs with their slim bellies would overeat, expel the food and gobble it again. But *Inupiat* knew to nibble just a little right at first; then more, until the shrunken stomach could acquaint itself with food once more.

Kiti quickly checked the remainder of the encampment. Six among the eight cold *igloos* contained the husks of fourteen *Inuit* with spirits gone. The remaining two snow houses, both deserted, looked as if their occupants had planned their leaving, for no provision or weapons remained and no sleds but only *kayaks* were nearby. In the village was no *umiak*, the big round whale boat which Kiti thought would normally be brought out to a seal or whale or walrus camp on ice.

Kiti returned to the original snow house. Nothing was here to fear, for the dispossessed spirits would by now have wandered far across the ice and onto prairie beyond. Could it be that those straying specters were the very reason she had found no food? She retrieved the other seal from that first *igloo;* then could not resist opening the *Big Feed*—in this place, it was a black basket artfully woven of darkly gleaming whale baleen. Inside were treasures quite different from those Pichikut had hoarded. Kiti removed a handsome white bear pelt. The coarsely worked amulets of walrus ivory, she left on the *iglerk* with the people. These were some *angakok's* domain, not hers. A neatly sewn little pouch of ptarmigan hide contained strange green stones. She examined them in lamplight, and each seemed to possess a glowing spirit within. Finally, she pushed the puzzling packet into a pocket of her parka to be studied later. She looked around for lashings, found two long braids of split walrus hide, coiled them around the *Big Feed*; then dragged the whole bag outside. Certainly she would use the container. She would plan her sled space after checking other *igloos* in detail. At present, she was carrying on Palunga's sled only robes, the sleep nest, her hunting bag and what had been Pichikut's *Big Feed*. Energy from food and burgeoning excitement coursed through her, and she interrupted her exploration only to feed the dogs again and nibble some more, herself. Then she stood tall and strong and faced the crimson lights dancing on the north horizon. She grinned at them; then opened her mouth wide.

"Ai-ee-ee-ai-ee!"

Life returned on that day to her and to the team. They stayed at the dead village for three days and nights. Between meals—and meals were many!— Kiti sorted, considered carefully, and then took all she needed from the six *igloos* where inhabitants were spiritless. She did not touch the contents of the two abandoned snow houses. She packed her sled with food in bladders which, remembering *kapvik,* she had this time placed in thick hide bags double-tied secure, and scentless as such a bag can be. She collected stored seal blubber from pouches in the various snow houses. This she cubed as she had done with Tuk; then stuffed it into many small, well-scraped bladders to await its transformation into golden oil for the lamp. She packed one sturdy pouch made of caribou hide full of nothing but rope and lashing, tough split walrus and the delicate, more elastic strips of seal hide. She selected two more soft robes in addition to the splendid white bear fur.

What has happened here? she wondered. The people did not starve, for food was plentiful. Their bodies were well padded, faces peaceful. Here was a mystery, she realized, for which she was unlikely ever to learn the answer.

As vitality and clear thought returned, the girl considered all that would be lost in this place when spring tides came. At season's change, deluges would break up thinning ice in this dead camp. What did not sink as the melting islands upended would surely float away. So before continuing north, she spent her last dark day in using a village sled to transport everything she could onto a land ridge high above the ice. She took weapons, lamps, stone food bowls—and every bit of food that she and the dogs were unable to consume and could not fit onto her own sled. She built a stone cache for the edibles—and then still remembering *kapvik* as well as the predations of unwatched sled dogs, all of whom take pleasure in chewing up animal hide, she added all the extra robes to the top of the well-protected cache. These would also muffle the scent. She wished there were some way to let travelers know that they could have whatever they needed without the usual obligation to replenish everything at first opportunity.

She could have her choice of sleds, several with runners of carved driftwood. But her own sled was lighter, and it was Palunga's. Besides, she was uncertain about methods for icing wood, even though she had observed Tuk prepare his driftwood runners. In the end, she piled sleds and *kayaks* and weapons on and beside the cache. But then at the moment of leaving, she retrieved a sturdy little *kayak* that she tied across the top of her own sled. *Ahmi,* who can predict the future?

"Nakorami, Thank you!" she told the spirits hovering near the cache; then repeated her thanks, as swith the sled and frisking team, she hissed north in darkness on sea ice past the silent village. She was more at ease, now, less leery of traveling near open water. For one thing, deep winter was upon them, so that ice should be very thick indeed. Also, she knew that the

village was built by coastal *Inupiat* who knew much about the sea. If the ice could hold them and their snow houses, so Kiti reasoned, then certainly it could support one woman with dogs and a laden sled.

Oomingmak

At her camp and before sleep, under the flow and churn of pale spirit lights on a windless night, Kiti sat talking to Arajik, to Nuna, to the team. She wished that someone could speak back to her. Arajik responded with a chortle. Then he laughed aloud, jumped up and down in her lap as she braced his arms. He wore a miniature tunic and feet-in trousers that she had finished making for him only one sleep ago. She had used hides gathered from the dead village, delicately cured caribou and hare pelt for trim. What a pleasure to make clothing for this baby! What a comfort he was!

Even so, at times—and this was one of them—she would give all her food and half her robes to hear her native language from lips other than her own. She wanted to *discuss* things. She wanted especially to hear another person's guess about the village that had saved them. She wanted to plan with someone to hunt for Sedna's large sea mammals. She had heard walrus barking and bellowing on floes for two sleeps, now. Yet she knew it would be foolhardy to take the new *kayak* into the lead for walrus. The huge males were peevish when disturbed. Or so she had always heard, and so her brothers said. But if another person were with her—perhaps someone with a big stable *umiak* to accompany her *kayak*. . . .

The team stirred, and Nuna gave a low grumble, looked toward the northwest prairie; then subsided. After a time, Kiti saw a slash of sled and dots of dogs backlit by the swirling pink and green of gentle spirit lights. One person with a large team came forward. She hefted the harpoon from her sled, grasped a sharp skinning knife in her left hand, and watched them come. Why did her dogs not give alarm? She tightened with dread. Their silence would mean that they knew who now approached. Her father? Oojulit?

At first, she did not recognize Tuk. The confident stride had vanished. This person's footsteps faltered as he slowly staked his dogs; then lurched toward her lean-to. Not until he crept into the lamp glow and released the hood string on his parka did she realize that she knew him—and even then could not be certain.

116

They stared at each other. What she saw made her lower her weapons. Dark pockets shadowed sunken eyes. The pads on his cheeks had vanished, the bones of his face now thinly fleshed. He stood weaving in the light, dull eyes fastened on hers. She took a folded robe out from still unloaded sled gear, spread it thickly on the ice before the lamp, and motioned him down.

He dropped wearily. She stood watching him. His eyes closed, unmittened hands working into the warm fur, bringing the lush folds around him. "Someone saw lamp glow on the ice," he muttered at last.

That was all. He didn't *care* that she might kill him. Or perhaps he knew she wouldn't? No, he could not know that. *She* did not know that, not until she saw his condition. Once more, she walked over to the load still stacked on her sled. She unwrapped seal meat, sliced off a large chunk and handed it to him. Then she went back, dug deeply until she uncovered choice *muktuk,* crisp whale skin with blubber attached, a special crackling treat she had found in a *Big Feed* at the dead village. She rustled for a slim stone bowl she had also found there, heaped more food upon it and set the dish before him.

When Tuk saw the mountain of good raw meat, his mouth fell open and his eyes widened. His hand came from the furs to slide into his tunic pocket and retrieve his sharp little knife used for eating.

He shook his head in wonder, glancing up before he grasped the whale. "Where? How?!" But he waited for no answer, only fit a corner of the frozen delicacy into his mouth, hacked it off at his lips. She noticed that both of his hands trembled—not a good thing for someone wielding an *ulu.*

Kiti turned away, picked up her skinning knife, grasped another split seal and dragged it out to feed Tuk's dogs. If *he* was hungry, so must they be also.

It would have been companionable for her to lay out lots of food, then sit and eat with her visitor. Not many moments ago, she would have given much to find someone to share the whole evening. Now, though, she quivered with strange, conflicting feelings, which put an uncomfortable echo into her belly. Also, she churned with questions that could not be asked. So she busied herself around the camp, expanded the lean-to and then played with Arajik. At last, she lowered the lamp wick, spread an extra robe for Tuk, and then rolled up wearily in her own sleep furs, one hand kneading at her cold ear lobe.

Nearly asleep and strangely relaxed, she realized that those few words Tuk had spoken . . . even in such unsteady voice . . . eh, a wonderful sound. . . . She would get him fed and warmed, back to himself once more. Then— should she let him stay? Would he want to? Should she *ask* him to join her camp? But he had come here, had he not? And come straight in, despite her prior threats.

Once more, her imagination leaped to and lingered on the worst possible scenario she could conjure. He might still be a threat. He knew where she came from—might now be in communication with Narluk after this time of travel, even if he had not formerly.

But a persistent, wily voice inside brought another view. *All right, if she had to believe that Tuk truly was in some way connected with her family; then why should she not have him right here so that she could keep an eye on him?* Yes, she liked that thought. Besides, he could have taken Arajik earlier, quite easily as she reviewed their time together, might even have hurt the child—or Kiti—if he had been told to do so by his shaman . . . but he had *not*. Perhaps his task, if he had one, was only to find her and report back.

So where had he been throughout these many sleeps?—and this she needed to know. How could he possibly have visited a village recently, especially *her* village, and then arrive back here in this condition? True, it would be far away from here. But her people would not have let him go without plenty of food. He would have hunted with a group, had he joined any village at all; then shared what was captured regardless of who had thrown the killing spears. And successful on the hunt or not, any but a starving group would have provisioned him before he left. *Peeusinga, the People's Way.*

But no. He came hungry, worn out, perhaps ill—and something else, besides. She could feel a sadness in him. He may have risked his life to find her camp. Or any camp at all? Right now, he seemed not to care whether his spirits stayed or fluttered off forever. He seemed to be heavy with *Perlerornaq*—eh, the weight of life, the futility of drawing breath. Tuk would not be first among *Inupiat* to succumb to this shadow on the spirit, this strange rapture that beset a person who followed a lonely trail in solitude. The everlasting darkness of deep winter. Such isolation on the trek that blurs senses and free will diminishes, even that innate determination to survive. How often she had heard of this mortal malady from tales dramatized beside the lamp? She wondered if she had, herself, come close to this condition before she stumbled on the dead village. No. Her perceptions had been mischievous and misleading, especially her vision and hearing. But no, she had not once thought life too troublesome to be continued. Of course, she had Arajik. No doubt, he made a great difference in the strength of her purpose. Too, she must remember that her guest had been upon the trail longer than she. Nor may it have been his choice to leave family behind.

She needed to know about Tuk. Why did he say nothing? Time, talk, good food and warmth—right *now!*—would surely chase the shadow from Tuk's soul. Perhaps this time she could wait patiently for him to talk. But this new woman Kiti, unfortunately, was no more patient than the old child Sukitilan. She really must learn to exercise more discipline . . . and soon.

* * *

They remained in camp while Tuk ate and slept. His dogs, as it turned out, were hungry but not starving, slim but not emaciated. And very little food, both seal and fish, still remained on Tuk's sled. He wanted her to use it with her own. She smiled privately. She had so much, thanks to the silent village, and he so little. The young man's pride returned. He was recovering.

"One found no helping spirit anywhere," he related over a meal three sleeps later. "Nor is this hunter strong enough to go on and on without the sight of other *Inuit.*"

Kiti remembered the strange visions she herself had—the imaginary creatures and active, fur-clad hunters on ice—during the time of great hunger after the wolverine destroyed their provisions and before they came upon the village of the dead. *But that invention was from lack of food,* she told herself now. She remembered how she had yearned for another human voice on the very evening Tuk appeared recently. *But that was preference and* **desire***, not* **need***, certainly not* **necessity***,* she decided. Could it be that Kiti was becoming independent? If so, Pichikut would be pleased. True, they would have starved had the village not appeared. But so would any hunter unable to find food. That no game had come to give itself had little to do with her growing self-reliance.

Resilient as all *Inupiat,* Tuk rapidly gained energy, strength and vigor. His hearty spirit returned. He now spoke more readily than before, as if he and Kiti were long-time friends. Or perhaps it was only that Kiti listened better, for she reveled in the sound of *Inupiaq* spoken in another's voice.

He told her, "It happens that even wind and sky are enemies when too long in one's own company."

Kiti smiled, raised her brows in agreement. She was determined to let him do the talking so that she could learn everything possible. She could not, however, keep her mind from formulating questions silently. Where had he been? What was his destination as he wandered in the blackness of mid-winter? *Did he know her father?*

". . . When the gale drones words that *Inuk* understands; then madness is nearby," Tuk told her thoughtfully before the fifth sleep time since his return. He was now up and energetic, had gone hunting alone inland that very morning, not successfully. Nor was Kiti fortunate on the ice she chose to search. Still, much food remained available to them at her camp.

At the end of the next full day, Tuk described his futile efforts to find game after he left her so many sleeps ago. "Near the end," he told her, "even though some food remained, this *Inuk* could not eat or sleep or think in a straight line. He could not plan or hunt. Often, he had to remember even to draw breath."

She smiled at him encouragingly, sympathizing without speech. This was not the time to mention his *perlerorneq,* that terrible weight of life which can overtake a solitary hunter on the dark winter trail.

She had by now decided that no, she herself definitely had not had such a problem. Or if so, she had handily laid it to a different cause. Her difficulties came from trying to hunt on ice and land when both were bare of life. His dilemma? The same, or only loneliness? A matter of perception, she decided— how two separate people interpret an identical situation differently . . and both, she decided with an audible snort, may be incorrect. The true picture might be something else entirely.

One evening, Tuk finally unraveled a part of the tangled straps of his origin. "When a young man's family died suddenly—both parents and a young sister, as well. . . . Did someone tell this tale before?"

Kiti dropped her eyelids, *No.* By the intensity of his voice, Kiti knew that her visitor would soon reveal a reason for his sadness. "A woman never asked," she told him, suddenly ashamed. Certainly she had been saturated right from the beginning with curiosity about this young man's beginnings, reasons for his current solitude. She still was. She slept poorly when he was in her camp because she kept going over and over the possibilities—mostly dire in her sleep time imagination. She had maneuvered from him instruction on hunting seal, on better ways to load a sled—even some information about *Inupiat* routines when living by and on the sea. How could she not have managed to get from him some answers to the truly vital questions?

Eh, she knew why. She had not wanted him to have such information about *herself,* so she avoided altogether the subjects of origin and current isolation.

"It happens that the family was far inland as winter began," Tuk told her, "because they had gone south as summer ended to follow the beasts called *tuktu*—caribou. But then they returned too slowly, long past time of tundra snow. Still, transportation could be rapid for that very reason, now able to use sled and team. Here was an adventure. A father found a sun-dried caribou carcass to make a sled, hitched up the team and started for the familiar village by the sea.

"But still far out on barren ground, it happened that a family came upon two coastal *Inupiat*. Both strangers, and they seemed frightened."

Kiti waited while Tuk stared into the fire for a long time before continuing.

"At first the two gave no explanation for their traveling west when others of the coastal folk had gone to meet the sunrise at least a moon before. Most by then would be already at the sea in freshly built villages."

Kiti's mind flashed a memory of the two deserted snow houses in the village of death. "On the ice," she stated, an obvious query tucked into the words.

Tuk raised his brows to show assent, but his voice continued hollow, echoing: "One day, the beloved family was vigorous. Then a little coughing on the sleep ledge in the night. The next day, their spirits fled."

He raised his mitts on either side, palm up and empty, looked at each. "One day, four happily together. The next, one sadly alone."

His eyes were tormented when he looked at her, his jaw working. She wanted to comfort him—clasp him to her as she would Arajik. Who would not in such circumstance fall prey to *perlerorneq*? Of course he was melancholy!

"So it happens, Tuk did not choose to be alone on the prairie," she murmured.

"Who *would!?*" he gasped. "Did Kiti?"

She hesitated, realizing for the first time how well her mother had equipped her for this trip. Not only skills, but also how her mind worked—the pride in doing for herself, the determination to rely on her own reserves so far as possible.

"Yes," she told him softly, "Kiti selected solitude from among those morsels offered in her food bowl."

He frowned, staring over at her, but did not comment further. And he did not ask.

* * *

The musk oxen were on nearby prairie. *Oomingmak,* the creature with skin covered by shaggy beard. Tuk said he had seen some, or *thought* he had, before he found Kiti on the ice. These were the only living creatures, he told her, that he had seen in many days. And they were not considered possible targets for capture by a solitary hunter.

Big hoofed beasts built more roundly than caribou? *Ai-ee-ee!* Kiti's mouth watered. How could anyone resist, so much food with a single thrust of the spear. Of course, the two of them must search before Tuk went away.

"Coastal people do not pursue them," he warned her.

"Nor do those of Kiti's old village. But why not? Does it happen that the flesh is foul, like wolverine?"

"*Owka,* No. For if this were so, then someone would have said it."

". . . Then perhaps they wait for two young hunters who have sufficient desire."

Tuk's hand on her sleeve to caution her, Kiti now gazed with awe over the top of a rise at the small group of *oomingmak* below them to the south. Bulky creatures, adults at the shoulder seemed high as Kiti's head. Their cascading coats were luminous under the filmy pink and green swirls still lighting the northern sky at a time that would be dawn if it were springtime. A fur skirt commenced beneath the chin with streaming overfur that seemed to Kiti as long as her arm. This joined the rest, all flowing in the wind, nearly hiding those delicate legs slim as a ptarmigan's tarsus. All the adults, male and female alike, had downswept horns that curved back up to swing out sharply at eye level. What looked to be the largest males had a thick plate above the brow.

Kiti had of course heard of muskox in lamplight tales. *Dangerous creatures, fierce and swift, to be feared and left alone.* So said the storytellers. But none professed ever to have actually *seen* one up close, only herds in the distance and then but rarely. Often, Kiti had plucked from tundra grass and rocks their clotted clumps of wool discarded lavishly during spring and summer. The long dark overhairs could be twisted to make a strong thread. Or handfuls could be stuffed into *kamik* for fine effect to insulate against cold. The shorter underfur could be hand- wound as elegant trim for parkas and trousers, and she had seen it used that way. Contrary to its coarse appearance, the material when washed was softer to the touch than the most delicate belly fur of a young rabbit. But preparing and working it into a design was more demanding, to Kiti's mind and to her mother's also, than mere beauty was worth.

These animals they saw grazed placidly, five adults and three juveniles, at lichen sites that they had bared beneath the ice. Kiti moved up toward the crest of the bluff to get closer. But she found Tuk once more grasping the sleeve of her parka.

Softly, *"Owka.* No."

She glanced at his anxious face; then retreated to where the hill crest hid them from the creatures. "They are violent?"

"Ee-ee, when they feel threatened." He sounded unsure. "Like all beings including *Inuit,* large fear becomes great anger. And musk oxen are said to be suspicious by their nature."

"But good to eat?"

"Opinions differ."

Kiti chuckled. "And had any who had opinions tasted the flesh for himself?"

The corners of Tuk's lips turned up. "None I heard ever spoke of doing so."

Both were quiet, and then Kiti grinned over at him. "Can it be that two mighty seal hunters will capture *oomingmak* on this day?"

Without answering, Tuk squinted and eased upward to peer once more over the top of the hillock. Then he slid back, picked up his spear.

Kiti clasped her own bone weapon, as well as the big harpoon she had lugged from the sled. *A large creature is worthy of such a projectile,* so she reasoned.

Just before they crested the hill, Tuk reached over in curiosity to heft the harpoon. A quizzical look swept across his face. Although small for a harpoon, it was still quite heavy. But he did not laugh.

"It may happen," he said softly, "that someone could move more easily with only the spear." He pointed his nose at the sharp implement she held in her other hand, raised his head rapidly.

Kiti's jaw tightened, especially because she had to admit to herself the truth of his words. "It may *also* happen," she retorted, "that the spirit of one's grandfather who made this harpoon will aid the granddaughter in its use."

Tuk shrugged. Who could argue?

Now why did she say such a thing? *Ananak* had always maintained that her father—the ice island grandfather whom her children never saw—was a terrible hunter. A good weapon-maker, yes, but a hard luck *Inuk* on the trail. It was for this reason that Pichikut had to take responsibility for feeding her family.

"Should a shaggy skin attack," Kiti continued, "this woman will throw the harpoon and retreat swiftly."

He motioned her back to whisper again. "Tuk has not hunted for nor eaten of *oomingmak*, this is true," he said. "But from a safe distance he *has* observed angered bulls outrun wolves easily and use those sharp horns to send their spirits flying forever!"

Kiti's eyes widened. "Then it happens that puny *Inuit* cannot outdistance it, should one attack?"

"So it's important that no reason for anger be given."

As if this provided all the instruction Kiti needed, Tuk returned to the crest and then inched down toward the beasts. Kiti watched him creep forward. In fact, she had trouble seeing that he moved at all. But she followed his lead, fancying herself a boulder set in the hillside *here* and then *there at this lower place* and now *here in this new spot*. At this pace, Kiti decided, the juvenile musk oxen would be fully grown before the two swift hunters ever reached the herd.

Halfway down the little hill, the two were perhaps eight sled-lengths from the nearest grazing animals. Tuk's hand again was on her sleeve in warning as they crouched there, the strong south gale in their faces so that they remained downwind, peering at their quarry.

"Now what?" Kiti finally whispered into his ear.

Even that slight sound, however, was picked up by the sharp but invisible woolly ears below. The biggest animal wheeled to face the sound, and the hunters crouched motionless, twin shadows against the snowy land.

Let the bearded ones see nothing but furry boulders. Kiti concentrated fiercely on the idea, just as she had focused on becoming a seal when she hunted on the rocks. *See? Here are two stones covered with animal pelt,* she amended her first thought, *set firmly in the earth.* She lowered her eyelids so that the whites would be less likely to reflect what little light there was. She tried not to blink or even to breathe, for fear some ripple of parka fur unnatural to the wind might betray her. She wanted to see what Tuk was doing, but dared not look. She knew the creatures could not scent them, for they had staked the dogs well back and taken pains to keep themselves downwind.

Yet, the herd knew something was different. They sensed some small change in their surroundings. With no signal Kiti could distinguish, adults in the group went together haunch by furry haunch, youngsters tucked between and behind, all facing the hillside where the two *Inupiat* hunkered stiff as rock cairns.

The big heads tossed. The ends of the line backed around to form a half-circle, arcs swinging back on either side of what Kiti took to be the one boss bull. Juveniles peered out curiously from among their full-sized kin.

Now came a timeless period. The *Inupiat* crouched motionless, furs blowing. Five bearded adults also stood on planted hooves, noses testing wind, eyes rolling, skirts flowing in brisk breeze.

The spirit lights gradually faded and disappeared while the hunters waited. Now a bank of black clouds which had hidden moon and stars passed by, and the sky afforded to the stationary scene a cold blue light. Perhaps a glint from one of the smooth weapons gave them away. Or even the sparkle of an eye. Whatever it was, the bull suddenly fastened his gaze on them. He snorted, pawed with a front hoof, rubbed his muzzle on his foreleg.

Neither Tuk nor Kiti moved. The girl felt her stomach lurch to the base of her throat as the whole herd advanced a sled's length forward, still in that curious formation. Then there was no more movement for a time. One of the smaller beasts suddenly broke free of adults and darted toward them. A full-grown muskox surged out to nose the youngster none too gently back behind the rank. That movement, and the small one's squall of protest, broke the spell only for a moment. Then all was as before. Standing. Staring. Breathless crouching. Fur rippling. Kiti slowly closed her aching eyes completely to keep them from watering and freezing. As she did so, every other sense sharpened. *Here is a good thing to know,* she thought, *and applicable in other circumstance.*

She became restless. Her muscles ached from holding still. Ice underfoot breached the moss lining her boots, and cold gradually numbed her feet and legs to the knee. Knowing what she now knew, she wanted to go back in time to the moment when they first saw the musk oxen. Then, having seen them, they could return to their teams and take the trail to hunt elsewhere. And before the sleep tonight, they would then have that unusual experience of seeing *oomingmak* to muse and mull over at the lamp.

She was the one who had pushed for seeking out muskox, she now recalled; and their dilemma, therefore, was her blunder. Neither of them had any idea whether these beasts were even good to eat. Neither knew how to catch them. Of two things she was certain. Only a *soospuk* would try to capture musk oxen in a herd. And she also knew that in this situation, the hunters were far more at risk than any of the creatures that they hunted on the flat below. *Another good thing to have learned,* she thought, wondering whether she would live long enough to apply this new wisdom to the trail. *Truly, could a small herd of musk oxen dispatch a whole pack of wolves?*

125

The two different species, human and beast, studied each other for what seemed to Kiti at least three sleeps. She felt herself become a lump of ice before the big leader turned and walked away with grand nonchalance. The herd broke rank immediately and returned to feeding without another look at the interlopers. Tuk and Kiti were forgotten.

Chock-chip, a sharp hoof dug through snow. *Smoo-oosh,* a blunt muzzle bent to snuffle and scrape noisily, and then move on. *Much sound, little food,* Kiti thought as she watched the creatures graze slowly south to greater and greater distance before the intrepid pursuers dared to move away.

She was startled when her parka slid back as Tuk put his mouth to her ear once again. His question reached her more as thought than sound. "Does someone see the lone beast on the next rise?"

She looked to the west, across the narrow valley and up another shallow hill. Yes, a solitary creature stood in silhouette against the deep black-purple of the starlit sky. She raised her eyebrows to let him know that *Yes,* she saw *something,* anyway. And that bit of movement, just lifting her brows, was a vast relief. She took a deep breath, turned to put her own lips to Tuk's ear.

"Can we reach him?!" She knew that somewhere near most herds of caribou—the only other grazer that she knew about—one or several exiles can be found. Usually, these will be old males, probably no longer vital enough to challenge other bulls and win cows, yet unwilling to leave their kind entirely. Or, the solitary animal could be a scout. Who knew?

Tuk raised his eyebrows, *Yes.* "Perhaps when the herd has moved further away."

"But won't the single one attack?"

"It happens, *oomingmak* is not foolish. Here to face him are two, he but one."

Kiti thought about this but said nothing. The male she had seen up close was more than equal to the two puny *Inupiat* who observed him. Even from such distance in poor light, those twisting horns looked very sharp. She pictured in her mind the demise of one ferocious pack of wolves . . . their carcasses careering high, one by one arcing to fall inert.

Still the hunters waited as the herd moved off. Kiti felt herself an extension of the frozen ground and not much warmer, either. Tuk kept shuddering, an arm moving up spasmodically, a foot changing position. *Is he cold also, or only restless?* Kiti wondered.

Suddenly, he spoke with a full voice. "One more thing is known about a herd of bearded ones which no longer feel immediately threatened," he said.

Then he braced his legs and took a deep breath. *"Ai-**EE-EE**! Ah-ah-**AI-EE**!!"* He jumped up and down, waving his arms.

Startled, Kiti watched him for a moment, and then sent her own howls upwind. The shouts still echoing, they watched when the herd well south in a deepening valley wheeled as a single creature and thundered off to oblivion.

Kiti glanced up. The shadow on the hill crest to the west remained exactly as it was. The wind was shifting, now beginning to rise out of the northwest. It would have blown their shouts south and east toward the moving herd, opposite from the solitary muskox. The two hunters walked down to cross the frozen prairie.

"If a woman still wishes to take this animal . . . ?"

"Yes." The two teams of dogs were going rapidly through her food supply. Tuk's provision was gone entirely, and they had not yet captured any fresh game. They could backtrack south to find the cache near the village of death, but Kiti would consider doing this only if she were truly desperate. Besides, she needed skill and knowledge in the capture of *every* creature. This attempt to take muskox would be part of her education on becoming completely self-sufficient. She had already learned—just today!—not to approach a herd of *oomingmak* unless accompanied by a whole village of well armed hunters. Even then, she would know to be most cautious. *A **whole pack** of clever wolves!*

"The creature may easily become provoked," Tuk warned. "A solitary herding beast is not a bachelor by choice—so is rarely pleased with his fate." They had reached the other side of the shallow valley, had circled around to be downwind, and were now ready to climb the hill on which the lone bull still stood foraging, head down. Sounds of his *chock*-ing ice and scraping at the lichen came to them on the wind. Tuk searched without explanation among rocks and boulders which had rolled down, what must in summer be a streambed, perhaps becoming a waterfall in heavy rain. Two giant stones leaned against each other at the foot of the dry course. The tops met, but a spear-high fold gaped narrowly from the ground to form a deep person-high triangle. Into this opening, Tuk pressed himself. Kiti heard him laughing, and he still chuckled as he emerged.

"One hunter will draw the beast, and then fly into these rocks for safety," he told her. "The second will be hidden above and will step out to plunge the killing spear as the creature charges the first hunter."

Just like that. Kiti looked at Tuk with new respect. A plan. She thought a moment; then snorted. "And which hunter will do what?"

"This decision belongs to Kiti," he told her.

"Who drives the spear more strongly?" she asked, as if she did not know.

"And who can run more nimbly?" he asked, with a crinkling grin.

"Phfft! Kiti's decision!" she laughed. Then soberly, she handed him her harpoon. "Might this be better?"

He studied it, turning it thoughtfully in his mitts. "The grandfather will continue to aid in the weapon's use when another hand holds it?"

"Perhaps as much as if the one were kin," Kiti heard herself say. She put a bare hand up inside her parka to rub her ear. *It is unlikely that the spirit of Kiti's grandfather could help regardless of whose hand holds his handsome harpoon.* And here she was, sinking in the muck of her original lie and unable to retrieve herself.

"Eh, and perhaps *not*," Tuk mused. He leaned the harpoon against one of the boulders, far back by the hill so that she would not stumble over it as she dived for the opening. "The spear man is likely to have but one opportunity. He must use a familiar weapon."

Kiti put her own spear carefully on end inside the safety gap. She started up the incline. Tuk followed. She selected as she went what was likely to be the surest path to take down the snow-covered ice on rocks which made up the streambed. Her descent would be at full speed, and likely not knowing whether the creature followed. She must memorize the most stable route. From time to time as they climbed, Tuk would grunt and point out some jagged stone or possible dark sink hole that she might not have noticed but needed to avoid.

As they neared the crest, they crouched low. They were silent in their stalk, cautious—once again nearly motionless, so slow was their crosswind approach. The solitary bull was unaware as he snuffled in lichen graze he uncovered.

At last, the hunters were at the top of the hill, two sled lengths away from where the creature stood with his shaggy backside to them. Rocks and a few boulders still lined even the upper waterway. Behind one of these latter Tuk now positioned himself, pulling Kiti toward him, once more placing his mouth at her ear.

"A hunter should not get too close before she lets the creature see her," he warned. "Someone needs wings for a flying start."

Kiti raised her eyebrows, *Yes*. Based on what she saw when the whole herd whirled away, a runner on flat ground would have no chance at all. A thrill of excitement accompanied her fear. She shivered, grinned. Now she moved away from Tuk to let him hide himself.

She straightened up suddenly. *"Hoo-oo!"* she called tentatively from downwind, feeling like a child play-acting, unsure of her voice. The creature did not move.

"HOO-OO!" she tried again. Nothing. He was intent on feeding. The blast out of the north caught her words and carried them away.

She stepped closer. Then she drew a deep breath, flapped her arms and jumped. *"AH-AI-EE-EE!"* she shouted.

The animal leaped straight up, came down turning toward her, bellowing, feet churning ice. As Kiti dashed down the streambed, she wondered whether he was annoyed enough to follow.

He was. He did.

She did not know when she passed the place where Tuk hid. Rocks skittered beneath her boots. She fell and rolled, got lightly to her feet, continued. She heard a crash behind and above, but dared not turn to see what happened. Perhaps *oomingmak* had fallen as she had. Perhaps Tuk had taken him. Perhaps Tuk himself was down. Rocks rattled behind her, passed her on their descent. Was it she or the animal that had disturbed them? She raced to the boulders, slid smoothly inside, hunched far back to make herself unreachable by horns, if not invisible.

Except for stones that rattled down the streambed—first many, and then few, finally none—she heard no more. No sound rode the wind—no bellow of angry beast, no shout of triumphant hunter. She waited for what seemed a long time before she peeked out and around; then emerged. Nothing. Staying by the gap, she shouted. No answer. She waited. Impatience overtook her. She could not remain here through a sleep. Whatever was to happen had by now occurred. Tuk might be wounded. Might be spiritless. The beast was either mortally injured, dead—or had long since run away. It certainly had not followed Kiti all the way down, for she had watched from safety and would have seen him pass.

She picked up her spear and knife, and left the harpoon for later. She needed to investigate. She also needed to get back to Arajik and the team, regardless of what had happened in this place.

Cautious, quietly as possible, she clambered up the streambed. Every sense was alert to possible danger in the black of early afternoon. But no sound came. Perhaps a smell of blood reached her nostrils. At the crest, she saw a large dark shape lying on the snow. *Oomingmak,* the bearded one, was down.

"Tuk?!" Her own soft voice startled her.

No answer came, nor did the creature stir. She moved closer. Blood that pooled from underneath the beast showed black upon the shadow of snow, spreading still, frozen at the edges, crystals sparkling in starlight. She removed a mitten, touched the muzzle. Cold, with a frothy, frozen pale mucus at the nostrils. She replaced her mitt, walked around the animal to observe. A broken spear shaft extended from under the creature. She kept walking. Something irregular caught her eye as she got to the belly side. She bent down to peer more closely.

A *kamik,* Tuk's fur boot. . . . She reached out to pick it up, found it attached to a foot, heard a muffled sound from beneath the animal.

"Spirits, help me *now!*" she beseeched as she backed up to the carcass and dug both of her own boots into the snow, pushing against the dead weight with all her might. She barely nudged the big muskox. Now she put her spear deep as possible under the belly, careful not to puncture Tuk or the creature, and then pulled up on the end until she knew the weapon strained and was ready to snap.

"Wait!" She raced to the other side, pulled out the remains of Tuk's spear and took it around. Then placing the handles of both weapons together and bending low, she pushed them far under and lifted once again.

This time, the big body shifted. She pushed back for fresh purchase, and lifted steadily.

Tuk's boot and leg wiggled. While she levered part of the weight, he crept out from under, spitting wool and sneezing. At last he stood free, plucking away whole handfuls of qiviut fur from face and ears and tunic. The pale light overhead showed him to be unharmed. The black smears of blood appeared to come from wounds inflicted on the beast.

The two thanked *oomingmak* for allowing himself to be taken. Neither *Inuit* was certain of the conventions in this instance, but their prayer of thanksgiving to the creature spirit was sincere.

Afterward, Kiti fixed Tuk with hard eyes and a set mouth. "Why is it, the hunter did not move out immediately from beneath the creature? Did not at least manage to call for help?"

Tuk raised his mitten, palm up to her. She placed his broken spear shaft into it, and he examined it ruefully.

"At first, the muskox still possessed fierce spirits, who knew how strong? The spearman dared not move."

"And after? A woman hiding below thought all was lost."

Tuk sucked in breath—yes, she had a point. "Later, as it happened, and for the first time since the sleep, the mighty hunter found himself to be . . . eh, comfortably warm." He looked across at Kiti with embarrassment, raised his eyebrows, and then his shoulders helplessly, and kept staring at her.

She was encased in snow where she had fallen on her trip down the hill. She resembled a delicate white she-wolf, head up, alert—and very shaggy. Tuk's lips twitched, and he held back the rising chuckle with a strangling sound. . . .

The woman looked at him. She knew that her anger issued from anxiety— fear for his well-being—not real annoyance. Wads of wool remained on his hood. Shreds that he had missed in his hurried scrape-off stuck out everywhere. She snorted. The young man stood before her like a spring-molted white sea-bear, clasping in his mitts the useless shank of a broken spear.

She grinned.

He continued to stare with grave dark eyes until he choked on his laughter. After that, he raised his woolly chin to the sky and bellowed.

Suddenly, both were rolling in the snow, smothered and helpless with mirth and relief and triumph and joy following a successful hunt.

The meat was edible if not exactly delicious. Thus, the first solid food for Arajik turned out to be muskox. Kiti thought this a good sign—exotic fare for an uncommon child. She cut the flesh into fine pieces, stirred in still-warm tallow from the thick layer of fat under the creature's skin. She had to heat the meal near the lamp, for Arajik of course knew only warm sustenance. Then Kiti mushed it with a rock she had picked up at the stream bed, a smooth long stone rounded on both ends, a cobble that fit her hand perfectly.

Interestingly, alluvium had slid down the streambed behind her rushed retreat. Or had been uncovered by her fall and slide. When the two brought in the sled to pack out the carcass, spirit lights were rippling. In the pastel flicker, both hunters took time to look through the gravel of rocks and pebbles. Beside the natural pestle and a small soapstone having one concave face— exactly right to hold her brother's food—Kiti picked out the clearest from among a great many of the translucent green minerals such as she had seen only once before. Back at camp, she added them to those in the pouch she had found at the dead village.

Tuk discovered a largish lump of pale, slick mineral which he turned over and over in his hands, feeling its smoothness and observing its shape from every angle. He was certain, he told Kiti, that the bearded one, the spirit of the very *oomingmak* of their chase, was hidden here within. The creature only wanted Tuk's chipping knife and hand stone mallet to release him.

Tap-tip-tap. Tuk was intent on this liberation of a shaggy beast before the sleep when Arajik dipped his fat-cheeked face into the new bowl of freshly warmed meat. The baby brought his head up, snuffling and snorting, but with wonder and delight making his eyes sparkle. Meat and tallow were thick on nose and chin when he looked at Kiti and laughed aloud, spraying a share of his meal. Then he dived back to the bowl as if someone might take it away.

Tap-tap, went Tuk's chipping knife. *Tap-tip.* "One questions," he said mildly, and pointing with his chin at the child, "whether that one can ever now be satisfied with only fish and seal."

Kiti giggled when the grimy face came up again for air. "Arajik must not get attached to muskox. This hunter has small desire to capture another."

"Hoo-oo!" Tuk said, in mock distress at the thought. Then, slowly, "Will it happen that *two* hunters can see the baby grow in these next moons, or only the child's mother?"

He was asking whether they might stay together for a time. Kiti was pleased at the thought, and then confused by that very pleasure. She dipped a warm, wet ptarmigan cloth from a bladder suspended over the lamp on a caribou rib and scrubbed at Arajik's protesting hands and face.

"Eh, this on the outside cannot be saved to later go inside!" She kept washing and murmuring to hide her strange sensations. Perhaps Tuk would not notice that she had ignored his question. In most ways, it would be good to have him with her. Easier—for he was knowledgeable and strong, could and would share work along the trail. Safer as well—for two could help each other in a time of trouble. She no longer feared him. Together, they had faced danger without fleeing, and together they had laughed often. . . . They were in harmony. Too, he had given seal oil generously at their first meeting when she had been without heat and light for half a moon. He had also been liberal at that time—despite her loud hostility—about leaving so much seal from his own capture. . . . That *kapvik* had promptly ruined it was not Tuk's fault.

Kiti reflected now that she too had shown good faith, despite her misgivings and threats of violence, by ministering to him seven sleeps ago when he came off the trail confused and half starved. Even if the worst were true—even if he were Narluk's spy or emissary—there was a kindness to this young man . . . and something else she could not yet name. Something good and mysterious and tantalizing. Something still forming richly in her perception. Perhaps she would invite him to share her body on this night. . . . What a very pleasant prospect!

But wait. He was an enigma still, even though he had explained his circumstance. She sighed. And had done so without requiring that she reveal her own situation. Despite his tale of tragedy—and yes, she did believe him— some questions continued to plague her. For example, why—after his family died—did he not go back to his village directly? Or at least find some people? He was not a person to thrive in solitude—perhaps he did not know this when he started? And also, since by his own admission he knew her village, how could he *not* know Narluk? Was it possible to be there and not meet her father? And even more confusing, was it possible to be there, meet him— then *not* know, at least from other villagers, that Narluk's daughter had vanished with *angakok's* newborn son? How much was known by those people there— how much Narluk had said—she had no way to tell.

She wondered where Tuk went after she sent him from her camp following their capture of seals. Not her concern, she realized—not unless. . . . *What if some treacherous sinew really did tie this man to Narluk? Was it not more prudent to continue as they were, hunt together by day and sleep separately at night? Then what? It would be easier, that way, to send him off alone when both had provisioned themselves. But Tuk was not someone pleased for long in his own company. And why did her logic go in circles each time that he visited, with always the same questions about the same unknowns and too few answers?*

Eh . . . and *why does Kiti continue to say nothing about her own circumstance?* She had good reasons. . . . But he did not know that, and yet he never pushed. Eh, supposing Tuk as well had solid grounds . . . ?

Chip . . . tip-tip,tap. . . . "It may happen, someone's husband would not wish for Tuk to join her on the trail," the man continued as he worked.

Ah, this gentle probing on his part invited but never did demand that she explain her domestic status. Of course he must suspect by now that no husband would be coming. Kiti felt heat rise in her once again, fury like all anger born of fear. *Be done with him,* she told herself. *Don't take chances when Arajik is at stake.* Still, if she knew the answers for questions about Tuk, then she might freely explain her own situation, might even permit—no, welcome!— his joining her while their coastàl routes converged. Yes, if perfectly at ease, she would open her sleep robes to him. A quickening overtook her when she got to this phase in her revolving fancy and recognized that this was no new thought conjured up today. In fact—automatically, her right hand reached for her ear. *The white bear peacefully asleep within the ice is not to be disturbed.* Who had said that? Not Pichikut. But never before had the young woman anticipated the *player* above the *process.*

Hoo-oo! No words to Tuk about this matter. She would not wish to make herself more vulnerable than she already was. Any *Inuit* alone for unlimited time outdoors in winter dallied with disaster. Pichikut hadn't said that, either. But Kiti's brain told her that a woman like herself was at risk . . . young, inexperienced . . . with an infant . . . her family probably still searching and perhaps with violent intent. And these were not matters to be *thought* on at one time, let alone to be spoken to a stranger.

*Well then, let Tuk be for you **not** so much an outsider.* Perhaps this man chipping on a stone only awaited opportunity to reveal himself. What question had he only just now asked? Ah!

"Any husband would want companionship for his wife on a long and lonely trail," she said. *Just as any wife who could not go herself because of late pregnancy or illness would want her man to take a woman with him for comfort on the trail.* Such selfishness would be unimaginable in either situation.

No response.

She would provide Tuk with another opening to reveal more: "Still, a man's village must be worried even now about his welfare."

"Owka, No," he said mildly as he tapped the muskox stone and turned it in his hands. Eyes half closed, he seemed to perceive the mineral with all his senses rather than merely observe it. "One knows the beast is there. But how is it placed within this rock?"

Kiti chewed her upper lip for patience. "Perhaps the people of his village will send someone to search for missing members long overdue," Kiti persisted.

"Eh, they will believe that it is by *choice* that a whole family has not returned. Families after summer can go anywhere. . . ." His voice trailed off but the chipping did not slacken.

Kiti raised her eyebrows. "They may believe that someone chose to join another village?!" Her own people usually stayed with the same group unless there was serious dissension. Or unless it became necessary to find a group with other sons and daughters of marriageable age, she remembered. Would her own family have changed villages when Narluk decided that his daughter really ought to take a husband?

Tuk made no response. His mind was not on her words *or* on his village.

134

It was on his carving, his releasing of the troublesome muskox.

"Hoo-oo. . . . Where's the *head* for this creature?" Tuk inquired of the soapstone.

"Otherwise," Kiti concluded, "some villagers would have searched for and found Tuk by now."

"This is true——*ai-ee!* There the horns! The brow! The muzzle!" Tuk moved closer to the lamp and bent forward to his work. Kiti watched as he chipped and tapped rapidly, patiently. Small bits of brittle stone flew up. Half hypnotized, Kiti saw the head of *oomingmak* emerge from the rock and as time passed gain realistic proportions. This young man possessed an artist's skill.

Finally involved, Kiti focused on Tuk's project. Several of the men in her village carved in stone or more often bone—usually to enhance the appearance of some useful tool, a spear or knife or certainly an amulet. Women did not. But then, such activity took place in spare moments. Women processed and mended hide in leisure time.

"How is it that someone can invent creatures from stone?"

He frowned over his work. *"Owka,* not invent. The creature lies within and fully formed. The artisan only chips away all that in this instance is *not* muskox."

Kiti thought about that for silent moments as bird flesh pricked up on her arms. *Would this long winter trail be the craftsman that chipped from Sukitilan all that was not Kiti?* She wanted to free the thought into the air for Tuk's consideration, but then compressed her lips. For what reason should she say such a thing? Neither of them had lived long enough, neither had observed the ways of life sufficiently, even to make a guess.

Before plucking up Arajik and rolling into sleep robes, she tried one final time to give Tuk a chance to disclose himself and the nature of his extended travel. "Even so, one supposes that Tuk's village is concerned about his absence."

Tip-tap, went the mallet. *Pop-chunk,* went discarded pieces. Tuk smiled as he worked, confident now, fully at ease. Kiti tied a soft bird skin filled with summer moss around Arajik's bottom, smoothed the sleep robes as she crawled in and tucked the child into the layers with her. She had, in fact, nearly forgotten her last words when the young man finally spoke.

"As one supposes Kiti's village concerns itself with her."

She did not respond from the depths of her robe, only reached up to finger the slick lobe of her right ear.

* * * * *

135

There followed eight days of successful hunting. Neither had enjoyed great fortune on the trail in the moon apart after their first meeting. Did they now bring luck to each other? Far more likely, Kiti thought, that sea and coastal creatures have a rhythm of appearance, like sun and moon and a woman's blood. Cycles with a pulse unknown to *Inuit* or at least unknown to her.

Throughout the time of their success together with the spear and fishing line, both tried to get the other to reveal personal circumstances. Kiti smiled grimly as she thought back. She knew *her* reason for being so close mouthed. But Tuk—*who was he really*? Again, the thoughts were circular, as usual involving home and family, but ending nowhere. Mostly conjecture about Tuk. Like her thoughts about Narluk and her brothers—their whereabouts and their intentions. Perhaps her father knew somehow that she was on the coast? Given that Narluk still searched. Given that he wanted to send out someone familiar with the prairies by the sea. But why would he use someone so young? She kept getting back to that. Because his daughter, too, was young? That worked well for Kiti's reasoning—but Narluk was not likely to trust such youth, and especially not a callow stranger. She knew him well. Besides, none of this surmise fit easily into her heart. Not the idea that her father still searched. Not the concept that he would embarrass himself by telling others what had happened. The great *angakok* unable to control his own daughter? What rode least easily in her head was the idea that he would send any emissary rather than come himself . . . or at the least send her brothers. The Narluk she knew—father and wise shaman—would tend to keep a family matter within the family.

Was Tuk capable of trickery? She did not believe that the open-faced, kind young man she knew *could* deceive for long. Although she became ever more certain of Tuk's integrity, day by day, her mind continued to advise caution.

And soberly, in a last talk on the final night they spent quartered together, they agreed that they should take their own trails. Or was it that Tuk respected a decision Kiti made? He was, after all, the guest in *her* camp. . . .

At least, he did not argue. The next day, each prepared sled runners and loaded up, harnessed teams and started north. Tuk went far out toward the black lead, Kiti along *tuwak*, that stable grounded ice near shore. In winter's daytime darkness, the young man soon disappeared.

Before leaving the camp, she picked up the muskox from where Tuk had discarded it in the snow on the very night he finished it. It fit neatly in the palm of her mitt. She was not sure why she wanted to keep it. After all, the carving was complete and therefore without value. It was a bit of Tuk, though—attractive and pleasant and skilled—a reminder. She wondered as she admired the craftsmanship whether the artist himself were not constructed in the same manner—graceful, intricate parts that revealed themselves slowly to a patient artisan. Oh? And did the young Kiti who traveled endlessly on ice consider herself sufficiently skilled? *Patient*—now or ever? She folded the piece deep into some *oomingmak* wool and dropped it into her hunting bag. *Ahmi.* Who can know the future?

Part III
COLD SWEEP

Defender

Dark, dark. Kiti tried to imagine summer sunshine, attempted to find at mid-day some hint of light on the south horizon. Sometimes she clenched her eyes shut during a rest time when she rode the sled, telling herself that all she need do now was open them to be dazzled by a brilliant day. These inventions amused her as she moved north, but of course they must not become real. She knew that if spring were a reality, the ice would thaw. *Tuwak* would be unsafe. Her speed would dwindle when she took her team onto rocky terrain that lined the shore. She would spend much time mudding and icing runners, and then would finally halt entirely because too little ground cover remained. More time would be spent building a cache for sled and all provision that she could not carry on her back—that would be *most* of it. Food for Arajik, for her dogs and for Nuna and herself would depend on what she captured daily. Only a *soospuk* wished for summer sun. . . . Besides, she could not with Arajik and the dogs reach ice islands when open water separated them.

Eh, and when she finally reached Pichikut's home at the top of the world, should sunshine arrive now, she would be able to see the shrinking ice islands, yes, but not reach them until next winter because the bridge of thick ice would be treacherous or gone. And should she decide to abandon her dogs— something neither she nor any *Inuit* was likely to do under any circumstance— and should she paddle the small *kayak* to those dots of tide-washed land— she would find no people. Had *Ananak* not warned her? *Within half a moon's time following appearance of the full sun arching the south horizon, ice island Inupiat will be gone to summer themselves on the mainland.*

She must find Pichikut's people—or some far-north village of people who could direct her—before spring break-up. How fortunate she was, to have come so far in only two moons. How lucky to have at least one more moon cycle of good ice in which to reach her destination. Ah, but she was truly weary of darkness.

She took from the sea enough for needs day by day and when possible a little more—something to save in hide and bladder bags against times of storm or places where game became scarce. On her sled was a fine stack of packets, mostly seal and fish, also what remained from her share of the muskox. Although some food still stemmed from the dead village, much of what she had now came from those days when she and Tuk had been so successful together on the hunt. The whale *muktuk* from the silent village was gone, unfortunately; but she, Tuk, and especially small Arajik had enjoyed each morsel. Meantime, her half of recent capture meant she was well provisioned at this time. *Ahmi,* who could ever say the future?

The young woman loped along beside the sled in the darkness of day, Nuna pacing her on the other side. Arajik poked his hooded head from her *amaut,* jabbered ceaselessly and punctuated the stream of sound with whoops of glee and howls of merriment. How he loved the bouncing trail. . . . He reached up now to pull at Kiti's own hood, managed to get toeholds in the pouch, enough to let him pull around to her face and grin. Then he braced himself back at the top of the pouch and shouted at the dogs. This Arajik would be a great traveler, Kiti knew. A strong dog handler, besides. So very much alive. . . . Eh, if Narluk could see the boy, would he—no. Kiti must not allow her thoughts to take that twisting track.

The nine dogs pulling Palunga's sled were trail-hardened. So was Kiti. *Kringmerk* were solid and dependable. Kiti hoped that she was, too. Iyarpok would never get the team's respect as Nuna did. But the dogs *feared* him—so the result in pulling day by day was nearly the same. Most of the team also put up with young Ajak capering beside them, took in stride the pup's teasing, her playful yips and nips. Iyarpok, though, would tolerate none of this. Ajak learned rapidly and painfully to give him space.

Kiti studied the rangy lead dog. He was normally good-tempered, patient—named as he was by Palunga for an innate sense of humor. Iyarpok, the *Laughing One* . . . but not these days. He still must remember that Nuna was lead before maternal duties claimed her. He had no intention of giving his position over to her—as he quietly continued to let her know. He would crowd away any dog that approached her to show friendship. A team when it was feeding normally allowed a nursing female to keep a bear's share uncontested. Iyarpok, though, would corner for himself the choice and largest portions of meat thrown to the dogs—not knowing that Kiti fed Nuna privately, better and far beyond what went to the pack. No fish for her while rich mammal flesh and blubber were available.

Iyarpok would not attack Nuna outright nor let himself become the object of her wrath, for he was no match. Carnivores appeared to know each other's limit without full test, Kiti reflected. The cheekiest crow would never taunt an owl. Nor would the most rapacious wolverine directly challenge a healthy adult bear. A pity that people did not have this special sense fully developed.

Nuna ignored Iyarpok. With Ajak weaned and fairly independent, the bitch was devoted to Kiti's little brother, permitting only the girl and Ajak to get close . . . *and* Tuk, when he was present. Now here was something to consider, a thought process far more useful than trying to conjure up sunlight in her memory. *Why does Nuna allow Tuk to touch Arajik?* Kiti should have factored in her dog's acceptance of the young man at her time for decision-making—but she had not. No matter, for she was not likely to see Tuk's face again.

And just as well, she told herself then and now. In fact, she told herself often. Odd moments, frequently just before sleep, Kiti would run her finger along her ear lobe notch and wonder what Tuk was doing, where he was *right now*, what had become of him . . . then tell herself once more how good it was that he was gone.

Strangers, visible in starlight, traveled up from the southwest in late morning. From an *aglu* far out on grounded ice, Kiti saw them in silhouette as they drove the crest on a prairie hillock parallel to the sea, passed her by and disappeared. Two *Inuit,* one long sled with a high, flat load, more dogs than she could count at such distance . . . a great herd of *kringmerk,* she decided. Twenty? More? How could someone feed so many? Worse even than Tuk's mob.

Then the travelers must have swept around, for she saw them later coming toward her from northwest across the ice. She with Arajik and Nuna were still at the seal hole when the men drove up boldly between her and her team. They stopped. Their dogs growled and her team howled. Kiti silenced her own group. The shorter of the two men shouted at his *kringmerk,* finally used his whip with speed and skill, but struck directly on the flesh of his dogs with no prior *snap* and *snick* in the air. Nor did the newcomers make any move to change the awkward placing of their team.

The girl stepped away from and folded up her bear rug, collected her crosspieces, pulled apart her harpoon, put everything into the hunting bag. She was annoyed. She had waited many hours at this *aglu* already, and now no seal could be captured today. The strangers lacked consideration.

Nuna grumbled far back in her throat, a sustained bubble of sound, as the two men came toward Kiti. Then the huge white dog went forward and stood between them and the young woman, her feet planted solidly, hackles high, muscles rippling and at the ready. Her mouth was agape, nostrils wrinkled high, fangs showing.

Both men stopped. The shorter one raised his spear, looked at Kiti and lowered it, smiled.

Smiled? The girl was close enough and sufficiently intent to see the glittering cold eyes that made a liar of his mouth. Kiti walked forward cautiously to stand beside Nuna, her mitt resting on the dog's head. She did not smile. She, too, could be discourteous.

"Hush!" she murmured to Nuna.

The growl ceased, but the stance continued to send a hostile message: come forward at grave risk.

"Some travelers wish to rest?" Kiti asked in a neutral voice

The taller man stepped up. "Great weariness caught us on the trail." He looked around.

"A woman's poor camp is on ice not far from here," she told him. She returned to the *aglu* to grasp her hunting bag, and then circumnavigated the strange team to reach her own dogs and sled, all the time hanging onto Nuna by a strap she looped around her neck. The men made no move until she was underway, and she was uncomfortable to have them behind her. She forced herself not to look back, for to do so might reveal the apprehension she felt but must conceal. Or might indicate to them a congeniality which she did not wish to convey.

Kiti's instincts this time were clear and exceedingly strong. They told her to fly. Leave the snow house and its content, all that extra food she had been saving . . . take the team, the sled with its precious nest and hunting bag, go as far and fast as possible.

Kiti has been too much alone, her brain objected. She was unaccustomed to strangers. *And besides, Kiti cannot outrun them, should they decide to follow.* True, her dogs were fresh. But theirs were many, and with two people besides—one to push the chase while the other rested. *And if they did not follow, there was no reason to run. . . .*

She pulled to the far side of her *igloo* before halting the team. Her animals still in harness, she went back with the driving whip to be sure the other dogs gave her team space. No one needed a dogfight on the ice. It was well she interposed herself, for the big team did not slow until she first put out her arms to give the signal, and then finally brandished the whip. Even then, the lead and both wheel dogs peered back for their driver's instruction. Kiti did not move, and the dogs halted. At the sled, the two men spoke rapidly, voices rising as if in argument, but Kiti could not distinguish words except to know with certainty that they spoke with the cadence of her own inland people.

She staked and fed her team without offering hospitality to the great throng of new canines, then rolled away the outer ice block and entered her small snow house. She sighed. Certain conventions of the trail had to be observed. The strangers must be permitted to share her shelter if they wished. To make space, she stacked deep into the harness porch the packets of seal she had left inside her *igloo*. The men need not know the extent of her provision. She felt niggardly to harbor such a thought. *What is happening here?*

The lamp glowed cheerfully, and Arajik was playing on the robes with his foster family as the men crawled in, each coming down the tiny tunnel and through the baffle. The girl put a hand on Nuna's head to keep her still. But the dog still stood with nose wrinkled, muzzle lifted to show her teeth as she stared unblinking at the strangers, first one, and then the other, back and forth. Nuna disliked them equally. Her hackles bristled.

"Eh. . . . The woman has a child!" Both men seemed genuinely surprised.

Why? Many women have children. If these two were sent by Narluk, they would know about the baby, Kiti reflected. Unless, on his assumption that the infant had perished, they were not told of its existence. *And unless they were not actually sent by Narluk.* She forced a smile, telling herself that she should feel relief at their lack of information. And telling herself also that she must not imagine every male on every trail to have been dispatched by *angakok.*

"The boy is *Arajik,* and his mother is *Kiti,*" she informed them.

The men exchanged glances, but the girl could not read their expressions. The taller one had to stoop inside the snow house. He promptly sat down on the ice floor, using the robe she spread for him. She did not offer the *iglerk.* Anyone could see that it was too small for three. Besides, the one on the robe might expect her to share more than the *iglerk* later in the sleep time.

The shorter, somewhat older man who had earlier drawn his spear on Nuna now stood up just inside the baffle, kept his eye on the dog, said nothing. Kiti was relieved that he did not offer up another ghastly smile.

"One's silent companion is Odlerk," the first man continued. He twisted to look at him. "Someone should go to the sled for seal—" he turned back to Kiti—"and perhaps *muktuk?*"

145

The prospect of such unexpectedly fine fare—the latter always her favorite and also always in short supply among inland *Inupiat*—thrust a smile onto her face despite the resolve to be formal and grave.

"For the child!" she blurted. Arajik seemed to have the insatiable appetite of his foster mother and her kind. When Tuk had introduced him to *muktuk,* the whale meat with its attached blubber, the baby had savored it even more than the flesh of *oomingmak.*

Nearly a moon ago, that would be. She wished Tuk were here at this moment; and this time no prissy inner voice interrupted her thought to say how good it was that he had gone. Kiti's right hand darted up to her ear while her left placed food into Arajik's little stone dish kept warm on bone rails above the lamp.

The blocky stranger named Odlerk returned in a few moments with a split of frozen seal along with a bulging leather pouch. From this he withdrew the promised whale blubber.

"*Nakorami,* thank you," she told him as she cut off a small chunk, and then pulverized it with the pestle in the warm dish. "The babe will enjoy it."

"Take some for Kiti as well." Odlerk spoke for the first time with a voice half-growl, a thick grating sound unpleasant to her ear.

"Take *all* of it for this household!" Tonratu corrected.

Kiti intercepted dark looks between the partners.

The evening was short and quiet. Iron rules of hospitality required her to offer shelter certainly and food if she had it. Not just surplus. Any food at all was to be shared with visitors. Kiti had plenty at this time, and she offered much. In normal circumstance, she would be proud to have such bounty. With these two, she was reluctant even as she chided herself for selfishness. Ultimately, her need would be far greater than theirs, with only herself to find food and much trail time still ahead.

More, she wanted to possess nothing and do nothing that would make them remember her. To the extent possible, nothing must set her apart from any other *Inupiat* they might meet on the trail. Kiti refilled the lamp as she thought these things, and twisted the wick to bring up the light. She was glad that her face was hidden when the absurdity of her wish struck her, for she nearly choked on sudden laughter rising from nowhere.

Of course she was unremarkable. What could be more ordinary than to come upon a young, solitary woman having a small baby suckled by a dog, the tiny party on ice near no village whatsoever . . . with full team in mid-winter dark? Kiti planned to make herself invisible? She coughed several times, cleared her throat to chase back her private amusement at the irony.

As it turned out, the guests chose to eat exclusively from their own supplies—an ungracious gesture on their part—rude—which nevertheless suited Kiti well. It was not essential in the name of hospitality that she feed their dogs, but certainly this would be the friendly thing to do. She did not. It was necessary that these visitors not feel too welcome, she reflected even as she deplored her own mean-spiritedness. She wanted them to move on.

Kiti managed that evening to keep Arajik from nursing Nuna while the men were in the snow house. She dreaded sleep time. The dog must stay in at night for the baby, and Nuna was warming to the strangers even less than Kiti. Besides, the *igloo* was far too tiny for five.

Tonratu got up at last and solved the problem, oil from the meal glistening on his skimpy chin hairs in lamplight as he stood hunched over beneath the low curve roofing Kiti's shelter.

"The night will be fair," he told her, "for the sky is clear. The unloaded sled of the visitors is vulnerable to loose dogs and wild creatures."

"Yes," Kiti agreed, not quite daring to hope where his prediction would lead.

"The two visitors have built with hides a lean-to for sleep outside." He got down to crawl past the baffle, and the woman dared to relax a little. Then he added softly, "It happens that a larger snow house will soon be built."

Kiti gulped. Good news, that they would stay outside. But a larger snow house? For them, perhaps. Not for her. *Hoo-oo-oo,* they planned to stay so long? She picked up the robe Tonratu had sat upon and spread it with others on her own shallow sleep ledge. She covered both Arajik and Nuna when she did so, and the baby shouted with laughter.

"And does it happen that a woman's husband will return from hunting by the sleep time?"

Kiti jumped, unaware that Tonratu had not yet left the shelter. How dare he ask such a blunt question, as if she were a child?

She gazed at him steadily to let him know she disapproved. "Perhaps not."

"Ai-ee-ee!" the man said softly, but Kiti caught laughter in his eyes. "It may be that a visitor will ask a question when the man comes back." His lip rose on one side to form a smirk.

Kiti flicked up her eyebrows, not long enough to indicate agreement, only sufficient to let him know she understood his words. She gave no other response. He was telling her that he wished to ask the husband if he might sleep with his wife. And why the unpleasant smile?

The strangers must leave very soon, she decided—so they need not trouble to build a new snow house. Or *she* must move on quickly. So long as they were not sent by Narluk to find her, they would not think it odd that she anticipated a husband's return. Nor would it be strange that he did not appear. Hunters were delayed more often than not.

Eh, that Tonratu thought her to be accompanied by a husband gave a glimmer of reassurance . . . unless that ancillary smile came from satisfaction with his own deceit. The other one, Odlerk, was large and brutal. But Tonratu appeared clever and so had to be feared particularly. His words were sharp on both ends. He might at first sight be less unpleasant than Odlerk, but something in his voice put her off balance—a mockery, as if he harbored some dark private joke. As if he played a game of fox and lemming—enjoyed each cut and leap, anticipated some future final pounce.

"This lemming," she later told Arajik softly, "will dig in too deep to unearth."

Tonratu had disappeared through the baffle to join Odlerk outside, to tend their dogs—to sleep elsewhere. *Pirtok.* Whoever they were, wherever they came from, the men were here and she did not enjoy their company. She realized as she rolled the ice lump door into place that the men would have to sleep doubled up if they tried to lie down within. She smiled. She must remember to build such tiny dwellings always.

The next day and the next, Kiti left early with sled and team. Alone, she went far out toward the lead to seek seal. Both times, she wound up only fishing through ice. Nuna showed no interest in searching out *aglu*. She was nervous, kept her pup nearby and continually checked Arajik on the sled. She would stand motionless for a long time peering west, and then south and finally north, her ears pricked forward, to see that no one approached. She paced restlessly between every such inquiry.

Later, the woman fed her team far from camp and then returned long past the sleep time. Her message to the visitors was clear: *be gone*. But still, the interlopers were there—bedded and silent when she returned.

It was late during the third sleep time, long after she had collapsed into her furs, that Kiti awoke suddenly. A blast of cold was coming down the tunnel of her snowhouse past the baffle. *Someone has moved the block.* Among the blankets, she reached first for Arajik and then flailed out with both hands to find Nuna or Ajak. None but herself were in the folds of her bedding. More, the lamp had gone out. She came alert fully.

Holding her breath, she listened for sound, aware that the stream of cold air was no longer noticeable. *Now someone has replaced the block.* She heard scuffing steps on the ice floor.

"Nuna!" she called softly. Why would the big dog take the babies from their furs? And where would she take them? No dog could roll away the big ice block.

Then the furs above her lifted and a human hand pressed her down.

"*Suwit?* What does someone want?"

"The comfort of a woman for the night." Tonratu's voice.

Kiti tried to sit up, but the man's palm held her back. "This is not acceptable. No one has asked a woman's husband, and the husband of course has not asked his wife whether—"

Tonratu laughed. "The visitors know well—" and his voice ceased as Kiti stiffened beneath his hand. Then he began again. "The visitors believe that no husband will appear at this ice camp."

"A hunter is delayed." *What is happening here? And what is well known by the unwelcome visitors? And where was her small family? She must find out.* "Arajik . . . the dogs!"

"The unnatural child is with its dog-sister and the nursing bitch."

Again, Kiti tried to rise, and again his hand pressed her down. Se reached out to remove it and he slapped her fingers away, then placed his fist against her stomach with great pressure. She could tell from touch in near-total black that the man wore only underfurs—his *illupak*—and these were askew, half open. As he bent close above her, she could smell his flesh—warm and moist and sour.

"—But the child and two dogs—*where?!*" Never mind the discourtesy of asking a direct question. His hand restraining her, his rough swat on her fingers—these were violation far beyond discourtesy, surpassing all she knew or had ever heard about.

"A white dog would not easily be taken from the *igloo,*" she said. *And never by you,* she thought but did not say.

Tonratu hoisted himself fully onto the ice shelf and kneeled above her; then yanked her soft *illupak* trousers down so roughly that she heard the sewing sinew break. Then she felt herself torn from the robes and thrown to the ice floor. She twisted and crawled toward the baffle. If she could reach the weapons in her hunting bag—

The man scrabbled after her in the darkness, grasped her leg, and jerked

149

her back. His rangy strength overpowered her, and she did not understand what was happening. If Nuna were here—but she was not. Kiti was dizzy, jumbled thoughts hissing past rapidly like a poorly-packed sled pulled by forty dogs on slick sea ice. Too fast to capture one idea and examine it closely, too jumbled to make sense of anything. She raised her right hand to her ear lobe, pinched it painfully. Better. But nothing she had ever heard prepared her for this, and nothing Pichikut had told her—resentment rose in her briefly. Not so much of the man behaving so strangely—for his actions were despicable— but rather of her mother. *Why did* Ananak *not tell of this? Why not prepare her daughter for this horror?* Perhaps because her mother did not know that such could occur. . . .

When her brothers brought some woman to the *iglerk*—and such a person would have to be from the trail, some other village—for no young or even half-young women outside the family lived in their own community—both were happy at the prospect of uniting. And when Narluk and Pichikut copulated, usually with each other, they did so with affection and mutual respect. And when Kiti—eh, *Sukitilan!*—came together with a man, it was a time for experiment and laughter, for hearing and heeding instruction, for general joy.

No *inuk* ever need take any woman by coercion. For anyone on the trail—woman as well as man—common hospitality at any village will produce for someone so inclined a choice of willing partners for the *iglerk* at every sleep time.

What of some creature like Tonratu? Yes, she decided. For village wives would be curious even if repelled by his manner. Variety and new experiences are generally welcomed as enrichments to the chapter of one's life. Then she realized with a shudder that the *Paija* spirit of the monster above her had interest not in copulation but in violence and power. She inhaled slowly and deeply as possible, fighting panic.

Kiti tried to steady her breathing, tried to listen beyond the drum of heartbeat in her ears. *This cannot be happening*—yet she knew it was no dream.

"Enough!" she told Tonratu firmly, once again attempting to sit up. This time, though, he grasped both her shoulders and slammed them onto the ice. She waited for the pain to subside, for the shock to recede, for rational thought to be possible. *What can someone do in this situation?* She felt the man's *ussuk*—his penis—probe her *uttuk,* the sensitive woman's portal, the vulva. *No. . . . The Inupiat woman has a right to choose. . . .* And she did not choose Tonratu.

150

"Kiti is unwilling to *kaoyuk* with this man!" she quaked.

But he ignored her, placed a hand at the opening to facilitate entry.

The woman tried to roll, but the fist only increased its pressure. She could think of nothing except to get away. She reached one hand down to find the tender place between Tonratu's legs, fumbled to grasp his genitals and twist.

"OwKAH! No!" he growled, and capturing both her hands with one of his, forced them up beside her head.

"Pinnak! Don't!" she told him.

His whole body held her down, but the fist and its pressure were gone.

She could try to take a full breath now. Perhaps he had not understood her before. "A woman chooses not to copulate," she gasped.

She heard the unpleasant laugh once more, and then felt a strap encircle her left wrist, stretch across her neck and loop the other wrist. The man pulled the binding tight, and again she fought for breath.

"A strangle thong around the neck will coax cooperation from dog or *inuit,"* he panted. She twisted to loosen the strap, but it held and she felt her body stiffen with horror. *Would he kill her now? Had he already killed Nuna? Arajik could not survive without the nourishment she provided. Had he killed all three?*

When the man ripped apart her lower *illupak,* she wrapped her legs around him and clenched hard with full and considerable power.

He grunted, and then his right fist pounded at her ribs. As her breath left her, she felt and heard something within her crack. At the same time, tension on the strap increased, and she gagged. She relaxed her straddling grip.

She tried to draw breath as the line across her throat loosened slightly, but then stopped short as new agony shot through her when she inhaled. Her ribs. . . . He had battered the cage of bones with his fury. *Now she could not breathe. . . . And if she could not find breath, how could she live to care for Arajik?* She tried to calm herself. As she pushed frenzy away by strong will, the space it left open filled with hot anger. Rage flowed through her mind and her body like seething spirit lights. The man was inside her. *How dare he!*

Here was violation of her body and of her spirit. An end to what she was before—that *Kiti* she had been testing and exploring—and doing so with delight, she realized. Liking much of what she discovered. And now—*how could someone do this thing?* Starvation was a natural finish on the trail. Or becoming the meal for a white sea bear. Even floating far and finally on a broken bit of independent ice. These and other such calamities, she could and did expect and would accept. *But not this. . . .*

The snarling man who strained and grunted at her here could not be real. He must be an emissary—not of her father Narluk but of *Paija,* that queen of evil deeds. A malevolent trail spirit is here, she assured herself, not *Inuit* and surely not *Inupiat.* She wondered at the distended *ussuk.* A spirit was equipped thus? She felt the tearing of her own *uttuk* as the creature pounded on her body.

For this one, she was prey. And Arajik's life—if Arajik still lived—depended on her survival in whatever form she now must take. *How dare this Tonratu do this to her? Pichikut, help me find breath.* Again she tried to expand her lungs, and the pain on her left side made her gasp and need even more air. Sharp sleet swam across her closed eyelids. She felt rivulets of perspiration roll from her head and into her ears, drip from her jaw. And she felt herself withdrawing. . . .

No. . . . Stay alert. Try to make the anger monster go away, for that one also requires air. Do not mind the pain. Breath is more important. She forced her mind to full awareness and once more inhaled, this time slowly, and felt her lungs expand. A miracle of comfort came with what she had always before thought her due. Blessed air. She breathed again, wincing with the anguish of the movement.

How did this devil get Nuna out without Kiti's hearing in what must have been a battle? Her imagination flashed a rapid chronology of images before her eyes. She pictured Tonratu rolling inward the ice block up at the end of the tunnel; then cunningly scratching on it enough for the dog to hear but not enough to disturb the human occupants of the *igloo.* She envisioned Nuna as she left the sleeping shelf to go investigate. Imagined Tonratu ready with a strip of walrus hide—probably the very thong against her flesh throughout this ordeal—to rapidly encircle and jerk tight at Nuna's neck. She could see her dog being dragged out through the opening, all four legs stiffened against the pressure of the pull, breathless, unable to protect herself or vocalize alarm. Where had he staked her, still choking, while he re-entered the *igloo* for Arajik and Arak? And where was Kiti's sled with the nest *right now*— how far from here, how safe?

With fury still foremost and strengthening her, she focused on the creature hovering above and pumping at her savagely. The demon had mastered her, but he would never be her master. Perhaps the new *Kiti* was not ended. It might be that this horror when it passed would leave her fully except in memory. She breathed again, cautiously, shallowly, triumphed in the seep of air. She gathered the anguish of her broken side into a small, tidy packet, consciously wrapped it tight and placed it mentally into a bladder to be examined later. Once more she inhaled. Better. *Now breathe again.* How soon before she could rise and dress and walk out to assure herself that all was well with Arajik and the dogs?

At last, Tonratu seized and grunted like a gut-shot caribou. She felt him shrivel immediately, even as he withdrew. *Eh, this is no true man!*

He pulled away the strap and left. Kiti heard the rustle of his clothing, listened as he crawled past the baffle and up the tunnel, moved the block without replacing it, for chill swept into the *igloo* and did not cease. The woman lay shuddering on the ice floor. The anger remained, but it did not heat her. Thoughts fled from what had happened most recently and centered instead on what she must do. Dress for the cold. *Illupak* and *silipak.* Inner wear—she had that of her adolescence with which to replace her own until it could be mended. The old *illupak* would be uncomfortable—too tight, short at the crotch, high above her ankles. But it would temporarily do its job—wick moisture from her skin and hold close the heat her body generated. And its discomfort would remind her to mend the one that fit. She was fortunate to have the spare with her—for she had been unwilling to leave it with her family as a reminder—unsatisfactory as it was bound to be. Most people had but one, and the *illupak* was essential. Without it, someone would freeze on the trail. It struck her now that Tonratu would believe she had but the one underfur—yet he put her at grave risk by deliberately tearing it.

And she must get her hunting bag and dog hitching from the storage bubble. Have weapons ready if Tonratu or Odlerk should try to stop her. Carry the harness. Take her team with their sleep time leads well away from camp—along with her sled if it was there. Go find Arajik and Nuna with her pup. If she was successful and they were well, she would plan only to leave this place. If her family could not be found or found but dead? She would return to this camp—to kill her visitors or die herself in the attempt.

Shaking with cold and the outrage of this night, she tried to rise but was caught short by the sharp pain of injured ribs. She rolled onto her right side; then slowly brought herself up to a sitting position. Taking shallow but frequent breaths, she placed both hands on the sleeping shelf, to draw her body over and ease herself onto the robes. She reached out to cover herself.

Only a few moments for warming. Someone needs to review once more the actions to come. While she waited for her body to stop shaking, she went over her plan. Hunting bag and harness. Weapons and underfurs—

full dress against the cold. Team. Find her family if possible. Return to pack and leave camp or return to take vengeance.

All done silently as possible, she reminded herself as she left the furs, wincing, and went for clothing first; then her hunting and harness bags. At least she would not have to deal with the effort of rolling away the heavy block at the doorway.

Recognizing her, neither team gave alarm as she padded painfully around to collect her own dogs on the leads which anchored them at night. Her sled was gone, and this fact reassured her. The warm nest was on it. Perhaps the babies were in their *upluk*. She knew that Nuna would have had to be tied. Did Tonratu use another choking strap? It would require that to insure silence. Slowly, each breath agony, Kiti led the team and carried the harness away from camp. She watched the dogs for any signal of what direction to take. The outdoors was moonlit, seemed bright after the blackness of the *igloo*. The hummocks showed detail as she passed, and the black of open sea glistened in the distance.

Close to the black lead, Kiti found her sled, Arajik and Ajik asleep safely in their nest. Nuna stood silent at the end of a choke leash that the woman released with a single flick of the *ulu* always in a pocket.

Kiti stayed out for the remainder of the sleep time to reassure a distressed Nuna and to calm her own troubled spirits. Movement and drawing breath especially were painful. But the woman realized as she assessed her situation that she was still—amazingly—the same *Kiti* she had been before. More experienced, now—and some inner wisdom reassured her that such expansion was bound to have value in the future. Gullies of perception had been deepened. The sleep time had contributed greater terror than she had ever known before. Not so much for her own well-being—one life has small importance—but for Arajik and for Pichikut's Plan. Too, Kiti was for the first time beset by abiding pain, anguish connected with simple acts like moving and drawing breath. Would this discomfort pass with time? She would learn in the days ahead. And finally, overriding all other sensation, was a white-hot calculating anger that swelled once more into rage. Energy rocked her. She wanted to race to the western horizon. To lasso the moon with the long cracking sinew she used to guide the team. To dive into and collect the spirit lights and force them to do her bidding . . . all if only she could walk and draw breath without torment.

She returned to her ice camp in mid-afternoon on that day, determined to pack up food and go. But as she came closer, she saw that her small snow house was demolished. She gasped in dismay, mouth open. Ruined blocks lay strewn haphazard across the frozen sea. Glistening in the flickering reflection of spirit lights was a large new *igloo* having a porch, a long tunnel and a large extra storage room that formed a doorless blister on the side. In debris tossed over the ice were Arajik's little food dish and Tuk's muskox stone-carving. These she picked up and dropped into the hunting bag still on her sled. The strangers with their many dogs were nowhere in sight. Once more, Kiti felt violated.

Nuna refused to enter the new house. She stood beside it and stared at the structure, fangs bared without making a sound. Kiti rolled away the door block, crawled down through the tunnel. Inside were her robes and lamp and packeted food, including what she had stowed in the harness porch. Her tools were there, and both *Big Feeds*—*her* property that no one had the right to touch without express permission. Fresh anger made her so warm that she threw back her hood. Everything not presently on her sled—or discarded among the ruins of her igloo—was now mixed with belongings of the men . . . food, lamp oil bladders, blankets, extra clothing. *What were they thinking?*

She hauled her robes outdoors and stacked them beside the sled. Still fuming, she pulled out the lamp and food pouches, and then the extra *amaut* belonging to Pichikut. How *dare* they? Why would anyone destroy the home of another? True, they had built one far grander—but for the two strangers to sort her belongings—actually decide between them that *this* item had value, *that* one not . . . . *Hoo-oo-oo.* . . . Never mind, she was going far away.

The girl went back to drag out food, careful to take only what she was certain had been hers. The whale *muktuk,* she left inside even though it was given to her and even though Arajik and she both loved it. The way of these men was not *peeusinga,* not the *Inuit* way. Even though they spoke *Inupiaq* perfectly with the inlander accents most familiar to Kiti. This folly today was no more acceptable than their interrupting her above a seal hole when they arrived. Their placing of the huge team between her and her own dogs and sled. Here was insolence, a show of flaunted power—blatant contempt. Nor was it *peeusinga* to have, at the edge of camp, their frequent private chats and arguments and sometimes laughter, often looking in her direction.

And the horror of last night was not even to be considered. The reason for her pain in walking and drawing breath was beyond her power to address on this terrible day.

This afternoon—now!—was the perfect time for her to go with no further loss. But before she could bring out the last of her bladders and food packets,

155

her dogs began to bark. She plucked her spear from the hunting bag; then turned to gaze south across the ice, the direction which was their source of alarm. The big sled came in with only one driver—Odlerk. He slowed the team, halted, walked toward her, kept coming closer, too close. She realized that she had not studied him before. No taller than she, Odlerk was thick of torso but short-legged with inordinately long arms. He had a low forehead, she saw as he shrugged off his hood. A few black hairs of finger length drooped from a dark mole located on his lower cheek to the left side of his mouth. His eyes were small, close together, glinting darkly in the flicker of lights high north and overhead.

Kiti could turn her dogs and run, as her heart told her, for they had been resting in their traces and were still harnessed and ready. Arajik was in her *amaut*. But she had not yet loaded and tied on what belonged to her. What she would need on the trail. Almost everything was stacked beside the sled. She'd soon be short of food if she left now. She and Arajik could not survive without the robes still piled on ice. Odlerk was examining her preparations, and she saw his eyes narrow. Given the desire, he could overtake her easily with his huge team. Or the men together could find her later, if they wished, tracking at their leisure and relentlessly. *But if they did not wish to chase her down,* so her brain informed her, then *she had no reason to bolt.*

She was still disoriented from the events of this past sleep time, and tired besides. And she was now further incensed over the destruction of her snow house over the vaunted lack of respect for her and her belongings. And besides that, she was furious with herself for feeling fear. Lips drawn tight, she marched up to make the gap between her and Odlerk even narrower—an impudent act, especially given the difference in their ages and the fact that she was female. Nuna insisted on staying ahead of her, and Kiti restrained her by looping a section of the whip loosely around the dog's neck.

"Does it happen that someone marvels at such a comfortable new home?" Odlerk taunted in his grating voice.

"Hoo-oo!" she disapproved.

The man brushed against her as he might a boulder along a narrow trail. He walked on past to reach her sled and team. He gazed for a few moments at the dogs, then walked around and inspected very slowly and deliberately every article on and beside her sled. Although he did not touch anything, he kept slapping his driving whip against the fur on his right thigh—*sluck, thwap, sluck-sluck, thwap!*

Nuna's deep bubble of disapproval began anew, and the girl moved up to

156

cover the dog's muzzle briefly with her mitt. The sound ceased, but the canine muscles remained tense, hackles quaking half-high. Nuna and Kiti together moved up toward their sled and the man beside it.

He turned. "And where will *Sukitilan* go now?" Odlerk sneered. "Back to her father to beg forgiveness?"

Every thought in Kiti shattered as she stared at the man. The ramifications of his words left her shuddering. All that early suspicion so unfairly misplaced on Tuk? And then followed by mostly ignored instinctive apprehension with arrival of these two men? To be a *soospuk* can be fatal.

She smoothly removed the strap from Nuna's neck and rested her mitt on the broad shoulder. Waiting for Odlerk to make the next move, she recalled how she first saw the men come from the southwest. Then, not knowing or perhaps not caring that she had seen them earlier, they pulled in as if to arrive from the coastal prairie northwest. Even though she had noticed all this at the time, she had consciously marked only that they were inlanders, barren ground *Inupiat* who spoke with familiar intonations. Yet, she realized now, their doubling back to reach her camp had niggled at her from the start.

"The people said the unnatural babe would be dead long ago," Odlerk continued.

"And Narluk—?"

"—The great *Angakok* is unknown to this person." Odlerk shrugged. "As is also the dark spirit named *Tonratu* met wandering on the trail."

Kiti was silent. *The two are not friends then, only travelers who met by chance. That would explain the constant differences of opinion. And if this irritable man uttered truth, then Narluk has not sent him.* She chose her next words carefully. "And now it happens that two men can find favor."

"—One man only. . . . *Ingminek* . . . .This one and no other!" His eyes disappeared when he scowled. "Someone does not reveal private plans to evil that walks on two legs."

So he has not spoken of this matter to his companion? "But Tonratu"

"—Now walks alone, and may his legs—!" Odlerk's voice broke. He spat on the ice and did not continue.

Kiti looked beyond him, but saw no shadow approaching. "A shaman did not send a traveler to find his daughter," she said, "and yet the traveler knows her childhood name." This today was by far the most speech the two had exchanged. Nuna remained tense under the woman's mitt. But, Kiti reflected, this dialogue was almost cordial although everything in her warned her to be wary. Also, the effort to pull air for talk and the pain of making that effort were taking a toll on her energy and patience.

Odlerk continued. "It happens that all *Inupiat* know of the willful woman's defection. Narluk will be pleased to have his female child returned to him."

What a soospuk *is this woman to have relaxed.* . . . Kiti drew herself up and inhaled deeply despite the pain. "Someone can see that a woman stands here. Narluk has no female child. Nor is the adult once called *Sukitilan* someone to be 'returned' like a borrowed sled."

The man's face darkened, eyes obliterated by lowering brows. He stepped forward, and Nuna rumbled. His face lowered to the dog, but his right hand came up with a broad knife of sharpened bone. "The seal should never taunt a walrus." Again he glanced at Nuna.

"—Go!" Kiti shrilled; then caught herself. "It happens that someone needs to find his friend and leave this place," she told him in low, emphatic tones.

Odlerk stepped even closer, the corners of his mouth turning up in that cold smile she had disliked from the beginning. Kiti put the mitt resting on Nuna to her side, the fingers clenching into a fist. Her right mitt grasped more tightly around her spear, but she did not raise it. Time stopped; all motion halted. Even the spirit lights towering above seemed to cease swirling and appeared to glow steadily while the woman collected her thoughts.

Odlerk spoke at last. "And Narluk will, no doubt, rejoice to have the spiritless babe disposed of as he should have been—"

"—The boy Arajik has **strong** spirits," Kiti told him softly, "and he is now son to the *woman* Kiti."

As if he followed the dialogue, the sturdy child pushed himself up in his hood bag so that he could regard this man with the rough voice.

"Give him over," Odlerk rasped. "We'll see how easily such powerful spirits can be dispatched."

Kiti and Nuna stood motionless side by side, the child still perched at the top of the carrier on the woman's back. One practiced shrug tumbled him deep into the *amaut,* and he objected loudly. Still, Kiti reflected automatically, it would take time for him to climb again to the top.

It was at this moment, with Arajik howling and Odlerk watching them expectantly, Kiti and Nuna standing silent together as they waited for Odlerk's next move, that small Ajak decided to attack the threatening man. She gave no warning sound, only flung herself at him, grasping and chewing fiercely with her sharp teeth at the knee of his fur trousers.

Odlerk grabbed her up with both hands, his face filled with rage, his eyes bulging. Kiti heard the man's clothing tear, and she gasped. The tiny teeth were still fastened in a portion of trouser hide when Odlerk raised the puppy above his head and dashed her straight down onto the ice; then kicked the small body two *kayak* lengths through the air. Ajak made no sound. She did not move from the spot where she landed.

Nuna was aware of what had happened, but for a wonder did not stir, while energy poured into every muscle of Kiti's frame. She felt her *kamik* seem to rise off ice, her body float on air—able to spring forward or race away, unrestrained by any normal law of weight. Her mind considered and discarded first this action and then that. She must not be precipitous. Must wait to see what happened next. Be ready to respond. She knew that she was no match for Odlerk physically. Her fingers tightened on her spear, but still she did not raise it.

The man frowned, glanced past her with an anxious, jerky movement, his eyes straying back beyond his team in the direction from which he had come. *Is he making sure Tonratu is not here to see?* Kiti wondered. Then Odlerk shifted his spear into his left mitt and took from the pocket of his *silipak* a killing knife. He held it before him, flat and ready.

"Give over the child!!" he growled, lifting the weapon.

But before the words had fully left his mouth, Nuna was on him—all fur and fang and fury. Her great forepads hit his shoulders and he toppled backwards. Her gleaming incisors closed around his trachea before he hit the ice, and the man's startled bellow became a gurgle.

Kiti tightened the grasp on her own spear and hurled herself into the battle. Odlerk was down, thrashing, his right mitt still holding the knife, stabbing in wild arcs at the dog above him. Kiti looked for a body target not dangerous to Nuna; then plunged her spear sideways, under the man's left arm and through his ribs, deep into the place where his evil spirit dwelled. That done, she dived across the dog, caught Odlerk's right arm and pinned it to the ice, finally. She kicked the knife from his fingers, and threw it far. The man's movements weakened; then ceased altogether.

Kiti crept around the still form to pull her spear out. She watched blood follow it from the wound to darken the ice and freeze. Blood bubbled also from the neck, around Nuna's teeth, dribbled from the mouth. But then the woman frowned as she realized that Nuna lay motionless across the chest of the downed man. Dark splotches were now blackening her pale fur. Kiti knelt to encircle the dog's middle and tug gently.

"This matter is concluded," she told the big dog, but the creature did not respond.

"Come!" The white dog twitched and quivered as Kiti loosened her teeth from Odlerk's neck and pulled her away from what was clearly nothing but the husk of a brutal *Inuk*. Kiti leaned over to inspect the man. His throat was torn open, the now-bloody mole hairs rested across it and crystallizing as she watched. As a result of Nuna's attack, the spirits of this man might have been soaring even before Kiti thrust her spear. She hoped not. She wanted to—no, she *needed* to be part of his finish.

Nuna collapsed beside her, sank to the ice when Kiti released her grip—motionless. The woman ran to the sled for a robe. This, she worked under the dog; then brought up the edges for warmth. She pulled small bladders from her hunting bag, got out certain summer moss and from a neat birdskin packet some web material to put on the dog's wounds. These would stop the blood and soothe the pain. If only.... She spoke gently, but the dog did not respond, shallow breath rasping high in her throat. When Kiti finished doing all she knew to do, she found her own body quaking. She was grateful that Arajik had subsided, was aware that the infant was at the top of the *amaut* again, taking in all that was happening, and for once without sound.

Kiti went over to Ajak, the small blizzard, and lifted that valiant little body now limp and spiritless, cooling rapidly. She carried the pup back to the team, laid her gently on the ice; then sank down onto the sled and wept for the first time she could remember. The speckled snowstorm had resembled her dam not only in having a tender heart. She also had her mother's fierce loyalty, the instinct to protect at any cost—but sadly without Nuna's restraint born of experience. Kiti removed her mitts. She rested her left hand on Ajak.

After a short time, the girl realized that she must mourn the pup later—possibly mourn Nuna as well—but not until they were safely on the trail. For that matter, she had never taken time to grieve about her own mother—but that loss was not the same, for Pichikut had not gone far. Or at least not for long. Right now, though, Kiti must plot for the survival of her family. She grasped her ear lobe with a bare right hand and rubbed slowly. *Think,* she told herself. *Go step by step without mistake. . . .*

Where had the men gone after building the *igloo*? Why did Odlerk come back alone with the full team? Where was Tonratu at this moment? Why, for that matter, would those two dare to be away when she returned from fishing? Would they not know that she would take what was hers and run? *Or perhaps they thought her so simple as to welcome their destruction of her inferior igloo and replacement with such a grand structure? Thought her so bland as to be undisturbed by their heavy-handedness with her belongings? Or . . . they were secure in knowledge that they could catch her whenever they wished—again like a fox with a lemming.*

Kiti got up, loaded the sled, and circled the team around so that the *upluk* was close to Nuna. She placed another blanket over the unconscious creature. It would be far better for the dog's recuperation—assuming that mending was going to be possible—if they could stay right here. But she dared not remain unless . . . kill Tonratu if and when he appeared?

That she had helped the dog slay Odlerk gave her no conscious distress, at least not yet. But the idea of causing more human bloodshed deliberately—even with the memory and abiding pain connected with this man's obscene assault during the sleep time—such behavior was beyond her. Odlerk had indicated that neither man knew her father. If she could believe him—and the creature seemed too doltish to be cunning—Odlerk by himself had planned to take her back to ingratiate himself with the *angakok*. More than ever with passage of time, Kiti believed that if Narluk required destruction for Arajik, and possibly serious retribution for the father's wayward daughter, he would undertake the job himself. Maybe—most unlikely—he would charge her brothers with such a task of family honor. But he would not commission strangers—she was now quite sure—regardless of his wrath. And certainly he would not delegate such men as these. In fact, men like Tonratu and Odlerk would not be tolerated long by any village that she had ever known or could imagine. Very likely, both were banished *Inuit* who happened to meet on the trail afterwards, who cached one sled and merged their teams. Two together on a winter trail were safer. This explanation accounted for their lack of agreement on practically everything. And miscreants like these were never welcomed by reputable *angakok* anywhere. No wonder Odlerk decided to bestow personally a great favor on Narluk. Such a powerful *angakok* could perform large service, and Odlerk meant to obligate him. The man had needed all the help he could get. No, she could not picture Narluk entering alliance with either of these scoundrels.

After easing Nuna up and onto the sled, Kiti hovered over her gingerly not only to observe the dog but also to assess her own condition. The cage of bones protecting Kiti's chest was sending out sharp signals. *Don't lift. . . . Don't draw breath deeply.* The woman placed her eyelid above the dog's nostrils. Nothing. Kiti removed her left mitt, touched with her warm hand the dog's cold nose, then the closed eyes. Spasms jerked the long legs suddenly.

Nuna was not dead, not yet.

"Only breathe, take air in deeply, and then push it out." Kiti in sympathy inhaled slowly, long and painfully. *Breathe.* At last she perceived the slightest movement of the dog's chest. Shallow respiration, one ragged breath drawn and then released. "Now another," she urged.

The girl got up, replaced her mittens. She had devised a plan that must be executed quickly. Hidden behind some ice ridge or hummock nearby, Tonratu might be watching the camp at this very moment. First she went into the new snow house and there cut an empty bladder into strips. Why had she not thought of this before? Then she removed her clothing and wrapped the bands tightly, tucking in the ends. Drawing breath still hurt, but the supporting bands let her move more easily. Now she went outside to organize and pack and lash her sled. She would bring out more food packets if time allowed—Odlerk's share. She built up a new, secure *upluk,* a big nest near the antler hand-grips so that she could keep a watch over Nuna on the trail. On this circling of robes she managed with great struggle to drag up once again the fur hides containing the mortally injured dog. Should Tonratu suddenly appear, the sled could now go. A warning moan or howl from even one dog, and she would bolt.

Now for her plan, *Kiti's Plan*—this time not Pichikut's—one remaining all-important set of tasks. She hurried back into the snow house and searched through every bag and pouch, collected all the harness and sled strapping, every heavy sinew—anything that could be tied or knotted. She emptied out one of the sturdy hide bags containing Tonratu's food. Into this, she stuffed every thong collected. Now she dragged the bag outside, stopping only to replace the ice block door. Tonratu—if he returned—would have great need for what remained inside.

She left the bag with straps and harness open on the ice while she dashed over to the strangers' team. Out from a parka pocket came her sharp skinning knife. Moving from dog to dog, she cut away the neck strap and released each beast. She hauled all the lines over to the open bag, and then dragged that bag out to the lead.

"Eh, Sedna—see what someone offers!" She upended the bag and dropped all contents into the black water.

Several among the freed dogs had by now bounded off to disappear inland. Most milled aimlessly about, and these she ordered away—chased them and shouted, threatened them with her whip. Confused, they scattered reluctantly. *It happens that* Kringmerk *know food comes only from those they serve,*

162

she reflected.

At her own sled, she stroked Nuna's head and spoke to her while she checked the injuries once more. No fresh blood came from the webby wounds. She would not move the dog from these warm robes unless necessary. Nuna must, however, endure the jouncing of the moving sled. The dog still did not respond to Kiti's touch or tone. Her breaths were more frequent now, seemed regular but still too shallow, and she felt warmer to the touch of a bare hand, even seemed more relaxed. *Or are Kiti's hopes becoming palpable in false perceptions?*

At last, the girl looked around her. Spirit lights rippled softly, a bright violet strip surging and fading at the base. Did she have time to drag out and tie on more food? One or two of the men's robes would not be amiss, she decided. Odlerk had no further need for robes. And it was Odlerk's knife which caused Nuna to require separate space and extra warmth. Kiti remembered the tense words and black glances exchanged so often between the two men. She wondered once again if Tonratu were still alive. She decided that he was not likely to be spying on the camp. If so, he would have intervened when she destroyed the trace lines.

He would have to walk from wherever he was in order to get here. And if or when he returned, he would find his partner dead—at least missing, if a predator had come. He had no means for transportation. Should she take time to drag the sled out to give to Sedna also? Eh, Tonratu could go nowhere without harness. She would make one more trip into the *igloo*, and then move out slowly on the trail to give Nuna as much ease as possible.

At last, she crawled up through the tunnel dragging behind her two robes wrapped around a little more food. Here in this place were food, shelter, and warmth enough for Tonratu. He had tools and weapons. He could remain until just before the ice broke up in spring. For now, his dogs were scattered. But most—those that did not starve or fall prey to predators—would surely return. Still, Tonratu would have no way to follow and harass Kiti, at least not anytime soon. His trailing her on foot would be futile. He was cruel but not stupid.

Her team became restless. They peered off to the south, in the direction from which Odlerk had arrived. Did new travelers approach? Not likely, for whoever or whatever came this way did not move rapidly or the dogs would show alarm. Tonratu? Yes, perhaps a man walking.

Kiti signaled, and they started smoothly. Arajik had fallen back into the deep hood long ago, was silent in the warm little nest of his *amaut* . . .

163

Arajik. . . .

Kiti's breath caught in her throat. *Ai-ee-ee . . . Nuna must not die.* How could she have overlooked something so important? Up to her ear went her mitt—*pat-pat.* . . . Arajik still depended on the dog for milk—*had* to have Nuna's milk, did he not? The girl fought the trembling which jolted her suddenly. She set her jaw, drew herself up, coiled the whip, forced both hands down to grasp the antlers. Was this son of Kiti old enough to live on solid food? Probably not, at an age of fewer than three moons. He had enjoyed the fatty mash she warmed for him while Tuk was in her camp—but more for the warmth and mess than any bits he swallowed. Then Kiti consoled herself. Pichikut would surely help him adapt to what they had. *And Arajik's many mothers were fortunate in the hunt!*

They hissed north on sea ice with no actual sleep times, only short rest breaks. The tight bands had relieved the pain from motion, and Kiti had learned to inhale with care. Twice, she had stopped to start a fire so that she could offer Arajik a warmed gruel of pounded flesh and fat. The first time, he had accepted a few bites; then howled to join Nuna. The second, he had turned away utterly. Perhaps, the girl thought, he will eat when he becomes sufficiently hungry. . . .

But he did not. Even if Nuna lived, Kiti realized now, her milk would be gone. And if Kiti was forced to stop to find food for the team—and if she had good fortune in the hunt—*they still must find a village soon.* Someplace with a woman—or even with another gentle bitch, she supposed—one lactating for her pups. Kiti must move steadily, not taking time to hunt unless they became truly desperate—*for Arajik **must** have milk.* . . .

As they skimmed a trail on sea ice, the girl set her priorities. For now and until they found people, Kiti herself must stay healthy and strong or all was lost. She did not, however, require great amounts of food. Arajik was paramount, of course. And Nuna must have steady provision to speed her recovery. Could Kiti masticate solid food for the baby? Feed him like a small wolf? Would he accept her doing that?

It was after five sleepless nights on the trail that the impact of what she had done finally filtered through her anxiety about Arajik, her distress over Ajak, and her continuing worry about Nuna. Kiti realized gradually that she had left more than small Ajak back on the ice. For she had now destroyed a living creature, a human—at least, that had been her intent; probably the fact—and done the deed for reasons other than to capture food.

Eh, where was the horror she should feel? Where the terror of his dispossessed and angry spirits wandering on the ice? Instead, she felt so . . . very . . . blank. Like an overcast spring day when sky and land on every side were blended grey and featureless.

And yes, she would do it again. Given the same circumstance, she would take a human life without regard. *Indeed* yes.... She could sleep as well at night as ever. . . . How could this be? She raised her face high to the rippling spirit lights and shrieked. *"Ai-ee-ee-ee!!"* And then again, long and quavering, *"Ai-ai-ai-ee-EE-ee-EE!"*

The howl bounced off nearby pressure ridges, off hummocks and coastal rocks. Coming to her ears as echoes, the sound was of a solitary seabird—a powerful, predatory creature that kills to keep its family and itself alive.

Epiphany

The blackness overhead reflected Kiti's prospects. The sled hissed north and slightly east. Nuna lay unconscious but alive. Kiti forced food into her each day by opening the dog's mouth and placing seal fat far back on her tongue; then softly rubbing her throat to get the swallowing response. At the very first, Nuna still had a little milk. Kiti found that she could take it from her nipples gently; then give it to Arajik. But now the dog had nothing in those glands, which had been generous for so long. If Nuna regained health, she would be able to offer Arajik only affection. The baby rejected solid food, even though Kiti carefully pre-chewed the bits of muskox and seal she tried to feed him. He drank more than usual of the melted ice she always gave him to cut the richness of canine milk. But nothing satisfied the little one; and although he seemed always to be hungry, he consumed very little. His eyes sank back into his head and lost their luster. The pads on his cheeks dissolved. He no longer shouted and laughed or—lately—made any sound at all except sometimes a hopeless hiccup that wounded Kiti's soul.

She rested the dogs every few hours, then continued north . . . north . . . *north to Pichikut's people*? She traveled on smooth sea ice, on *tuwak,* for Nuna's sake and for speed and to save the dogs' feet as well as her sled runners. But she kept as close to shore as possible and peered inland through eternal darkness until her eyes ached. She was trying to find some friendly snow house glow. She had seen not even one village on the long trip since she left home except for that silent *Dead Village* on the ice. Not that she had been looking for one *until now*. Not that she would not have gone out of her way in order to avoid a village—*until now.*

For the first time since seeing Narluk and her brothers and calling up the storm, Kiti was haunted by doubt about the wisdom of her travel. Would she ever find her mother's islands? Did they still exist? Where were the villages she should be seeing along the coast? How far north had she gone? How much of "north" remained? Perhaps no one lived at the top of the world anymore. She realized that, going along the coast this way, she would see snow houses—

166

if at all—only if people had not built on the far side of a rise protecting them from sea winds and seasonal tides . . . only if lamps were lit . . . only if air were sufficiently free of fog and mist . . . and of course, only if the village were *there* . . . .Or was she blindly passing all the people?

Owka! No. Her mother's coastal *Inupiat* were somewhere still to the north and slightly east. She had to believe that, or she would cease to struggle.

Except for what little remained of food saved back for Arajik and Nuna, her provision was gone. Desperate at last, she stopped her journey to hunt. But she found no *aglu*. No fish came to her spear. If Pichikut's people—*some* people—did not soon appear, her long trip would be ended.

Sometimes, during a rest period when she mustered energy to think beyond the moment, she remembered the pride-filled young woman a few moons back who, after a few successes on the trail, was certain that she was now independent. was positive that she needed no one's help. True, two or three could starve as easily as one where no food was to be found. Also true, decisions were made faster with one alone and no need to discuss or compromise. Quicker decisions—yes, but not necessarily better ones. The spirits within, Kiti realized now, grow dreary in their own company hour after hour and moon after moon in solitude.

She drove right through most storms. Or if winds were too fierce, all including Kiti herself would dig into some drift on the lee side of a hummock and wait until the violence was spent. On one run, a ferocious northerly swept in a layer of frozen fog that burned the face and scoured the eyes, peeling back the lids. She lost all sense of direction. Progress was impossible. She could easily drive her team and herself into the sea.

Kiti veered to land and had the great luck of finding a fair-sized cave. It was so large that she brought the team in, too, before she ice-blocked the opening. They slept—all of them together. She remembered awakening only once, aware that the air was warm but stale. She got up to plunge her snow knife through chinking at the opening to give the cave a *nostril*. She remembered satisfaction with the *whoo-oo-osh* of air exchange. Then, because it was so quiet and because she was so weary, she returned to her robes. She did not remember covering herself.

When she awoke much later, the team was refreshed and ready for the trail. Nuna breathed more easily after rest without motion. But Arajik's eyes were even more deeply settled into his small face. Kiti tried a warm mash of herbs and water, but the boy abandoned it after one taste. How long they had slept in the cave, she did not know.

Outdoors once again, and into the darkness of another winter day. Mud and ice the runners. Return to a smooth sea trail. Run north by northeast, parallel to what now passed for the coast. Stop. Food for Nuna. Create something appetizing to offer Arajik. Liquid. Rest briefly. Hunt unsuccessfully, always unsuccessfully. North again—north by northeast. Darkness. Stop. Food for the two fortunate ones. Try, try to get Arajik to eat. Darkness, always and abiding darkness. The roiling spirit lights no longer gave her comfort. They seemed bleak and impersonal, far removed from her world of cold and hunger and everlasting dark.

She loped ahead of the team to break trail on new snowfall, and she tried continually to remember the *sun*. A great burning ball—yes, and she must imagine it above her, lighting this unbroken trail. When the real sun returned near the end of the season, where would she be? And where would Arajik be? No, she must think of something else. Hunt—hunt. Capture something, anything at least some fish for the team. Nothing, nothing. Move on. . . .

North by northeast. The food saved back for her brother and Nuna was finally finished. She could try those honored two on seal oil—she still had plenty of that golden fuel, largely because she seldom lit the lamp. She would happily give over her bladders of oil for one frozen fish right now. A single char would keep Nuna alive for a long time—and Arajik, too, if he would swallow it. Neither the dogs nor she had eaten for so many sleeps that she could not remember. Was it important? She had no appetite, anymore, but chill was in the very juices of her bone. And in this second time of great hunger in her short life, she noticed growing lethargy, found herself caring about nothing much, doing automatically whatever must be done.

Should she stop and stay until hunting became successful? But what if no food existed in this place and at this time—then what? Every moment spent on anything other than discovering a village—*any* village!—gave fading Arajik that much less opportunity for survival and put all the rest of them at ever greater risk. So no, don't stop, not yet. Not until the dogs begin to die. Or until she herself expired. Here was surely one of those decisions better made by several people.

The time for dying arrived in less than half another moon. How could she have been so foolish as to think that her team and its driver could go forever without nourishment? She tried to find shelter on land. But wind had scoured the plains clear of snow, and she could not take the sled to find a cave. So she returned to sea ice. There, on the side of a pressure ridge, she found snow right for building a snow house and energy to help each dog dig in separately. She staked them well apart, for they were so ravenous by now that they could no longer be trusted near each other unless harnessed, pulling and supervised.

Nuna was finally conscious but weak as hoarfrost, unable to so much as lift her head. Certainly she had no milk for Arajik. And Arajik—increasingly fragile and listless, existing on water warmed in Kiti's mouth—steadfastly turned away when Kiti spoke to him.

The girl barricaded Nuna inside the *igloo* whenever she left to hunt, for the dog was helpless to protect herself if a predator came by or if one of the starving sled dogs slipped a collar and attacked. Nuna was, in fact, totally inactive—and therefore the only creature in the camp, animal or human, still in good flesh.

Kiti stayed on ice to hunt. She took Iyarpok first; then two other dogs one by one, to search out seal holes. They dragged along beside her—hungry, resentful, dispirited. How could she explain to them that finding a seal hole might mean an end to the gnawing in their bellies?

At last, she abandoned the idea of taking dogs. She would rest a few hours; then go out with the baby in her *amaut*. Repeat the process. She fished through ice; then tried to bait them while she tottered directly at the lead; but nothing found her hook. She walked in an aching crouch to locate a seal hole. The dogs could smell them, if they would. But they refused to try, and her own nose revealed nothing.

Now, as hours and sleeps passed endlessly, she began to see odd things. A wolverine peered at her around an ice hummock, and she grasped her spear and automatically moved toward him. She would by now savor his flesh, as would the dogs—stink and all. Out he came, but not to attack. Rather, he was harnessed with two more of his kind to a splendid sled all carved of ice and glistening in moonlight, the spirit lights reflected in dazzling colors. Kiti's brain told her that what she saw did not exist. But her eyes and ears and nose told her that this was real. When she smelled the odor—with that very nose which gave no help in finding *aglu*—she actually perceived the rank scent given off and had a difficult time accepting that nothing at all was there.

On another hunt, a gigantic white bear came from nowhere to tower above her. He was so large that her spear thrust upward from where she stood would not even reach his stomach. She stared at him, awed by his size and stunned to silence. Then as she stared at the furry white mountain overshadowing her, its head suddenly elongated and was drawn up into the sky, the body swooshing after, like a deflating bladder. She laughed, and the sound of her laughter frightened her as the bear had not.

The time came when she could do no more. Kiti's energy was gone completely. She expended monumental effort to bring the ice block into the snow house doorway one last time. She uncovered Arajik's face from the robe and looked down at him. Would he have been better served if left on the hillside where Narluk placed him? But she remembered his laughter, his new joy following each sleep.

"Owka, that was not the time for a babe to die," she told him. "It happens that *this* is his finish, and Kiti's as well."

Perhaps it was another strange vision among those which had her seeing *kapvik* harnessed to grand sleds and *nanuk* turned to liquid draining into the sky. But there in the dim snow house, using her seal oil in volume for the first time since fleeing Tonratu, her small brother's eyes seemed to hold more vitality than she had seen for days.

"Eh, a daughter has done what she can, and Pichikut knows this to be so," she told the bright spirit peering from Arajik's face.

Then the girl patted Nuna and made sure that all the robes were tucked in snugly. Next, she poured into the travel lamp as much seal oil as it would hold. *"Ee-ee,* we shall close our eyes to a friendly glow," she announced. Then she lay down and clutched Arajik to her, brought the remaining robes around them, put her right arm up to rest at the notch of her ear. She closed her eyes. Here was a finish then, to this particular block in the *igloo* of their lives.

* * *

Kiti choked on a thick, warm liquid that dribbled down her throat. She coughed to bring it up, then swallowed it. Somewhat salty, and delicious. Too weary to open her eyes, she nevertheless heard unfamiliar voices chattering familiar words. The sound filled her with a leisurely, disconnected sense of well-being. Again liquid touched her lips, and this time she sipped with enthusiasm. Laughter, more sound. She floated in a cozy broth of contentment. Gradually, after many sips of the thick soup, she began to track meaning in the words floating about her. When she heard *baby,* she came alert.

She heard a seared voice ask, "Arajik? The child?!" She tried to look about her, but a great rock rested on her head and kept it pressed against the fur on which she lay.

Laughter, chuckles of delight. "The woman awakens!" echoed around her in different voices. Here were the good *people* sounds that she had yearned to hear and now remembered from some distant past. Where was she? Someplace comfortable and warm. Finally, a ***village!***? Or perhaps another waking dream? Let it continue then.

Suddenly, a woman's face came close to Kiti's, for she could feel the warmth. "The babe is well. That little one is a ravenous wolf cub!" She laughed.

"Arajik," Kiti told the voice without opening her heavy eyelids. "The baby is Arajik."

"Indeed, we know!" The same woman, her voice gentle but filled with laughter, too.

"Nuna? What of Nuna and the team?"

"Eh, *Kringmerk* . . . dogs . . . and the wounded white bitch?"

"Yes!" Still her eyes would not open. With mighty effort, she brought her right hand up to touch her ear.

"A treasured creature. All have seen her strong spirit. It happens that a village son has taken her to nurse to health. Already, she *walks.* "

Kiti sighed in relief. She wondered if she herself could walk—not likely, not with this boulder lying on her head. "The other dogs?"

"—Are well . . . nine?"

Kiti raised her eyebrows. Incredibly, her team had survived!

"—And all becoming fat on walrus meat."

Walrus. Kiti's mouth watered. She had eaten walrus flesh but once before, and remembered it as rivaling whale *muktuk*. The blubber and meat were usually not available to people inland; but her brothers traded on the trail for those thick walrus hides that they could split for making harness and sled lashing, could twist and braid for whips. One time, a bit of meat was included in the exchange.

"The broth that someone served," Kiti said later, "so good. What?"

No hesitation. "Blood."

Kiti came alert. Narluk always said that blood was best to bring back any *Inuit* near death. And Pichikut always boasted that her people kept it frozen for emergencies. With great labor, Kiti gradually opened her eyes enough to be half-blinded by the lamplit walls that arched above her. It was a relief to let the lids fall back. Others were in the *igloo,* for she heard the talk and enjoyed the cadence of her mother's coastal *Inupiaq*. But no one had been standing nearby.

171

"Please? Someone?!" The woman who had been feeding her returned, for the girl recognized her smell. "How long has Kiti been in this place?"

Laughter. Rapid talk to others. "She wants to know how long she's been with us!"

"Tell her our children have all grown and learned to hunt since she arrived!" More laughter. Warm, caring, comforting.

Then the woman's face came from directly above her. "Ten sleeps—"

"—*Ten!*"

A chuckle. "Ten for villagers, but only one sleep time for the starved, exhausted patient who lies here."

More merriment from others in the snow house. Kiti tried to rise but fell back feebly.

"*Hoo-oo!*" the woman chided. "Someone must give her spirits time to gather."

Near tears, Kiti slowly raised her eyebrows, *Yes*. "Arajik? *Where?*"

"Here!" The boy's face was brought down close to hers, and she heard his laughter and delight as he recognized her. She opened her eyes to slits once more. His cheek pads were back, and the glimmer was in his eyes. Held upended as he was, he dripped saliva on her face. He jabbered at her, and the sound was music. She smiled, felt the corners of her mouth turn up before she surrendered once again to the weight that pressed her head and pushed against her eyelids.

"Someone is awake?!" The broth woman introduced herself as *Pusik*. "Three young women, here, have babies of their own."

Kiti smiled. Here was good news, but she could not remember why.

"Continually, they argue over which among them is to feed this new child."

"*Hoo-oo!*" Arajik. Arguing was *not* good news. Were the mothers short of milk then? Kiti's mind was misting.

"Each wants him at her breast many times each day!"

Good news after all. Kiti smiled. Good news . . . good news . . . good. . . .

Later, she awoke and drank more of the warm soup, even swallowed a few bites of flesh offered. This time, her eyes would open and her mind felt clear, although her arm was too heavy when she tried to lift it. She looked over, and Arajik lay asleep on it. She heard an argument among women somewhere in the snow house. Not bitter, for they were laughing, and their tones were low. She listened. Yes, the words were those of all *Inupiat*, but the tongue was far back in the throat like . . . Tuk's . . . and similar to her mother!

She opened her eyes. "We are on ice islands?"

The woman Pusik was still nearby. *"Owka,* no. The edge of land, but not yet the islands that float."

Kiti let herself sink back. At least, Arajik and she were *somewhere*—and in the care of compassionate people. For now, only those facts were important.

Again, she raised her brows. *"Nakorami,* thank you. The people of this village are kind." She closed her eyes, drifted off once again.

Later, "A son from our village told us, *Kiti* is a precious one." Pusik laughed. "That's why he took his village out on ice to search for her when she did not appear."

"This same village son who has Nuna," said an unfamiliar voice.

"Yes," several agreed.

"And it was he who brought the people to rescue those dying on the ice."

"Yes . . . the brave young traveler named Tuk."

But Kiti was asleep. Pusik stood looking at the dry, sunken face of her patient. She wondered if she, with all the others could feed and love this skeleton of a female back to the grace and dignity Tuk said she once possessed.

Walrus

Kiti dipped her paddle timidly, then again. For several summers, she had used *kayaks* to seek out likely fishing spots on inland lakes. Salt water seemed more resistant than the familiar fresh water, so that she went farther with each stroke, but that appeared to be the main difference—that and knowledge that she was paddling on top of Sedna's nearly bottomless salt sea. This small craft from the silent village fit her still-emaciated body especially well. She had wrapped a soft fur inside, around her feet and legs. Her hunting bag, she had thrust back down into the stern of the hide-covered boat. Low fog layered above the water in moonlight, but—so long as she stayed close—she had no trouble following the others in the swirling after path. She had no intention of being left behind.

She experimented to see how quickly her little boat responded, found it obedient as a friendly, half-bright dog. She had insisted on going out with the village hunters for walrus, the giant *aiverk* of the floes. Some suggested that she ride with her harpoon in the *umiak,* the rounded and more stable boat that the broad-chested harpooners used. A sturdy boat without a rudder which would be used later to tow the walrus catch to ice.

She was indignant. The men patronized her, indulged her as if she were fragile. But she was strong and healthy, these days, rapidly regaining lost padding—and bustling with her old energy. Restless, too, from so much time spent in the village. She had built her own snow house and made it comfortable for Arajik and herself. She had practiced quite enough of household management. Most of the time, she even managed to keep a lamp going. In fact, she had done for far too long the woman things with which she still had too small patience.

Nuna? People said she remained with Tuk and was recuperating. Him, she heard *of* frequently but had not seen until today on this hunt and at a distance. She was distressed that he had not come over to see her.

In the argument about her going on the hunt, Pusik spoke up for her. "Two other women, as well, take part in this hunt. And both in *kayaks!*"

174

Grumbling by a few men. Old Anjuk, the village expert on *aiverk* capture, declared that women—any women—would make the whole hunt futile. "Spirits of the big bulls are insulted to be sought by a female," he declared slowly and loudly. And *annoyingly,* Kiti added silently, even though the smooth-jawed, toothless fellow had been nothing but kind to her on other matters.

Fortunately, Anjuk was the accepted authority on *walrus* but not on *spirits.* So thanks to Pusik and the two widows customarily permitted to hunt with the men, Kiti was here. She wouldn't be, if anyone knew she had never before dipped a paddle in salt water. The people assumed that because she carried a *kayak* by the sea, she possessed the skill to use it there. A half-inflated sealskin was fastened to her harpoon line and rested on the back of the craft. The harpoon itself lay on top along one side, at the ready, her spear along the other side. Except that her *kayak* was smaller, it looked like the others. Her hood was empty, for once. Arajik was at the village in the care of his milk mothers.

Kiti expected to be equal to whatever must be done during this hunt. And so long as she managed not to disgrace herself, she would at last be earning some of the vast amounts of food given so generously to her and to her dogs. For more than a moon, now, she chafed at being dependent when she was capable of securing her own food if creatures were available.

And may the clever daughter be successful in the hunt. . . . Eh, spirits of Pichikut, come nearby to help Kiti now. . . .

The paddlers closed on a cluster of floes in an unusually broad portion of lead northeast of the village. Anjuk with two other hunters reported last night before the sleep that these low ice ledges were floating in together. *And* that the men had heard conversational barks of *aiverk* bulls echoing back and forth among the islets.

"That means the sun will soon return," Pusik assured Kiti when they heard about the walruses.

Kiti did not know what one had to do with the other, but she was certain to enjoy the presence of both. As so often before, she tried to remember that bright globe in the sky, not only the look of it and its brightness on land and water and the sharp shadows it engendered—but also the *smell* and *feel* of its warmth on her nose and cheeks and chin, its heat on the fur of her parka.

Once again, Kiti had strong arms, which now used the double-blade bone oar on first one side, then the other, to make her *kayak* dance lightly through surface ripples. Moonlight filtered through light cloud cover to brighten the mist that swirled in the lead. It dazzled her eyes as she peered through the churning paths to stay with other hunters.

She swiveled her head to pick out craft around her, then suddenly bumped to a stop. The bow of her *kayak* had come against a floe. And peering at her wild-eyed was its walrus inhabitant. The two stared at each other in mutual astonishment. Then the huge beast bellowed, and Kiti back-paddled to get clearance for a turn. As she pivoted, she saw the creature lunge into water and come for her. She dug her paddle in deeply, trying to keep her eyes on the walrus behind as well as the water ahead. He was gaining.

Terror brought vast power to her strokes, but the animal pursuing her was better fitted for the sea—and angry besides. He was but half a *kayak*'s length behind when Kiti made a decision and veered to another floe nearby. Just before her bow rammed it, she jerked back with all her weight and gave a mighty pull on the paddle. The small craft leapt up onto ice and slid fully from the water before it tipped sideways on its rounded hull. She looked back in time to see the walrus swerve away and start back to his fellows, evidently satisfied with merely chasing the interloper from the water. Then she spilled out of the hatch.

She stood up and looked around. Well, here she was—high and dry and oh-so-very safe. Her first walrus hunt, and did she lift her harpoon? Did she thrust out with even the smaller spear? Oh no, she merely managed to irritate one of the huge beasts; then race away like a *kussuyok*. She hoped that she could refloat her craft without anyone knowing she'd paddled herself right out of the sea.

She saw no *kayak* in water nearby. But through the bright mist swirling, as she looked in the direction of sudden sound, she saw that she was sharing this much larger floe with a clustered colony of *aiverk*. Gradually, she made out the dark forms huddled well across from her, barely visible in the fog, at least ten *kayak* lengths away. They appeared to be disturbed by action in the lead nearest them. They complained with grunts and neighs, an occasional fierce bellow. Perhaps they as well were vexed about her presence. They must have felt the bump through the ice as she bounced up into their territory.

Then, while she watched, some person walked among them. An upright figure, a hunter from the village. The grumbles and bellows increased. And then she heard a sharp howl, and the figure went down. Kiti grasped her spear in one hand, her harpoon in the other, and raced toward the herd. The seal float attached by a long line to the head of her harpoon trailed after her, snagging and bouncing along the ice.

She took a moment to find the hunter before she waded into the herd. The animals were pressed together so closely that she finally jumped onto one broad back and then another, dropped down to ice in a clear place, then leaped back onto another beast. The creatures grumbled, but a walrus is cumbersome. She moved so fast that their angry twists and lunges occurred after she was gone. Now she stood in the middle of the herd with one *kamik* atop the back of one beast, the other on the haunch of another, and both animals packed so tightly together with their companions that they could do nothing in protest but grunt and cough. Before her was a huge bull. And in front of him—down on the ice—rolled the hunter she had seen.

Kiti lifted her harpoon as high as she could. "Grandfather, *help!*" Then she jumped onto the beast and thrust the stone head into the killing spot, following through on the plunge with her whole body. The tip imbedded deeply, separated as it was meant to do, and Kiti scrambled to get clear of the great bellowing creature as it pushed past the downed hunter to flop to the water in agitation. The bull dived and swam. The attached sealskin float, snagging and popping across walrus backs, followed wildly until it bounced down to zag along the surface of the sea.

Kiti looked to the hunter fallen on ice. A young bull was making for him now, and she raised her killing spear and struck him behind and slightly above the right flipper. Blood bloomed on him and then onto ice, and the beast made no more effort to reach the man. Walruses near the lead were sliding into the sea, but perhaps thirty creatures remained in the big herd, most milling frantically and grunting with frustration while they tried to separate themselves from each other.

Kiti pulled her spear from the smaller bull, which now lay motionless. She lifted the weapon high and thrust it deep into the ice, so that it stood upright. The harpoon shaft lay behind her. She bent to the groaning hunter. He managed to stand when Kiti pulled his left arm across her shoulders and stood up. He was not safe here among the disturbed herd. She half-dragged him rapidly as possible through, and around, and occasionally across the shifting beasts.

When they were clear, she lowered him to sit on ice. Then she looked for damage. His right arm hung useless within a torn parka sleeve—a mortal accident, had he been alone, for he would freeze.

"Cold. So cold!" he quaked.

"Yes . . . wait here," she told him. He'd be cold not only from wind coming through his ripped furs but also from the shock of being wounded and in pain. Back at her *kayak*, she snatched the lap robe from the hull, raced back. She tucked the big fur under and around him snugly.

"Someone will come," she promised him, then loped toward the herd, her weapons, and the open lead. Perhaps she could hail a paddler out there in the water. At least twenty walruses remained clustered on the floe, bellowing and annoyed, all seeming to tangle themselves further as they tried to separate, their confusion blocking her path. She picked up her spear and thrust it at first one and then another of the largest and therefore most formidable of the beasts, and finally at any creature who lay with its killing spot visible. She felt invincible, as if no hooking tusk or flailing flipper could reach her. She leaped back and forth among the creatures, thrusting and then pulling away her spear, springing lightly away to thrust again.

At last, those walruses still alive were in the sea, plunging noisily but then diving down with grace to disappear. Only silence came to Kiti's ears. She walked to the edge of the lead, waited until a *kayak* appeared in the mist, then waved her spear high in the air. "Please help!" she shouted, and in only moments, not one but two craft drew up to the floe. She steadied the bow of the first while the paddler pulled himself onto the ice. Then she tugged the light boat up from the sea while the first helped the other get out. She noticed a dead walrus lashed and floating beyond the stern.

"A hunter is wounded," she explained, looking over to the place where she had left the man. But he limped toward them now, her robe wrapped closely around his tunic.

He peered at everyone. "Not badly hurt," he assured his rescuers. The two men hurried over, unwrapped the robe, examined what they could see of the bloody arm. "This clumsy *Inuk* slipped and fell," he apologized, with embarrassment evident on his wry features.

Kiti raised her eyebrows as she walked up. She knew how easily someone could slip, for the ice all around was fouled and slippery. Besides, had she herself not managed to fall at the seal cliff where only a few creatures rested? And the mellow seal could not be compared with walrus.

One of the paddlers looked here and there at motionless beasts scattered about. *"Ai-ee!* That *Inuk* gave a good account of himself before he went down!"

"Eh?" asked the wounded man. He peered around him—rapidly at first; then slowly, with disbelief. He shrugged, turned to frown at Kiti, his mouth falling open.

The other paddler started back for his craft. "This man goes to find the *umiak.*" The big boat would be needed for the injured hunter and also for lashing up and towing carcasses, once the large animals were hauled to water's edge.

The wounded man spoke with a deep rumble of consonants far back in his throat, each syllable coming out slowly. "It happens that someone fell even before his weapon could be used. What is visible on this ice gave itself to the woman."

Stunned silence followed his words as the two newcomers took in more carefully the scene of carnage.

Kiti grew uncomfortable, and she picked up her spear and the shaft of her harpoon to start back for her own *kayak*. Then she paused. "The huge bull that caused the trouble—" and she pointed with her chin to the wounded man—"is somewhere in the lead with a float attached."

* * *

She could *feel* an awkward silence surrounding her. People of the village visited in hushed tones as they gathered around fourteen walruses laid out respectfully on the ice. Enough to feed everyone for the rest of the winter. Hide for *kamik* soles and lashing to be used in years to come. Even the most generous of lamp legends would not dare to describe such a feat. Anjuk gave a ceremony of thanks. He laid for a few minutes his mittened right hand on each beast, one by one, starting with the smallest cow and working up to the great bull long as any one-hatch *kayak*, the beast that had wounded the hunter. Before the old man removed his hand, he gave a brisk rub on the forward haunch.

"This fine creature left the water for air and for close mingling with its kind," he murmured, "then delivered itself to capture by a village which had need." When each animal in turn had received his touch, Anjuk looked up. "We thank all the noble creatures and their ocean queen Sedna for these great gifts."

Kiti had tasted walrus meat only the one time before recently having it almost daily at the village here. She had never before today seen a live one. Now she watched as the old man removed one forward flipper of each. He called out the name of the hunter who had speared the beast and gave to that person what he had cut away. Kiti decided that the right front flipper must be considered the choice portion. The remainder of each beast, save a symbolic organ or two, would probably go to families in the village according to their requirements. The second name called was Tuk, and she flushed with unexpected pride as he went forward to claim the heavy prize. After a woman of the village was called to claim the fifth flipper, Kiti heard her own name.

She went forward and dragged back a flipper almost as heavy as herself.

But then her name was called again. And again. When Anjuk grated out her name once more, Kiti hurried over to Pusik, begging her to come along.

"*Owka,* no," that woman said. "It happens that Kiti must do this thing alone." The girl thought her friend eyed her strangely.

Kiti was called nine times. She was flustered and embarrassed and exhausted when she had a mountain of walrus flippers piled around her. This ritual complete, the people of the village chattered and laughed happily among themselves while loading their sleds high with steaming meat as it was cut.

But silence surrounded Kiti. No one included her in their delight. *What had she done wrong?* The flippers alone seemed too much for her sled, not counting flesh and blubber brought over as her share and now accumulating on the ice as the careful butchering progressed. What she had here was far too heavy for her small team, but no one offered help. The meat would go to Pusik anyway; for it was with Pusik and her husband Itok that Kiti continued to take her meals. But those two were happily intent on getting their own walrus loaded. Kiti watched sleds leave one by one. She wanted to hug Tuk when he came to her after most of the heaped up sleds had hissed off across smooth *tuwak* toward the village.

He looked at her sad eyes and grinned, but she could see that he was uneasy. "The woman hunter shamed the men, today. It happens that the village has a convoluted knot to untie."

Kiti only stared at him, still dazed by rejection from people so friendly before. "Eh?"

"Anjuk was humiliated most of all," Tuk explained, "and yet, no one could wish to be without what was captured by the fierce woman hunter."

"Someone did not intend—" Kiti began, then broke off and tried again. "Tuk would have captured as many," she insisted, knowing it to be true, "surely even more, had he been in that place and time and circumstance."

"Perhaps . . . but Tuk was *not!*" he said softly, "nor was any other, only Kiti. A mysterious matter."

"Mysterious? The people think . . ." The woman's voice trailed off. She looked around. All but Tuk and she were gone and she could speak freely. "They think Kiti is some violent trail spirit? Not possible. . . . The people plucked this woman from the ice when she was close to death."

"Yes, *near* death. Not dead."

"And had they not brought her to their homes, had they not warmed and nourished—"

"—Eh, they do not fear Kiti. They know that she feels kindly toward them. But they are awed in the presence of what is thought to be—what *they* think is—!" This time, Tuk had to leave his thought unfinished.

Kiti smiled, shook her head. "If they could know how *very* human is the stranger in their midst!"

Tuk studied her with no expression she could read. After silence, he continued. "A thing noticed. In Kiti's presence, *five* seals upon a rock were taken. By two hunters? Unusual indeed!"

"But they—" Kiti began.

"—And does someone recall a time when two inexperienced hunters could not capture the powerful musk oxen in a group? And then they *chose* to go away?!" He laughed. "And it *happened* that another of the creatures—only one—stood nearby and anxious to give itself."

"—But an outcast male of any grazing kind often stays near—"

Impatiently, "—Perhaps . . . eh, *ahmi*. . . . Who can say what wonders will yet occur?"

Kiti was silent.

"Some women hunt, and the villagers accept this. Unlike some places, perhaps because of our young widows, Tuk's village allows women to use the spear."

"Truly, for none among grown women in *Kiti's* old village may accompany—"

"—Allow someone to finish while the thought is on the trail. . . . Some women know the motions in the hunt, are even useful in the group. Then rarely, some one female wins the *Smile of Fortune*. This one becomes the female hunter not often seen but heard about in legends."

"It happens that Kiti often enjoys success in the hunt," she told him. This she knew without his saying, had known for a long time . . . except of course when her luck ran out, as recently. . . . *Hoo-oo, but a happy fate did **not** desert her*, she thought now. *Was she not rescued in the end? And with Arajik, Nuna, and all her team surviving?*

"Yes, good fortune in many ways." He laughed, now more at ease simply from their exchange. "The beasts on land come to Kiti's spear, now also *puyee*, the great sea creatures. Yet this young Kiti was born to inland *Inupiat*. Here, surely, is another riddle with no simple resolution."

The girl stood tall, her right mitt brushing the ear within her parka. She studied the steady eyes of her friend. "Only know," she told him now, "that Kiti is no trail spirit."

He did not speak as he turned to help her heap and lash the nine flippers onto her small sled. He loaded separately, upon his own, her share of walrus hide, meat and blubber.

Feast

A special *igloo* was built for a feast to celebrate success in the walrus hunt. Every man, woman, child and infant of the village attended. So did travelers, invited as they passed through and several hunters met recently on ice and coastal prairie. One village to the south, only a sleep away, had also been summoned to join the merriment and share the food. Ultimately, all would be in the big new snow house where five large seal oil lamps cast conflicting shadows of human activity on the arching walls.

Outside at the beginning of the celebration, Kiti had watched the blanket toss—youngsters in their parkas with faces peering out through furry *nuilak*. These children resembled bright plovers as they tumbled and swooped gracefully above the taut, tightly sewn and hand-held skins which sent them vaulting into the sky. They shrieked with joy and excitement as one by one they soared, competing with each other in the number and intricacy of acrobatics they could complete before gravity claimed them.

Kiti had listened for a while to the drum duel that had been going on for much of this special day, taking place in a circle heeled out in snow. Here were two young men, antagonists from the village who worked out their differences with dance and drum and clever poetry chanted or sung—the creative breath of *Inupiat*. Village spectators would finally judge on the basis of their performances who in the ring was innocent, who guilty—to what extent and with what punishment meted to the one found culpable.

But Kiti did not know the people or the issues. She was too excited to stay long. She didn't want to miss anything, not outdoors or in. She went over to watch the wrestlers. . . . Here were two good-natured opponents pitting speed and strength and cunning to determine which would finally lose balance, stumble or even fall and thereby forfeit the competition. She stayed for three matches by three different pairs of opponents. Rapt, she barely moved but finally succumbed to the deepening cold, the rising wind and the beguiling sounds and shadows from within the special snow house.

Now Kiti sat inside on a robe with Pusik and her husband Itok along with

Tuk. As her chilled body warmed and as her eyes and other senses adjusted to the dim shadows and chaotic sound, she reflected on what she had already seen. Certainly, she had attended such celebration feasts at home. But this one was different. Unlike her own small village composed of older people, young couples with a fair number of children lived in this larger hamlet and seemed to blend well with those of the guest village so that running and shouting were a continual part of every moment. The high spirits of children around and on the blanket toss had been infectious. Too, drummers at the duel seemed wittier here. The wrestlers seemed stronger and more skilled as they courteously circled in the snow ring to find a single grasp to cause that one all-important misstep by the opponent. Or was Kiti imagining increased vitality in this place to avoid yearning for her own home and the more familiar faces?

Inside, she saw upon white arches all around her and above the active silhouettes of men and beasts. The outlines of fully animated creatures were fashioned by agile hands interposed between a lamp and the wall. These figures swayed and gesticulated, every move attended by laughter as the hand shadows of different people interacted, the creators vocalizing wild, spontaneous dialogue back and forth as they went along. Sitting cross-legged on robes, people with flashing fingers wrought intricate string figures—sometimes with an accompanying tale—that brought *"Ai-ee!"* from appreciative spectators. Mimics in the laughing games seemed funnier than those at home, somehow; their masks and those of dancers, too, more intricate than she remembered, more colorful than any she had seen before.

Ah, *not* homesick. She realized, as she relished her surroundings that she was truly comfortable in this place. She felt as if *she* had grown up in this village instead of Tuk. When he returned without parents, the village had adopted him, despite his advanced age—and he belonged to every family, now, received their warmth and hospitality, their love, and was called their *Village Son.* He lived alone and separate by choice, his *igloo* some distance from the others. He continued to be inseparable from Nuna as she slowly healed, and he reported her progress to Kiti. But families argued over who would get to have Tuk enjoy a meal with them. Women vied with each other as to who would mend his clothing and check his *kamik* daily to be certain no seam leaked. The young women in the village were affable as well. Kiti often saw him emerge after the sleep from one or another snow house not his own. She still wondered what he would be like as a partner on the *iglerk.* But then she pushed the thought from her mind. *Remember Tonratu,* she would tell herself and touch her still-tender left rib cage. She tried to imagine some future time when the act of *kaoyak* would be other than appalling. *So unfair,* she scolded herself. *Comparing Tuk to Tonratu is like comparing Nuna to a wolverine.*

Pusik and then Anjuk, himself, had eventually told her their versions of the reason people left her alone on the ice that day of the walrus hunt. They corroborated Tuk's guess. People were afraid. She was a newcomer, after all—who knew but that she might not be *Inuit* but some palpable strong spirit? It was Tuk, they informed her, who did his best to still their fears. But Kiti knew that even Tuk had been wary. Was he still? She understood his hesitation. He remembered her emerging not only from the sea where she had fallen but also, after the storm, from the cavity of the big seal. And now after the walrus hunt, he must wonder about her especially in the solitary musings of a sleep time . . . if any of his sleeps were solitary.

But here at the feast, half a moon after the taking of walrus, everyone was friendly. All detail except the resulting largesse was forgotten or put aside. Kiti would be hesitamt about leaving here and starting north again when Nuna could take the trail. Pusik had already suggested that she join the village permanently, and she was tempted. Arajik was well loved in this place. And yes, Kiti felt at home.

Now Tuk beside her at the feast jostled her elbow for attention, then pointed with his chin at two young girls kneeling on heavy bearskin, arms across each other's shoulders, mouths fitted against each other.

"Katajak," he told her. "Throat throb."

By ignoring crowd noise, Kiti was able to pick out snatches of the gasping, bubbly sound that came from them. They produced their percussive, tuneless *wind songs* when each used her own breath to play upon the voice box of the other. Kiti had heard from her mother about this kind of music created in the high northeast. Pichikut had tried to describe it, but how? Kiti found herself caught up completely in the pulsing sound. Now she knew the reason for her mother's difficulty in explaining, for the timbre and the tones were utterly alien. Hypnotic.

"They practice for the woman-changing game to come," Tuk told her.

She knew this game, for her own village often finished off a feast in the same way. Gatherings like this followed a hugely successful hunt, and usually took place at the time festivity was most needed: in winter darkness. Truly large feasts that involved several villages might even last for several days and sleeps. Only few adults slept. At the very end, late or soon, all village lamps in this place would finally be extinguished as the *Great Sound* commenced. The sustained background at home was produced either by drumbeat or an oldster's wailing chant. In either case, it was a continuing cadence that pounded rhythm through the skin and into the life-blood trails of every *Inuit* who heard it. Used often here in Pichikut's northeast, so *Ananak* had promised her daughter, were these wild wind songs Kiti saw now in rehearsal.

When the *Great Sound* started up, and during the hours it continued, every married and unmarried woman and girl whose moon cycles had started— at least all those who wished to play—would be chosen and chased by some unidentified man or nubile boy. The impromptu pairs would hurry off in darkness to some sleep ledge in some snow house—it did not matter whose. Not knowing who the partner was at the time or ever after filled the whole event with magic and delight. So said the pleased participants. Kiti herself had played the changing games only twice, for feasts of plenty were infrequent among her own people. And while she remembered the thrill and the delicious mystery of a partner unknown at the time and forever unidentified, she would not participate on this night. She would roll up in a robe on a far corner of her *iglerk,* as would the young children here, throughout the extended time of continuing noise and frenzy.

Kiti realized suddenly that Tuk was watching her. She stretched out her arms, yawned. "It happens that someone grows weary," she told him.

Disappointment crossed his face. Then, "A story comes soon. Kiti will wish to hear it, for it is the tale of a powerful huntress."

But Kiti was not thinking about hunting or story-telling. One day, she would need to have experience once again of a man who was not violent. *Tuk?* She removed her mittens, drew her hands across her face, rubbed at her ear lobe. She found it to be very warm in this place.

"Ss-ss-ss!" The crowd grew silent. The wind-singers pushed away from each other and sat quietly on different robes. So did others drop down onto furs or stand behind those sitting. Everyone moved well back to let the storyteller be active as necessary and visible to all.

In came an old man, deep laugh furrows stretching down from the outer edge of each eye and disappearing under the circle of each cheek. His parka was trimmed with insets of different color, and the furs of his *silipak* rolled and draped when he walked, lampglow richly emphasizing every fold. He looked as if he were accompanied by clinging, undulating creatures of the trail.

"Kanerk," Pusik murmured aside to Kiti, "relates his tales with cunning."

The storyteller lowered himself onto the white bear pelt which the wind singers had vacated, built interest and suspense as he took time to carefully smooth out his parka and then his trousers, looking around and flashing funny faces at the audience. A helper handed him a small drum, a moon of tautly stretched hide well stained with oils from use. He put the beater on his lap and started a tentative rhythm on the rim with his bare fingers, beginning slow but soon settling into a regular cadence. The snow house went absolutely silent. He gave no word or look to signify his commencing, seemed to be talking to himself. But his voice rose up deep as storm gale pounding waves on lakeside cliffs. . . .

"Chikut, for that name was spoken at the moment of her birth, entered this world as the scrawny, half-starved only child of an old mother and even older father. This baby was for them the only glory in their miserable lives. The mother was a friendly crone, but never clever in the ways of sustenance. Her lamp wick always flickered. The robes she cured shed pelt-hair handfuls at a time. The fur boots she sewed lapped up water like a sled dog under summer sun. Oh, she worked hard enough. But what she did hardly ever worked!"

"Yet, she was a miracle of success when compared with her husband. Old Munkut was a hunter, of course, and he did indeed hunt like the others—but alas, he did not find. Seals in winter abandoned their breathing holes forever when they saw his shadow on the ice. Whales postponed their spring trip south if Munkut waited in his kayak. Caribou at summer's end changed migration patterns when they learned the man awaited them."

"Hoo-oo. . . . Ai-ee-ee!" breathed the listeners, as if the story were new to them. Kiti knew *she* hadn't heard this tale before. But a strange restlessness grew in her as Kanerk continued.

" Chikut was a gaunt little girl with dark eyes and a runny nose. At eleven winters, she decided that she had listened to her belly groan for long enough. She spied upon the village hunters, thereby learning to make weapons for herself. She watched them handle dogs, observed the ways they captured food. Now she went out alone to hunt with a small bone-and-sinew sled and a ragtag team of outcast mutts. She found herself successful."

With as many bends and lateral wanderings as a child lost on trackless tundra, the tale centered around a hot spring beneath a prairie sinkhole. And around Koloki, the water serpent which the spring contained. Chikut drank

187

and bathed in this pool each day before she started on her solitary search for food. She washed herselt in aromatic liquid which spit steam into the cold air . . . water warmed by the fiery center of the earth. Here was a phenomenon Kiti had heard talked about but which no one professed ever to have seen, not even Narluk.

"Villagers were curious. One who followed her reported. 'This has someone witnessed. . . . Before each hunt and after, the child goes to a strange smoking pool, removes her clothing—'

"'—Takes off her furs!"—the listeners interrupted—'in winter?!'"

"'—And there she steps into the pool!' the speaker finished."

"'She . . . no! Deliberately moistens her body?'"

"—not moistens—wets. . . . The child immerses herself from head to foot—"

"'In water!? The one to report such a spectacle must have been undergoing raptures of the trail. Immerses!?'"

Thus went the dozen voices as they gossiped. For none listening to the storyteller had ever had a bath beyond the time of birth—nor known of anyone who had. Hand fishing streams in summertime—walking into hip-high depths— they might get somewhat dampened in the process. But deliberately to remove the rich oils from the skin—and in the winter. . . . *How could someone stay warm?*

The story continued with Kiti now listening closely. *Chikut.* **Pichikut.** This youngster, Kanerk said, fascinated the serpent Koloki from the start.

"As years passed, the scrawny child hunter became a graceful maiden. The village men grew too old to hunt and perhaps a little lazy. They depended more and more on Chikut, each dark winter, to supply their food and hides for robes and clothing. Throughout this time, the serpent took many forms and did great deeds first to protect the young woman and finally to attract her. In the end, after fabulous acts involving earth and sky and sea, the serpent spirit chose to take human form permanently—for this shape once chosen could not be reversed.

"He wooed and won her when he became a handsome and mysterious **angakok.** *Together, the mystic huntress and the sorcerer left the ice islands at the top of the world to go south inland for their new life. Neither was heard from again."*

Kanerk the storyteller looked around at people and flicked his eyebrows. The tale was told. He got to his feet, folded the white bear skin with dignity— and left the feasting house. Only as he got down to crawl out through the tunnel did people free themselves from his spell enough to stamp their feet and clap their hands and shout his name, "Kanerk. . . Kanerk!"

Astonished since halfway through the story, Kiti turned to Tuk. She had trouble keeping her voice steady. "Where would Kanerk learn this tale?" He must forgive her asking so directly.

The young man shrugged. "Where does any storyteller? 'On the wind,' or so it's said." He raised his eyes to watch on the ceiling the massive shadow of a masked female who twirled and leapt as she danced. Soon would come the wind songs with woman-changing, Kiti knew.

She turned to Pusik. "Does it happen that someone knows where a storyteller got the tale he told?"

"Most times, no. They come from the fogs of distant days. But this one Kanerk related is not so old. It is said to have started in a village to the north."

"How far north?!" Kiti demanded, exasperated, and then remembered herself. "Someone would like to know the trail time involved."

The older woman's eyes narrowed as she turned her face to Kiti. "Too far to visit easily. The legend comes from isles which float upon the frozen sea."

"Can it happen that someone here will instruct Kiti on how to reach this place?"

"Perhaps some other from further to the north and east." Pusik shrugged. "Only a tale—" she laughed, "—for who could possibly believe such a strange account?"

Kiti startled both companions when she stood up abruptly. *"Nakorami,* thank you," she smiled and abruptly left the feast.

Later, her hands trembled as she trimmed permafrost spread across her sled runners. The only child of older parents? A lucky hunter? Married to *angakok*? A combination of facts . . . surely more than mere coincidence. Plus of course the remnant of a name. . . **Chikut**.

The snow house lamps went out and the wind song throbbed and churned in the dry air, sweeping out across the snow and up to join and pulse with flowing spirit lights north and overhead. Kiti tensed when she saw Tuk approach, his eyes narrowing at what she was doing.

"Can it be that someone plans to travel?" he asked, as she started the layer of ice.

"Yes." She spat and then rubbed vigorously with the furry tail of a white fox. Here was the perfect rub, presented to her by Anjuk as a peace offering after the walrus hunt.

"A village wishes to have Kiti stay with them," the young man said earnestly. Then, "**Tuk** wishes her to stay, as well."

Kiti sensed a new note in his voice, and she felt a warm response within herself. Perhaps it was the rush and blow of the wind song pervading all. The girl stopped her work and turned to him.

"It happens that Arajik can take flesh for his meals, now," she told him. Arajik was weaned, thriving on a mushy version of Kiti's own daily fare. "A woman *must* go north to find a certain village," she told him. Tears sprang to her eyes and strangled her voice.

Tuk waited silently and without expression until she could speak further.

She dropped the water bladder and the fox's tail, let the sled slide to the snow. Then she put an arm on each of Tuk's shoulders. She swallowed, found her throat constricted, swallowed once again. "Kiti's mother was named **Pichikut**," she was finally able to say. "Perhaps *Chikut*? A hunter woman from ice islands far north who left her home to marry *angakok*." She paused, bit her lip. "Kanerk's story is surely about her."

* * *

Tuk piled additional food onto the sled. "Twice has Kiti known deep hunger on the trail. It is not good to tempt the hunger-beast too often."

The girl looked longingly at Nuna; then harnessed Iyarpok as lead. Her big white dog would have to stay here. When villagers rescued them, that dog was nearly dead. Too far gone to worry about, they thought. But Tuk had quietly taken her to his own *igloo*. At first, he used his intuition and the simple remedies of his people. Later, with Kiti's help, he ministered to the dog from the girl's supply of herbs and what seemed to him her amazing knowledge of shaman lore. Knowledge which he now understood. And although Nuna was recovering from the grave wounds made by Odlerk's knife, she was not yet fit for the trail.

Certainly not strong enough to pull a sled. Now that maternal responsibilities were past, she would be content on the trail as nothing less than leader. Her heart was ready, but not her body. She could not yet thrash Iyarpok. He would kill her. Besides, the valiant creature looked as if she might be readying herself to produce a new family.

"Is it possible that Tuk can keep the white dog safe until he comes north to visit or until Kiti returns?"

His face split into a broad grin. *"Ee-ee,* and someone will take this for an invitation."

Kiti smiled. "Naturally. But the present journey must be made alone."

Kiti said a brief but warm farewell and *nakorami* to the villagers; then started north that very night. Soon, the sun would actually begin to show rather than send the few moments of pale glow they now welcomed daily on the south horizon. No one she asked could say how long her trail would take. Smiling, humming, running along without effort as if born by the hefty south wind *Nigituk,* the young man with his own sled dogs and Nuna accompanied Kiti for two sleeps.

"Remember—if someone allows it, Tuk will go north all the way," he kept reminding her.

Kiti could not invite him, for she knew this to be *her* journey, hers and Arajik's, as pledged to their mother. Who could predict what awaited them? And who knew if she would ever find Pichikut's village? Who knew if the place still existed? *Ahmi.* Who can know the future?

By day, they loped along beside their sleds or else took turns breaking trail for the teams. Then before the sleep time, after a meal, they sometimes talked. The ice wall that had separated them was thawing, becoming more transparent. Perhaps if the events involving Odlerk and Tonratu had not occurred, Kiti thought, she would by now be speaking freely to this pleasant acquaintance. She had earlier done him grave injustice, she knew now with certainty, for Tuk would not—*could* not!—deliberately deceive. Yet, here she was—and here *he* was—and her tongue still frozen in her mouth. Hiding behind that ice wall were not only her own domestic situation but also the recent experience with Tonratu and with her father's self-appointed emissary. *Kiti has killed a man.*

The woman reminded herself continually that Narluk had not actually sent those two to find her. But their appearance meant that her flight had become so widely known that others like them might yet appear. For *all* such matters were talked about if known. News traveled between villages and across the tundra like a blizzard borne by strong gales. All right, Narluk would never set such violent strangers upon his daughter. But who could say what conduct others might take upon themselves?

Hoo-oo, so much had happened. . . . Now, besides her domestic misdeeds, she had killed a man. She found it impossible to disclose such an intensely personal matter to Tuk or to anyone. The young man knew the pup Ajak to be gone, but he thought she had starved. Just as he thought Arajik was her own. If Tuk knew her truly, would he not turn his face and go away?

Yet Kiti's brain kept pestering, even though she trusted the man completely. "Does Tuk know Narluk?!" He knew of Kiti's village. How could he *not* know the shaman? On their last night together on the trail, she asked him.

"Narluk? *Ee-ee,* it is Tuk's great pleasure to have met the great inland *angakok* and his two sons as well."

Kiti stiffened. But Tuk's face was without guile as she studied him in camplight, and his words were open. She was still speechless, examining his features, when he continued.

"When his family died," Tuk told her on that night, "the son believed his own spirits would soon flee. He built a stone cache above the bodies; then stayed by it to await the snow-walker for himself."

"How frightened someone must have been!" Kiti sympathized. No one feared death, of course; but only the very old might wish to die alone.

"Tuk fed the dogs and starved himself," he laughed. "No reason to waste food on someone who is soon to perish. Then after several sleeps, it was evident that Tuk's spirits were in no hurry to depart. By then, little food remained. So someone searched the tundra, but without success."

"The man was distracted," Kiti observed, "and only small creatures are easily found inland when winter comes."

"It happened that the family of Tuk had been waiting for hard snowfall so that their teams could take them home. When it came, finally, the winter season was well advanced. Now only Tuk remained, and he dared not go to any village. He sought out and spoke only to hunters he met upon the trail— and even so kept distance from them, always downwind."

"When Tuk found a village," Kiti asked curiously, "he dared not enter?"

"He must not take illness to them, and it was not possible to keep the friendly people from coming close."

"Yes." Kiti understood.

"But by inquiring of hunters *near* villages, Tuk was able to find the shaman Narluk."

The girl shuddered. Why had he never before admitted that he saw her father?

Hoo-oo-oo. . . . *How was he to know that Narluk **was** her father?* Nor did he know now.

Tuk did not sense her uneasiness. "The great *angakok.*" Tuk chuckled. "Imagine. . . . Here is this young stranger on the trail. He walks up—but not

too close—to the huge shaman others extol. He asks—artfully, of course—*'How long must someone wait to die?'"* Tuk laughed loudly.

Kiti smiled in courtesy, although she was too preoccupied to grasp the humor, then waited for him to collect himself. "And Narluk responded."

"He said, *'A person waits throughout his life for death.'* Truly, this was his answer, for he knew nothing of the circumstance." Tuk was still chuckling.

That sounded like her father. Kiti's lips twitched. "And then a young man explained."

Tuk shrugged, nodded. "He asked how many sleeps since someone had buried his family."

"And Tuk knew." Kiti herself knew something about sickness brought to *Inuk* from Sedna's strange dog-people who appeared in their huge *kamik* on the sunrise sea.

"Sixteen," Tuk remembered.

"Narluk used this information." Kiti was pleased with herself for getting answers without asking a question. She was improving.

"He said he did not know. But he suggested Tuk avoid breath contact with any other person for one full moon more."

"And Tuk did this."

"Yes, but it mattered little. One traveled east by northeast to the coast, a trail never overburdened with people—or with anything else, as it happened. The hunt for food along the way was not successful until the young hunter reached the sea . . . and found Kiti that first time. Eh, a woman is always fortunate in the hunt. Like the girl in Kanerk's story." Then, "A girl who it may happen is like her *ananak?"*

A shiver racked Kiti as she once again heard Pichikut's refrain: *"And may the clever girl be successful in the hunt.* To Tuk, she said, "And so the meeting with Narluk was before the meeting with Kiti."

Tuk raised his brows for affirmative, then hesitated. "He had observed the woman on one night, true, but not *met* her, never spoken."

Kiti clenched her jaw. Let him speak of that night once again. She would listen for discrepancies.

Tuk explained with detail. Every hunter he met on the trail directed him to find Narluk for an answer to his question about contagion. At last, he approached the shaman's village deep in the sleep time. Two or perhaps three shadowy rises before he got there, he spied in moonlight a beautiful maiden suckling her child. The woman was accompanied by her guardian spirit, as he then interpreted the scene . . . a huge, ghost-white dog. He chuckled with embarrassment. Nuna, he knew now.

He laughed as he continued his tale. "As someone knows, the view beneath spirit lights can easily mislead. Still, Tuk followed the young mother to the village, saw her harness a team to a sled already loaded, watched her silent departure."

Blustering with a whole new set of questions, Kiti forced herself to wait. *Someone may be learning patience at last.*

Tuk continued. He had slept all too well later that night and awakened tardily. By the time he got back to the rise overlooking the cluster of snow houses, as close as he dared go, whole family groups—the entire village, as it turned out—were taking the trail. He stopped one sled and then another to inquire about Narluk. All said the same. The village was moving because of death in an unsealed snow house. *Angakok* with his family, though, must have gone out earlier, south and east, must have left late in the sleep. Thus, the young man was obliged to go off in search of Narluk once again if he was to get information about bad spirits he might carry.

"Following six days of tracking," Tuk went on, "and two more of wandering—after a storm swept away the tracks—Tuk found first what turned out to be Narluk's sons, Oojulit and Pajuk. Finally, the great man himself."

The girl considered. "So it happens, Tuk never did *follow* Kiti."

Tuk responded to her tacit interrogative. "Never. That night he saw her, his focus was on *angakok.*"

"And thus, it was coincidence that a young man first came upon Kiti's camp?!" The girl once again wondered if she could believe entirely these earnest assertions. She wanted to. Her spirit said "Yes!" But now her brain remembered Odlerk and Tonratu. The great white tundra stretched in all directions from her village. Here on the coast was endless prairie to the west. Saltwater ice swept up and down the shore, stretching far out east to an invisible sea where in some places no lead cut toward the shore. *Happening* to find anyone seemed so unlikely—unless one followed tracks or knew the person's destination in advance.

"After that first meeting, though, her camp became his ultimate goal," Tuk confessed. Then he smiled and lay back in his coverings, pulling the furs up to his nose.

Kiti was pleased. "When sleep time is over on this night, the two great hunters have long but separate trails to follow," she murmured as she curled herself around Arajik in the warm robes.

But still they talked. Quite sure about Nuna's gravid condition, they agreed

194

that the dog should definitely stay with Tuk. Could the pups be healthy? Never mind, she had earned her right to have a litter without human intrusion. Kiti would someday soon collect her.

"And collect Tuk as well, someone wonders," the young man murmured softly and with great hesitation, as if he feared the response. Kiti rubbed her ear lobe invisibly beneath the covers and pretended not to hear. He did not repeat his thinly veiled query.

After long silence, giving the young man plenty of time to drift off in slumber, Kiti spoke aloud to the still night and to the spirit of Tuk within it to tell about her mother's death and of the daughter's own responsibility. Voice tight and low, she described the Plan. She did not describe the extent or status of her family, certainly did not mention her brothers or Narluk by name, did not allude to her father's vocation, although she had already laid claim to Kanerk's feast tale.

After even more silence following her saga, a period so long that the girl was certain her companion had slept throughout, he spoke. "Then it happens that Kiti must find the village of her *ananak*." Any promise to someone dying became a sacred pledge from which, of course, no release was possible.

"And does Tuk agree that Arajik is now Kiti's own son?"

"As if the babe emerged from her very loins," Tuk assured her. *"Ee-ma, absolutely."*

Part IV:
ICE SONG

New Faces

On the trail north. Thanks to Tuk and the walrus hunt, Kiti need not spend her time hunting. Sled runners sizzled on smooth sea ice that *cra-acked* and *groa-n-n-ned* nearby and in the distance. The mighty pops and booms, the great percussive concert of ice, were pressure adjustments between tide and land, Kiti knew now—not a result of her presence with team and heavily burdened sled. Over and around ridges they swept, up and across occasional hummocks of hard drift. When clouds permitted the sight, a watery crescent of sun showed on the south horizon for a very few more moments in the middle of each day.

Kiti awoke after one sleep to the sound of her staked dogs wailing and the sight of a white sea bear in moonlit silhouette atop the next ridge. The creature stood on all four legs, nose weaving slowly on sinuous neck to test the air. The camp contained a large quantity of food. The girl rapidly packed and iced her runners, and loaded up. Before they left, she put down onto ice the walrus meat and blubber from one big bag. She hoped that *Nanuk* would know this to be fair. Kiti possessed food and perhaps he did not, right now. But he had far greater ability to secure provision.

Near the end of another day's run north by northeast, Kiti saw the glow of lamplights coming from inside a dozen snow houses. The village was far, for air was crisp and clear. She decided to feed and rest the dogs. She and they would go in fresh after the sleep.

The next morning, remembering the tale of Chikut and wanting to appear her mother's child, she melted a little snow above the lamp and washed her face and hands. *Brr-rr-rr.* But in this way had *Ananak* met the world. She peeled away from her face the coating of instant ice. Such personal cleansing was not something to be done with frequency. Then she drove into the new village. People crowded around, for hunters had not yet left on their day of foraging, and the rare visitor was a welcome novelty, even or perhaps especially, a woman alone. After introductions, Kiti spoke privately to an old woman hovering nearby.

199

"It is possible that the people here know the legend of Chikut."

The woman frowned at first; then brightened. "Yes! a visitor means **Pich-i-kut!**"

"Oh yes!" Kiti breathed.

"The tale is enjoyed—especially because it came originally from a village not so far north."

Always, *always* north, Kiti thought wearily. "And it may happen, someone in this place will know the trail." A *soospuk* statement, a silly one. For if people knew the village to be *not so far* north, then certainly someone had been there. And any *Inupiat* who has ever been to a place will forever know the way.

The woman laughed, and people gathered. Someone located clean snow and squatted to draw a map. Others made suggestions. In a short time, Kiti had the trail clearly in mind.

"A young woman will need to hurry," remarked someone in the group. "People on those ice islands go inland early. It happens that they must cross much frozen sea before ice rots."

"—Then return late in the season to be sure *tuwak* is thick," added someone else.

Excited, Kiti took the trail without staying even for a meal. She had to promise the friendly people that she would stay with them for several sleeps when next they met. Up the coast she went and onto ice that stretched beyond the sight of land, stopping briefly at this village and another, getting reassurance in each place that her destination was not far.

* * *

Two hunters came to meet her as she approached a sparkling set of igloos in the still-brief but now dazzling light of mid-day.

"People here may know the legend of Pichikut," Kiti said.

"Yes," with pride. "And of Koloki the frost serpent, as well, for Pichikut was of this place."

The girl grinned with pleasure. "It may happen that this visitor can add some more to the tale." She explained her relationship to the heroine of their people.

The villagers welcomed her and Arajik as if the two were highly valued citizens misplaced temporarily and finally found. Perhaps we *are,* Kiti reflected as she used her *ulu* to cut away at her lips a mouthful of *muktuk*. Eh, and—hard to believe!—a welcome change from walrus!

All was flurry in the village as people absorbed the traveler's news while they prepared to go for summer camp. Kiti tried to trade her ubiquitous walrus for seal and whale meat. The whole idea of *exchange* was alien here, although the concept of *giving* was strong. So the girl arranged to *give* walrus meat and split hide, both prized here at the top of the world so late in the season . . . to some who would *give* her seal meat and *muktuk*.

One woman who exchanged gifts generously was Ertok. Wrinkled and tattooed, a withered little bunny in white furs, she was nevertheless as spry as any adolescent, and could pace the lead in a fast team. She remembered and was anxious to describe Pichikut as a child. Ertok and her husband Pomakut appointed themselves to accompany Kiti and Arajik with the village on the long trip south and west when it began after two more sleeps. It was on this trail that Kiti had a chance to hear about her mother.

"One remembers that tiny, half-starved child," Ertok told her. *"Ai-ee,* and all who lived then can recall how readily that child found food!"

Pomakut was not so wizened as his wife, and neither was as old as they looked, Kiti suspected. Across the man's head, bare in the snow house, were a few strands of what looked like smoke-blackened sinew. His jaw was smooth, and his pleasant face a plump, rosy pad.

He, too, recalled the remarkable child who finally left the village. "This man who speaks was but a youth," he told her, "a *nukapiak*. At seventeen winters, fewer than Kiti's age now, he had been a boy practicing to become a great hunter. Naturally, he observed the little girl."

"That tiny Pichikut discouraged everyone. The child would come back with her sled piled high even when the fathers and grandfathers found nothing at all!" His naked brows rose high as he laughed; then he shrugged. "A marvel it was that all the men did not give up entirely!"

"It was said that food creatures flocked to give themselves to her," Ertok added, "that a tame spirit on the trail made magic only for her."

"Some few uncharitable men blamed her and the helper for their own lack of luck," Pomakut put in, "said that she took all that was available and left nothing for the rest."

"Still," Ertok said, "no one ever refused what she generously provided for the village."

"Yes, they enjoyed their share—and most were properly grateful." Pomakut frowned. Then, thoughtfully, he added, "Men find it difficult to thank a woman who exceeds them on the trail."

Kiti nodded, remembering the walrus hunt. She understood completely.

"Some tried to accompany her," Ertok remembered, "but she permitted no one to join—"

"—Perhaps she knew, the mighty hunters of the village would be embarrassed," Pomakut went on, "by the amount of game which gave itself over to her spear—"

"—And perhaps she truly *did* possess a helping spirit," Ertok concluded, "a creature that could be dangerous for others."

"Whether or not a spirit was used, *the girl was most fortunate in the hunt!*"

Kiti stared at the man. A tremor that started at the neck and shoulders jolted through to her toes. Here, again was her *ananak's* wish expressed so often.

After an awkward silence, Pomakut cleared his throat politely. "Someone wonders if it happens that Kiti—eh . . . *hunts?*"

"Not quite enough to stay alive on a recent trip," she replied.

Both Ertok and her husband stared at her and waited for an explanation that Kiti did not supply. She was still trying to piece together what had happened.

"Ye-es, then. She hunts," Pomakut said thoughtfully. "And could someone say that the daughter of Pichikut is *fortunate* on the trail?"

Another shiver went through Kiti. *"Ye-es-ss,"* she answered softly, "someone might say that she possesses far more luck than skill."

Pomakut chuckled. He asked Ertok, "Can this be Pichikut's child?!" Then he shouted with laughter, so that others looked over and several joined them at their travel lamp. But they spoke no more of Pichikut that night.

On the trail inland to make summer camp, Ertok saw Arajik and a small village boy named Isumak playing with the muskox carved by Tuk. When they abandoned the stone figure, she picked it up and inspected it closely. Smiling, she turned to Kiti. "Pomakut, too, is expert with releasing that which hides within a stone." And later in the evening, "The *oomingmak* carried by a young woman is done by someone having patience and great skill. . . . Permit an old woman to guess—Kiti's father?"

"Owka, no." Kiti could not imagine Narluk even *searching* for a creature within material someone might give to him—let alone spending time with a knife to *release* whatever it might be. And his digging at inland streambeds or searching along coastal gravel to find likely minerals was impossible to picture.

Patience of this sort was not a quality Narluk possessed.

"A brother, then. . . . Does Kiti have brothers?!" Personal questions. But Ertok was old enough and Kiti young enough that the woman had certain prerogatives.

Kiti laughed. "The only one who seemed to have such skill—Palunga—is now gone."

"Ah, Kiti does have brothers, then." Ertok was understandably curious about the family of her old acquaintance as well as her new friend; the family beyond Pichikut regarding which Kiti had spoken nothing until now.

The newcomer must not seem to be unfriendly, Kiti chided herself. Slowly, "It happens that someone has had—" she hesitated. Should she count Arajik? No, he was now her son. "—*Five* brothers. But only the youngest took time to carve."

Ertok frowned. "Someone **has had** brothers in the past but not—eh. . . . All are left behind her on the barren grounds."

Why did coastal people—even Tuk—always think inland tundra to be grim and hostile? Kiti shrugged. True, she supposed, that all of her brothers were gone. . . . Except for Arajik—and be*cause* of Arajik—her family was lost to her. Loss of Pichikut still made her sad, and she tried not to think too deeply on that subject. Loss of the three who had disappeared was also painful—particularly, always, the loss of Palunga. This topic of Kiti's family Ertok steered toward repeatedly—while Kiti wished to paddle past without stopping. To change direction in the conversation, she reached deeply into her parka pocket to draw out the bag of green stones and hand them to the woman.

Ertok peered into the leather pouch, then poured two pieces into her hand. She smiled broadly. "These must come from inland."

"Some are from a place near the stone in which the carved *oomingmak* hid—a steep stream bed where inland tundra meets with coastal plains. Does it happen that a wise woman knows what they are?"

Ertok held the two closer to the travel lamp, and Kiti could see their glow. The promise of a tundra summer lay within each. Hard, dry and sterile, yet green as prairie grass.

"One cannot be certain until a scrape is made in sunlight," Ertok told her, "but they appear to be what the whalers call jade."

"Jade." The girl repeated the unfamiliar word. Was it truly stone or did it only seem so? Kiti was reminded of the partially digested green matter often found in the stomach of a captured caribou. Like that, this material looked delicious, and her mouth watered. Eh, ice island *Inupiat* like these must rarely taste the long-legged deer, might not know of the belly delicacy. Yet, Ertok seemed to know about this *jade.*

"Can one somehow eat it?" Otherwise, it held small value. Far too heavy to make a sled, even if one could find it in such bulk.

Ertok laughed. *"Owka,* it's only mineral. But it's strong and beautiful in sunlight. Somewhat hard, useful to make light tools. Often, small but elegant creatures of the fancy conceal themselves within."

"It happens that Pomakut would like these." A question was implied.

Slowly, "Ye-es, yes he would. But so would whoever released that muskox."

Ertok was probing, and Kiti chuckled. She tried to think back. Tuk knew nothing of her find at the *Silent Village.* But had he seen her pick these up on the day they took *oomingmak*? Eh, he was always absorbed in finding likely bits of soapstone.

The older woman laughed. "And Kiti will not reveal the artist? *Hoo-oo. . . . Ungayok.* She must love him!"

Kiti reached up to finger her right ear lobe as she felt her face grow warm. She said no more.

"These stones," and Ertok gently replaced those she held and handed back the soft hide bag, "have value in the making of strong harpoon heads. Also fine amulets, since the stone carves well."

None of those items interested Kiti. But she did retrieve from the pouch two of the largest pieces and handed them over. "For Pomakut," she said.

"Owka, No. The gift must come directly from the giver." Ertok smiled. "A girl will give them to him from her hand—perhaps sometime when his spirit is dark and restless."

So went time pleasantly as the village moved off the islands and onto mainland. Soon they arrived at a place where a decision must be reached. Melting snow cover meant that they must either set up here for summer camp or carry on their backs what they had to have and then cache their sleds along with extra provision for the trip home. There was much discussion. Kiti was amused. When her village looked for straggling caribou in summer, Narluk as shaman *told* people where to stop. And she as Narluk's daughter knew—but never, ever *said,* of course—that whatever reason he might give for his decision, camp was always made in places likely to produce the healing herbs he needed.

Following hours of high poetic drama and eloquent sarcasm, the favored methods for discussion, people agreed to stay where they found themselves. An old caribou hide was discovered, and some caves lay above a thawing lake. Were these not auspicious omens? Was this not a hospitable place?

* * *

Days turned light and long, some few with brilliant sunshine, many more with cloud cover and a slow, drenching rain. All days had wind, sooner or later. Nights got even shorter until no darkness came at all. Insects swarmed—biting, stinging, each trying to live a full life within its short breeding season. Berries ripened on the blooming, buzzing tundra, and these were gathered mostly by women and children.

Kiti and Ertok turned for home one dazzling afternoon. Young Isumak was with them, a chattering child of three winters who liked to play with Arajik. Kiti's boy, by this time, was asleep in her *amaut* bouncing along on her back. The women's skin bags were stuffed with bearberries and sourberries, and Isumak's broad face was smeared with evidence of liberal sampling.

"Look!" Ertok pointed with nose and chin into a nearby soggy valley they had avoided for fear of deep bog.

Kiti followed the point. An upright figure was there, tall but far too slender for a brown bear. As she watched, the creature took several steps toward them. *Inuk,* human. A head looked in their direction, and arms waved in the air.

"Eh, perhaps a spirit," Ertok muttered.

"Spirit man!" Isumak proclaimed loudly.

Kiti wasn't certain she believed the hunters' tales about walking, talking, visible spirits on the trail. She knew about hallucinations, yes. And she knew from her experience, and certainly from Tuk's, that days and nights of solitude could produce unpredictable *raptures* within the lonely soul. But Pichikut always laughed at spirit tales—said they were a man's creation to boast of his bravery. Trail dreams to fill the long, eventless hours and days of isolated hunting in a broad, featureless land. Such *spirit* persons, Kiti would have to see for herself in order to believe.

"Someone from the village who left early?" she asked now.

"Owka. Who would go on treacherous marsh alone?"

Kiti knew no one so foolish.

205

"Spirit, spirit, spirit man, see the spirit man!" Isumak chanted.

The women left the boy with the bags and an enticing pile of berries to eat. Then they walked out toward the stranger. He fell, lay still for a few moments. But as they approached him, he raised himself to hands and knees. Now he staggered up once more to lurch forward. The women picked a way carefully through the valley marsh. A misstep could mean sinking into deepening muck above permafrost—a cold, messy ooze even in summer. The man had fallen again by the time they reached him. Kiti squatted to turn him so that he did not lie face down in wet ground cover. Ertok helped lift him to a sitting position.

"Ergh . . . eh!" said the man, and the women looked at each other. He was long but lean as a clean-picked caribou leg. Stringy, matted hair hung across a broad face covered with scratches and running sores. An angry crimson gash came down the left side of his face from hairline to jaw. His beard was splotchy, louse-infected. His body stank. He wore underfurs only, *illupak,* at least the filthy and torn remains of rabbit and fox skins. Kiti could see, though, that the cut and arrangement of hide were similar to that which her tundra people made for wearing at all times, under *silipak* and within the *igloo* and under sleep robes at night. Here was no animal but a human, an *inuk,* and an inland man. . . .

Kiti put one of his arms across her shoulder, waited for Ertok to do the same. Slowly, with the stranger's limp body dragging and bouncing along the ground between them, they picked their way through the slough to go back for Isumak and the berries. Then they returned to camp. The man's mouth made strange noises all the while. Sometimes, his legs moved in effort to support the long body. Mostly, they did not.

After many days of continual care, it seemed that the newcomer might live. Since he did not supply a name, they called him ***Adla,*** the *Stranger.* Kiti applied herbs to the sores, and they gradually scabbed and healed. She privately thought, however, that Ertok's thick red soup made the vital difference. The man's eyes cleared. The crust which had encircled them was wiped away and did not return. But the snowy mist fogging the eyeballs was replaced by a hard, reflecting glare. Adla's eyes rarely blinked. Nor did understandable words pass through now-healing lips.

One sunny afternoon, Kiti put Arajik down to sleep on a fur in the shade of the cave mouth. She stayed nearby to brush away mosquitoes and the triangle flies that stung so painfully. Everyone in the village was gone except for her,

Arajik and Adla the *Stranger*. Some hunters were out to search for caribou. Most children and women looked for berries. All others hand fished at a stream which fed the lake. The baby dozed and Kiti herself was half asleep in sunshine.

Suddenly, something sharp poked her back, and she sat up, instantly vigilant.

"Agh-rr-rr!" said the *Stranger*, lurching around her. He was completely naked. "See the wild one!" he said then, in perfectly understandable *Inupiaq*. Familiar speech . . . in a familiar voice? She shook her head to clear the odd illusion. Of course his pronunciation was familiar; for unlike the others, he was of the tundra.

His eyes glared as he waved what Kiti recognized to be her own spear. She gazed at him sternly, since the jab had hurt. It had certainly torn her light *illupak*, and the small wound was probably bleeding. When he pulled his eyes away, they seemed to bounce everywhere—to sky and cave entrance, to the lake below. Finally, they fell upon the baby. He raised the spear, and Kiti shot up.

"See the savage stranger capture food!" he told her, and he drew the weapon higher.

Kiti crashed against him, easily knocking him down. She pulled her spear from his weak grasp; then forced herself to speak soothingly. "The man must be gentle with a child," she told him. "And he must let Kiti help him back to his robes."

He was limp and listless as she hoisted his slight weight. Tears flowed from his eyes. *"Issumariyungnaerpok*, Forgive . . . forgive," he murmured all the way back to the cave where he had been. He slept for the rest of the day and through the night, not rousing for a meal.

* * *

"He must be washed," Kiti declared to Ertok and Pomakut. The two women had fashioned for Adla a complete new set of underwear, *illupak*, from hare and weasel trapped recently. They were now planning *silipak* and *kamik*, outer garments and boots, so that Adla could strongly meet the coming snows. Summer was passing. Although sunshine remained generous, a chill haunted the air. Cold rains came more and more frequently, and only last night did sleet ride the wind. Ertok finally agreed that Adla should not put on even his new *illupak* until he looked and smelled better.

"But how can he get clean?" Ertok wondered aloud. "He is asked to accompany the villagers for fishing, but he ignores the invitation."

Kiti dug into her hunting bag for certain herbs. Some she had collected this summer from tundra soils and grasses. "It happens that this can go into his food," she said as she used her pestle in Arajik's bowl to crush fleshy stems.

Ertok watched with interest, then awe, and finally with fear. "Kiti is *angakok?*"

The girl laughed. "Kiti is a dabbler, a *cook,*" she told her friend. "This will go into some of Ertok's good soup heating in the sun. Adla will sleep well on this day."

That late afternoon, people returned from fishing and hung their gutted catch on tall bone drying racks. Adla lay in the sun at the opening to his small cave, asleep and snoring raggedly. Ertok and Kiti stripped the rags from his still frail body and bathed him with warm water. Kiti saw on his chest and thigh more of the puckered red scars, these also on his left side. She rubbed a frothing herb on the man's face, and Pomakut used his sharpest knife to shave away the thin, vermin-infested beard. He did such a good job that Kiti begged him to trim and comb out the man's head and pubic hair, as well.

"Perhaps the biting creatures will leave if their nests are disturbed."

"He's *young!*" Pomakut exclaimed, as he finished. For everyone had thought the stranger to be wizened with age. Dirt and matted hair removed, only scars and unhealed wounds remained on face and body.

"Hardly more than a boy," Ertok agreed. "Surely not more than twenty-five winters."

"Such serious injuries," Pomakut remarked, "might be from struggle with a bear."

Kiti said nothing, but she stared at the man with foreboding. Here was no hoary elder having confused thoughts. When healthy and strong, this man could wreak damage. She had never spoken of the spear attack from half a moon ago. Something else. Something about this Adla was familiar. She tried to imagine him *without* sores and scars.

The three of them—with Isumak and even small Arajik helping—plucked and snapped remaining lice from the scant hair upon the body. At last, the light new clothing was pulled over the bony limbs and rib-lined torso. They laid him on a clean robe. The other robe, they scraped and brushed and then hung out beyond the reach of dogs on a rack to bake in sunshine. Adla would surely be astonished when he awakened in the morning. He smelled much better, and no great number of flies swarmed around him.

If Adla noticed the change, he gave no indication. But from the day after his cleaning, the man's appetite improved as did his physical health. He ate ravenously, and flesh began to pad his skin. Strength developed. He spoke *Inupiaq* clearly and distinctly if not sensibly. Sometimes he smiled. Those who saw the smile looked around to find a reason. The expression itself was more grimace, as if the corners of his mouth were attached by sinew which was lifted or lowered by whim. The strange glare in Adla's eyes did not fade. Nor did he seem to *notice*. He responded only to what he saw as obstacles to progress when he walked through the camp. With no word of displeasure, he would kick out viciously at anyone or anything in his way. He showed no interest in going out with hunters, although he ate with gusto the good freshwater fish and occasional caribou that everyone contributed.

Sagak was the wise one of the village. He was not very old, being still a vigorous hunter. But he was a thoughtful *Inuk* from youth, so Ertok explained, and people tended to listen when he spoke. "We shall give this youth our food and time, also tender care," Sagak said. "One has observed this illness in the past—always by solitary *Inuit* found wandering on ice or tundra. His enraptured spirits are starved and frozen. Let them feed and thaw."

Others were content to feed the stranger, to smile and try to talk with him. Still, as sleep times passed and then another moon, they grew discouraged and might have given up.

"Nothing is lonelier than a human spirit encircled by a season of empty horizons," Sagak reassured everyone. "His soul is badly bruised, and time is required to blot the discolor."

209

Reunion

For Tuk, an odd summer followed a peculiar spring. Food creatures were generous that year, especially those of the sea, so that his village stayed not far from the coast. Small herds of caribou drifted north and—never completely predictable—moved east for calving. People built their summer *igloos* high on rolling prairie, this season, instead of among rocky outcroppings on soggy inland tundra. They erected hide tents and sod-walled lean-tos only far enough inland to escape the mighty summer tides. Yet, they could easily tramp to shore—since sleds and teams were useless without snow and ice—and search out seal or walrus. These big mammals love to sunbathe in summer and let warm beams scour saltwater lice from their hides. On shore, they enjoy safety from the insatiable black-and-white whales that cooperate in packs to tumble them from floes.

During low tide, *kayaks* went out for fish, day and night in endless light, to fatten new caches that for once could be conveniently located. Sometimes in the sea, someone spied a solitary tusked narwhal or even a mighty bowhead tardy in migration. Then came great excitement, and if the tide were right, a launching of *umiaks*—the slow but sturdy, rudderless boats of thick hide. Rarely was one of the huge mammals captured, in fact none that summer, but anticipation and imagination lent magic to each sighting.

From a high coastal rock, Tuk watched a broad lead nearby where a herd of twelve spotted white narwhal dived. Their graceful, wraithlike forms danced down to disappear in clear green water. Much later, when he thought he had somehow missed their return for air, he saw a great cloud of ocean cod come boiling up ahead of the narwhals. The fish leaped clear before flopping back motionless to the surface. Cod lose consciousness when herded rapidly from great depths. Not only the herding spear-toothed narwhals but also seals and birds—jaegers and shrieking gulls—fed greedily on the fish before sense returned and survivors could dive to safety.

Tuk was restless. Energy crackled through his body, and he seldom slept. When the village first moved, the bachelor hut he built backed onto a shallow, broad-mouthed cave. From this base he careened out with hides draped on whalebone. Space enough for half a dozen people, or so the others teased him gently.

Much rain fell in summer. How was the young man to keep collected water from collapsing his roof?

"Hoo-oo. . . . Someone plans to hold a drum-feast day and night."

"Does it happen that this Tuk will surprise the village with a family previously hidden?!" Much tittering followed that question, for people believed Tuk and Kiti with Arajik to be a likely unit sometime soon.

He laughed with his friends good-naturedly and looked at the vast shelter. Yes, he realized suddenly. A *family* was badly needed here.

"Eh, Nuna," he told the dog where others could hear, "come live with Tuk a while." Actually, she bore six pups soon after the camp was established. And she *did* bring her litter inside. There, with this trusted temporary master, the little ones were dry during downpours and swirling gray mists, and then at other times protected from relentless, burning sun.

Food was easy now—berries, fish, small creatures from the prairie. Tuk went out with village hunters and was successful. So successful that on most days he did not hunt. Fish swarmed the rivers, and everyone waded in to spear them, ate the smaller ones or fed them to the dogs; then helped with drying the largest fish as a buffer against the long winter to come.

But nothing truly satisfied Tuk. Extra energy continued to course through him. He knew that Kiti, for some unknown reason, kept and prized the carved muskox he had freed from rock. Therefore, his seal oil lamp, every manner of bowl, certainly each weapon and utensil he owned became enhanced by carving. The crudely stitched rawhides of his lean-to carried outline pictures from the hunt, and these were much admired. Even so, as spring passed and summer moved to its zenith, the ground all around his hut was strewn with finished, useless and therefore discarded separate carvings, often stone or bone. He remembered how much Kiti liked those slitted spectacles made of wood, those *idjak.* He would spy bits of driftwood as he walked along the shore, dry it in sunshine; then if large enough, would turn it into cunningly decorated *idjak.*

"What manner of beast is this that Sedna has rejected?" Kiti always asked when she admired Tuk's sled or some tool made from driftwood. Neither *Inuit,* of course, had ever seen a tree, and no summer berry bush was

211

supported by more than a spindly stem or vine. Kiti thought the material most beautiful when carved. Both she and Tuk agreed that *idjak* made from driftwood instead of bone fit more comfortably on the face. But the source of this mysterious substance was just one more of many secrets guarded by Queen Sedna and the sea.

If the bit of precious wood retrieved was too small for practical use—as a spear, a runner, a crossbar, a harpoon—then Tuk was secretly pleased. He would turn the piece in his grasp slowly, study it from every angle; then easily free from bark and pith whatever hid inside—often some sea mammal, some *puyee*. From one, though, emerged a kittiwake—the slender, gull-like bird he often saw attacking cod brought up by narwhal. He charred the legs and wingtips to make those parts black as raven quills. Finished, he discarded the piece—or as he thought, *released* it.

On side-hills along the shore, he would find shiny soapstone uncovered by fierce tide. During the bright night while others slept, he worked this material with knives and mallet. He labored long over his carvings, whether wood or mineral . . . and he *thought*. The aching pain from loss of family had subsided. But anxiety and restlessness dwelt within him just as this form or that one dwelt uneasily within the materials on which he worked. He could liberate the creatures, but who could release the tension in Tuk's own muscles and tight belly, the stiffening of his neck, the dull pain across his shoulders?

With Nuna, when she could leave her new litter so long, the young man walked out on isolated prairie. One day he heard a distant hail and looked about. Even the dog was mystified. On a hill to the south he finally made out two figures walking, unaccompanied by dogs. Tuk watched as they descended and then reappeared on the next rise. One was tall and slender, taking long strides. The other was shorter, broad, quick-paced, a hurrier. Each carried a bulging pack high on his back and braced with a band across the forehead. As the two came closer, their tempo increased. Did they know him? No one would shout out a name, for no *Inupiat* would tempt malignant spirits hovering in the air. But something about the visitors tugged a cord linked to his memory.

Ah, Narluk's sons. . . . He trotted forward to meet them.

Pajuk arrived before his brother, but was overwhelmed by a leaping, licking Nuna. Tuk watched in awe as the normally stand-offish bitch rose up to put her paws on Pajuk's shoulders. She whined and gave low, joyous barks. Her tail became a blur of rapid movement. Clearly, those two knew each other.

Then Oojulit was there, laughing, undergoing the same treatment. Nuna dashed back and forth between them, as Tuk observed with open mouth.

"Nuna, drop!" Pajuk commanded, grinning happily.

Hoo-oo. . . . They knew her name—eh, of the same village, so naturally they recognized each other?

"It happens that two young men have trailed far north inquiring of the coastal boy named *Tuk,*" Oojulit said.

"—But then to find as well the pride of one's own family team—!" Pajuk stooped to caress the wriggling form.

"It happens that a long search may now be finished." Oojulit smiled.

Tuk did not respond. Narluk's sons were looking for *Nuna*? Surely not for Tuk alone, as they professed. . . . But how unlikely that anyone would come so far—and risk travel afoot so late in the season—to locate a mere *kringmerk,* however magnificent that dog might be.

Pajuk looked up, shining dark eyes fastened on the boy's face. "Where is she?"

"She?" Tuk stammered. Nuna was right here before them. How did they know her so well? And how did Nuna know them—far better than merely coming from the same village, he decided. These three had shared a trail more than once.

Oojulit prompted him. "The sister of these two brothers who stand before you."

"Sister," Tuk repeated in confusion.

"Sukitilan, of course," Oojulit said.

Tuk echoed, "Sukitilan."

Oojulit finally read the bewilderment on Tuk's features. His face darkened. "This Nuna dog was found where?"

A ray of light came into Tuk's mind—one slash of brilliance surrounded by murky fog. Details came to mind. His early observation of Kiti's exodus from the village while others slept. Her present name. Such unreasoning anger as comes only from fear when he had said he planned to return Arajik to that very village she had left. And always—the distance she maintained in conversation with him and with others, the careful weighing of what little she revealed about herself.

"We took the dog off the ice, half-dead of wounds and hunger," Tuk responded slowly. His stomach roiled with the discomfort all *Inupiat* feel about being less than fully honest.

Oojulit looked at Pajuk, and despair was exchanged in that grim glance.

"She was alone in her anguish," Oojulit said softly.

"True," Tuk agreed, but now more confused than ever. Such compassion and sorrow for a dog seemed unlikely. But then, these were *Inupiat* of the inland caribou. He must try to console them. "Still, she has had someone with her and caring for her at all times ever since her rescue."

"Not the dog!" Pajuk told him. "The daughter of Narluk, the small sister of these worthless brothers who stand before you."

"Small sister," Tuk repeated.

"Practically still a child," Oojulit said, "and very timid."

"A timid child." If the Kiti he knew was this *Sukitilan* they sought—and considering Nuna, how could she *not* be?—then the young woman they described must have been away from home for longer than the one full season he presumed. Perhaps she only passed through on that night when he saw— no! She was accepted by the dogs. She had collected a team there. But the daughter of Narluk? Surely these two spoke of someone else.

The mystified young man changed the subject. "It happens that the village of Tuk is not far away," he said, "and a man has space and food—poor though it is!—for these most welcome travelers."

He turned back to take the brothers to his people. He did not worry that villagers would reveal anything. Neither Oojulit nor Pajuk was likely to ask total strangers about their sister *Sukitilan,* now that Tuk was found. These two evidently believed her dead, only Nuna remaining. As might truly be the situation now, Tuk told himself, for all anyone here could know. . . . Except, he was certain that *he* would somehow *discern* her finish just as he had picked up on her distress before he went with villagers to search her out on ice. No, Kiti was alive and healthy. Somewhere. And although he held these two and their father—Narluk was Kiti's *father?!*—in high esteem, he respected Kiti's reasons for leaving her family and resolved not to disclose her presence among the ice islanders.

In the next days of never-ending light, sunshine broken by frequent rain and wind but never darkness, the three walked out together. Gradually, Tuk understood that these were indeed brothers to Kiti, and that they were genuinely saddened by her disappearance. Mighty Narluk was her father. She had deliberately hidden this fact from Tuk. He wondered why.

"The male parent has never been the same," Oojulit told him gravely, "since those two sweet females departed his *igloo* and his life."

Two abandoned his *igloo*? Perhaps the father and his sons were not as pleasant when nested in the family unit as they seemed upon the trail. Eh, and if their Sukitilan had an older sister *Kiti*—

"—A mother died," Oojulit explained. "A young sister found it necessary to take the trail."

"Was *pushed* to do it," Pajuk agreed with such bitterness of tone that Tuk stared and Oojulit cleared his throat uncomfortably. Pajuk continued. "A child forced onto a black winter trail by a family without understanding."

After walking a long time in silence, Oojulit spoke. "It happens that someone so young could not possibly get this far—"

"—Yet, a family's chants went out to many spirits for a miracle," Pajuk said.

"—Only a child," Oojulit resumed, "a pampered female who never had needed to endure hardship."

"Helpless and ignorant alone on a trail," Pajuk said with an air of finality.

Tuk spoke no more. Even if the brothers *did* ask villagers, this child they described as their Sukitilan could not easily be linked to the fierce and confident huntress *Kiti*. Through Nuna? Still, so far as people here could know, Nuna had been picked up along the trail and added to Kiti's team. They did not know the dog had nursed Arajik. In their view, two inlander friends of Tuk would be visiting to learn from coastal people the skills of harvesting an iceless sea. People here would be delighted to show these affable visitors ways to stalk seal and capture walrus.

Still sleepless at night, Tuk pondered. Neither Oojulit nor Pajuk had asked about a baby. Yet, Arajik was born *before* Kiti left her people. Still another mystery.

After five long nights of continued deception with his guests, Tuk could no longer digest the food he forced himself to eat. His belly ached. He felt dizzy. Nothing seemed real. He watched and listened, even spoke, with a growing sense of detachment—he was the useless flapping strap on a stranger's sled. He felt himself to be *present* but no longer *part of* what went on around him. The time had come, he decided late one sleepless night, to go find Kiti. She would summer with her mother's people if she had ever found them. And she must have done so, for she had agreed to return to his village if the trail northeast concluded without success. Therefore, she must be with one or another of the ice villagers. But on what pretext could he go? He could not track her down and suddenly appear, saying only that his soul had become restless. Nor was it credible to contend that their paths just happened to cross.

Hoo-oo. . . . He had his reason for seeking her out—a reason far more important than that Nuna was ready to be returned to her. Kiti must be informed that her brothers were nearby—that they in fact thought her dead. Then she could herself decide whether to make her existence known to them. But somehow, someway—for curiosity chewed him without mercy—he must find out why she had left her family.

At the end of his sleep time without sleep, he made a backpack by using thongs to bundle some robes wrapped around food for a walking trail. His spear lay beside the burden he would carry. When the brothers awoke, he spoke softly to them. "Someone makes a journey."

"Let Tuk add the company of two brothers," Pajuk suggested, "two who have nothing to do until winter trails can be followed." The young men had been making gifts to villagers of caribou they captured with experienced skill on inland forays. In reciprocation, village folk had promised them this extra dog and that one in order to make up their team when ice and snow arrived. The brothers were using sinew on bones from a beached whale for runners and sun-dried antlers from caribou as cross-pieces to make ready a magnificent sled for their return. Meantime, villagers were enjoying the extended stay of these vigorous aliens from inland.

Tuk said, "It happens that this travel must be made alone." Would Nuna be permitted to go with him? She was in his care, after all, and he was responsible for her safe return to Kiti. But Kiti being absent, the dog obviously belonged to the two young men.

The brothers made no protest when their host insisted on making his trip unaccompanied—for they were still weary of foot travel and enjoyed the hospitality of the village. Oojulit shrugged when Tuk said he wanted to take Nuna with him. Although the two quietly claimed her, they agreed to let her stretch her legs after confinement first with wounds and then a litter recently independent and distributed. Tuk was careful not to say he would bring the big dog back—and Kiti's brothers did not think to ask. Why would they? After all, their friend promised to return well before the snow. Meantime, the two could stay here and care for Tuk's team. They could continue to learn from enthusiastic villagers the ways of finding provision in the sea. And they could try to stockpile food against their long journey to come.

So Tuk with Nuna set out northwest. A rising wind at his back, Nigituk hastened him on his way.

216

Justice

Kiti's early thought about the identity of Adla, after his cleaning, was based entirely on his appearance. His healing and weight gain strengthened her earlier notion. She had no doubt but that Adla was—well, *had been*—her brother Palunga. As the days passed, though, anticipated joy was replaced by deepening dread. The wit and humor of the brother she once loved best had vanished with no trace. Yes, of course she recognized this strong, physically healthy man. But the essence of her youngest brother was confused by raptures on a trail too long solitary and by grim events no one would ever know. Was his condition permanent? This question haunted her. At least, he was no longer *Adla the Stranger*, not to her.

In the sunshine of night during sleep, she awakened to his shadow crossing her face as he walked alone. She checked to see that Arajik slept soundly before she herself got up and padded outside after the man. He sat on the lakeshore embankment. She touched his shoulder and spoke only to let him know that she was there, then sat beside him. For a time, both watched the water.

Kiti finally cleared her throat. She turned to watch his face. She tried to ignore the ugly silver scar. "Palunga," she said softly, "a sister welcomes her brother back."

Not so much as a narrowing of eyes betrayed his hearing let alone his understanding of her words. He continued to stare straight ahead at the riffling lake surface while Kiti waited.

At last, she chanted in a low voice, "Palunga . . . *Palunga* . . . PALUNGA!" She continued to watch the face for response of any kind, but nothing happened. "Fifth son of Narluk and Pichikut . . . brother to Sukitilan . . . and named Palunga."

The mouth of the man beside her began to work, twisting and opening several times before words would come. "This one is *Adla the Stranger*, the *Wild One*." Then he turned to look at her and a grin sliced his face below

217

glowering eyes. Suddenly, he grabbed her, forcing her shoulders to the gravel. He stared down at her; then fumbled with her *illupak*. She tore herself away and stood over him higher on the bank.

"Kiti is someone's *sister!*" she scolded. Every *Inuit* knew that such coupling is prohibited.

He lurched up from the ground to grasp her wrists.

"Palunga!" Again she twisted away and ran fully up the bank. There she stood with hands on hips. "Someone forgets himself!" she told him, her eyes flashing anger and her feet ready to run. How strong and quick he had become since his healing.

He blundered up toward her, then stopped, mouth open. His head cocked, then jerked to another angle. His eyes narrowed, a single line of concentration deepening between his brows. And Kiti watched as tears collected and trickled down his cheeks. "Forgive, forgive, *issumariyungnaerpok,*" he told her as he turned, slid hurriedly down the bank, dropped once more onto pebbles beside the lake.

Back in the lean-to and rolled into light robes with Arajik, Kiti trembled for a long time before sleep would come again. Not fear, but a vestige of anger and mostly something else . . . hopelessness finally admitted.

The next morning in a gloomy drizzle, Adla walked away from camp. A rumor that he had made himself a knife alarmed Kiti. Ertok told her that the man had gone toward the place where *kringmerk* were staked. *He has been with the village long enough to have the smell of the camp on him*, she thought, *and the dogs will not bother him*. Still . . . *ahmi,* who can say what is to happen? She armed herself and followed at a cautious distance, Arajik in her *amaut*.

She arrived to see Palunga standing perfectly still and looking around at the dogs.

"Iyarpok?" he asked. Kiti remembered once again that her own team's *Laughing One* had once been Palunga's lead dog. Of course he knew that name even if not his sister's.

The dog looked up when his name was called, wagged his tail tentatively as Adla hurried to him. The big dog was in a far better mood, these days, now that Nuna was not around.

"Iyarpok!" The man got onto his knees before the staked dog, and put an arm around his neck. Kiti saw movement at her brother's side, one flash of motion, no more. But the creature fell to the ground when Palunga raised his arm. Kiti hurried forward, then stopped.

"Iyarpok? Iyarpok?!" The man lifted one of the dog's legs, watched it fall back limply when he let go. The other hand held a bone knife with blood dripping from its point. Palunga stood up. *"IYARPOK!?!"* He kicked at the body. No response.

Then he dropped his head and Kiti heard his gasps for breath. She knew that tears were falling once again. "Forgive!" sobbed this Palunga who was not Palunga. *"Issumariyungnaerpok!"* He grasped the dog's neck, raised the body to hug the creature with both arms.

Kiti felt tears dampening her own eyes as she walked up, and she knew that she did not grieve for Iyarpok. Together, Adla and she removed the dead dog's neckstrap. They helped each other carry the creature to a hillock above the lake. And together, wordless, they dug down to permafrost; then afterward laid rocks over the husk of what had been *The Laughing One.*

The sun now hid for hours in the middle of each sleep time. This was a cold night with the wind moaning outside the lean-to. Already, a few flurries had come to presage winter. The village was ready to move back to the sea as soon as hard freeze and snow cover promised a base for sled runners. Everyone yearned for home. Two dozen caribou hides stretched and cured on high bone racks. Kiti had helped with strategy for capturing these long-legged *tuktu* who had dared to lag on green tundra behind their migrating companions. Countless firm-fleshed whitefish were sun dried and cached ready for lashing onto sleds. Handsome pelts from small game, too, awaited final processing to be used for *illupak* and clothing trim. Stacked and ready to load beside individual sleds were bladders and pouches stuffed with dried berries, herbs and mosses, and sturdy bags of permafrost as well.

On the day Iyarpok died, Kiti and Arajik ate their meal before the sleep as usual, with Ertok and Pomakut. After, Kiti stared into the lamp as she told these friends about Adla and the dog; then about the scene at the lake and finally about the spear threat to Arajik more than a moon ago.

"Hoo-oo!" Ertok breathed, and Pomakut echoed that response.

They decided to consult Sagak, and that man once again advised patience. "In summer can come madness from unending sunlight," he told them. "Soon will arrive the cold for which *Inupiat* was made. The useless *kringmerk* will work again and our own legs will stretch beside the sleds. Displaced spirits will settle into place. Let the people watch and be wary but tolerant."

Kiti tried to stay alert, but most days she went out, Arajik in her hood, to search for stragglers among end-of-season caribou. The great southern migration of these beasts had ended. Or she went to fish with sinew at the edge of the lake, where hard ice was beginning to form and where the water was too cold for wading and hand fishing. Adla's new parka, trousers and boots were ready long since because village women all helped with the curing and careful assembly.

One day while most of the village was gone, Adla raped an old widow who had remained in her tent because, as she explained that morning, her bones creaked with the change of season. Kiti, when she heard of this on coming home, found herself sick in the stomach. She left the group to retch over and again, cold shivers wracking her and birdflesh rising on her skin. Part of what she felt was fear. She remembered Tonratu. On top of the terror she felt guilt. Adla had displayed before now the strange predilection for violence so unlike his former self. And although Kiti had ultimately described those events to Sagak and her friends, she had warned no one. That late afternoon, when she had finally relieved herself and soothed her roiling stomach, she went immediately to the victim.

The sweet old grandmother was not injured, she told Kiti. Not hurt at all. Her reaction was, in fact, a combination of surprise and amusement. "He was gentle but persistent," she said. The language *Inupiaq* has no word for sex against the will because it does not ordinarily happen. Among people who enjoy the pleasure of each other's bodies from childhood, the idea of taking someone sexually by force is unthinkable.

The woman's eyes glittered as she gave a dramatic account. "And afterward, the boy called Adla cried true tears and said, 'Forgive, forgive!' A strange happening."

Later, the people turned to Sagak.

He wrinkled his small nose to show disapproval. Most of the villagers did not know of Adla's earlier transgressions. "It happens that this is not a good thing," Sagak told them. "A savage specter remains within the young man's healthy body."

"Yet, he asked forgiveness," the old woman reminded him. "Is this not honorable?"

Sagak looked at Kiti, and she dropped her eyelids down for a long time: *No. Asking forgiveness is not honorable when someone fails to change behavior.*

"Now everyone knows of the tortured person in our midst, this Adla," Sagak said at last. "He shall continue to receive tender regard, but all must be vigilant. No one should be alone at any time."

Good snow finally fell. Temperatures plummeted. Planning to leave for the coast within the next few days, villagers became intent on preparing sleds, planning, packing for the journey. Arajik bounced up and down in Kiti's hood and amused himself as she filled the last bladders with dried fish and arranged bags and pouches for her sled. No one paid attention to Isumak, the only youngster in the village permanently out of the *amaut*, a boy who seemed to be everywhere, chatting and laughing and asking questions. But people paid attention when the evening meal time came and Isumak did not appear.

The question went around the camp, "Does it happen Isumak is in someone's *igloo?*"

"No? Then where must he be?"

They found his body beyond a rise, near a frozen streamlet that dropped into the lake. He had been strangled. Pomakut went to find Adla, who came willingly enough.

When he saw the child, he cried. Great, aching sobs tore from his throat. "Forgive, forgive!" he said, over and again.

The people turned away. Isumak, this time on earth, had drawn breath for a mere chink in the snow house of his lives. All went to comfort his parents.

That night brought howling wind with ice particles that swept parallel to the ground, intense wet cold. Every villager assembled in the larger of the two big caves, one several openings from where Adla had slept since late summer among other unmarried men and boys. He himself was invited to attend, but his was not among the solemn faces gathered around the seal oil lamps.

"If he were *kringmerk*," said Pomakut, "we could bind his limbs until good spirits returned."

"Hoo-oo!" the people disapproved. A shocking thought unworthy of consideration for any *inuk*.

Sagak cleared his throat for attention. "But everyone knows that *Inupiat* cannot live in a condition of restraint."

"It becomes necessary now to say," Kiti announced clearly, "that the stranger is Kiti's brother."

"Ai-ee . . . Ai-ee-ee. Hoo-oo!" Surprise and dismay.

"His name is *Palunga*. He is the fifth son of Pichikut. He disappeared two seasons past from tundra far south and west of here."

"Ee-ee," sadly. That explained it, certainly—a whole winter of solitude

221

added to the summer before. How did he survive at all? Silence and gloom were in the group, sympathy, no sound. Based on long experience as well as the recent actions of a physically healthy Adla-Palunga, villagers agreed that no hope remained. Such a man was not *Inuk* now, but rather *Paija's Person*, violent at the core, a danger to all and to himself. He would forever be feral and frenzied, would never be predictable.

At last, Sagak spoke up once more, his eyes on Kiti. "The body is Palunga's, but the spirits within will ever be *adlait,* strangers in battle with each other and the world."

Kiti's hand found the notch at her ear, tugged it unconsciously. Now she sucked in a long breath to show that she heard and accepted Sagak's words . . . and also that she reluctantly agreed. She stood up, as did Ertok and the other women. She was grateful not to be involved in what would come next.

As she pushed past the baffle to enter her own lean-to, carrying Arajik, she heard the village males file past to go down the embankment to the lakeshore. There, she knew, they would select fourteen small smooth pebbles and one larger, uneven one. They would station themselves well apart and privately near water's edge. There in the stormy night, Sagak would pass each man to drop a rock at random to sink into the shallow snow before him. Whoever then retrieved the large pebble would do the deed, and only that one man would ever know. Responsibility for the act rested with every member of the group. Her brother Palunga—now again Adla the stranger—would not live through this night. *Pirtok.* One cannot ever, ever change what has occurred.

* * *

A little later, she came awake in darkness to feel a hand on her shoulder. She sat up, clasping the robe to herself tightly, for the cold on this stormy night was intense.

"Come out," whispered the familiar voice. Kiti checked Arajik, arranged one furry robe around her shoulders and took time to pluck up her sharpest skinning knife.

She had no words when finally she got out and braced herself against the fierce wind. Sleet whirled everywhere and stung her face as she looked at the dim shadow close by. She could not see the features of that once-loved face, and she was glad.

Palunga too clutched a robe. He bent over her to speak into her ear and be heard above the gale. She clung tightly to the handle of her knife, had it outside the robe but hidden in a fold. "Sometimes comes a moment's memory," he hissed, "of dear family and good times before the loneliness."

His recollections were returning. Was this not a healthy sign?

"Palunga!" she groaned. "Come, the brother and sister will go together from this place. The two will leave tonight!" Her mind was racing. Here might be hope for him . . . but not so much that she could endanger Arajik. *Leave the baby!*? Ertok would take him—but where? Of course, to *Tuk!*— all she need do was tell her. Then she heard her brother's voice once again in her ear.

"*Owka,* no, for strong evil lies within the man who stands here . . . a burning presence churned at the hot center of the earth. . . . *Sukitilan,* forgive!"

He dropped his blanket, stepped from his *kamik* and flung away his warm new furs, then stripped away his underwear. With no sound or backward glance, he raced naked away from camp to the heart of Ooangniktuk, the powerful north wind.

Quest

Kiti was numb for the first days of travel on the return to ice islands. She grieved silently, even knowing that her doomed brother had made a sensible choice at the end. Ever since Palunga originally left the village and did not return, his fate had been to her a strip of pelt that flapped upon the drying rack but never tempered. His tale was now a seasoned hide—true, not her choice in outcome but at least a finished event. She wondered if spirits of enraptured *Inuit* would heal in the sky and then return as protectors. Palunga's would if any could, she decided, for the brother she remembered had once possessed a graceful manner and a loving heart.

The weather was terrible for their return, day and night producing great blasts which carried sleet and frozen fog. The hours of darkness increased—a result of storm-saturated overcast and a portent of black winter to come. White-outs and shrieking blizzards forced frequent stops. Wind picked up snow previously fallen, coated it with sharp new frost; then churned it like a thousand tiny knives into the face and eyes. Frigid gale carried gusts that whipped at nose and mouth, rimed the lining of the lung.

Overland toward the coast contained rough terrain with sharp rocks jutting through still insubstantial ground cover. Many stops were necessary to pack and re-ice runners. Everyone carried a bag of permafrost inside the *silipak*. To build a melt-fire in the lamp between sleeps along the way required too much effort. And here on the rock-savage felsenmeer, jagged edges were insufficiently ice-glazed and snow-covered. Such conditions forced every driver to fit hide bags around the bleeding pads of *kringmerk*, slip-string each canine *kamik* tight with sinew. Kiti kept unfrozen in her tunic pocket an herb paste she used to treat wounds on paws of all the suffering dogs. On whim, Kiti placed at the sole of each boot for her dogs a bit of qiviut from the muskox Tuk had taken. *Where is Tuk right now?* She hoped that he would not go alone for dangerous *oomingmak*. . . . Tuk and Kiti hunted well together, did they not? *And Nuna—where is she?* Kiti needed the great white bitch. With Iyarpok gone, her team which had previously performed as one creature of

224

one mind was now confused. She kept testing different dogs in lead position, but without success. Individually, all had proven themselves valiant and hard-working; but none so far had the necessary strength of will overlaid with intelligent sensibility. Yes, Nuna is needed, here. *And Tuk.*

Kiti shuddered as she ran beside her sled. *And Tuk?* Why would she think that? Nuna, yes. But if Tuk wanted to be here, he would come. And if he did not then he was not needed!

So cold. . . . So very cold. . . . She must turn her thoughts to overcoming the snow walker in this first severe storm of the season. Here was a circumstance during which each *Inuk* must tighten *nuilak,* the fur trim of the parka, so that only the tiniest peep-hole remained, and that obscured by hide hairs. Those fortunate ones with *kapvik* on their parkas—with rich, frost-free wolverine pelt—need not forever slap away accumulating ice. Much as Kiti missed and yearned for Nuna, she had to admit relief overall that the white dog was absent during this painful trek.

The villagers fussed over Kiti, especially Ertok and Pomakut. They worried, she knew, that she suffered greatly from the shock of losing Palunga. Sagak one night came to her tiny trail *igloo* just before the sleep. He coughed courteously before crawling through the baffle. Suspecting that she chewed interminably on this last occurrence as well as other events unknown to him—for she must have endured hardship to come alone to search them out—he spoke to her directly about the recent tragedy, something no other villager would invade her grief to do.

"Even the great disasters in our puny lives are small ones," he told her, "when someone looks to the circling horizon with all its pain and joy. And that ring itself is trivial within a sky that may peer down on *countless* horizons under myriad suns and moons, each sharing as many seasons as there are sand granules on all the summer beaches."

Inupiat have always known that the earth circles the sun while the moon circles the earth. Have in fact always taken pleasure in the roundness of it all. For several moments, Kiti envisioned herself as a single hair on an *iglerk* full of fur. The fantasy helped, and she summoned that very perspective often in days to come. *The sadness of this puny woman will pass.*

At last, and after many sleeps, her grief could be managed. She had six brothers. Three were surely dead, and one was now her son. Therefore she had two brothers. To continue her inventory, the old Sukitilan had two parents.

The mother was gone, but the spirit of *Ananak* was nearby. Nearby to Arajik and to Kiti, that would be. So then, did Kiti have two parents? The father. *Hoo-oo*. Here was a matter for study at a later time, when Kiti's own soul was not so troubled. Perhaps, as sleep times and as moons and seasons passed, she would understand.

Meantime, Kiti had proven herself *to* herself, in making the long trip from family and village. In being independent. In fulfilling the pledge to Pichikut. So now once again, back to her mother's village . . . to **Kiti's** village . . . to the rest of her life and of Arajik's? *Ahmi*. Who can know the future?

* * *

She came awake suddenly in the tiny trail igloo she had built the night before. Someone—some*thing!*—fumbled at the robes where she and Arajik lay. She jerked up, Tonratu uppermost in her blurred consciousness. She had the sharp knife in her hand and was trying to focus on form visible in a pale shadow from the flicker of spirit lights above. Her team was staked just outside the entry. Why had they made no sound? Even now, her dogs were quiet, unalarmed. Unless they were dead? She raised her knife high over the shaggy creature beside her—then felt a wet lick on her cheek. Another. She lowered the knife slowly.

"Nuna?" Kiti asked.

Awake, Arajik shouted with joy as he recognized first the name and then the touch and smell of his foster mother even from under the robes in darkness.

The girl saw the hide baffle at her doorway push up, recognized Tuk crawling through. In hot confusion, she reached out to raise the sinew in the lamp—but then remembered she had made no fire for the trail hut. She felt a chaos of conflict. Her first impulse had been to raise her arms and clasp this man to her tightly and forever, take solace and strength from his presence. Why? Her second impulse? To dismiss him, just order him away. *Again* why?

Ah, Nuna. How she had missed the dog—and Arajik longing for her even more. The small boy was tangled and half out of the robes, his bare arms and fists pummeling the creature. Nuna put down a paw to anchor him, then nosed and bathed him excitedly.

Still muddled, Kiti turned back to Tuk, trembling, frowning. Had they not agreed that she was to make this journey alone?

"It happens," he told her with a slow, uncertain smile spreading across his face, "that someone brings news."

Nuna leading joyously, her old position no longer contested, Tuk and Kiti shared her sled to go with her village back to the ice islands.

"Hoo-oo!" Ertok teased at first. "Here is a fine young man whose existence Kiti hid away!" Others also tried to joke with her about him while Tuk was out with the men to find provision for the trail. But banter gradually ceased when the girl did not respond. She showed no anger or embarrassment over their friendly jibes, but no particular pleasure, either. People noticed that although the two spent trail time together and ate their meals with Ertok and Pomakut, they continued to build separate little *igloos* for the night.

Kiti could not talk of her visitor even to Ertok, because the girl was in a drift of confusion. She tried not to let herself *think* about Tuk, for he only complicated the quandary in which his news had placed her. Should she make her existence known to Oojulit and Pajuk? What of Arajik, if she did? Should she let them know of *his* survival? And if so—for it would be hard to hide him if she herself appeared—might she then endanger him?

No. She remembered the threats of Odlerk, and she recalled her automatic and violent response to those threats. Nothing would happen to Arajik. She would not let harm come to him. Whatever was necessary for his safety, she could do. Narluk was not here with his sons, Tuk said. Surely her brothers would not have walked all this way simply to harm a child they believed dead long ago. . . . So why *had* they come? *Hoo-oo,* yet another question. To compel her to return? But she would never again live with Narluk and her old village. . . . Should she tell her brothers about Palunga?

No. Why cause new pain needlessly?

As she made her way with Tuk and villagers to the east and north, always heading for the spirit lights and sunrise sea, she devised a plan and discussed it with Tuk. When they finally reached the coast, he was to take her team with Nuna southeast to his village, she continuing north and east, sharing sled and provision with willing Ertok and Pomakut. Tuk would tell Oojulit and Pajuk that their sister was alive. Then—if they wished to see her—he would see to it that they went to the ice islands or else found her on the trail. She wanted to meet with them—if at all—in the company of her new people, those from their mother's original home.

The child in her, the frightened young woman who had started this long, uncertain trip almost a dozen moons ago, wanted someone else to take responsibility for that first encounter. But the mostly confident person she had become was grateful to Tuk. Not only had he protected the secret of her existence and of Arajik's, he had also left to her those decisions that affected her, since it was she who must live with the results. What an unusual man, this Tuk. How sensitive to her situation, now that he understood at least a part of it.

She realized at last that her long-standing resentment over what she thought to be his many *mysteries* stemmed mostly from her own unwillingness to talk, her own lack of trust, her fear of Narluk and of an unknown future. Unjustified as she gradually knew her caution over Tuk to be, she had continued to closely screen her speech. Now, though, without restraint, she told him everything about her family circumstance as they moved along the trail. All the pieces he had heard before—and all that he had surmised from observation—now were lashed tightly with the sturdy sinew of total truth. Pichikut. Narluk. The *Dead Village*. Yes, Tonratu. Even Odlerk. All, all, all. . . .

The young man followed closely her words and her countenance. His own features betrayed no surprise or chagrin or pleasure. He was the perfect listener as Kiti shared her secrets of fact and fancy.

Ertok had been first to mention Tuk's special qualities. "The person who released *oomingmak* from the stone," she said of the carving Kiti kept, "possesses not only skill but great patience as well!" *Skill and patience with carving, yes*, Kiti thought, *and with Nuna. And with people. Especially with Arajik. And with Kiti herself—even when she was angry and unreasonable. Hoo-oo. . . .* Such thoughts made her restless.

Later, they agreed that Tuk should not mention the baby to Oojulit and Pajuk. If they came north to see their sister, Arajik would be with her, and they would then of course see him and deduce his origin.

"It is fully agreed then," she said once more to Tuk before he left, "that Arajik is none but Kiti's son?!"

"Yes, as said before. No mother could care more."

Snow fell and drifted. At the last sleep time before Tuk left the group to return to his own village, the two by tacit agreement built but one small trail snow house. Kiti cut extra blocks while Tuk layered from the center. When the woman crawled inside, her head bumped the sleeping shelf, the *iglerk*. The ice ledge claimed four-fifths of the *igloo*.

"Hoo-oo! It may be that half the village will join us tonight in the sleeping robes!" She rubbed the top of her head.

Tuk grinned. "And it may also be that they will *not!*" He plumped and then smoothed the many robes piled on the shelf.

This, then, was what *nuliakpok* could be. The coming together of a man and woman who cared deeply for each other. Kiti felt Tuk's nose nuzzle the hollow between her own nose and cheek. The patient man with the delicate touch. An artist whose medium was his body on this night. What did his artistry see within Kiti? What would he release? Here within the furs was something unique and of great value among her life experiences. Here was more than joy. Throbbing, she pulled him close to make every bit of this man a part of her.

In the short light of early winter mid-day, two sleds came up the trail behind the moving villagers. All stopped and waited. Pajuk, with a ragged fan of obviously still unfamiliar dogs, pulled around the lead to approach first and start the process of staking his team well behind the barking, snarling village dogs. Next came Nuna, jauntily leading Kiti's own team—and with Oojulit driving them. Anxiously, the girl scanned the trail behind the sleds. *Where was Tuk?*

Kiti took her hunting bag off Pomakut's sled, and set it in the snow after grasping the spear. The meeting would be cordial, she decided, quite formal on her part at least. *What is their true reason for coming so far?* After one last search for Tuk along the back trail, Kiti walked over to release Nuna from the team. The big white dog beside her, the spear clutched in her right hand but pointed to the ice on which she stood, she turned to meet her brothers.

Ertok had been carrying the baby, and she padded behind, dragging Kiti's hunting bag. Now the older woman brought Arajik from her own makeshift *amaut,* stood him on the ground. A vigorous toddler, these days, he broke away and half-crawled, half-ran to reach an enthusiastic Nuna.

Ertok followed the boy to the small group collected near the teams. Kiti had told her that her brothers might be visiting, although she had not explained the circumstance. The woman introduced herself.

"It will be better," Kiti told her friend, "for the village to keep moving and use wisely the gift of such good weather."

Ertok caught her eye sharply, and the younger woman smiled. "As can be seen, Nuna and the team have arrived. These two hulking men—" she glanced at Oojulit and Pajuk—"are also testing dogs to make a team which will take them back." Anyone could see that the *kringmerk* of Pajuk's team were motley and mismatched. Where had the brothers found such creatures? Pajuk was the better trainer, Kiti knew. But both had much work in front of them before this bunch could become even a passable unit to break a tundra trail south and west.

Ertok gave Kiti a slow smile, then went forward to confer with others in the village. She returned almost immediately. "It happens that Kiti's people—" and she looked soberly at the brothers—"will continue slowly along the trail." Then the woman reached down to collect Arajik.

"The child needs to stay," Kiti told her friend softly.

Ertok hesitated, then seemed to sense the need for privacy, so wheeled and trotted up to join the others. In a moment, they moved north and east along the trail. Kiti swung a protesting Arajik into her hood. Oojulit and Pajuk stood before her, watching mutely. Nor did Kiti speak, for she could think of nothing to say. Questions lay crowded on her tongue like red-billed terns on a cliff face—but she was determined to contain them. She lowered herself onto the familiar robes that Oojulit had strapped to her tidy sled. Palunga's sled. It would be good to have her own coverings at sleep time. She had wondered in past nights how much time would pass before she could reclaim the sled and tested team—and of course Nuna. As she lowered herself, Arajik scrambled nimbly from the *amaut,* dropped down to join the big white dog once more.

Oojulit and Pajuk also chose to sit, one on each side of their sister. If they thought it odd that she sat unresponsive, clinging to her spear, impassively watching the antics of the child and dog before her, neither said anything. In fact, they too watched closely as Nuna and Arajik tustled on the ice, rolling and diving at each other with canine yips and childish crows of merriment. Over and again, Arajik tried to climb onto Nuna's back. They romped for a long time before the action mellowed and finally ceased as dog and child crawled onto the sled together, curled up and closed their eyes contentedly. *Now what,* the girl wondered.

The brothers shifted their attention to Kiti, and Pajuk finally spoke. "It happens that a snowhouse is needed here to contain the three great talkers."

Kiti looked for the first time at his face and caught mischief in his eyes. With no responding smile, she added, "And for the smaller two who love deeply without words."

"A cozy *igloo,*" Oojulit added as he stood up and took his own hunting bag from the sled, pulling out the broad snow knife, "because it is likely going to take some time for these great talkers to begin."

Relieved to have activity replace the uneasy silence, Kiti found freshwater ice in a draw, cut a rough circle of it and carried it to her brothers for use in making an eye for the snowhouse. Then she unloaded from her sled all that Oojulit had packed while she waited to chink the blocks. She was relieved to see that he had brought food. With the villagers gone, she had no provision.

After a silent meal, Kiti sat on the *iglerk* to mend her left *kamik* snagged on a sharp rock by the pool where she got ice. She chewed the hide patch to soften it so that it would fit smoothly into the repair. She had to consciously hold back from inquiring whether her brothers had damage that required a woman's attention. Then she had to bite back a giggle. She would and did regularly sew and patch—like any *Inupiat* woman—for any villager whose clothing or *kamik* needed maintenance, also for Tuk, even for a stranger on the trail who had no woman to do the work. She did it not because it was a woman's job, but rather because only a woman had been trained from childhood to do it properly. A poor patch on clothing and especially on *kamik* could mean death to the wearer if he or she were on the trail. And yet—Kiti would *not* on this day offer aid to her two brothers?

Eh, and not tomorrow, either. First they must *ask!*

Oojulit and and Pajuk sat on folded robes in the middle of the snow house floor, watching her; then watching Arajik lie with Nuna. The two men traded bewildered glances from time to time, but Kiti had no sense of secrets or signals being exchanged. Clearly, they had arrived upon a situation that they did not expect.

Now Kiti lay down her mending and turned to her hunting bag. From it she finally found and withdrew the mortar and small pestle she needed to prepare Arajik's food. She used her knife to slice off layers of seal from the split Oojulit had brought in. Now she mashed the flesh and blubber for warming it in the stone bowl that heated above the lamp. Arajik must have his final meal before the sleep. Kiti kept her features serene. She ignored her guests except, of course, in wildly churning thought. She would not ask, must not ask, absolutely refused to ask any of the hundred questions seething in her. She amused herself by imagining ways to phrase them elegantly so that they were not questions but rather comments that did not absolutely require response. And she fastened her upper teeth along her lower lip to keep from blurting out a likely phrase. She would not so much as clear her throat. They must speak first, these two, for they had sought her out.

Oojulit and Pajuk looked at each other. Where was the fragile sister they had known? They did not doubt but that this was Sukitilan. Yet the person they saw held her head high, moved with certainty, possessed a thick hide of independence that was hard to pierce. Kiti sensed their thoughts, drew herself up even more strongly and busied herself on several tasks not absolutely necessary.

"Pichikut's child?" Oojulit finally punctured the silence.

"Yes, the child who died on ice now lives." The girl gazed at them with unwavering eyes. "And is *son* to the woman called *Kiti.*"

"Hoo-oo. . . . Kiti!" both breathed out softly, nodding, their eyes fastened on her.

After another uncomfortable pause, Kiti allowed herself one word. "Narluk."

Oojulit's face clouded. *"Angakok* has become a feeble man."

"Skin hangs in wrinkled folds across his shrinking bones," Pajuk added.

"Yes, and a frozen fog sits silent in his eyes," Oojulit told her, "ever since he lost his *two* sweet women."

"Hoo-oo!" Kiti flared. "One lost, the other pushed away." Had they come to retrieve her then? And did they think to force her return by filling her with pity for her father? Eh, she could speak her thoughts now, she decided. In a few bitter words, she described what she had seen as they passed her on the trail eleven moons before. "Narluk was strong and vital then. He was determined to do as he thought he must. So intent on slaughter that he ran before the sled, pacing the lead team."

"No." Oojulit spoke softly. "Until this very day, all thought the babe had perished on the ice where Narluk left him."

Pajuk stood. "Yes, and so the search seen by Sukitilan was for a young woman, Narluk's only daughter." He took a step toward Kiti, reached out with both arms.

Kiti stood still, eyes narrowed and cold. She would not retreat, but her stony stare stopped his advance. *Eh, Koloki. . . . And at the end, does a frost serpent regret mortality?* Perhaps not.

"It happens then, that a father has sent his sons," she said. Would they take her words as the question they were meant to be? Had Narluk sent them to find her?

Rebuffed, Pajuk walked over to sit on the sleep ledge. He placed his hand softly upon the boy's head, and Kiti eyed her hunting bag against the wall. Never mind, Nuna would not permit harm to her foster son—not even by other members of the family she loved. Probably not even by Kiti. The dog's

232

head went up, alert, her muzzle busily nosing Pajuk's hand away.

"It may be that a father and two brothers were wrong, Sukitilan—"

"—*Kiti*! Remember that this woman before you is *Kiti.*" She drew out the two syllables with equal strong emphasis on each.

"The boy—"

"—*Arajik.*"

Silence. Pajuk studied his sister, his hand once more resting soft upon the child' form beneath the robes. Then he looked over at Oojulit before returning his gaze to his sister.

"The dog, though—" and Pajuk lifted his fingers to scratch one of Nuna's furry ears—"is *Nuna* still?"

Kiti glared at him; then softened when she saw the twinkle in his eyes.

It was Oojulit who responded to her earlier statement. "Narluk has asked his sons to find his only daughter, if she is still alive—and to request her forgiveness."

Kiti did not respond other than to search their faces for a measure of their sincerity.

"Each night before the sleep," Oojulit continued, "he tells his two worthless boys how wrong it is to do a thing blindly and for no reason other than that it has been done so in the past."

"'Peeusinga is not infallible'—Over and again, he tells those brothers," Pajuk said, "until his sons would have taken the trail anyway, just to be away from him." He sighed. Like his father, Pajuk exercised patience only with difficulty.

"Yet, he himself put a son on ice to die," Kiti said harshly.

"Yes," Oojulit said softly, "he tells his sons so often *because* he cannot accept the revulsion of his having performed that very deed."

"He learned late in life, he says, and at great cost." Pajuk.

Her brothers went foraging with her in the stormy, darkening days that followed. Two teams must be fed. They hunted following the sleep; then took the trail northeast for some hours before building a single *igloo* to share. Now they traveled coastal prairie ridges and finally *tuwak,* a safely frozen sea. Kiti saw her brothers become increasingly comfortable. Not meaning to, she daily exhibited her skill in coastal searches. And her *luck* revealed itself. As winter settled in, the ratio of grounded sea ice expanded. The three of them used trail time and leisurely evenings to visit, to let Kiti rebuild trust slowly, watchfully. The pressure ridge of resentment she had nurtured now for nearly twelve moons gradually subsided.

Neither brother questioned her leadership in this setting, but rather remained in awe of it, despite their recent instruction and practice at Tuk's village. It was Kiti and not they who readily found sea and coastal game. It was she who could approach and capture it. What had been an observation evoking mirth and banter at home—that their younger sister saw prey faster and more frequently—was now a sober fact. Her speed and expertise dazzled them. Nor did any remnant remain of her old hesitation to strike when opportunity came. She did not seem to take pleasure in killing, but she got much satisfaction from harvesting their surroundings for food. And she did by now know uses never dreamed of by the two inlanders for the various parts of marine creatures.

These days of hunting were for Kiti a balance of anxiety and routine. She fought the growing warmth for her brothers by reminding herself of how they ignored her distress when Narluk took the baby, of how they followed their father to track her on the trail. In fact, after a dozen sleeps—her new village by now far ahead and perhaps settling for the winter on their former island—she wished that the brothers would move on. The three of them had made peace, but all knew by now that the fabric of family was torn irreparably. Oojulit and Pajuk accepted that she would not return to Narluk with them, never live at her former home permanently. They could observe daily how much at ease she was, how self-reliant, here at the top of the world. Nothing was to be gained by their lingering, and they had far to go.

Besides, Kiti awaited Tuk without admitting this fact to the brothers or even to herself. At first, she was sure he would soon arrive. Each passing day, to her thinking, made it all the more certain that his return was imminent. She scanned the south and west whenever she could do so without being obvious. As time passed, though, she tried to contain her disappointment. After all, she warned herself, he *did* have his own team.—and she had hers, along with Nuna. There was no need for him to seek her out.

She had learned only since they arrived that her brothers had been with Tuk throughout much of the past summer. That they had packed and carried on their backs from inland their hunting gear, their winter clothing, only a little food, and a few small items for trade. And satisfying her great curiosity, she had learned that her brothers' second sled—the one handled by Pajuk; not her own, with Oojulit on the lines and Nuna at the head—was drawn by *kringmerk* put together from gifts and trades made in Tuk's village—very young dogs or quite old ones, and some few troublesome creatures as well—

all now being taught to work together under Pajuk's firm control. Two of Nuna's last litter scampered loose with the working team, and these were especially prized by the men.

At last, Kiti accepted that Tuk was not going to come. He knew that her brothers would find her. Perhaps he thought that all of them together might wish to return to their tundra home and to Narluk, after all. A cohesive family unit. The woman sighed. Not possible now or ever.

"Those in Tuk's village know of no Sukitilan," Oojulit told her one night before the sleep. That day had been unusually successful, with three seals taken while basking on a flow, two by Kiti. She would happily lash all three to their sled if only the brothers would go back now.

"Tuk, though, must have known." Her eldest brother was asking a question.

"He heard that name first when two brothers inquired," she assured him.

Pajuk spoke up. "The villagers there did say that a woman called *Kiti* is valiant in the quest for provision."

"—And lucky," Oojulit added. "It is said that at one time she captured more walrus than all the rest of the village together—"

Pajuk broke in. "—That she is extremely fortunate in the hunt."

Those words again. . . . "Someone's helping spirit—" Kiti began, then ceased. The stronger and more independent they thought her, the more likely that they would leave soon and peaceably without her.

As if to read her thought, Oojulit continued. "Following this sleep, it happens that two brothers must take the trail for their own village inland," he said. "It may be that Kiti will wish to go as well."

Like a sunbeam descending from the sky, the girl suddenly saw her future— not events so much as circumstance. The ice island here was to be *her* home, the people here surely *hers,* unless . . . until. . .

"Owka, no," she told her brothers, "for it happens that Kiti has something she must do."

She watched both faces darken with sadness but not anger or even surprise.

"A father promised not to seal his *igloo* before his sons returned with news," Pajuk muttered.

The girl smiled. No Narluk she recalled would die so passively. She did not doubt but that he had *threatened* such a thing. "The sons may tell their father—"

"—Not Kiti's father also?" Pajuk prompted.

"Narluk is father to Sukitilan, not to *Kiti."* Her face held no expression.

"And Sukitilan. . . " Pajuk's voice dwindled to a stop.

235

"—Sukitilan no longer exists. But the sons may tell their father that Kiti with *her child* will come to visit—"

Oojulit smiled. "—Soon?"

The woman lifted her eyebrows, *Yes*. "Before the snow of this next season is gone," she promised.

Oojulit and Pajuk took their sled southwest on sea ice to make a final provisioning at Tuk's village. A direct path on smooth ice would mean an easier trip than the one coming north to find their sister.

On that same day, Kiti with Arajik started due south with the team led by Nuna. She had decided not to follow the clear trail northeast left by the villagers. Not yet. Instead, the young woman embarked on the most important journey of her life. Nor did she care how long it might take.

Just now starting her twenty-first winter, Kiti knew what she wanted. Not the *where* or the *when* or even the *how,* exactly. But she had a clear quest and determined focus. She would find Tuk and let him know how she felt. *Eh, Pichikut? Eh? Smile on Kiti to insure that a daughter has great good fortune in the hunt!*

Epilogue

The villagers sat rapt as the storyteller continued his tale.

. . . Kitilan lay upon the surface of the sea.

Sedna saw her there. "This one, we will take," she decided.

But Ooangniktuk, the north wind, was in a temper. He was, as usual, warring with Nigituk from the south about—also as usual—who was strongest.

"No!" he blared, just to be contrary. Then he blasted a breath beneath Kitilan that flung her looping high into the air and back onto the icy ledge from which she had fallen.

The girl snatched breath in the clashing gales and looked about for shelter, but saw only the five seals captured before she fell. She shivered. Ooangniktuk swept frozen fog along the ground. Nigitook answered the power of the north wind with a blizzard having frozen flakes so tightly packed as to be blowing drifts.

Kitilan drew from her icy parka the long, jagged tooth of a Greenland shark. Fighting the gale, she lurched to the biggest seal, sliced open his belly and hauled out steaming intestines and large organs. Then she crawled inside.

"Now shriek, thou windy two!" she muttered before she pulled in close to her the cut flap of skin with its heavy blubber. She curled down into the warmth of her well-insulated refuge. "Let them rage," she murmured once again before she slept.

Glossary

- *aa-gii-ii!*   *no (emphatic)*
- *adlait*   strange
- *aglu*   seal's breathing hole on ice
- *ahmi*   no one can predict the future
- *ai-ee-ee!* **(or similar)**   exclamation of surprise or horror
- *aiverk*   WALRUS
- *alertik*   house shoes/slippers or stockings
- *amaut*   woman's extra hood for carrying baby
- *amoutik*   women't parka built to accommodate amaut
- *ananak*   mother
- *angakok*   shaman healer, sorceror, philosopher, spiritual leader
- *ee-ee*   yes
- *ee-ma!*   yes absolutely! (emphatic)
- *Hoo-oo!*   interjection to express surprise or disapproval
- *idjak*   slitted spectacles for snow (to prevent snow blindness)
- *iglerk*   sleep ledge in igloo
- *igloo*   any shelter, lean-to, hide hut, snow blocks, wood, reinforced concrete—whatever
- *illupak*   light undergarments worn inside shelter
- *ingminek*   one's self alone
- *inueruttyok*   the people are (all) gone
- *Inuit*   general term for people formerly known as Eskimos
- *Inuk*   one individual Inuit person
- *Inupiaq*   language spoken by Inupiat
- *Inupiat*   Inuit of NE Canada, Greenland, certain parts

239

	of Alaska, Siberia
• *issumariyungnaerpok*	forgive
• *kalunait*	"heavy-eyebrowed" people (westerners)
• *kamik*	custom-fitted, warm, waterproof boots for winter wear
• *kaoyok*	to copulate
• *kapvik*	WOLVERINE
• *kargolarpok*	what a great smacking of lips (good manners)
• *katajak*	the "wind songs" of wind witches; throat music
• *kayak*	small, enclosed canoe
• *kinaowit?*	what's your name?
• *kringmerk*	SLED DOG(s)
• *kussuyok*	coward
• *nakorami*	thank you
• *nanuk*	POLAR BEAR
• *nathek*	true (earless) SEAL
• *Nigituk*	The South Wind
• *nipjarnok!*	Shh! Be silent! (command)
• *nuilak*	any fur trim on parka
• *nukapiak*	male youth
• *nuliakpok*	copulates
• *Ooangniktuk*	The North Wind
• *oomingmak*	MUSKOX
• *owka*	no
• *Paija*	spirit goddess who incites evil deeds
• *peeusinga*	culturally "correct"; the way of the people
• *perlerornaq*	how very wearisome is life
• *permafrost*	permanently frozen earth which in Arctic may go down many meters
• *pinnak!*	don't!
• *pirtok*	no one can change what has already occurred

- *puyee* — (big) sea creatures
- *qiviut* — muskox underfur
- *siku* — nomadic (ungrounded) sea ice
- *silipak* — outer (fur) garment, often just trousers
- *soospuk* — nitwit
- *suwit?* — What do you want?
- *tokoyok* — dead people/village
- *tuktu* — CARIBOU
- *tullimak* — rib/rib cage
- *tuwak* — grounded sea ice
- *ulu* — sharp, circular knife used for eating
- *umiak* — sturdy, relatively large, rudderless "women's boat" or "whale boat" (rounded)
- *ungayok* — love
- *upluk* — nest
- *ussuk* — penis
- *uttuk* — vulva
- **[eyebrows raised]** — yes (non-verbal)
- **[sucking in breath]** — yes and agreement (nonverbal)

Acknowledgments

My thanks go to Sallie Swanson Blank who had faith even back in the Pleistocene (something worthwhile rarely happens fast) and patiently typed my left-hand scribbles onto bright white pages. Thanks also to the visionary Dr. Anwar Dil, who dispatched me to the Arctic; and to Dr. Edmund Carpenter, who made me feel at home there. I am indebted to Dr. Olav Oftedal at the Smithsonian for so graciously sharing his expertise on lactation.

Great gratitude goes to Jenny Kay, who read forever among successive versions. To Chicki Mallan for years of tough criticism and well-placed kicks along the way. To Claire Braz-Valentine for encouragement, professional suggestions and a telling tweak. To Karol Saritas , who supported unfailingly and got me through technological vicissitudes. To Kent Brisby for examining possibilities and providing assistance. To Walter M. Mayes, who years back told me, "Go for it!" To Sultana Saritas and Kalí Lowe-Brisby, who now know more about the Arctic than they ever thought they wanted to. And to the CSUC writers who endlessly critiqued and unselfishly aspired.